Praise for

THE SIXTH FLEET Novels
by David E. Meadows

"An absorbing, compelling look at America's future place in the world. It's visionary and scary."

—Joe Buff, author of *Deep Sound Channel*, *Thunder in the Deep*, and *Crush Depth*

"If you enjoy a well-told tale of action and adventure, you will love David Meadows's series, *The Sixth Fleet*. Not only does the author know his subject but [his] fiction could readily become fact. These books should be read by every senator and congressman in our government so that the scenarios therein do not become history."

—John Tegler, syndicated talk show host of *Capital Conversation*

"Meadows will have you turning pages and thinking new thoughts."

—Newt Gingrich

"Meadows takes us right to the bridge, in the cockpit, and into the thick of battle. Meadows is a military adventure writer who's been there, done it all, and knows the territory. This is as real as it gets."

—Robert Gandt, author of *The Killing Sky*

"Meadows delivers one heck of a fast-paced, roller-coaster ride with this exhilarating military thriller."

—*Midwest Book Review*

Berkley titles by David E. Meadows

DARK PACIFIC
DARK PACIFIC: PACIFIC THREAT
DARK PACIFIC: FINAL FATHOM

THE SIXTH FLEET
THE SIXTH FLEET: SEAWOLF
THE SIXTH FLEET: TOMCAT
THE SIXTH FLEET: COBRA

JOINT TASK FORCE: LIBERIA
JOINT TASK FORCE: AMERICA
JOINT TASK FORCE: FRANCE
JOINT TASK FORCE: AFRICA

DARK PACIFIC

FINAL FATHOM

DAVID E. MEADOWS

BERKLEY BOOKS, NEW YORK

THE BERKLEY PUBLISHING GROUP
Published by the Penguin Group
Penguin Group (USA) Inc.
375 Hudson Street, New York, New York 10014, USA
Penguin Group (Canada), 90 Eglinton Avenue East, Suite 700, Toronto, Ontario M4P 2Y3, Canada
(a division of Pearson Penguin Canada Inc.)
Penguin Books Ltd., 80 Strand, London WC2R 0RL, England
Penguin Group Ireland, 25 St. Stephen's Green, Dublin 2, Ireland (a division of Penguin Books Ltd.)
Penguin Group (Australia), 250 Camberwell Road, Camberwell, Victoria 3124, Australia
(a division of Pearson Australia Group Pty. Ltd.)
Penguin Books India Pvt. Ltd., 11 Community Centre, Panchsheel Park, New Delhi—110 017, India
Penguin Group (NZ), 67 Apollo Drive, Rosedale, North Shore 0745, Auckland, New Zealand
(a division of Pearson New Zealand Ltd.)
Penguin Books (South Africa) (Pty.) Ltd., 24 Sturdee Avenue, Rosebank, Johannesburg 2196,
South Africa

Penguin Books Ltd., Registered Offices: 80 Strand, London WC2R 0RL, England

DARK PACIFIC: FINAL FATHOM

A Berkley Book / published by arrangement with the author

PRINTING HISTORY
Berkley edition / June 2007

Cover art by Studio Liddell.
Cover design by Richard Hasselberger.
Interior text design by Kristin del Rosario.

ISBN: 978-0-425-21600-2

BERKLEY®
Berkley Books are published by The Berkley Publishing Group,
a division of Penguin Group (USA) Inc.,
375 Hudson Street, New York, New York 10014.
BERKLEY is a registered trademark of Penguin Group (USA) Inc.
The "B" design is a trademark belonging to Penguin Group (USA) Inc.

PRINTED IN THE UNITED STATES OF AMERICA

10 9 8 7 6 5 4 3 2 1

This book is dedicated
to our children
Sara Meadows and Nicholas Meadows

Acknowledgments

It is impossible to thank everyone who provided technical advice and support for this book and my other action-adventure novels. I deeply appreciate their advice, support, and technical competence. I also am always appreciative of those who visit www.sixthfleet.com, read my columns, and sometimes disagree. Your comments are welcomed and for those who send e-mails, I do try to reply personally to each.

You run the risk of missing someone when you are acknowledging contributions, technical advice, and support, so I apologize up front if I did so.

In these three books of the *Dark Pacific* series, I wrote a lot about the F-22A Raptor. The F-22A Raptor is the most technologically advanced fighter aircraft in the world. All the information in the books on the F-22A is easily available on the Internet. Without reserve, my great respect to the men and women who take this phenomenal weapon of democracy into the hostile areas of the world. Writing about them and trying to extrapolate how they fly and how flying those planes is different—from those who sit in the cockpit, who know what they are doing, and use the advantage of the technologies and avionics of the stealth fighter to control the aerial battle space—I ask their forgiveness if, for the sake of literary ease, I mixed up the cockpit controls and capabilities of the aircraft.

There is another group of individuals who should be recognized for their contributions to the Raptor. This group is the men and women of Lockheed Martin, Boeing, and Pratt & Whitney, who built the F-22A Raptor, integrated the technologies, and designed the avionics that gave this aircraft its superior position in the history of military aviation. Without them, this aircraft would never have left the enterprising desk of some Pentagon defense requirements person.

The Joint Strike Fighter (F-35), also in this series, is being flown by our closest Navy ally, the Royal Navy. Lockheed Martin leads the Northrop Grumman and British Aerospace Systems (BAE) teams in building this stealth fighter. When accepted by the Pentagon, the Joint Strike Fighter will join the F-22A as another premier battle space fighter to be flown by the United States and some of our closest allies, including Great Britain.

The information on the Fast Sealift Ships was gained in an afternoon of trekking across the deck of the USNS *Denebola* with the master of this gigantic aircraft carrier–size ship, Captain Joe Gargiulo, and Mr. Matthew Cull (PM5 Sealift Surge Detachment). Other information came from personal research, which included libraries, the Internet, the handouts on the ships. The *Denebola* is representative of all eight of the Fast Sealift Ships. It is over 946 feet in length. The newest aircraft carrier, the USS *George H. W. Bush,* is 1,092 feet in length—a difference of less than 150 feet. The *Nimitz*-class aircraft carriers, of which USS *George H. W. Bush* is one, have a crew of more than 5,500 people, with ship's company and the air wing embarked. The USNS *Denebola* has fourteen merchant marines manning her while in port, growing to a maritime complement of about forty when she is under way.

My thanks to Terry Smith, Vincent Widmaier, William "David" Cross, Amanda Roberts, and Angela O'Neal for their security insights and recommendations. For technical advice and support, my appreciation to Tim Bovill (may he enjoy Norfolk), Jerry Bechlehimer, Mark Thomson, Christine Weston-Lyons, Mary Forbes, Shirley Cool, Bonni Rae Lamson, Sue Abbott, William "Bill" Gaul, and Bill "USNA class of '74" Hall. And, of course, three of the most powerful women at NIS: Cassandra Mewborn, Brenda Williams, and Jessie McAliley. Then, of course, every retired sailor has ole shipmates who keep in touch. My thanks to Paul and Karen Ratkovich, William J. "Hawk" McDonnell, and Marcus "Narwhal" Williams for their comments and support.

As always, my continued thanks to Tom Colgan for his editorial support and to his able right-hand person, Sandra Harding. And my thanks to my agent, John Talbot, for his advice and guidance.

Rest assured any and all technical errors or mistakes in this novel are strictly those of the author, who many times wanders in his own world. Please keep in touch.

David E. Meadows

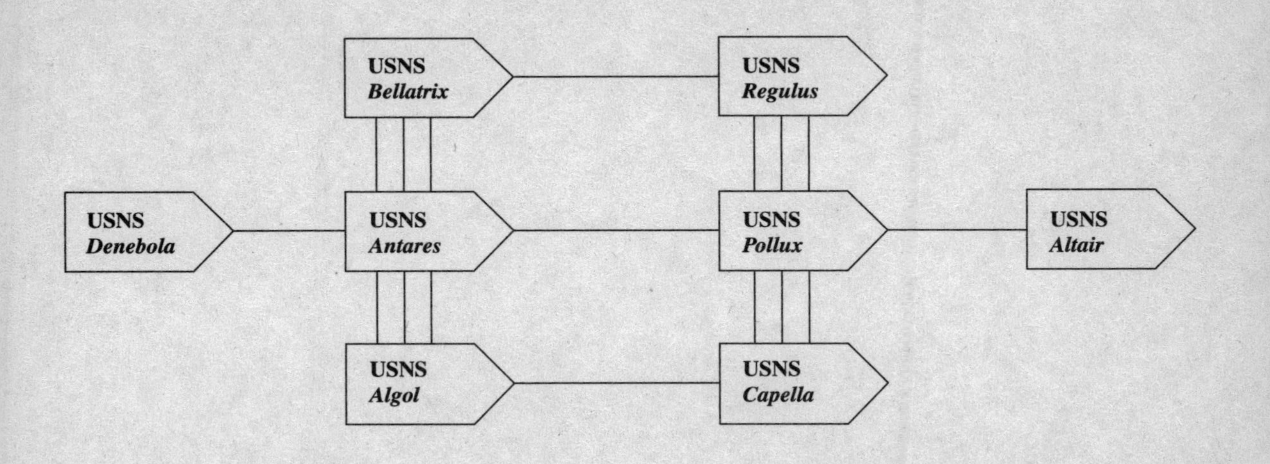

Figure 1. The Sea Base foundation.

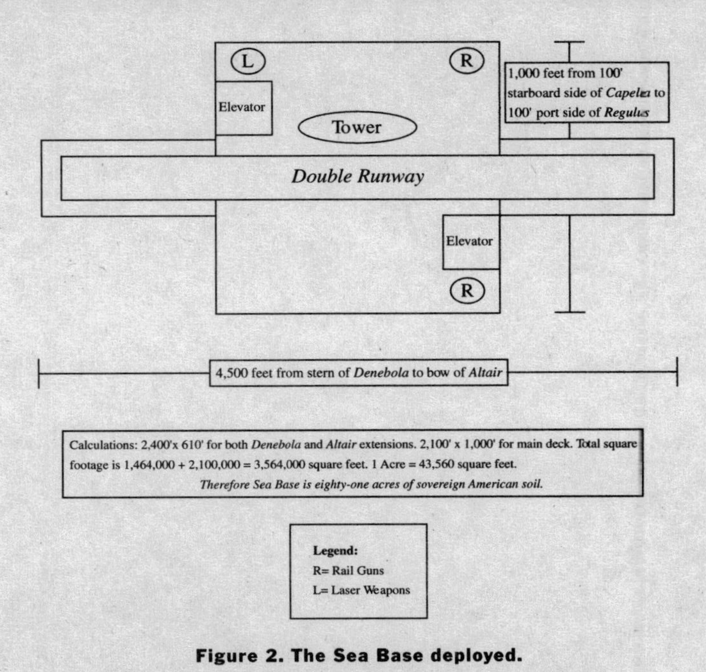

Figure 2. The Sea Base deployed.

ONE

The hammer clicked on an empty cylinder. Andrew jumped. His eyes flew open. Beads of sweat raced down his cheeks. His breaths were short, rapid, and panicky with relief. The steady outward appearance of calm moments earlier vanished. His body shook and he nearly tumbled off his knees. He closed his eyes and bowed his head slightly, knowing those watching believed him to be praying. Andrew fought to stop the trembling, slow his breathing. He recalled his father's warning about how he should act once the selection process finished, but it was easy for his dad to tell him for his dad never had to do this.

The pressure of the barrel shifted off his temple. When the handler pulled the pistol up, the cool air circulating through the shadows of the barn brushed like a circle of ice across the red pressure spot on his temple. His eyes followed the pistol as the man placed it in the case carried by another man.

"It is God's will," the crowd said in unison.

"Like his brother," someone said.

"The pistol!" one of the deacons shouted.

"The pistol!" the crowd shouted, taking up the cry.

The man who moments earlier had pulled the trigger while

the gun was against Andrew's temple reopened the case and took the gun out of it. He pointed it upward and pulled the trigger. The gun fired. The bullet shattered old wood shingles as it penetrated the roof. Andrew jumped at the noise. The smell of cordite drifted across his face. Small splinters drifted down onto the crowd.

"Amen," came a smaller chorus from the deacons surrounding the pit. "Praise the Lord."

Four more shots followed the first one. More small pieces of wood rained on the crowd.

The congregation went wild with cries, prayers, and shouts of praises for God's grace on Andrew.

The pistol was laid reverently back in the case. Then the man locked it, nodded at the man holding the case, and the crowd watched as the person carrying it walked up the steps leading from the pit. Andrew watched along with everyone else until the case disappeared within the crowd, the man carrying it heading toward the area where earlier Andrew had hugged and left his father.

Two pairs of hands grabbed Andrew under the arms, pulling him to his feet. He opened his eyes and glanced at the two men. Their lips moved. They were speaking, broad grins stretching their faces. He smiled. He knew they were praising him, shouting thanks to the Lord. But the words flowed around him like a bubbling stream, failing to penetrate the frightful haze still enveloping him.

His knees buckled, their hands tightened. He was numb from kneeling so long as the congregation prayed for divine intervention. Upright, he was a good six inches taller than the two men holding him. His weak smile faded, removing all expression from his face.

The hands tightened slightly and the two men turned him toward the steps. He took a deep breath. A few tears edged from the corners of his brown eyes, trickling down across day-old growth of dark stubble. He wanted to fall back onto his knees. Take more time to regain control of his body; show his composure; impress the congregation—not disgrace his father.

Andrew shut his eyes for a brief moment when he reached the first step, causing him to trip slightly on the rough rise of the concrete pit. The pressure from their grasp increased enough for him to regain his footing, keeping him from falling, as if they knew he had no energy to stop anything that might happen now. *When God pulls you back from the abyss of death, there is a great weakness surrounding the body in the knowledge of His power,* thought Andrew.

Three slow steps later, he stood at the top of the pit. Gradually, they let him go. He swayed to the right. The man there touched him briefly on the shoulder, steadying him. Andrew grimaced, bending his knees slightly to relieve the itch and pain of blood flowing into the numbness. He turned slowly, testing his feet, prepared to fall, even though the two handlers remained alongside him.

He turned and looked down at the pit behind him. Ten feet from one side to the other, the ancient pit canted toward the far side, where drainage ran across a rusty wire grating covering a twelve-inch iron pipe that carried the blood and runoff of the old slaughter pit from the barn.

As a lad, Andrew had followed the course of the pipe. It ran under the nearby dirt road to an overgrown drainage field created by the runoff from it and the septic tank of the nearby abandoned farmhouse. The stamped, ancient straw stomped into the bottom of the pit was soaked in fresh blood. Andrew looked at the drain cover at the far end where earlier in the day four other disciples had preceded him. Pieces of white flesh hung on the cratered edges of the drain cover.

God had not intervened in His display of love and worship for the four who preceded him.

Andrew stared for a moment, looking at the imprint in the blood-soaked straw upon which he had knelt for what seemed hours. He stopped a quick impulse to look at the knees of his blue jeans to see if the blood of his fellow believers had soaked into them. He knew it had; he didn't need to look.

He turned away, nearly falling, but his handlers took him gently by the arms, softly offering gratitude to God. He was too unsteady. He'd fall, or the handlers would grab him again. The travail wasn't over. He had to accept this as God's will.

The gun had five bullets along with an empty chamber. Holding the pistol by his side, the handler had kept turning the cylinder throughout the hour of prayer—one spin after the other, over and over again—never looking to see where the unloaded chamber came to rest. The sound of the spin, the smooth clicking imprinting itself in Andrew's memory, drawing his attention to the cylinder and away from his prayers, and still God had intervened to choose him.

Each of the young men chosen for the selection, the Lord had turned His back on. Then, without warning, his father had volunteered Andrew. He should have known eventually he would be chosen to go through the selection. His father had taken him for a walk this morning talking about God's will and how the Bible many times required God's followers to demonstrate their faith through sacrifice. He should have figured it out, but his father was forever sharing his thoughts with Andrew in their many walks. It was good he didn't fully share this one.

A clear insight rushed through Andrew. His father had had little choice but to send him into the pit. The past few weeks had been a jumble of pastoral maneuverings that his father believed were leading those who oppose him into replacing him with another. When mumbling turns to whispers, the leader has little choice but to offer a sign of his faith before the whispers become shouts and fist-waving demands.

Andrew was that sign. As others in the Bible had offered up their firstborn as a sign of their love for God, so his father did with him. His father preached to all to never worry that God would be with them always.

But his father hadn't been the one on his knees hearing the spin of the chamber or surviving the click of the hammer. Suddenly, his bladder was full and Andrew had an overwhelming urge to pee. He tightened, forcing the urge down. Joshua, his brother, probably had had no doubt he would survive the selection process.

Now, since Andrew was the Lord's chosen one, his father's—Ezekiel's—leadership would not be challenged for a long time.

Andrew looked at the crowd chanting his name. There were more than a hundred crowded into the huge barn in the woods of eastern West Virginia. Andrew breathed deeply, fear dissipating quicker as the joy of being alive raced through his body. A few tears escaped from his eyes. His brother had not cried. The chanting increased in intensity.

"The purity," someone said, and he knew they were referring to his tears.

"Holy."

"Acceptance of God's will."

Andrew nodded at his handlers, standing near him, ready to grab him if he faltered. If he fell, no one would think ill, for God had chosen him, but if he regained his composure and walked with confidence, then when his father fell, he'd assume the mantle of God's Army. The idea of replacing his father had never entered his thoughts until now. There was only one more trial to face, and then God's Army would be his. But not until his father, whom he loved and worshipped, passed into God's arms.

Andrew raised his arms wide, feeling the joy of his name being chanted louder and louder as the congregation swayed in unison to the love of God. His arms felt heavy as he held them aloft, and he fought the momentary urge to lower them; holding them in this position for a few minutes before bringing them down.

Andrew's eyes roved over the crowd, stopping when he saw his father standing in the rear. His father's trademark thick dark beard with streaks of white hair running down from each side of the chin, tracing a path like a waterfall to the beard's very edge, which rested on the second button of the white shirt. Ezekiel's eyes were hidden beneath thick eyebrows forever brooding.

Looking at the old man's face, Andrew wondered if this man he called Father had cared whether he survived the selection, or if his father had been willing to chance Andrew's survival as the only option for maintaining sole control of the people. It might not have been his only chance, but it was a quick one if Andrew survived, and survive he had.

"Sir . . . ," one of the handlers whispered. "The Bishop waits."

The Bishop waits. His father would never willingly give up the title Bishop. His father communed with God. He spoke with Jesus. Ask his father, he'll tell you. His father preached the righteousness of his faith. A faith grown from a handful when his father started God's Army, to encompassing nearly six thousand in less than eight years; dedicated to whatever his father wanted. And within that six thousand were the core one hundred who plotted and planned the coming Armageddon. The core one hundred who sent followers across the globe to start the world toward Armageddon.

The Bishop preached, and they all believed, that with anarchy and the growing radicalism of Islam, the return of the Messiah would occur sooner, wiping bogus religions from the face of the earth and bringing peace for a thousand years. Ezekiel preached that the key to releasing the demons of Revelation was to rain destruction upon the world. The explosions at North Korean embassies in Canada, New York, and London had nearly achieved that goal. Alert police in France and across Europe had stopped the others—others who now languished in jails around the world, but who would die rather than betray God's Army. They knew that when Armageddon came, their freedom would be assured.

If this first march toward anarchy had been successful, God's Army would have led the people of America toward salvation as they waited for the return of the Lord.

A handler touched him slightly. Andrew nodded and started forward. The crowd shuffled apart, creating a path through which Andrew and the two men walked abreast. Someone tossed a small bouquet of flowers into the path. As Andrew passed, worshippers fell to their knees, giving thanks to God. A God looking down who had taken His finger and touched Andrew as the most faithful, most pure of the five men.

The scuffing of shoes disturbed the mildewed straw, stirring long-idle dust. Years of dried manure crumbled, joining the sharp mixed coppery odor of blood rising through the lantern-lit barn. It was the smell of God's creation, which was why his father liked this abandoned and long-forgotten farm. *Blood and manure—the beginning and the end—the Alpha and the Omega—the Ying and the Yang—for every start there is a finish.*

Each step brought more confidence. Andrew's pace quickened to a normal gait. His smile broadened and his tears stopped; only moist streaks remained on his dust-covered face. He raised his right hand as if blessing those who knelt in honor of God who had chosen him.

A few feet from his father, he met the old man's eyes, and saw anger in them. His knees weakened for a moment, and then coursing through his body was the realization that with the click of the hammer he had both become his father's successor and his father's adversary. Only hours earlier, Andrew had been the Bishop's eldest son. He thought of Joshua for a moment—now Andrew was his father's only son.

His father reached out and touched Andrew on his shoulder with his right hand. Even through the light shirt, the calluses on the hand were rough against Andrew's skin. Calluses that told of the hard labor of many years put into the fields of the farm and the cotton mills of the South. The Bishop looked upward, lifting his left hand, waiting for the prayers and chanting to stop.

Keeping his hand on Andrew, Ezekiel stood. He looked down at Andrew, their eyes meeting briefly. "My son, I am proud of your goodness and faith." His father looked at the congregation and continued. "Pride is something God forbids in the faithful, and for that pride I accept the small sin for what I feel for my son. God has reached down." He looked at Andrew. "He has touched you with His spirit and He has returned the son I offered as a sign of my faith and love."

Andrew dropped his gaze. His father dropped his hand. Andrew cut his eyes upward, watching his father. His father's head turned slowly as the old man surveyed his loyal followers. In a loud voice, his pastor's voice, his father took a deep breath and addressed the crowd. "This is a sign. It is a sign that God's Army continues on the right path. I offered my son to the Lord to prove my faithfulness to Him. To prove to those who think that God's Army needs a new Bishop, that God's Army is moving too fast or too slow to hasten Armageddon, and that our direction is too radical for a country founded on the Bible. Let me say and ask each of you to carry this story forth. Carry it to your own congregations. Let it be known that Bishop Ezekiel offered God his remaining son and God, through His benevolence, rewarded my faithfulness by sparing Andrew."

"God shows His love," the congregation said in unison.

He patted Andrew a couple of times on the shoulder while never taking his eyes off the people surrounding him. "We will do what God has approved today. We will destroy the evil taking hold of this country—the evil growing in our enemies around the world. We will see the prophecy fulfilled and my son, through His selection, has become a holy weapon for this fulfillment. For without God's intervention, Andrew would be dead, so his life now belongs to God. He must prove worthy of this selection."

Prove worthy? Andrew would have laughed if he had the energy. He tucked his chin deeper into his chest and shut his eyes, knowing those nearby watched. He kept the small smile frozen on his face, lifted his head, and turned to face the congregation. *Never underestimate the old man.* His father didn't create this Biblical following by being ignorant or stupid. His father would never allow anyone to replace him, least of all his son. When his father was ready to lay down the mantle of the Lord or the Lord laid it down for him, Andrew would be there to step up. To grab the reins of God's Army and continue the Lord's march to anarchy and a thousand years of peace and love.

This day, he knew this. He could and he would, with patience as the path. His wearing of the mantle would wait until his father drew his last breath. And when that last breath expelled, Andrew knew his father would die without ever identifying a successor, for his father believed God would never allow him to die. But he would die. Everyone dies.

Andrew raised his face high, looking upward as if seeing something others in the congregation couldn't. Other eyes followed his, staring at the roof of the barn, seeing the stars poke through the holes weathered through the aged wood or scattered by the numerous bullet holes. Eyes turned away from his father to follow Andrew's unspoken bidding.

Andrew's smile broadened. He hoped his countenance shined in the faint light. Strength was growing with each passing second. He was the chosen one. He detected a slight disruption—a slight hesitation in his father's words. It was small—barely detectable—but it was there. And Andrew had caused it.

His father could preach for hours, so he stood listening to his father explain that he—not Andrew—was the beneficiary of today's miracle. Swaying those who whispered for a new Bishop. Swaying them back to the continuing leadership of the founder.

Andrew had never had so many epiphanies at one time. God truly reached down and touched him. The people. His father. Everyone's true purpose glowed in clarity.

Andrew turned and looked up at his father, knowing his face reflected love and respect for everyone to see, even as he thought through about how his father had miscalculated.

It was the anger Andrew had seen moments earlier when he approached him that had revealed to Andrew that his father had also fully understood what had happened. Throwing his son into the selection—watching his son nearly fall from fear as he was led into the pit—all to chance God's mercy so his father could keep the leadership. In doing so, his father had unwittingly allowed God to identify his successor. It was as if those maneuvering to replace his father down one path had been stopped because God had chosen a quicker, easier one.

"ANDREW, sit down," Ezekiel said, motioning him to the couch. Even in the small living room, his father's deep bass voice resonated.

Across from his father, on the other side of the unlit fireplace, Thomas Bucket sat in the straight-back chair brought from the dining room. Bucket's legs firmly together, his unsmiling face and dark eyes followed Andrew as he crossed the room. Andrew was uncomfortable around Bucket. The man seldom spoke unless asked a question. Usually, the answer was a monotone "yes" or "no." If more was expected, Bucket would fold onto his knees and entice you to join him as you both asked for God's guidance.

It wasn't the taciturn nature of the man that made Andrew uncomfortable. The man had killed at the whim of his father. Bucket was the most loyal of Ezekiel's disciples, willing to prove his loyalty and worship for the old man whenever asked. If Bucket thought Andrew was other than the loyal, loving son of Ezekiel, Bucket would wrap his large work-strong hands around Andrew's neck and with the strength of those sinewy arms, snap his neck with as little emotion as that of a chicken chosen for dinner.

"Andrew, God Bless," Scott Temple said as Andrew walked by the heavyset man.

"God Bless," Andrew replied.

Scott Temple sprawled on the right side of the couch. The rich black beard of the forty-something disciple failed to mask the smile of a man happy with himself and happy with his God. Like Bucket, Temple would execute Ezekiel's words without question. These two men were the power behind the throne. Andrew wondered briefly as he sat down what were the last thoughts of those whom these two disciples had dispatched to God's kingdom on the whim of his father.

"Thanks be to God," his father said, remaining seated.

Andrew joined the other two men on his knees, and as his father led the mantra of God's Army, he repeated it along with Bucket and Temple. The words were so ingrained in his mind, they came easily as he thought of other things, relived the near-death experience of earlier.

In the background, as the men prayed, Andrew's mother talked softly to the two men's wives in the kitchen. The sound of a knife slicing through something on the carving board—handed down from his granny—came faintly from that direction. Making sandwiches, he told himself, causing him to realize how hungry he was. His stomach rumbled.

He had refused breakfast this morning, knowing his father had called for a selection. He never ate when his father called for a selection. Andrew was a creature of routine. He washed before going to bed at night and again showered when he arose. His pants hung in the closet on the left side and his shirts on the right. Coats and suits hung in the hallway closet of the small three-bedroom farmhouse. Andrew expected his mom to have coffee ready by the time he dressed. He only expected it because his father demanded it. His underwear was divided into briefs on the left and undershirts on the right. Everything had a time and a place, his father taught. Andrew had yet to reach the age where such meticulous attention had turned into a full-blown phobia.

Selections were emotional days. Someone always died. The selections disturbed Andrew's sense of order. So, this morning like others, Andrew took the obligatory solitary walk of his developing phobia along the path leading from the house, past the barn, listening to the chickens rising, the clucks announcing fresh eggs filling the nests. Two roosters parried in the corner for master of the roost as he passed. Life was a cascading waterfall of complexities. His twin sisters were already gathering the eggs, waving at him as he walked past.

From behind the barn, Juan had emerged. Andrew had waved at Juan as the hired hand led the two cows into the barn, their bells parading tones in front of them. He could almost feel the man's rough hands on the teats pulling forth God's bounty. This smell of the fresh morning air mixed with the rich odor of manure, and the faint rustle of the dark leaves of the nearby wood, accompanied him, surrounding his solitude of thought, as he walked to the spot above the stream. The heat and humidity of the summer morning had already stained the underarms of his shirt.

"Amen," his father now said, bringing Andrew's thoughts back to the living room.

Andrew repeated the word with the others. He took a deep breath, finding ease in the situation as he leaned back onto the couch. His father was speaking, but Andrew's thoughts returned to his walk.

He recalled how upon reaching the huge rock jutting out over the stream, he had bent down and run his hands over it feeling the moisture blanketing the moss that covered it. Andrew and his brother had played many times on this huge rock, playing Indians and cowboys as children. Scaring each other with tales of gore and wild animals when they camped upon it. It was here he had fallen, gashing his forehead. He touched the faint scar above his eyebrows, feeling the long indentation that ran from above the left eyebrow to the top of his forehead on the right. The thin line blended with his face except when he was sunburned. Then the scar glowed in brilliance across his forehead, drawing pitying comments from his mother. His brother and he had fished, swum, and camped on this huge rock, scraping their initials in it. It was here while camping one night that his brother had taught him the fine art of masturbation.

"Andrew, you listening, son?"

Andrew shook his head, shooing away his thoughts and bringing his attention back to his father. "Sorry, Father. I was thinking of Joshua."

His father nodded. "Not a day goes by that I don't thank the

Lord for the time He allowed us to have your big brother." He sighed.

Andrew had walked his life in the shadow of his older brother. Joshua's death while in the Navy had devastated Ezekiel. Andrew never understood why Ezekiel sent Joshua into the Navy.

He looked across the room at Mr. Temple. Then his eyes rested for a brief second on his father before shifting to Mr. Bucket. He was surprised to see Bucket returning his gaze. Their eyes locked for only a moment before Andrew quickly lowered his in deference to the older man. There was coldness in the man's eyes, as if he enjoyed the tasks on which his father sent him more than for the purpose of the tasks.

These three men had a plan to hasten Armageddon, to bring God's kingdom to earth during their lifetimes. Many a night, as a young lad, Andrew had fallen asleep listening to the men dissect Revelation, fighting to understand the meaning. To find the secret that was intertwined in this Holiest of Holies within the Bible. Along with the theological discussions had gone hours of prayer, until one night as he lay in bed listening to the men begin their studies, his father had announced that God had visited him.

Andrew lay in bed listening to his father tell the story of how a few hours earlier, God had seized him in the barn and when he revived hours later, the vision had been given to him. The prayers had been quite loud that night, as if the three wanted to ensure that God was aware of their faith and love. Andrew had quietly joined them, muffling his voice with his pillow. He had peeked several times from beneath his pillow to glance at the moon, afraid each time it would be a bright red, the sign of the Lord's imminent arrival. He loved the Lord, but he wanted more time on earth before joining the heavenly Father.

The morning after his father's vision, the three men packed their camping gear and disappeared along the Appalachian Trail. For two months they vanished, sending his mother into a panic. When they returned, they were surprised to discover how long they had been gone. It had been their trek into the wilderness to understand God's message and His love.

For him, Joshua, his mother, and his twin sisters, Mary and

Charlemagne, it had been a time of deep sadness and loss. It was as if they had no path to follow. It had been the time when Joshua discovered how to comfort his sisters, and watched as he brought Andrew into the comforting.

The day of his father's return, he had dismissed with a wave and impatience the family's concern. Ezekiel and his two disciples had sat down at the kitchen table as if they had been outside for only minutes instead of being gone for two months. The light in his father's eyes that day seared a spot in Andrew's memory, for as his mother rushed around the kitchen making food and coffee, Ezekiel announced that they carried the plan to fulfill the prophecy of God's return—a prophecy given to his father in the vision. A prophecy refined with his two trusted disciples. A prophecy burst forth in glory and vision during the wilderness months in the Appalachians.

Andrew blinked a couple of times, realizing his father was speaking to him. His thoughts returned to the living room.

"Andrew, I *said* you need to listen and pay attention to what we are going to share with you. You understand?"

"I always understand, Father."

Ezekiel's eyes narrowed. "You do not fully understand, son. It is your youth speaking. Do you understand the vision?"

Andrew bent his head in deference. "Yes, Father."

Ezekiel shook his head. "No one but the three of us, and now you, will understand the vision. A vision entrusted to me by the God Almighty. A vision only myself, Thomas, and Scott fully understand." The Bishop leaned forward in his chair, his elbow knocking the empty glass of iced tea off it.

"Sophie!" his father shouted.

His mother appeared in the doorway, wiping her hands on a kitchen towel. "Yes, Father?"

"I've been a clumsy fool again, dear."

His mother saw the ice on the carpet. She smiled. "No bother, Nate . . . I mean, Ezekiel," she said, hurrying over to the spill, squatting to use the towel to push the ice cubes back into the glass.

Andrew saw the moment of fear wash across her face, but his father only nodded.

"We will speak shortly," his father said to him and the two deacons.

"There," his mother announced as she stood up. "Spick-and-span again."

His father reached over and patted her hand. "Thank you, my dear."

His mother's face glowed. Andrew could count on his hands the number of times he'd seen his father show his mother affection. Affection was a word Andrew doubted the old man truly understood. Loyalty was something he truly understood and demanded.

At the door, his mother turned her head and said brightly, "We'll have sandwiches shortly, gentlemen." She looked at Andrew just before disappearing from sight, mouthing the words "Love you."

"My apologies for my clumsiness," his father said. He leaned forward in his chair. "Andrew, today is the day you become a sharer of the prophecy of the vision. There are things within the prophecy that must be fulfilled for God. He is counting on us to do that."

"Yes, Father," Andrew said, his voice respectful. He uncrossed his legs and sat up straight. The vision was what guided God's Army. It was delivered to Ezekiel directly from the lips of God. Everyone knew of the vision, lived the vision, and believed with their hearts and souls it was divine guidance necessary to bring God back to earth. Everyone also knew that parts of the vision were secret. The secrets were designed to keep the unbelievers from disrupting the prophecy. Only two leaders were privy to Ezekiel's secrets within the vision, and they sat in this room alongside Andrew.

Andrew had become more than the Bishop's son. Today, he had become a pawn in the vision.

Ezekiel talked, the words rolling off his tongue, and as he shared with Andrew the secrets for fulfilling the prophecy, the two deacons prayed quietly. Periodically during Ezekiel's testament, as he called it, the two would say "Amen" in a slightly louder voice, background to the secrets.

Andrew tried to swallow when he heard of the carnage that would happen to the world. His brother had been a member of this inner sanctum. Andrew had thought his father was disappointed when Joshua disappeared one night and joined the Navy. His father was telling him that Joshua's actions were part of the vision. To bring anarchy and hasten Armageddon meant sacrifice. The selection was only part of the new covenant with God; there was a second level to which Andrew would now ascend.

"To come to fulfillment, we must bring the world into conflict. Do you understand, Andrew?"

He jumped. The question was unexpected. "Yes, sir, but isn't the world in conflict? Has been since I was born, sir."

Ezekiel nodded. "That it has, my son. It has been a world with small wars burning quietly over the globe. For the prophecy to be fulfilled, these conflicts must be brought together." He brought his hands together, bouncing the fingers against each other as if holding a ball between them. "The mighty must fall and throughout the world we must have a conflagration so when God shows himself, His presence will be spectacular."

It would be spectacular without conflagration, Andrew thought.

"It will be of such benevolence when He waves his hand across the world and every weapon, every bomb, every aircraft stops fighting. Weapons will cease to work. Soldiers will cease to fight. A thousand years of peace will descend across the globe and we shall be on His right, separating the good from the bad, choosing those who will live in His shadow and those who will die."

His father's eyes glazed as Ezekiel stared upward as if seeing something past the ceiling.

"Governments will evaporate. No need for police, prisons, or even cars. We shall truly be one world and one people on bended knee to the Almighty," Ezekiel said, clenching his fist and shaking it. He looked at Andrew. "If we did nothing, He would still come, but not in our lifetime. We are but hastening His arrival. Do you understand?"

"Yes, sir," he said, not truly understanding. *If God wanted to come, why did he need any preparation for a world which He made?*

His father leaned back in his chair. "The vision has identified critical nodes to be attacked, to be destroyed. Destroying them will escalate the world toward Armageddon. A world in chaos will bring forth the Lord."

Andrew nodded. He'd heard those words over the years, believing them, knowing them to be truly the words of God.

"Andrew, you will leave in the morning. You are part of the vision. You must prepare yourself for sacrifice if needed, as your brother Joshua did. In the past month our martyrs offered themselves to put the prophecy into action. They sought out and destroyed places of blasphemy and idolatry of a country that lacks the love of God and threatens those who do, North Korea. Thanks be to God for their actions. The dominoes toward Armageddon are falling, but we cannot sit back and think they will fall fast enough for God."

Andrew nodded, wondering if his own death was expected in the fulfillment of his father's vision.

"It will be hard for you as it was for us"—Ezekiel lifted his hand and waved it at the two deacons—"to come to terms with the possibility that we may wound or kill some believers, but it is God's will who lives and dies for He alone sends us into this world. Even if innocent ones die, they are immediately resurrected into heaven. It is a sin quickly erased by our beliefs."

"Amen," the two deacons said in unison.

"He alone decides who shall live and who shall die."

"Amen."

"He alone determines who will be allowed to participate in the prophecy."

"Amen."

"And He has chosen you." His father leaned forward and pointed a slightly bent finger at Andrew.

"Amen."

"Amen," Ezekiel said. His father leaned back into the soft cushion of his chair. "For you will take Joshua's place, Andrew." He turned to Tom Bucket. "You have the . . . ?"

In one smooth motion, Bucket walked across the room and from behind the couch where Andrew and Temple sat, he lifted a cardboard box and brought it into the center of the living room. He pulled open the sides.

"This is but a small part of what you will need as you go to do God's work," he father said.

Bucket pulled a smaller box out and opened it. He handed it to Andrew.

"You will take your brother's place."

Andrew lifted a military identification card from the small box.

"I will join the Navy?"

His father shook his head. "No, you will take the place of the sailor whose uniform is within the satchel," he said, pointing to a seabag leaning on the wall in the corner of the room. "His name was Albert Jolson. You will spend two weeks with Tom Bucket's son, Steve, who retired from the Navy. He will teach you what you need to know."

His mother entered the room. "Here are the sandwiches. Does anyone need a drink?" she asked.

"Mr. Bucket, I didn't know Steve had retired from the Navy. I thought . . ."

"He didn't retire. He spent his two years and was discharged. The Navy refused to have a believer who saw through their evil ways. He retired from following their ways. He knows what to teach you to make sure you pass as a sailor."

A few minutes later, his mother was gone. They ate and spoke for another thirty before Ezekiel announced the end of the visit. Andrew glanced at the clock. It was nearing eleven. He walked behind his father as they escorted the Buckets and Temples to the door, his father embracing each of them before they left. His twin sisters, Mary and Charlemagne, stood halfway up the stairs, coming down them, joining the family on the porch to wave and bid farewell to the guests.

Minutes later, the cars turned out of sight on the country road at the end of the long lane leading to their house. The small window in the top of the barn where Juan lived showed the reflection of a lamp. A long moo came from the direction of the barn.

"Come along, girls," his mother said as they turned back into the house.

His father beckoned Andrew into the living room. Behind them came the sounds of his younger sisters scrambling upstairs, laughing at something one of them said.

His father went to the bookcase and removed several books from the lower shelf. He pulled out a metal box. Andrew recognized the box as one of those inexpensive fireproof boxes designed to protect valuable papers.

Only, when his father opened it, where papers should have been was a pistol. "This is your brother's first gun." He lifted it from the box and set the box on the seat of his chair. Ezekiel took the gun in his right hand, deliberately keeping his finger off the trigger. "This gun he learned to shoot with. He shot his first squirrel with this gun, Andrew, and your mother—*bless her heart*—cooked it—fried in batter. I was so proud of him."

Andrew remembered the dinner. The display made over his brother. Until his brother was killed two months ago aboard this thing called Sea Base, Andrew had been a shadow to him. With the death of Joshua, that had changed. His father had lifted Andrew from the shadows, treating him as Andrew saw him treat his brother while growing up. Andrew had always been the one in the background. The quiet one. The morose one, as his sister Charlemagne whispered to him one night.

He handed the gun to Andrew. "This is yours now. When you arrive at your destination, you will find those responsible for your brother's death."

Andrew held the gun in his palm, looking at the small .32-caliber pistol. The six chambers held five rounds. "Five rounds," he said aloud.

"We never fully load a gun, son. God must have a way in which he may show us His will."

"Thank you, Father."

"There is more, Andrew. When you find these men . . ." Ezekiel pulled a photograph from the box. "This is one of them. You will kill him and you will kill anyone else you find to be involved in his death. You will shoot him with your brother's gun and you will make sure he knows why he is being killed and by whom. You will whisper my name so when he reaches hell, he can tell the devil who sent him."

Andrew nodded. He lifted the photograph and looked at it. Against the background of the ship, Joshua stood with other sailors. Beside them stood a tall, thin man wearing a khaki uniform. The man's hair was cropped close, and Andrew couldn't tell if it was red or brown.

"That is one of the men," his father said, pointing to the one wearing khakis. He handed Andrew a three-by-five card. "Here is the man's name. His wife's name. They have no children. His address is there along with his duty station. We have people in every military service. Even as you and I talk, in Millington, Tennessee, where the Navy has its military personnel command, a member of God's Army is writing orders—*I think that is what he said they call them*—to send you to Hawaii."

Hawaii. This I would like to see.

"When you arrive, you will become part of his division. This killer is part of the Navy experiment called Sea Base.

"There is another man who must die first, for he was the one who tossed your brother into the sea. His name is Jacobs. He is something called a master chief. Steve Bucket says he is something called a boatswain mate, which is what you will be when you arrive. Kill him first." Ezekiel raised the photograph. "Then, kill this man. It must be in that order, do you understand?"

"I do, Father."

"I know you will do it, Andrew. God expects it of you."

Andrew nodded. "I will, Father. Is this Sea Base part of God's will?"

"Everything is part of God's will. This Sea Base is another domino to hasten Armageddon. It is becoming more and more a part of it." His father leaned back in the chair and clasped his hands together. "When your brother was sent out to Sea Base, we saw it as just one of many dominoes for hastening God's return. Your brother was to destroy it and if it was God's will, he would have returned. The result was to be one more evil destroyed as we started executing the vision. He failed. Through our prayers, we know the failure was a bigger part of God's vision. The failure put this Sea Base against the God-haters of North Korea." He father stood suddenly and walked to the fireplace, putting both hands on the mantel and leaning against it. "Something happened out there. Something we don't know. Something this Sea Base did created the situation we hear about now with another country that knows not the love of God. China. Already, this Sea Base is moving toward Taiwan according to the papers, and for you to accomplish your mission of avenging your brother's death, you will have to journey into the same mouth of the beast as Joshua did. You will have to kill the men responsible for his death. You will have to do it so they know who killed them in the manner I described."

He turned and faced Andrew. "I want you to return to me, my son. You are the only one I have left to follow in my footsteps even as I hope that God will allow me to see His vision fulfilled. You must fulfill the vision I have seen for you and then return to me."

Andrew crossed the room and kneeled and bowed at his father's feet. "I will do as you ask, Father."

Ezekiel nodded. "I know you will, my son." He touched Andrew on the shoulder. "Stand," he said. "Son, it will be God's will if you come back to me. I will pray for your return. If it is God's will you go to His arms, then it will be with great sadness we accept that fate, knowing we will see each other in heaven, in glory."

"God's will."

"Yes, God's will."

"Am I to destroy Sea Base also as Joshua was instructed?"

His father's face twisted as if in deep thought. Then he shook his head. "Only if an opportunity presents itself. I think if the Lord had wanted Sea Base destroyed, He would have allowed Joshua to succeed."

Andrew nodded, relieved, as he had no idea how to destroy something as large as Sea Base.

"But if God wishes the destruction of Sea Base, He will tell you. If you do not see it as part of His design, you are only to try to sink it if you believe you can escape." His father moved toward the doorway. "While at sea, you will hear of explosions and carnage as we stir the world toward a global war. If you can sink this abomination so that those in Washington think a foreign power did it, then it will help our vision. Even if you are partially successful, whatever happens to this Sea Base will be seen as an attack by China. A war between China and America would catapult the world into Armageddon."

"How will I know what God's Army is doing elsewhere, Father?"

"You will know, Andrew," Ezekiel replied, smiling. "We will work here to stir up America over a Chinese attack. We will convince enough people that it is only days from attack. You will hear of the preparations and God will guide your hand. For the prophecy to be fulfilled, we may even have to allow our country to be attacked. If Sea Base should sink during this time, it would be seen as evidence of an impending attack. Then, there will be such a powerful reaction by our own mighty weapons, we will rejoice in how God's Army catapulted this world into Armageddon."

"Yes, Father," Andrew said, wrapping his palm around the pistol.

His father leaned close to him, his eyes wet, a tear escaping from the old man's right eye. "I want you to kill these men who took my oldest." He took the photograph and stared at it. "They both must die by your hand before you try anything against this Sea Base. I want these seeds of Satan shot with your brother's gun." Bracing his hand against the door facing, his father tugged Andrew down. "Let's pray for guidance."

Thirty minutes later, the two arose. His father slapped him on the shoulder. "Go to bed, my son."

Andrew nodded and started up the stairs.

His father stood at the foot watching him go up. "Andrew, you should stop in and see your sisters. Let them comfort you before you begin your long journey tomorrow."

TWO

"How are you feeling?" Agazzi asked.

Jacobs pushed off lightly from the safety railing of Sea Base. Alistair Agazzi, Senior Chief Sonar Technician, walked up beside him. "You know, Alistair, I hate to tell you this, but your red hair is migrating toward gray—hell, it isn't migrating, it's at a full gallop."

"What's this, you still feeling sorry for yourself? Deflecting my question?" Agazzi jerked his thumb over his shoulder. "I was down in medical. They said you won't do a damn thing they tell you since you returned from the *Boxer*."

Jacobs pulled a cigar from a small waist pack threaded onto his khaki web belt. He winced from the effort.

"You're not fully recovered from your wounds, you know," said Agazzi.

"I'm not?" Jacobs replied sarcastically. "I mean, it's only been a couple of months." He bit off the end of the cigar. "Go figure."

"You lose your clip?" Agazzi laughed.

Jacobs reached out and placed his hand on the safety line. "Yes," he said softly. "It bugs the shit out of me having this sling around my neck all day and not being able to do what I need to do. I got my boatswain mates offering me seats when I come up. Now, where in the hell does a boatswain mate sit when he's doing his job?"

Agazzi shrugged.

"He sits on the deck on his ass is where he sits. There ain't any chairs in a boatswain mate's work space."

Agazzi chuckled. "Seems to me they may be seeing through your master chief façade and recognizing what a great and wonderful guy you are."

"What you trying to do? Upset me? It's been a beautiful day so far, so don't come up here and try to ruin my lunch."

"Speaking of lunch, you going down to the goat locker?"

Jacobs took a deep pull off his cigar. "After my cigar maybe. Do you know how long it is going to take my First Division of boatswain mates to clean up this mess on the deck and get it back to Navy standards?"

Agazzi grinned as Jacobs ranted about the damage the burnt aircraft had done to the Sea Base deck. Keeping a ship at sea pristine was impossible. Salt air, wind, and waves worked together to grow rust on top of the Navy gray. Agazzi stood quietly beside the injured man, noting that while Jacobs had complained about the sling around his neck, his friend seldom used it. It hung there like some giant French *honneur de guerre*.

How long had they served together? Agazzi asked himself against the backdrop of Jacobs's monologue. It seemed to him they had known each other for at least twenty of his twenty-two years in the Navy.

They had steamed together and deployed together so many times in his career, he had lost count. Jacobs was always a pay grade ahead of him in the oldest rating in the United States Navy—boatswain mate.

Boatswain mates lived with the reputation of being more Navy than the Navy, tracing a tradition of keeping warships shipshape, fine-looking, and seaworthy. They fought the salt air, wind, and waves to remove the rust the elements left behind. Over the years as ratings came and went, the boatswain mate rating survived, even during the years of transformation when ambition and political favors turned the Navy inward upon itself.

Jacobs turned with one hand on the safety line, looking aft out to sea. Agazzi did likewise. His friend was still experiencing a lot of pain, but Jacobs hated sympathy almost as much as he hated a speck of rust on his deck.

"I understand the Skipper wants to hold a ceremony for your Bronze Star award," Agazzi said, interrupting Jacobs.

Jacobs stopped and smiled at him. "Did you glaze over again while I was talking?"

"You were getting too technical for me."

"How do you get too technical for a sonar technician, Alistair? What you mean to say is that I was getting too nautical for you."

"As I said, I understand the Skipper intends to hold a ceremony for your Bronze Star."

"So the XO told me."

"I would think you'd be more enthused about it."

Jacobs shook his head. "Alistair, there I was—*alone*—against the entire North Korean Army and armed only with a measly fire hose." He waved his cigar at his friend, his eyes twinkling above the smile. "A man can get hurt doing that shit." Jacobs pointed toward the forward portion of Sea Base. "I don't need no stinking ceremony. What I need is that fire-blazed stain off my deck."

Agazzi knew Jacobs would never admit anything worried him. Jacobs had been wounded fighting North Korean soldiers who had staged a surprise landing on board Sea Base in an attempt to replicate their capture of the USS *Pueblo*. Wielding a fire hose at the time, the master chief had used the water pressure of the hose to keep the North Koreans from assembling until bullets pierced the hose, draining the pressure.

"You know something, Alistair? You never think about your mortality until something such as this slams it against you." Jacobs turned, looked at Agazzi, started to say something, but instead just shook his head. "Wish I was on a real warship instead of this Office of Naval Research floating experiment."

Agazzi nodded. "Guess so. You don't have transport aircraft landing on warships."

"And," Jacobs said, jerking his thumb over his shoulder toward the forward portion of Sea Base, "you don't have a big black starlike stain ruining the starlike quality of your deck."

"Sea Base did pretty good in the Sea of Japan."

"Sea Base is a disaster waiting to happen," Jacobs harrumphed. The master chief smiled. "It's a miracle we aren't resting on the bottom of the dark Pacific with our story being told on the History Channel under *Great Military Disasters* or something like that."

Sea Base was a man-made island of more than eighty acres of a special alloy deck held aloft by eight of the largest, but oldest, Fast Sealift Ships in the Fleet. Ships that two years ago were headed for the mothball fleet, but thanks to this ONR experiment, had gained new life.

Banks of computers and servers filled the cargo hold of the USNS *Pollux*. Connected to the engineering rooms and bridges of the eight ships, they worked constantly to control the coordinated positioning of the ships.

Each Fast Sealift Ship was over 946 feet long, only a few feet shorter than an aircraft carrier. At their beam, they were 105 feet across. The eight ships were arranged with two sets of three holding up the main body of Sea Base, with the remaining two forward and aft of the six. These two ships held up the leading and trailing edges of the runway that ran down the middle of Sea Base. Both ends of the runway jutted out from the main Sea Base deck by one thousand feet.

ALONG with running the engineering and bridge controls, the bank of computers and servers moved huge sea anchors beneath the ships, continually adjusting their depth with technological direction to further hold the ships in place. Connecting each ship to the others were mobile passageways with rubber gaskets that stretched and contracted to the minute changes of position. No one enjoyed walking the passageways. They swayed like rope bridges over deep canyons. Many preferred to climb the four stories from the main deck of the Fast Sealift Ships to the Sea Base canopy and walk across the gray metal island in the open air to the next ship.

"I figured by now you would have painted over the stain," Alistair offered. "Then it would all be the same color."

"You trying to piss me off or something? You know that stain is made up of oil, burnt gasoline, and other flammables."

Jacobs turned and stared at it again. "I'll try sanding it down and see what happens." He winced as he lifted his right hand. "That hurt."

"It wouldn't if you kept it in the sling like the doctor said."

"He didn't tell me to keep it in a sling. He put this sling around my neck and ordered me to keep it on whenever I was awake." Jacobs lifted his left hand and flicked the sling. "Ergo, I have the sling on."

"I think I was there once when the doctor said the sling was for your right arm."

Jacobs turned back to the safety line. "I think you heard right. But he didn't tell me to keep my arm in it all day."

Jacobs pulled a lighter from his pocket.

"Didn't the doctor also tell you to give those up, at least until your wounds fully healed?" Alistair asked.

Jacobs grunted. "The doctor also told me that Helen said when I returned home I could expect her to wound me again."

"Yeah, Frieda sent me an e-mail saying Helen was still slightly upset over this."

Jacobs relit the cigar. "Upset is not the word I would have used. I think she threw the rest of my clothes out the window."

"She must have told *you* that. Frieda told *me* Helen spent the first few days worrying and crying, wondering how badly you were wounded."

"That's good news except . . . I think Helen wants me well enough to kill me herself."

Alistair laughed. "I suspect the neighbors have already given the cops a heads-up."

"I think I will too before we dock back in Pearl."

The two friends stood silent for a few minutes. Both looked aft across the Pacific Ocean. The slight wake of the ships working to stay in a constant position was the only disturbance to the smooth blue waters.

"The incident got to you, didn't it?"

Jacobs shrugged. "I'm a master chief boatswain mate. I'm not smart enough to let something like being shot, bombed, and tossed through the air get to me."

Agazzi jumped back from the safety line and put his right hand over his heart. "Methinks I am going to pass out. This did upset you," he said emphatically. "Finally, something that has made the boatswain mate master chief sit up and realize—"

"You know those sharks are still milling about in the shade under there," Jacobs interrupted, pointing below Sea Base. "I still have one good arm, which is enough to pick your hairy ass up and toss it overboard."

Alistair laughed. "Now, that's the Jerry Jacobs I know and everyone loves."

"Does the ancient nautical term of 'eat shit and die' mean anything to you?" Jacobs replied good-naturedly.

"Now that you mention it."

Jacobs pushed away from the safety lines. "I've got to get back to my boatswain mates. Doctor wants me to wait another couple of weeks. It's been a month now." He looked forward. "And if I don't get this deck shipshape, I'm going to go squirrelly."

"Who's running First Division now? Who's your LPO?"

"I guess Showdernitzel is the nearest thing to an LPO I have."

"You mean the one they call Mad Mary?"

"Yep. She comes down every afternoon before dinner and tells me everything that's going on with the division. She told me yesterday the old man is thinking of either putting a junior officer in or transferring a chief over to First Division until I get better."

"That should be all right."

"All right!" Jacobs blasted. "The hell it is. There's no telling how screwed up First Division is now with Mad—Petty Officer Showdernitzel running things. She's probably got them in flip-flops, short pants, and earrings. All I need is one of these ninety-day wonders or some hotshot Academy grad with visions of John Paul Jones running things." He pointed once again to the dark stain where the North Korean Y-8 transport had burned. "What the hell do they know about how to remove that burn stain and restore the deck to pristine Navy gray? You can bet your bottom dollar they don't know shit, and especially some junior officer who is still trying to figure out who is supposed to fold his underwear."

"Ah-ha! The truth comes out. You're worried someone will see how replaceable Master Chief Boatswain Mate Jerry Jacobs is."

"Alistair, anyone ever tell you what an asshole of a friend you can be?" Jacobs replied in a normal voice. "Just a big asshole."

Alistair raised his hand to shield his eyes from the early afternoon sun. "Looks as if the Air Force is tinkering with their toys again."

"That's Chief Master Sergeant Willard standing there with his arms folded. I'm told that him and his flight line crew fought the North Koreans also."

"From what I've read, they had M-16s and while you were washing them down, they were mowing them down."

Jacobs shook his head. "Alistair, how long did it take you to think that metaphor up?"

CHIEF Master Sergeant Johnny Willard stood near F-22A Raptor Side Number 223, arms crossed, looking up at Technical Sergeant Danny Grossman. A side panel on the nose of the world's best stealth fighter lay on the yellow mesh grating of the hydraulic platform. Grossman's head and arms were inside the opening.

"What does he think it is this time?" Sergeant Lou Thomas asked Willard.

Willard pulled a handkerchief from his back pocket, lifted his cap, and ran it across his bald dome. The six-foot-four-inch first sergeant of the Air Force detachment glanced down at Thomas for a moment.

"Who knows? Sometimes an aircraft is a Jonah, built to be a hangar queen; or maybe, as my first chief master sergeant once told me, there are aviation demons on every flight line looking for a home. I think ours have found theirs."

"It did fly for a few days," Thomas protested.

"Everything flies for a few days. This one keeps burning out the test chopper assembly. I have no idea what a test chopper assembly is supposed to do, but every time we replace it, we have to order it from the supply depot Stateside because of the cost. And every time we order one, we get a nasty message from the Air Force demanding to know what in the hell we're doing with them."

"Tell them we're trading them to the Navy for real food."

Willard's forehead bunched up, causing his heavy eyebrows to bunch into a V. "You don't like the food here?"

"Well, it's okay, if you like the same thing day after day, night after night."

"Gawl-damn it!" Grossman shouted from above, pulling himself out of the narrow confines of the opening. The screwdriver in his left hand fell, clanging on the metal grating of the platform steps until it clunked on the deck of Sea Base.

"Jesus, Danny!" Sergeant Melanie Parker shouted, jumping away from the bottom of the platform where she and Snaggles Cole served as safety observers. "You want to kill us down here?" Parker was slightly rotund, with straggly brown hair that always seemed to be trying to escape her head. When her cap came off, the hair flew every which way.

"Yeah, watch the tools, Danny," Thomas added.

Grossman looked down. "Chief, this assembly is a piece of shit," he pleaded. "And it's not easy to get out, much less put in."

"You did an excellent job replacing it last time."

"And did you see the nasty message—"

"I saw it, Danny," Willard replied. He tapped his finger against his massive chest. "Messages are mine to handle, not yours. You just fix the 223."

"The best way to fix it is to shove it over the side."

The noise of an aircraft drew their attention. Willard recognized the distinct rising turboprop sound of the transport even before he saw the venerable C-130 Hercules appear near the end of the runway. It amazed him the Navy kept flying the aircraft in every type of weather while at least the Air Force restricted it to the Air National Guard. He'd be on that proverbial rocking chair with a lap blanket spread across his legs, watching the days go by, and these aircraft and the B-52s would still be flying. The Navy and Air Force were going to fly the C-130s until they wouldn't fly any more; then they'd probably strip the wings off and use them as tractor-trailers. Someday, the Department of Defense was going to have to realize that even aircraft age.

The C-130 flew over the edge of the runway. It seemed to float down onto the runway, and the friction of the wheels when they touched the deck sent a brief wave of bluish smoke behind the aircraft. The flaps came up, the propeller blades rotated slightly, and the aircraft quickly came to taxiing speed.

"Well, looks as if our spare part is here!" Grossman shouted.

"How do you know it's on the afternoon run?" Snaggles Cole asked. Snaggles was the junior airman of the ground crew. A native of Chicago, he spoke as if the slow pace of words was in unison with his speed of thought.

Everyone smiled except Willard. Cole was a good man, but in the old Air Force—back before his time—Cole would have been a twenty-year airman. The man had been in the Air Force nearly four years, and had managed to make it all the way to E-3 before catching up with his expertise. The Air Force would allow him to reenlist one more time, but if Cole failed promotion, then it would be out on the street for the man. Too bad. Snaggles really loved the Air Force. Too bad he also had a crush on Parker.

A light blue pickup truck appeared to the left of the C-130. Up until a week ago, the only light blue pickup truck had had "Air Force" painted on the side and was parked a few feet from him. The Navy liked the idea and had shipped in a pickup truck for their use. The Navy did not like the light blue color that appeared when it was backed off the C-130. The Navy was trying to get another pickup painted Navy gray. He smiled at the irony of how much the two services were influencing each other during this deployment. Knowing the Navy, they were probably keeping a secret score somewhere. He also smiled knowing the Navy was stuck with the Air Force–blue pickup, and with their supply department much like the Air Force's, it would be a long time before they received approval for a second pickup.

The aircraft fell in behind the pickup and followed it off the runway to the apron. Willard turned and watched it.

"I said, how do you know our spare part is on it?" Cole asked again, shielding his eyes as he looked up at Grossman.

"RFID."

"RFID?"

"Yeah," Parker said, slapping Cole upside the arm. "You heard da man! RFID."

"What the f—"

"Eh!" Parker drew her hand back.

"—hell is RFID?" Cole finished, lifting his shoulder and raising his hand in defense.

Parker laughed and dropped her hand. "You dumb shit."

"RFID stands for Radio Frequency Identification. Kind of like those bar codes at supermarkets, except these bar codes react to radio frequencies," Grossman said. He squatted, then slid to the edge, dropping his legs over the side as he sat down on the platform. "I'm not sure exactly how it works, but instead of supply manifests, the supply weenies zap a load of supplies, and everything in it blabs back what they are and where they're supposed to be."

"So, you got one of those?" Snaggles asked.

"One of what?"

"One of those zappers?"

"Snaggles, is your brother an only child?" Grossman asked, shaking his head.

"Lou," Willard said. "Get someone over there and get our spare part."

"Snaggles!" Thomas shouted. "Go do your thing and get that chopper assembly before it gets lost in the Navy supply chain."

Cole gave a mock salute and took off. The last two times when the part was sent, Snaggles had met the aircraft, cut open the box, lifted the part, and brought it back. Later, Willard had straightened it out with the Navy Master Chief Storekeeper, who had to account for the six-digit-priced piece. There'd be griping and complaining, but the E-9s of the Navy ran it much like the chief master sergeants ran the Air Force. Difference was, the Navy recognized their E-9s by putting two stars on their collars, which came in handy on non-Navy bases.

"Okay, Lou," Willard said. "Did you finish the preflight check on 213 and 233?"

Thomas looked at his watch. "I did, Chief. We did it yesterday and we did it again this morning. Showtime is in an hour with a 1400-hour launch. Both aircraft are fully armed and fully fueled."

* * *

ANDREW bent over and turned sideways slightly to step out the small door onto the metal steps leading down from the body of the C-130. Why didn't they let passengers disembark off the ramp like the flight crew? The ramp was lowered. Everyone could have stood up as they walked off. He tripped on the lower rung, and would have fallen if a set of hands had not grabbed him.

"You okay there, buddy?"

The petty officer third class holding him was lean, his hands revealing a sinewy strength to them not readily apparent in the sailor's appearance. Andrew was proud of being able to recognize the rank by the emblem on the left shoulder. A month ago, this life as a sailor would have been confusing, but Steve had taught him what he needed to get by as a third-class petty officer.

"Excuse me," the woman behind Andrew said. The two sailors eased to the side, but not before watching the tall-drink-of-water lady swish by.

"Thanks," Andrew said, pulling away. He brushed the creases in his dungaree bell-bottom trousers.

The hands let go. "Just trying to help, buddy."

The two continued to watch the woman. The pants suit clung to her body. Both men knew a ten-hour flight in a C-130 would make everything cling.

"Wow," Taleb said softly.

Her red hair increased in intensity as she moved from under the shade of the wing into the bright noon sunshine of the Pacific. Two men met her. One was huge, with a waistline that cascaded over his belt, hiding the top of the pants beneath the folds. The other civilian was tall, slender, with the high and tight haircut of a military person.

"Nice eyeball orgy," Taleb said.

Andrew dropped his stare and glared at the man. The sailor who had stopped him from falling had a dark complexion. Short brown hair matched the man's dark brown eyes. Part Negroid, Andrew told himself. One of God's children to be led. He forced a smile as someone bumped into him, sending a surge of anger through him.

One of the flight crew shouted at him, "Move it, sailor, you're blocking the exit. Let the others out."

"Come on. What's your name?" the sailor asked.

"Al . . . Al Jolson," Andrew replied as the sailor touched him and motioned him toward the rear of the aircraft.

"Al Jolson! Wow! You must get a lot of joshing about being Jolson."

Andrew's forehead wrinkled. "Not too much."

"Here, follow me. They'll off-load the luggage at the rear and we can grab your seabag. You know where you're going?"

Andrew shook his head. As soon as he stepped out from beneath the shadow of the wing, the heat of the Pacific sun burned down upon their bare heads. He reached in his rear pocket and pulled out his ball cap. "But I'm wearing the same insignia you are."

"Yeah, we're boatswain mates, but most likely you're going to be with Master Chief Jacobs. . . . Hey! Don't put on the hat."

That was one of the names, Andrew thought when he heard Jacobs's name. He held the ball cap in his hand, looking down at it. "Thought we had to wear our hats at all times."

"Naw," Taleb said, turning his nose up and shaking his head. "Not on the flight deck. Too many opportunities for something built by the lowest bidder sucking it into its intake, blowing up, and killing people. When that happens, the Skipper tends to get pissed off. Hence," the sailor continued, holding up a finger, "no hats on flight decks is the golden rule. Now for you, most likely you're going to be with Master Chief Jacobs and his band of renegades. I work for another section of Sea Base."

At the rear of the C-130, a mixed line of personnel wearing flight suits, colored flight deck shirts, and dungarees stood in a line. Hand-over-hand, luggage emerged from the C-130, passing unceremoniously from one person to the next, until at the end, the luggage was tossed onto the deck for the passengers to sort out.

Andrew and the sailor stopped near the crowd.

The sailor stuck his hand out. "Name's Jaime Taleb. I spend most of my days around Combat Information Center." Taleb pointed toward the tower complex located several hundred feet off the port side of the runway. "That's where the true heart and soul of Sea Base is. Tours are free."

Taleb shook his head. "Damn, they're going to break something doing it that way." He looked at Andrew. "Best thing you can do, my friend, is to grab yours as soon as you see it; otherwise, if you have pictures of loved ones in your bag, you're going to be looking at them through cracked glass."

Andrew walked to the line, reached out, and pulled his seabag away from the sailor about to pass it along.

"Hey!"

Andrew turned, ignoring the sailor, who was quickly bumped by the next piece of luggage, drawing his attention away and back to the unloading.

"Wow! That's what I call God looking out for you."

Andrew's eyes narrowed. It seemed for a moment as if Taleb's eyes were boring into him. "God always watches over those who know His ways."

"Yeah, my old man used to say the same thing about Allah."

Andrew's eyes widened. Blasphemy. Equating Allah with God! Who was this heathen? Maybe this was God's test for him?

"Sorry," Taleb said. "Didn't mean to offend you."

Andrew shook his head. "No offense taken. It's just where I come from, religion is taken very seriously."

"Then, you'd love my father's country of Iran."

"Hey! You two!"

Both Andrew and Taleb turned. A senior chief marched toward them. "You two got your gear?"

They both nodded.

"Then clear the hell away from the aircraft. I don't have time for onlookers and grab-assers." He jerked his thumb toward the port side of Sea Base. "So, go find yourself some other place to trade your sea tales."

"I don't have . . ."

Taleb put his hand on Andrew's arm. "Where you want us to go, Senior Chief?" Taleb interrupted.

The senior chief spread his hands wide. "What the hell am I wearing? Does this look like an apron? Am I your fucking mother? No, I ain't, and I don't care where you go as long as you get away from my aircraft so me and the crew can offload this flying bucket of bolts and get off this piece-of-shit Sea Base before it falls into the fucking ocean."

Taleb leaned over to Andrew, looking up at him. "I think he wants us to move along so they can finish unloading and fly off the ship."

"What the hell did you think I was saying?" the senior chief shouted. "That's exactly what the fuck I said."

"Sorry, Senior Chief. Your description was so apropos, I wanted to translate it for my friend here."

"Get the hell out of my sight," the senior chief said through clenched teeth. He turned and walked away mumbling something about the Navy not being the Navy he'd joined.

Taleb grabbed the top half of the seabag, while Andrew held the thick cloth strap at the center. "Follow me!" And the two stumbled-ran across the deck, leaving behind a tense senior chief shouting something about deck apes.

"Deck apes?" Andrew asked.

"Yeah, that's what they call us boatswain mates: deck apes."

The soft breeze of the warm Pacific caressed Andrew's cheek, blowing his hair as the two men, laughing, moved across the deck. After several minutes, they stopped, dropping the seabag onto the deck near a line of fighter aircraft. He'd never seen something so huge and fearsome. Smooth lines that arched into sharp edges broke the symmetry of the fuselage.

Taleb let go with one hand and waved at someone standing near an opening off to the port side of Sea Base. Andrew turned and looked back at the aircraft.

"They're Air Force fighters—stealth fighters; called F-22A Raptors," Taleb offered. "We have eight of them on board, though the one with the hydraulic lift alongside seems to be broke all the time. It's one broke-dick motherfucker."

Andrew bristled. "You curse a lot, Taleb. Cursing shows a lack of education." He looked at the boatswain mate helping him. Something about the man's eyes bothered him. His father told him you could tell the depth of a man's soul by the brightness in his eyes. This man had no brightness. There was an evil behind those eyes.

"Sorry," Taleb said, his eyes lowering. "Didn't mean to upset you on your first day." He laughed. "It usually takes me two days to piss people off." He reached down and grabbed the seabag by the handle. "Come on and let's get you checked in with First Division and then I'll head back to my own work."

Andrew watched Taleb saunter off with the seabag swinging slightly from his left hand. Within that seabag the evil man carried were Andrew's Bibles. Inside one of those Bibles rested the pistol for his act of vengeance. He raised his head and took in a broad view of the man-made island floating in God's waters. It was both magnificent in its construction as a testament to what man can do when God wills it, and it was a blasphemy to God's plan for Armageddon by being the man-made instrument that might delay or stop armies from colliding.

"You coming?" Taleb shouted from about fifty feet away. "How you know I'm not some flimflam artist about to steal your seabag?"

Andrew lifted his hand and hurried to catch up with Satan's spawn. He wondered briefly before slowing to a walk alongside Taleb if this demon was able to sense the gun.

THE noise of the hydraulics kicked in, suddenly filling the Unmanned Underwater Vehicle compartment with sharp noise.

"You could give a sailor some warning!" Bernardo shouted from in front of the bank of servers that separated the line of UUV storage cells from the larger part of the compartment. He quickly placed his hands over his ears.

"Shut your griping!" came a voice from the other side of the compartment. "You got ears, pull them down!" Taylor shouted in reply. Ears was the military term for a set of muffling devices that resembled earmuffs. They were issued to sailors working around loud noises and on flight decks for the purpose of protecting a sailor's hearing. Few career sailors finished twenty years with their hearing intact. Ships and aircraft were noisy war machines. A constant ringing in the ears was something most career sailors learned to live with.

"Listen, Po-Boy; if I want shit out of you, I'll squeeze your head."

From behind the array of equipment separating the storage

area from the UUV firing cradle, Taylor replied, "If you hit me and I find out . . ."

"This isn't what I signed up to do," Bernardo said, looking at Keyland, who was bent over the computer console that controlled the overhead tracks and the UUV firing cradle. "This is something along Taylor's line of skills."

Po-Boy Taylor, the maintenance person for the sonar team, grumbled, "That's all I hear from you: gripe, gripe, gripe."

"And all we hear from you is 'mumble, mumble, mumble'!"

"All right, you two, stop the crap and let's get this last UUV loaded into the firing cradle. We left MacPherson alone with our two seamen too long. Makes me nervous," Petty Officer Keyland declared.

"Well, I can always run back and keep Jenkins company. That way you'd have two qualified operators on the job. Could send the two seamen, Calvins and Gentron, down here—"

"Just shut up for a while, Pope," Keyland pleaded. "Hard work for a few hours isn't going to kill you."

"But this isn't even my job," Bernardo said, tilting his Navy ball cap up off his forehead and running his hand through his long black hair. "I'm a sonar technician, not a torpedoman."

Taylor came around the corner. "Whoa!" he shouted, pretending to shiver. "I can't believe you're running your hand through that greasy shit you put on your hair."

Bernardo put his hands on his hips. "I put nothing on my hair."

Taylor laughed. "Then, maybe you should," he said, picking up something from his toolbox and disappearing around the corner.

Bernardo turned back to the leading petty officer. "Listen, Petty Officer Keyland, as I said before our high school dropout interrupted, I'm a sonar technician, not a torpedoman."

"Ain't no such animal anymore in this man's Navy!" Taylor shouted from the other side of the consoles. "And who you calling a high school dropout?"

"Cut it out, Po-Boy," Keyland said in a loud voice to Taylor. "And you, Pope," he continued, poking Bernardo in the chest once. "This may not be in your job description, but it isn't as if we have extra hands we can send down here to do this."

"The second UUV is hooked up and ready when you are," Taylor said in a loud voice.

"So, Pope, get your butt down there at the firing cradle and make sure it loads properly."

"Okay, I'm going, Petty Officer Keyland, but you keep your hands away from the button that opens the well deck. Remember what happened to that cat named Smith."

Keyland did remember what happened to Smith . . . or whoever the sailor had really been. He glanced at the walkway that ran around the upper level separating where he stood and the lowest level, where the firing cradle held eight UUVs ready for launch. Beneath the firing cradle was a well deck that opened directly into the ocean.

Smith had tried to kill Senior Chief Agazzi on the walkway. The sailor would have succeeded if Master Chief Boatswain Mate Jacobs hadn't decided to be his nosy self. He had knocked the faux Smith down onto the third level of the UUV compartment, where the man had rolled into the ocean through the open well deck. The sharks that now filled the shadows beneath this eighty-one-plus acres of man-made island had made short work of Smith, according to rumors.

Keyland turned around to the operating console that allowed manual firing of the UUVs. Senior Chief Agazzi had never spoken about the specifics of what happened down here, but if it had not been for him and Jacobs, Sea Base would have been resting on the bottom of the dark Pacific months ago. This Smith character had rigged C-4 on several UUVs. The UUVs were nothing more than sophisticated torpedoes capable of being computer-driven from the ASW control center by MacPherson or Gentron. Each UUV weighed over a ton with a five-hundred-pound high-explosive warhead. If Smith had not been stopped, the chain of explosions would have ripped the bottom out of the USNS *Bellatrix*. The large eighty-one-acre canopy held aloft by the Fast Sealift Ships would have started to collapse as *Bellatrix* sank. It would have been like a row of dominoes falling as Sea Base followed. Keyland shivered. He doubted anyone would have survived.

Bernardo's boondockers clanged on the metal mesh steps

of the ladder as he climbed down from the first level toward the second, drawing Keyland's attention back to the console.

He watched as Bernardo, halfway down, grabbed the metal railing and slid the rest of the way down the short ladder to the second level. The second level was a metal mesh platform that encircled the third and final level, where the firing cradle rested.

Keyland looked at the firing cradle, then down at the computer control. "Ready, Taylor?" he shouted.

"I'm out of the way. It's in the harness. All you gotta do is hit the button."

"You got the emergency stop button."

"I got the dead man's button. It's connected to the overhead tram and I'm holding it in my hand. As long as I keep it pressed, it'll keep moving."

Keyland pressed the icon. The noise of the hydraulics increased in intensity. He looked at the overhead rails. Within the exposed opening along the center, hidden partially by the shadows of the metal surrounding it, chains moved. The chains clanged against the sides of the metal railings adding decibels to the noise of the hydraulics.

"Jesus Christ!" Bernardo shouted, turning around and glaring at Keyland. The second class reached up and pulled his Navy ears down.

KIANG pulled the door to his stateroom closed. In his hand, he held several photographs from the North Korean incident over a month ago. This Petty Officer Taleb and he had spent that afternoon on the enclosed platform high up in the antenna masts over the tower, and Taleb had been bumping into his consistently since then. The man continued to pester him for copies of the photographs Kiang had taken that day.

He had tried to avoid doing this, but maybe if he gave the young sailor some of the photographs, the man would go back to his work and leave Kiang along. The last thing he needed was someone trailing him around Sea Base, especially some friendless sailor looking for an older mentor. The face of his handler, the colonel, interrupted his thoughts.

Whenever Kiang thought about a normal life, his captivity

in China under the machinations of the colonel brought him back to the reality of how the rest of his life was going to be. He had received a letter from his parents in yesterday's mail run. Along with the letter, written in English, were two photographs of his mom and dad visiting relatives in central China.

The difference was this letter held a message. The three pages had the second and last page interchanged. This was the second letter in a row with the same mistake. The first time, he'd attributed it to the censor forgetting to put them back in right order. For it to happen a second time meant it was deliberate. It could be the colonel sending Kiang a warning, but the colonel was not subtle about his warnings. Kiang's ribs on his right side had healed slightly askew. That was the colonel's idea of a subtle warning.

No, his father had done this. His father was a meticulous person. He ran their small shop in San Antonio with the precision of a major corporation. Nothing was left to chance. There was no way his father would have sent a letter with the three pages out of order.

He set the letter aside to play with later. His father was sending him a message with these two letters. So far, he had been unable to figure it out.

Kiang turned and shook the door. He glanced both ways down the passageway of the USNS *Regulus*. Seeing no one, he reached up and slid the thin wire into the crevice of the door. Less than a quarter-inch long, the wire would jump back flush with the door facing if someone opened it.

Satisfied, Kiang started down the passageway, passing other staterooms. He had seen one of the open-berthing areas on board the *Regulus,* and realized how lucky he was to have a private stateroom. The open-berthing areas had been constructed from part of the hangar bays on the Fast Sealift Ships. Each held fifty people of the same sex. A long row of two-high bunks lined each row of ten, each bunk with a mattress that seemed six inches thick to Kiang. The last row was only five double-bunks deep. A small lounge with a couple of couches and chairs surrounding a table and a television filled in the vacant space. The head was a hundred feet away in the aft forecastle of the ships. This meant the sailors, contractors, and merchant marines assigned to the accommodations there had to walk through about fifty feet of the huge hangar bay, then another fifty feet along a passageway, to shower, shave, and do their morning ablutions. Only the colonel could have kept him on board the *Regulus* if he had been assigned to one of the berthing areas.

Being a Ph.D. and a senior contractor helped, though he wasn't sure how. Most of the contractors on board "racked" in the open berthing area with the junior sailors. "Rack" was the nautical term for a bed, and "to rack" was the verb for sleeping on them. He could understand after seeing their construction why the word for a torture device of centuries ago applied to those beds in the open-berthing compartments.

He had a stateroom. Staterooms were the territory of the officers on warships. But staterooms on Fast Sealift Ships, such as the one he had on *Regulus,* put staterooms on warships to shame. He had overheard Navy officers talking about their accommodations. The staterooms on board Fast Sealift Ships made the Navy officers think of rooms on cruise liners. Twin beds, recliner rockers, lamps, private bathrooms with showers, and televisions. All that was missing was a bar, and Kiang wouldn't be surprised if alcohol was available somewhere on these merchant marine ships.

Kiang walked onto the main deck, pushing the watertight door shut behind him and pushing down the bar to secure it. He glanced up at the bottom of the Sea Base metal canopy that stretched over the top of *Regulus,* held aloft by huge masts that reached nearly four stories above him. The trapped fumes of the eight ships assaulted his nostrils, the dense sulfur burning his nostrils slightly as he breathed. Dusk brought the late afternoon ocean breeze through the underpart of Sea Base, cleaning out the trapped fumes, and enticing people to come out. The bow of the *Regulus* was usually free of the fumes because of where the ship was located: front port side of Sea Base with no other ship in front of it.

Shouting came from over the side of the ship. He walked to the edge to see what the noise was about. The side of the ship that in other days was used to drive military vehicles on and off *Regulus* was open with its ramp extended outward. Fishing contest. The big thing on Sea Base was the fishing competition. At sea level, the fumes never penetrated, but being at sea level was something he never intended to do.

He shivered slightly. The only fish beneath Sea Base were sharks. Big sharks, small sharks . . . he wasn't a marine biologist, but he had seen enough shark movies on the National Geographic Channel to know they were sharks. But you didn't need to see them to recognize them, for they were something people talked about constantly. When Sea Base was first set up nearly four months ago, the Captain had allowed swim call, but within days the first of the sharks had arrived. Then more. Within a month, the whole of the shaded area beneath Sea Base canopy crawled with sharks. When Kiang first saw the spectacle, his first impression was that there were so many of them, you could walk between ships on their backs.

When Sea Base left the western Pacific and moved slowly into the Sea of Japan, the sharks accompanied it, never leaving the shadows beneath the floating island.

The fishing teams below were wrestling a shark to the side of the ramp. He turned away. The routine was to kill the shark, weigh it, take the statistics for the games, and then toss it back into the ocean, where fellow sharks fought over the carcass. It was a cruel sport, he thought. And each time they threw the shark back to be devoured by the others, it drew more sharks to Sea Base.

The door to the staircase leading up to Sea Base had been roped open. He started climbing. Four stories later, he pulled himself up through the opening onto the main deck. The stifling heat from the open area below was blown away by the soft Pacific breeze arcing up from the south. There was still the summer heat, even if the calendar said it was October, but at least there was nothing deflecting the breeze as the clustered ships below did.

He saw the C-130, and spotted Taleb carrying the front end of some poor soul's seabag away from it. Taleb had told him that the two of them had met when Kiang returned from San Antonio. He didn't recall the meeting, but seeing the man meeting this C-130 helped confirm that maybe Taleb did speak to him when he disembarked from the C-130. Kiang had a lot on his mind.

The interchanged pages meant something. It was a signal. A message from his father. But what was his father trying to tell him?

Taleb waved, but kept on with the task of helping the new arrival. Kiang ignored the gesture and continued toward the tower.

THREE

"Captain in Combat!" the booming voice of the Chief Operations Specialist for Sea Base Combat Information Center announced.

Garcia found the rolling announcement of his presence wherever he went on board Sea Base different from the jobs he had had for most of his career in the Navy. The thing that shocked him was how much he enjoyed it. He raised his hand in acknowledgment as he turned and shut the hatch behind him. Walking across the hard rubber covering in the blue-lighted compartment, he felt the eyes of the Combat Information Center watch team on him. It had been like this since the fight with the North Koreans. His eyes were still adjusting to the blue fluorescent lighting that kept Combat in a perpetual nighttime environment when he reached the vicinity of his chair.

Combat Information Center: This was where Skippers, throughout the era of the modern Navy, had fought their ships and their battle groups. This was the nerve center of Sea Base. And he was the four-striper Captain who could with a snap of his fingers bring the whole experiment to its full war-fighting potential, or with the same snap, shut it down. Military equivalents in other services had little appreciation for the full range of powers a Navy Captain at sea held.

A petty officer appeared out of the shadows with a fresh cup of coffee. Garcia thanked the man and took the cup. He had been drinking coffee since reveille at zero six hundred. He could do without another cup, but since the fight in the Sea of Japan, his sailors had treated him as if he was . . . what? Their father? He smiled. He enjoyed the treatment.

Combat was on the second level of the tower construction raised on top of the Sea Base canopy. The tower was four levels high. Unlike the top level, the second level was windowless. Ships at sea had levels instead of stories. Ashore, the tower would have been a building and each level referred to as a story. But four stories became four levels once Sea Base left dry land.

Air traffic controllers and the Air Boss occupied the top level—called the Air Tower—with its slanted windows wall-to-wall around the four sides of Sea Base. Each window slanted outward to increase visibility in heavy rain and each window had its own set of wipers.

The scientists and contractors who designed and built Sea Base occupied the bottom level. The Office of Naval Research filled the offices and cubicles inside the bottom level, which, like Combat, had no windows. But unlike Combat, every office, niche, and cubicle within the ONR spaces had bright fluorescent lights to help them see as they analyzed every bit of data connected with Project Sea Base. They were the only ones that referred to the man-made island as Project Sea Base.

The third level was his. It was both the in-port and at-sea cabin for the Skipper, and it was the largest he had ever seen. It was more a suite than a stateroom.

Vice Admiral Dick Holman, Commander United States Seventh Fleet, said it was bigger than his stateroom on the *Boxer*. Garcia didn't know if the admiral was a little envious, or just making an observation. With Holman, you never knew when he was joking and when he was being serious. "I guess if he throws me overboard, then he's serious about something," Garcia said under his breath.

"You say something, Skipper?" Commander Stapler asked as Garcia reached his chair.

"No, I was just thinking out loud, Stan. My apologies for not making the 1000 briefing, got caught up in a teleconference with Admiral Holman and Admiral DeMedewe-Stewart."

"Another problem, if you don't mind me asking?"

Garcia shook his head. "No problem. Admiral Stewart, the British battle force commander, and Admiral Holman spent most of the time bad-mouthing the French and discussing battle group disposition."

Stapler ran his hand over the top of his head, stopping on top of the very short crew cut to scratch it a couple of times. "Don't understand why someone with a name like DeMedewe would take a dislike to the French."

"Don't know. I think when all is said and done, a lot of centuries of wars between them still have an effect today. I recall the admiral saying the name was ancient Norman."

"DeMedewe; sounds French to me. Commander Tyler-Cole," Stapler added, rolling the name around his lips as he pronounced it. "There's another hyphenated British name."

"The admiral said something about DeMedewe being handed down through the centuries. The admiral's aide referred to him a couple of times as Admiral Stewart, so I think we'll use Stewart. It's a lot simpler than . . . than . . . Oh, never mind."

"Is the admiral on board the *Elizabeth*?"

"That he is." Garcia nodded and then put his coffee cup in the holder on his chair. "By the way, the British have asked, if necessary, could they stage some of their F-35 Joint Strike Fighters on Sea Base. Told them we'd be glad to do it. I also approved them putting a liaison officer in Combat to help coordinate things."

Stapler's bottom lip pushed into the upper as his eyes narrowed, drawing his light brown eyebrows into a V. "How will I integrate him into Combat? They aren't going to want to control Sea Base, are they?" Stapler's eyebrows lifted. "I am concerned if we give up any control, Skipper."

Garcia shook his head. "No, no, no. Neither I nor Admiral Holman would ever give up any of our responsibilities. The British have the only aircraft carrier out here, and until the larger American aircraft carriers *George Bush* and

Abraham Lincoln arrive from the West Coast, Sea Base and the HMS *Elizabeth* are the only two fighter platforms near Taiwan."

"What do we do with the British fighters when the other F-22A Raptors arrive from Langley?"

Garcia smiled. Two months ago, most of the Navy had no idea what Langley was, much less that it was an airfield in Virginia. Now, the word rolled off the tongues of sailors as easily as the names of Norfolk, San Diego, and Pearl Harbor.

"It looks as if the Air Force squadron are going to bingo directly to Taiwan," said Garcia. "They should arrive within the next seventy-two hours."

"Skipper," the Operations Chief interrupted. "Air Force is preflighting the birds for launch. We have a two-flight escort mission scheduled for launch at 1400."

"Thanks, Chief," Garcia answered.

"That'll be all, Chief," Stapler added. When the chief left the immediate area, he continued. "We can handle the aircraft, but they are Joint Strike Fighters, not F-22As. There will be a problem with logistic support."

"Air Boss doesn't see a problem with us embarking them. I visited the Air Tower before coming down here. Sea Base could handle over two hundred fighter aircraft if we parked them correctly and did the right apron management."

"Sir," Stapler said, leaning forward. "Of course the Air Boss is going to say that. His job is handling aircraft and the more aircraft . . ."

Garcia raised his hand. "Commander, the purpose of Sea Base is to show how efficiently a floating island such as this can handle a larger number of aircraft and project power farther and faster than a three-carrier battle group. The Air Boss was deployed by Naval Air Forces Pacific and assigned to Office of Naval Research. His task is to prove the concept. My and your mission is to prove the concept also, even as we get sucked into this latest crisis."

"But sir . . ."

"No buts, Stan. Besides, handling the aircraft is his problem, not yours."

"It's also yours, sir."

"Every problem, every operation, everything that happens

on Sea Base is mine . . . eventually. Now bring me up to date. Where are we?"

"Aye, sir. We are making way at about eight knots on course 190. We should be in our assigned operations area by noon tomorrow. The British carrier, CVA-01 *Elizabeth,* along with its four warships and the USS *Stripling,* is two hundred miles southwest of us. They are flying the defensive fighter patrols between mainland China and us."

"As of this morning, the British have taken over responsibility for providing air protection north of Taiwan."

Stapler nodded. "We received the new Task Order a few minutes ago. With the British Joint Fighters flying DEFPATs along the northern portion of Taiwan, it frees the Taiwanese fighters to concentrate on the waters directly between Mainland China and Taiwan's west coast. The *Elizabeth* operations area is right around the mouth of the Taiwan Strait."

"We heard anything from the Canadian Task Force?" Garcia asked.

"The three destroyers led by HMCS *Algonquin* and an oiler are due to rendezvous with us tomorrow."

"Algonquin," Garcia said with a smile. "Probably the oldest warship in the free world."

"You know her?"

"I had a friend years ago who served on her and eventually returned about five years ago to be her Skipper. Originally commissioned in 1973 . . ."

"1973! Wow, and still steaming," Stapler said with awe.

"Look at the eight Fast Sealift Ships holding up Sea Base. They were all built around the same time. Guess they did better maritime engineering back then."

"Must have. Skipper, I received a message saying that when they get here, we're to replenish them and they were going to sail onward to join the British battle group."

Garcia nodded. "That's their ultimate destination. The British can't get additional ships here from Great Britain to flesh out their battle group, so the Canadian Forces are going to do it for them."

"Aye, sir," Stapler acknowledged.

"What time is the Rivet Joint due on station?" Garcia asked, referring to the RC-135 reconnaissance aircraft. The

RC-135 was getting long in the tooth, if you asked him. Unlike the aging EP-3E that was retired by the Navy a decade ago, the Air Force continued flying aircraft that long ago should have been in a museum. On the other end of the pendulum was the F-22A Raptor. The Raptor was the foremost stealth fighter in the world, capable of evading radars and with the avionics to take on ten adversaries simultaneously at long range. It is hard to shoot down an aircraft with a missile if your fire-control radars can't find it and the missiles can't lock on. It's even harder when missiles are coming at you seemingly out of nowhere.

"It's in the air now," Stapler said, jerking his thumb toward the Air Traffic Control station. "ATC has voice contact with it. We're coordinating the data-link integration." He took a couple of steps toward the operator and touched her on the shoulder. She eased her earphone off her right ear. Rich black hair fell onto her shoulder.

"Petty Officer Bonicella, where's the RC-135?"

She looked past Stapler and smiled at Garcia.

If he was twenty years younger. . . . He might be in his fifties and eyeball orgies might be as far as his fantasies took him now, but there was little to make a man feel better than a young woman's smile. Garcia nodded at the attractive brunette, and wondered how many hearts lay broken along her path through life. He looked away, his eyes skipping from one young sailor to the other. He smiled as he wondered how many heartbroken sailors she had cast onto the shoals of Sea Base during these past five months.

"It's three hundred miles out on a bearing of zero-four-zero, sir," she said.

Stapler turned back to Garcia.

"I heard," Garcia said. Not only did she have the looks and moves to break men's hearts, but she also had a voice like a siren song from a Greek tragedy.

"The C-130 will be launching in the next thirty minutes."

Garcia turned his mind back to Combat. "Sorry, Stan. My mind was elsewhere."

Stapler's eyes lifted. "I can imagine where, sir," he replied, smiling.

Garcia's eyes narrowed. "I don't understand."

"Sorry, sir," Stapler replied. "It is easy for the mind to wander in Combat. Lots of stuff going on . . ."

"Stan, there is a saying in the Navy that when you discover you're digging yourself deeper into a hole, to quit digging. You said the C-130 is about to take off. Seems to me, they don't take kindly to remaining on board long, do they."

Stapler smiled again. Twice in one day! What is Combat coming to? Garcia asked himself.

"Nope. They think Sea Base is an accident waiting to happen."

Garcia crawled up into his chair. "They aren't far wrong. If we lost the computers in *Pollux,* we'd have eight ships holding up Sea Base slowly going separate ways."

"Let's hope we don't. Does the Skipper have any other questions? Otherwise . . ."

"Yes," Garcia said as Stapler turned to leave. "Tell me the geopolitical situation since this morning. China back down yet? I presume no, or you'd have let me know. Talks still going on in Beijing?"

Stapler shook his head. "No, sir, to your first question and yes, sir, to your second. No big change. The Chinese are still slamming their fists on the table accusing us of sinking their submarine. The State and Defense Department negotiators are still trying to get the Chinese to focus on the growing crisis with Taiwan, and don't seem to be having much success. Lots of demonstrations in Tiananmen Square."

"Maybe this time they really do intend to use military force against what they view as a breakaway province."

"I saw a secret Naval Intelligence message this morning that said the Chinese know the North Koreans sunk the submarine."

Garcia crossed his legs. "Then why all this bullshit?"

Stapler shrugged. "I'm just a lonely old Surface Warfare Officer stuck on board something that's supposed to be the warfare platform of the future, Skipper."

"Stan, you're in a good mood this morning. Everything been going wrong?"

"No, sir," Stapler replied with a tight smile. "I think if you take the message at face value, it means the Chinese have no intention of invading Taiwan or fighting us. They're just using the submarine sinking to remind the world of their position and to flex their ever-growing military might. Flexing it shows the world what they could do, if they wanted to."

Garcia thought about what Stapler had said. He tried to recall an instance during these past five months when Stapler had been as open and forthcoming. He couldn't. "I hope you're right. If you're not, then we're going to have one hell of a fight on our hands."

"We would if we were on the ground. The Pacific Ocean is our friend for this confrontation. They have to come hundreds of miles to reach us."

"It's not us they're after. It's Taiwan."

"Could be right. Could be they're not after Taiwan. Could be they're going to teach their irate teenager neighbor—North Korea—a lesson."

"Why you say that?"

"Imagery is showing Chinese troops massing along the border with North Korea. All of this other stuff could be for show, or could be about showing the world they're a world power now. But it could be an Oriental feint and North Korea is their true target."

"They did that during the Korean War in the fifties, Stan. It was so they could join the North Koreans in fighting us and the Allies."

"ONI mentioned that possibility, but discounted it. The message goes on to say the Director of National Intelligence has information that the Chinese are using this as an opportunity to resolve the Taiwan issue."

"The Taiwan legislature is supposed to vote on independence this week. If they pass it, then I would submit DNI is right, Stan. The Chinese have been warning about that for decades, threatening military action if Taiwan ever voted for formal independence. China has its reputation to uphold for following through on its threats."

"Taiwan hasn't voted for it yet. It has never voted for independence. I think they just like to tweak the nose of their mainland cousins."

"Their mainland cousins, as you call them, don't have a sense of humor about this idea. They have staked their national honor on Taiwan being a breakaway province that will someday be restored to the People's Republic. You are right about them never voting for independence. Taiwan has always tiptoed around the issue while promising its people that eventually they'd be independent."

Stapler shrugged. "Don't know why we're involved in this, but then it isn't in my job description." He changed the subject. "I will have the watch bring you the Intelligence Board so you can read the message. ONI believes the Chinese are just beating their drums. If Taiwan fails to vote for independence—for whatever reason—then ONI says there are indications the Chinese may use the opportunity to resolve their North Korean issue."

"Others disagree with ONI."

"What do you think, Skipper? I think our Intel weenies have a point this time."

"You could be right, Stan. Meanwhile, our concern is Sea Base and the tasks Admiral Holman has assigned us."

"Aye, aye, sir." He turned to leave. "Captain, I know it matters little if they're right about the independence issue. Just because the Director of National Intelligence believes the Chinese are serious doesn't mean she's right. The President thinks the Chinese are blowing smoke and just using the occasion to remind Taiwan that they are still serious about reunification. I'll side with the Prez in this instance."

"Let's hope we can convince them to be less serious."

THOMAS nudged Willard, nodding in the direction of the female pilot heading their way. "Here comes the DETCO," Thomas said, using the Air Force acronym for Detachment Commander. "I thought you said the *real* commander was going to fly aboard, Chief. How much longer?"

"Watch your lip, Sergeant. We are proud members of the United States Air Force, we are enlisted, and we don't get involved in officer shit."

"Shit, Chief . . ."

"Lou, how's the replacement aircraft holding up?" Willard asked, his eyes never leaving the approaching Major Johnson.

"It's holding up now just as well as it was holding up

yesterday and last week, Chief. You trying to change the subject?"

"Of course. That's why they pay us E-9s, to keep you young wannabes out of trouble and from talking too much."

"High Pace's aircraft . . ."

"It's Captain Walters to you, Sergeant Thomas. Let the officers call each other by their call signs." A couple of seconds later, Willard added, "Besides, it's Fast Pace—not High Pace, and if you're going to try to ingratiate yourself with the officers, then at least get their call signs right."

Willard watched Major Louise "Pickles" Johnson, ignoring a spat of angry mumbling from Thomas. She was marching across the apron as if any minute she was going to break into a run. Captain Alex "Blackman" Franklin walked a couple of steps behind her to her left. He was watching her as if he expected any moment he was going to have to jog after her.

No one walked with Pickles. Willard smiled. Perceptively, she made a slight course correction and headed toward him. Why in the hell did he have to smile?

"I think I will go check the aircraft that replaced the one destroyed," Thomas said quietly.

Willard turned to reply, but the technical sergeant was gone. Willard looked both ways, then over his shoulder. Thomas was walking quickly toward the replacement aircraft. The sergeant threw his hand up, as if knowing Willard was staring at his back. Chief Master Sergeant Willard wished he had been quicker.

"Chief!" Johnson shouted as she neared. "Is the flight ready for launch?"

"Yes, ma'am. We fueled and checked both last night . . ." he started to reply, raising his right hand in a salute.

"Last night is unacceptable. How about this morning?" she asked sharply, returning the salute.

"And we did it again this morning. Sergeant Thomas just finished doing it a third time."

She had her helmet tucked under her left arm. Her dark black hair bounced a couple of inches above her shoulders, exposing small gold earrings. Willard watched her frown. Her lower lip pushed up and over the upper, as if waiting for tusks to appear at the corners of her lips. She was silent for a few seconds.

"Okay. I'll still need to preflight it myself," she said, the frown disappearing. She marched by Willard without waiting for a reply.

I hope to shout you will, Willard thought. For an instant, he saw the physical beauty of the woman, but shook his head quickly at the thought.

"I said, I'll still need to preflight it, Chief!"

"Yes, ma'am!" Willard replied. No pilot accepted an aircraft without a preflight check, even if every minute the plane had been sitting on the apron it was being checked. The Air Force held the pilot responsible for his or her aircraft, not the ground crew.

"Afternoon, Chief," Franklin said as he walked by Willard.

"How's Fast Pace, sir?" Willard asked quietly, falling in step with the wingman.

"He's still at the burn center in San Antonio. Looks as if it may not be as bad as we thought."

"He looked pretty bad."

Franklin looked down at Willard's hands. "How's the hands, Chief? I see you still have gloves."

"Inside the gloves, the hands are bandaged and covered with this slip-on latex gloves." He lifted his left hand. "This hand is worse. The right hand is about back to normal. Doctor said to keep making and unmaking fists to keep scar tissue from forming. He asked if I was allergic to latex. Told him if I had been, there'd be a lot of little Willards running around the world."

Franklin chuckled. "Glad you're okay."

"Doc says the hands are going to be an ugly sight."

"Hate to hear that."

Willard smiled. "Naw. It'll fit right in with being a chief." He raised his left hand and made a fist. "Ought to scare the shit out of junior officers."

"Well, I know it'd work on me."

Willard wrinkled his nose and shook his head. "I don't think so, sir. But some junior officers are beyond salvation."

Johnson continued toward the far aircraft. Franklin stopped at the one parked alongside hers. "I exchanged e-mails with

Fast Pace last night," he said as he squatted to look into the front wheel-well. "It was daytime in Texas and they're sending him home. That's the good news."

Franklin stood and walked toward the right wing, his eyes scrutinizing the fuel and flush panels for anything out of place. "Bad news is that he may never fly again. His wife is in Texas with him. Air Force has put her up at Lackland. Her folks are taking care of the children. He said the Air Force is going to let him go home at the end of the week and finish his recovery there. He said the doctors told him he could do his rehab at the Naval Hospital in Portsmouth. They'll fly back to Langley and they won't have to fly commercial."

"That's good. Too many stares for commercial."

Franklin touched the fuel cap. Satisfied, he put the cover back in place. "Civilians do tend to stare," Franklin replied. He let out a deep breath. "I miss him and I worry about him."

"We all do. It was a messy crash."

Franklin faced Willard. "That was a brave thing you did. Not many would have rushed onto a burning plane."

Willard turned red. "Good thing I didn't have time to think about it. Captain Nolan should be ready to fly again soon," Willard added, changing the topic.

"Doctor says he should be good to go in another week. Unlike your hands, the good captain had less burns on his."

"Without the two of us, we'd . . ." He felt his throat constrict.

Franklin slapped him on the shoulder. "I know what you mean, Chief. If you two had not ignored your own safety . . ." Franklin stopped. This was getting too emotional for him. Fast Pace was alive. He was Stateside. And he was with his family. He, on the other hand, had inherited the coveted spot of being the DETCO's wingman. For that, he would never forgive Captain Ronny Walters, near-death experience or not. "Chief, anything I need to know about my airplane?"

"Should be okay, sir. Sergeant Thomas has paid close attention to both."

A young female technical sergeant emerged from beneath the aircraft.

"Captain Franklin, this is Sergeant Norton—Kathy Norton. She came aboard the mail plane two days ago and is now a valued member of our ground crew."

Franklin nodded at the dark-haired, deeply tanned woman, and welcomed her on board. When she walked away, his eyes followed.

"Yep, she has that effect on people—especially us men. She has one of those bird tattoos on her right ankle. Quiet sort of a person."

Franklin brought his eyes back to Willard and started walking toward the rear of the aircraft. "Back to my fighter, Chief?"

"It's ready to go, sir. We've been over it, done our ground check, and now it's up to you."

"Good," Franklin said as the two men turned around the tail, heading toward the other wing. Franklin stopped at the tire and kicked it. He smiled at Willard. "I know what you're thinking, but it gives me great pleasure to kick the tires."

"Getting used to your new lead pilot?"

"Chief, don't go there," Franklin replied lightly. "We're still adjusting to each other. But you know something—she's not a bad pilot. Knows her shit."

"Chief!"

Willard turned toward Major Johnson, who stood with her hands on her hips facing him. "See you, sir," he said with a wave as he turned toward Johnson's summons. "Have a great flight and an even better landing. Remember the secret of a good flight, sir."

"The number of takeoffs and landings must be an equal number," Franklin replied.

Franklin watched for a moment as Willard walked toward the DETCO. *In five minutes, Chief,* he thought, *you'll still be here on the deck of this floating island, but I'll have three to four hours of fun flight time with her.*

"GLAD to have you aboard, Agent Montague. Hope your flight out was okay. It would have been nice if Headquarters had told us you were coming before the flight left Japan," Zeichner said. He pointed to the chair across from him.

"Please, Mr. Zeichner, call me Angie. We're going to be working together until Sea Base returns to Pearl or we catch the foreign agent working on board. This agent stuff makes it sound as if we're on an adversarial basis, don't you think?"

Zeichner smiled, knowing Naval Criminal Investigative Service headquarters had an ulterior motive for sending Montague. "You're right," he said after a few seconds. *What's your game?* he asked himself, his gaze fixed on her.

Gainer dragged a chair into the small compartment from the outer office, scraping it along the rough carpet that covered the metal deck.

Both Zeichner and Montague stopped talking and watched Gainer push the chair against the port bulkhead of Zeichner's office. Gainer straightened, cocked his head to each side once as if assessing the location of the chair, and then sat down. His eyes widened when he saw both of them looking at him. "What?"

"Nothing, Kevin. You comfortable?"

"Yes, sir," Gainer replied, gripping both arms of the straight-back chair and shaking them once. "As comfortable as Navy chairs will let you."

"They're not built for comfort," Montague added, and then turned back to Zeichner. "Agent Zeichner . . ."

"Please, call me Richard. As you pointed out, Angie, if the three of us are going to be working together, it would make it a little awkward in private if we kept up the 'Agent' business."

Montague raised her left hand, running it along the side of her head. "Yes, sir, but I would feel better . . . you're the senior NCIS agent on board the battle group . . . I'd feel better if you'd allow me to address you as either Mr. Zeichner or Agent Zeichner. I think it would be only appropriate." She looked at Gainer. "What do you call him?"

Gainer looked at her and then quickly glanced at Zeichner.

"Think of your answer carefully, Kevin," Zeichner said with a smile.

Gainer leaned back in the chair against the bulkhead. "I call him Boss."

Zeichner watched Montague. Unfortunately, he found himself liking this young lady. He leaned back against the chair, consciously keeping his full weight off it. The last thing he wanted in front of this beautiful . . . what was he thinking! Pleasant to look at didn't mean she wasn't sent here to screw him . . . figuratively speaking . . . and take credit for his hard work.

"Headquarters asked me if I would come out here and augment your efforts in discovering whether we have a spy on board Sea Base or not—"

"A spy," Gainer interrupted. "Sounds almost like a movie script or a good novel when we say the word out loud."

Montague smiled in acknowledgment. "It does, doesn't it? This will be my fourth time ferreting out traitors. Spy is too respectful a term in my book, as I am sure it is in yours."

Gainer blushed, stuttering slightly. "You're right. Spy is too . . ." His words tapered off.

"Kevin and I aren't completely convinced we have a traitor or a spy or whatever Headquarters wants to call this unidentified suspect. That being said, we have gone through the rosters of the ships and we have been keeping a travel log on several contenders." He leaned forward, giving Gainer a withering glance. "Angela, while I appreciate Headquarters' desire to help with this investigation, you have to know that I requested no augmentation. At this point in Agent Gainer's and my investigation, we have yet to come up with any strong evidence to support this idea."

"I understand, sir, but they sent me anyway. I hope you will allow me to work with you." She leaned forward, the loose blouse dipping down.

Zeichner deliberately looked at her forehead although instinct cried out for him to take a peep at the top of her breasts. "I have no intention of excluding you," he said. "We can use all the help we can get on board Sea Base. I hope you understand that I have no intention of limiting your work to seeking out what may be a nonexistent foreign agent."

She leaned away from the desk, looked behind her, and sat down in the chair near the door.

He brought his eyes down to hers. There was a hint of mischief in them. Without thinking, he smiled at her as if to say "Touché." She was smarter than she seemed and she was telling him as much.

"In this case, Boss, we have evidence to the contrary," she said.

"You want to share that evidence with us?"

She twirled her finger around the compartment. "What level of conversation can we have in here?"

"Secret. If it's higher than that, we will have to go up to radio, and if it's anything compartmented, then the USS *Boxer* is the nearest facility."

"I think secret is fine." She crossed her legs. "A fellow agency in the government has contacts within the Chinese Ministry of State Security. Information provided to NCIS reflected insider knowledge of Sea Base operations being provided to the Chinese."

"That information could come from Stateside."

"But it didn't. It came from on board Sea Base. The type of information confirmed it."

Zeichner shook his head. "That doesn't mean it came from someone out here. It could still have originated from Pearl Harbor, or Washington, D.C., or even one of the multitude of contractors who won bids to build this contraption."

Montague lifted her briefcase and unzipped it. She pulled out a folder and handed it to the head NCIS agent on board Sea Base. "These are photographs that the foreign agent sent along with his or her reports."

Zeichner took the folder and opened it. He lifted one eight-by-ten photograph after the other, slipping each to the bottom when he finished with it. Then he handed the folder to Gainer. Zeichner put his arms on the table and locked his fingers together. "I would say you have strong evidence, Angela. The question I now have is why didn't Headquarters send this information to us. Why are we finding out this from you?" He knew his voice was rising. He was angry. What in the hell was Headquarters trying to prove? Trying to prove he was incompetent?

"I believe it was because we knew the only two ways we could get the proof to you, sir, was either by sending it over communications, in which case we ran the risk of the sensitive information being leaked, or by sending it with someone they trusted. Ergo, I am here."

"What if I said Agent Gainer and I are capable of doing this on our own—we've been doing it on our own for five months."

Montague uncrossed her legs and in a calm voice replied,

"Then you can send me home, sir. But if we do have a traitor on board Sea Base, Mr. Zeichner, I can help you find him. And I do know how to work for someone."

"Or find her," Gainer added.

"It's a him," she said emphatically.

"How do you know?"

"You told me," she replied, turning her gaze back on Zeichner.

"We did?" Zeichner asked.

"You identified eight suspects earlier in your investigation." She touched her chest. "I am a trained counterespionage agent. As I told you, this won't be my first case."

"What number will it be?" Zeichner asked, his anger fading as he realized he could march her fancy butt up to the flight line and have her off Sea Base on the next available flight.

"I told you, this will be my fourth."

"And what is your success rate?"

"Two positives, one proven to be false, and the other one just petered out: unable to determine if we had one or didn't.

"Nationalities. France and China were the two positives. The French espionage was business-related. They just wanted to get some technological edges they could interject into their own businesses. The Chinese was a visiting professor who made the rounds of some of our universities. Unfortunately, they were universities that had government contracts and we caught him with his hand in the cookie jar. As for the unsolved one, we don't know," she said, shaking her head. "Someday, I will reopen the case."

"So, you think this is a valid one? And if so, what have you learned that we can put to use?"

"In doing those four cases, I discovered two things that seem to be heuristic—rule-of-thumb. One is that the first list of suspects is always wrong, too extensive, and most times only peripherally related to the event." She held up two fingers.

Zeichner noticed she had what was called a French manicure with the ends shaded white. They complemented and drew attention to her smooth hands and fingers. Fact is, he realized, she had long slender fingers that seemed almost too long. She wore a small diamond on the middle finger of her left hand.

"And second is that as the investigation goes along, if you haven't narrowed the scope so tight"—she held her thumb and finger slightly apart—"that you are certain who the primary suspect is, then you have to go back to the first list. He or she is most likely on that list, or someone with a strong personal or professional relationship to someone on that list is your true suspect."

"We have a primary suspect," Gainer interjected.

"I know."

"It's a professor . . ."

"You mean a Ph.D., don't you?" she corrected Zeichner.

"Yes, you're right. He has a Ph.D. in aeronautical engineering."

Gainer laid the folder on the desk. "The photographs tell us who the suspect is," he said.

She nodded. "I know."

Zeichner nodded. "Kevin, you're right. Only one person could have been in the position to have taken those photographs."

"Based on my review of your notes, I don't think we have to go back to the first list, sir. I discussed this with the boss before I departed Washington. She thinks as you do. Dr. Kiang Zheng meets the right profile."

"He is also the only person who has continuous access to the mainmast, which is the only place some of these photographs could have been taken," said Zeichner.

"They were taken during the day," Gainer added.

"And no one noticed anything unusual or reported it," Zeichner added.

"But he is first-generation American-born," Gainer added. "America has never had a first-generation American become a traitor."

"I guess Benedict Arnold doesn't count," Montague countered.

"He's not on board Sea Base," Zeichner said. "And it was before America was born. It was more during the birthing process."

Gainer and Montague smiled.

"Wasn't he born in England?" Gainer asked.

"No. He was born in Connecticut, but he died in England."

"So, Agent Montague—Angela—I guess we can't just march up there and arrest our good doctor based on these photographs and our investigation?"

"No, sir, and I know you know we can't. While we have evidence marking him as the prime suspect, we need concrete proof. We don't have the final link of seeing him in the act of doing it. The boss wants us to catch him in such a way we have the proof necessary to ensure a conviction."

"I would be very surprised if you didn't have a plan for ferreting out our good doctor; otherwise, Headquarters wouldn't have sent you. And from your reference to the boss, I presume you mean the Director."

"Yes, sir. Director Mullins sends her respects. Apparently, you and she have served together in a prior assignment."

"Long time ago." He patted his stomach. "Before I grew my friend here." Now, why in the hell did he say that? Men say the most asinine things when they're around beautiful women. Why didn't he just find a fire hydrant and hike his leg like a dog?

"She was very complimentary about you, sir."

Well, you know how to lie well, Agent Montague, he thought. He and Mullins never got along on their assignment. She was notorious for taking credit for successes and shoveling failures onto others. The bodies of her fellow agents lay along the side of her career. To her credit, Mullins made director by hard work, even if she used a little Teflon politics along the way.

"Well, she deserves congratulations for the recent appointment," he said. "The Director worked very hard for the position. She was about your age when she and I first crossed paths. But that's another story, Angela. Why don't you tell us your plan for catching the good doctor?" He leaned forward and nodded at her. "That is, assuming we have an agent of a foreign power on board Sea Base."

She pulled her briefcase forward and lifted it into her lap. The weight pulled the pantsuit tight against her thighs. Zeichner thought Gainer was going to pass out from lack of breath. He'd talk with the young agent later.

"In fact, I do have a recommendation for you, sir." She pulled a second folder out, laid it on the desk, and stood. "If I could show you." She stood, opened the folder, and started sorting the papers inside it on top of the desk.

Gainer nearly fell out of the chair getting to his feet. Zeichner stayed seated, focusing on the papers and trying not to look at the top of the loose blouse. Montague started to explain, her voice strong and sure. In minutes, all three agents were focused on the papers, and by the time she finished, he knew she was easily a future contender for Mullins's job. Thankfully, he'd be long retired by then. The plan was simple and it would work. The tidbit on Benedict Arnold marked her as a student of history. This idea showed she knew how to use history to their benefit.

The C-130 had already flown off by the time the three of them emerged on top of Sea Base. At the far end of the runway, two F-22A Raptors revved their engines, and in seconds were speeding down the center of Sea Base. Moments later, they lifted off. The three NCIS agents watched the planes as they flew straight ahead for about a mile before turning on their tails and zooming up and out of sight.

"Has Air Force headquarters given permission to do this?" Zeichner asked.

She shook her head. "They'd never approve. Besides, Mr. Zeichner, if we do it right, they'll never know."

They started walking toward the group of Air Force pilots standing along the flight line.

He had heard that statement so many times during his career. He glanced at her as she walked slightly ahead, black pumps peeking out from beneath the pants. Maybe she wasn't a future Gloria Mullins. Then again, there weren't many directors—male or female—who had the street smarts of Gloria.

FOUR

Ten minutes after taxiing and lining up, Johnson and Franklin were blasting down the runway. The two Raptors lifted off simultaneously. The last hundred feet of Sea Base runway rolled rapidly beneath them as the two F-22A Raptors flew straight, Franklin following one aircraft length behind on the left as they ascended slowly.

"Wheels up," came the voice of Major Johnson over the private circuit between her and Franklin.

Franklin acknowledged the unnecessary command, hitting the switch. The end of the runway passed beneath him. The slight drone of hydraulics vibrated through the cockpit as the wheels rose. The aircraft vibrated slightly when the three sets of wheels locked into the body of his Raptor. Out of sight beneath him, the three sets of wheels had merged into the fuselage, rough metal doors closing over them, restoring the smooth aerodynamic shape of the stealth fighter.

Wheels down affected the stealth of the Raptor, but once they were hidden inside the fuselage, the aircraft body disappeared from radar detection. Radar signals were only good if they hit something and returned to the point of origin. Finding the Air Force stealth fighter on radar was near impossible because radar signals were distorted away from the sender, sent out in every direction but the one back toward the sender.

Franklin drew his eyes to the heads-up display on the front of the cockpit window. The F-22A cockpit was a continuous piece of specialized tempered glass, giving Franklin a 360-degree view without any obstruction.

He looked at the weapons load-out, hit the status-check button, and was satisfied with the result. The Raptor had four internal weapons bays for missiles. For close-in combat and ground support for the troops, he had an M61A2 20mm cannon mounted in the wing root area. The barrel of the 20mm cannon was hidden behind a cover that opened and closed in millisecond synchronization with the bullets coming out. The finger pulling the trigger inside the cockpit controlled all of this. Raptor pilots wondered aloud what would happen if the cover ever failed to open in synch with the shells. But that curiosity never dampened their confidence in this phenomenal fighter aircraft.

Everything about the Raptor was designed for superiority in the air, much like the Navy's command of the seas. Everything the Air Force, the scientists, and the developers could think of for hiding the aircraft in the skies had been used on this aircraft, including locating the missiles and the cannon inside the skin of the Raptor.

Both he and Johnson carried a standard air-to-air combat missile load-out. His consisted of two Sidewinder AIM-9L and six AMRAAM 120C missiles. The Sidewinder was a legacy air-to-air missile still in inventory, upgraded with modern fire-control technology. Designed for rear-hemispheric attacks with its sophisticated infrared detection and lock-on capability, the modern Sidewinder also had an active seeker. If it lost the infrared signature, the missile started pinging with its fire-control radar. This was the same class of missile that had barely missed shooting Walters down, but did hit the burning North Korean Y-8 on the deck of Sea Base.

The AMRAAM stood for Advanced Medium Range Air-to-Air Missile. It had state-of-the-art active seekers designed to lock on and drive the missile to a target. The internal radar and logic head gave the AMRAAM the ability to act independent of the aircraft fire-control radar once it was locked on a target.

The pilot didn't have to keep his or her fire-control radar locked on the target. This gave the fighter pilot the fighting flexibility to launch the AMRAAM and go on to another target. It could fight its own air-to-air engagement. The AMRAAM was truly a "fire-and-forget" weapon. But the target was unable to forget as the supersonic AMRAAM 120C shot toward it. Whether the missile achieved its mission or not, while the AMRAAM was on its tail, the target was out of the combat picture.

The Air Force knew the value of both in combat and cost. The smaller, faster AMRAAM cost nearly $400,000 each, while the legacy Sidewinder cost a miserly $85,000 each. Both were supersonic and both were long: AMRAAM, the more sophisticated and costly missile, was over eleven feet in length, while the cheaper, slightly less technical Sidewinder was a little over nine feet in length.

These deadly missiles carried by the Raptor were arrayed internally. When the fighter pilot selected the weapon, the missile electronics prepared to fight. When the pilot hit the launch icon, the missile bay doors opened just long enough to fire the missile. The doors closed before the missile was an aircraft length on its journey. During this time when the doors were open, the F-22A was vulnerable to radar.

Thinking about the two Sidewinders caused Franklin to think of Fast Pace. He and Ronny "Fast Pace" Walters had been a team for over a year. The events that nearly killed Fast Pace were as fresh today as they were last month. North Korea beating its war drums. Sea Base sailing into the Sea of Japan. Everyone knew Sea Base was a prototype; an experiment; something unproven in combat. A Congressional pork addendum added to the defense bill to provide perks in forty-six states. It's hard to defeat representatives and senators aligned together from forty-six states.

Franklin and Walters had been returning from a defensive fighter patrol two hundred miles ahead of Sea Base. Both had been riding on fumes by the time they reached Sea Base. But Franklin had to bitch about low fuel, so Sea Base landed him first. His aircraft ran out of fuel as it taxied to the parking apron. Good argument for landing, but it did nothing to salve the feeling of guilt over what happened to Fast Pace.

So Walters, riding his own fumes, took the action against the inbound North Korean transport. It had been Walters's aircraft that had sucked in a piece of the Y-8 exploding as Walters's cannon tore through it. It had been Walters's engine the piece of metal tore up, creating a blaze that stretched for yards behind the Raptor. It had been an irate Sidewinder minutes later fired by a Royal Navy F-35 fighter chasing another North Korean transport that locked on Walters. The inbound missile forced Walters to take drastic maneuvers that sent Franklin's teammate and friend crashing onto Sea Base. A crash that burned his trapped friend for seconds—*long seconds*—before Chief Willard and Captain Nolan fought their way through the flames to pull him from the cockpit. In times such as that, time seems to slow. Seconds stretch into what seem minutes, and a minute seems forever.

Both Willard and Nolan carried the burn scars from the incident, a constant reminder whenever Franklin saw them. But they were nothing compared to the third-degree burns covering Walters's body. If not for the fire-retardant flight suit and the quick actions of those two men, it would have been a burned body carried from the aircraft.

"Blackman, wake up! Are you listening to me?" Johnson shouted.

"Sorry, ma'am; say again."

"I said it's time to show those squids what we can do," she repeated, miffed. "You ready or you daydreaming?"

"I will follow your lead."

"Eighty-degree angle."

The two aircraft turned on their tails. Franklin shoved the throttle forward, keeping position on the left side of Johnson's tail. Within seconds, the two aircraft passed twelve thousand feet, sparse cloud cover at this altitude quickly disappearing beneath them.

"I love this," Johnson said.

"Makes two of us, DETCO," Franklin said, squinting his eyes shut as soon as he said "DETCO." *Why me, Lord? Is this my penance for Fast Pace?* Johnson was the Detachment Commander, but demanded to be addressed as Commander. Not DETCO, the Air Force term, but Commander, which was reserved for the "real" Commanding Officer of the squadron.

Tradition is a hard animal to kill. Her being unpopular and going against Air Force tradition should be wearing her insistence down, but she persisted. After all, she was the DETCO—*oops!* The commander. Franklin smiled.

Several seconds passed; then Johnson's voice came over the circuit. "Call me Raptor Leader once we get off the private circuit, Blackman, or you can call me Pickles."

He winced. Another Air Force tradition rumor had Johnson thumbing her nose at. The pilots refused to call her Pickles. The rumor was she refused to accept the ritual naming tradition at the officers' club. She was awarded "Flat Cheeks," didn't like it, and changed it to "Pickles." Where in the hell she got Pickles from was the big question they would all like to have answered, but no way anyone would ask. They were afraid she'd tell them, and the idea of having to listen to the story appalled the men.

"When we level out, let's increase our separation. Half a length, left side about two hundred feet."

Everyone had a story. He'd like to know hers, but like the others in the Ready Room, he wasn't going to be the one to ask her.

"Raptor Leader, Raptor 10. Wouldn't separating that far increase our radar detectability?"

"Shouldn't, Raptor 10. It should increase our radar reduction profile because by separating we reduce the chance of radar signals bouncing off each other's aircraft and returning to the sender."

"I just thought . . ."

"I know. Conventional wisdom and all that bull. If it doesn't work, we'll soon find out. Sea Base and those Navy things boring holes in the ocean will tell us. Better to find out now than when we're in a hot situation."

"I thought we *were* in a hot situation."

"We're not going to fight the Chinese," she said.

He watched her shake her head.

"But I thought that was why we were out here," he replied, mentally kicking himself for continuing the conversation.

"We are here to convince the Chinese we are prepared to fight if pushed to it. They no more want to fight us than we do them."

He started to ask why when the bagpipe synchronization of another secure channel broke into their ears, saving Franklin. Over his headset and Johnson's came the voice of the Sea Base Air Traffic Controller.

"Raptor Leader, Raptor Haven ATC; level out at angels two two. The RJ is entering the northern edge of their track at this time. Come to course zero-one-zero; range fifty. Rivet Joint is at angels three zero. You copy?"

"Roger, Raptor Haven; we copy."

"Switch to Bravo channel at this time. Air Intercept Controller will take over. Have a good flight, Raptor Formation."

For the next fifteen minutes, the AIC talked Raptor Formation toward the rendezvous with the Air Force RC-135 Rivet Joint bird. The Rivet Joint was a vintage reconnaissance aircraft of the Air Force. With the Navy self-destructing its cryptologic and airborne reconnaissance capabilities, the Air Force had the only tactical and strategic assets to support a large-scale military operation. The sensors of the aircraft were state-of-the-art, while the avionics of the RC-135 were twentieth century. Regardless, the Rivet Joint could fly anywhere on a moment's notice, conduct its mission, and with an air-to-air refueling capability stay on station longer than any other country's reconnaissance aircraft. It carried up to thirty-five crew members and could detect, identify, and locate anything in the electromagnetic spectrum. With a superior communications suite on board the four-engine jet aircraft, the Air Force team could send information anywhere in the world to commanders it thought would be interested in what they were discovering.

The mission of today's flight was to see if the Chinese had deployed any additional warships in the Taiwan Strait. They would fly down the middle of the strait that separated Taiwan and Mainland China. China had warned against any foreign aircraft or warships entering the volatile strait.

Raptor Formation was the fighter escort for the northern half of the track. The British battle group operating at the mouth of the Taiwan Strait would provide the fighter escort for the southern leg of the track. Commander Lester Tyler-Cole from the British 801st Naval Squadron, embarked on the Royal Navy carrier *Elizabeth,* and his F-35 Joint Fighter wingman would relieve them about one hundred miles inside the strait. Raptor Formation would turn escort of the unarmed reconnaissance aircraft over to the British while the Raptors refueled.

"Raptor Haven, we have the RJ in sight," Johnson broadcast.

Franklin glanced at his radar, saw the return, and looked in that direction. The huge four-engine jet aircraft was flying straight and level above them. He imagined every radar along the Chinese coast was reflecting the Rivet Joint. The RJ was so humongous, radar was unneeded. A contrail stretched for miles leading directly to the tail section of the aircraft. The Chinese should be able to see it from the coast once they reached the center of the Taiwan Strait.

"Raptor Leader, Weasel here. We have you on radar."

"Weasel, Major Johnson here. We are your escort. Do you have us on radar?"

"Major, nothing escapes the Rivet Joint."

"Except oil," Franklin said into the private line. *What are you thinking? This isn't Walters. Keep your ad libs to yourself.*

"And hydraulic fluid," Johnson agreed.

Was that a bonding attempt? Wow! He'd have to watch himself. What Pickles said sounded too much like something Fast Pace would have said.

"RAPTOR Leader, I have you left and right sides. Be aware of the jet wash directly behind me. For escort duties, we'll remain on secure communications. Okay?"

"Roger, Weasel; secure comms. We're going up another couple of thousand feet to ride escort. I will be on your right side and Raptor 10 to your left."

"Roger. Be advised the British fighters will join our circuit in approximately three-zero minutes."

"Weasel, Raptor Leader; copy all. We will remain with you until ten miles of rendezvous with 801st, and then we will break off to refuel. Unless needed, we'll orbit around breakoff point for your return."

"Roger, Raptor Leader; our electromagnetic calculations balanced against today's weather, Raptor Leader, show that if you two stay above me, it should present only one radar reflection as a target."

Target! Franklin glanced both ways. *The Chinese would be very surprised if they thought they could come out and shoot down an RC-135. The surprise would be stupendous when one radar return turns into multiple missiles.* He smiled. He enjoyed surprises when they were his to give. Unfortunately, they would be late arrivals, because the British were going to do the bulk of the fighter-escort duties for today's mission.

"Roger, Weasel; we will station ourselves above and slightly to the rear," Johnson replied

"Oh, by the way, Raptor Leader, would you secure your air-search radar? It's interfering with our onboard radars and reconnaissance equipment."

No way! Franklin thought, pushing the talk button for a second, before releasing it. They'd be blind without their radar, depending on maintaining visual on Rivet Joint to keep them on course.

"We'll data-link our picture to you in receive mode, Commander. You two will see the same thing we do. We also have data link with our Navy ships and the British task force integrated into the overall picture. Should provide you more information than your onboard is doing."

Franklin switched to their private line. "Ma'am, we ought . . ."

"Weasel, Raptor Leader; will do."

He let go of the button. She didn't even discuss the idea with him. Walters and he would have at least argued a few seconds over opening their kimono.

"Stand by."

"Raptor 10, Raptor Leader; secure radars."

"What if we need our fire control?" Franklin asked, not trying to hide his displeasure.

"Then, I would suspect, Captain, that if we need our fire-control radar, the RJ will suddenly discover its mission is over and neither it nor us will be in proximity to each other."

"Roger," he replied, unconvinced. She was going to get both of them killed.

"Secure air-search radar," Johnson ordered.

Franklin reached forward and put the radar in standby. No

way was he going to turn it completely off. If he needed it, he wanted it to go back online instantly, not wait for the electronics to cycle through a diagnostic or to warm up.

"Raptor Formation, Weasel; you should have the data link now."

Franklin touched the icon. On the heads-up display where previously only the RC-135 was reflected, multiple contacts appeared. Some were hundreds of miles away flying along the coasts of China and Taiwan. *Wow!* was all he could think. Multiple targets, even if most were commercial. A fighter pilot's cataclysmic orgasm of opportunities. Like a payday Saturday night at the Officers' Club. Like a . . .

"Raptor 10, your data link working?"

"Yes, ma'am," he said, the awe in his voice.

A light chuckle came over the private circuit. "I know. I've worked with them on missions over Iraq during the invasion of Iran."

"How do they do this?"

"Not sure myself, but only two ways I can think of. I suspect multiple data links and multiple sensors all integrated into one all-source display is one way. We can't do it, but I understand on the ships and the ground, you can hook on each contact and it will not only tell you what the contact is, but course, speed, altitude, and who really has the initial reflection."

"What's the second way?" Franklin asked after several seconds of silence.

"Magic."

This was going to be a long flight. Johnson was sounding almost human. He must keep alert, he told himself, or he might forget the monster she becomes when the curtain opens on the leadership stage.

"Raptor Leader; this is the Weasel Electronics Warfare Officer. I want to draw your attention to the six contacts orbiting two hundred miles bearing two-four-zero degrees true from our position." The RC-135 EWO proceeded to read the track numbers to the two fighter pilots.

Franklin shook his head. Did the man think the two of them had the flexibility while flying the world's most sophisticated fighter aircraft to write down the data he was rattling off?

As if knowing Franklin's thoughts, on the heads-up display

a red line emerged from the center of the display and grew slowly in a straight line toward several contacts orbiting over Mainland China. Then, the end of the line grew into a circle encompassing the bogies. Franklin took his cursor and shifted it to one of the contacts. Even as the data emerged on his display, Weasel was broadcasting. The contacts were definitely aircraft because of their speed.

"They are Chinese fighters. We think they are the J-12 stealth fighter. We have known since 2000 the Chinese were developing them, but other than some overhead photographs, this will be the first time we have them flying. These J-12 fighters have exported or stolen Raptor technology applied to them. That will convolute your actions, if you have to engage them. Most likely, they are the sixth or seventh generation of the Chinese stealth program designed to catch up with you Raptors."

"Do they know we have them on radar?"

"They probably have the same indications you do. They know radar is pinging them, but like you fighter jocks . . ."

Franklin envisioned the man shaking his head and looking down at his flight boots.

"Sorry. Like you fighter pilots, they probably believe they're invincible and laughing about not showing up on radar."

"If they have Raptor technology on their hulls, then how can you show them?"

"Raptor Leader; if we told you, we'd have to kill you." The EWO laughed.

Franklin gave a wry laugh too. That expression had to be as old as his grandfather. He jerked his finger away from the talk button. It was too tempting to press it and say, *Just tell us a little bit; then you'd only have to beat the crap out of us.*

Seconds passed without Johnson acknowledging Weasel's comment, convincing Franklin she was one pissed-off bitch right now. He felt like singing.

Minutes later, Weasel broadcast a course change as the formation entered the track running down the center of the Taiwan Strait. Franklin looked to the right. Sparse cloud cover marked the line between the Chinese coast and the ocean waters. He looked at the heads-up display. The six contacts were still orbiting. An orbit was as good as . . . What? What was an orbit as good as? Well, he thought, it was good they were orbiting and not trying to disappear in the Raptors' direction. Six Chinese stealth fighters against their two might be an unfair advantage. He smiled. *Yeah, they'd be outnumbered.*

Franklin marked the relative bearing of the contacts and looked in that direction. Out of the corner of his eye, flying about a quarter mile away, was Major Johnson's Raptor.

No contrails marking the bogies broke the blue sky. None marked Johnson's Raptor, ergo none marked his, but he turned his head and looked behind him.

If any threat came after the RJ, it would be these sophisticated fighters. The Chinese would use this opportunity to demonstrate their air superiority. He turned his head to the left. The coastline of Taiwan was crystal clear. No clouds over it. He could easily make out where the waters crashed against the land of the breakaway province that was drawing America into a confrontation no one wanted. His earlier thoughts of Saturday nights at the Langley Officers Club drew his mind from the boredom of escort duty ahead. Moments later, Franklin was humming.

"SKIPPER, Admiral Holman called and asked you red-phone him back," Stapler said to Garcia.

Garcia pulled himself up into his chair.

The nearby Petty Officer of the Watch handed Garcia the red handset. "Sir, the POOW of the *Boxer* is on the other end."

The Petty Officer of the Watch; must not be too important. When it was important, you could bet money Holman would be on the other end. Garcia mumbled thanks and pushed the talk button. The synchronization of the bagpipe keying of the secure comms echoed in his ear. When it cleared, he told the petty officer on the other end who he was. Within two minutes, Admiral Holman was on the line.

"Hank, how is everything going over there? Sea Base making good time?"

"Still ambling along at eight knots, Admiral. We should be in our Op Area in the next twelve hours. We'll do a nighttime stabilization of Sea Base and when you wake tomorrow morning, Sea Base will be anchored—figuratively."

"Good. I think locating Sea Base a few hundred miles northeast of Taiwan should keep you out of range of Chinese aircraft."

"And North Korean."

Holman guffawed. "You never know about that country of bipolar leaders."

For several minutes, Holman and Garcia discussed the actions in the Sea of Japan a month ago. A couple of sentences about the large burnt spot on the Sea Base deck and the smaller one where Walters's aircraft had burned. For the first ten minutes, they talked about the previous action, the damage inflicted, and the condition of those medically evacuated. As Holman spoke, Garcia thought of how lucky he had been to have this leader with him in the Sea of Japan.

Holman was an old-timer. He had earned his four stars the old-fashioned way: combat. Weren't many "Holmans" in the modern Navy. Most earned their stars through a rote set of tours designed to show upward mobility and political astuteness. Political astuteness was a trait hard to find in the admiral's character. Garcia smiled at the image of the short "battling the bulge" admiral standing with him along the aft safety lines of Sea Base smoking his Cuban cigar. In today's politically correct society where even words were suspect, here was a person whose only safety was probably the sea. Holman was chubby. He was brusque. And he smoked. He had something for everyone to hate.

But this cigar-smoking admiral had fought a carrier battle group through the Strait of Gibraltar against submarines and mines to project American and allied power back into the Mediterranean. He had led a covert set of engagements with a French ally off West Africa, and done it in such a way that the quasi-war never left the area. For all of that, there were those in Washington who would dance and party for weeks if Holman failed. They'd probably name a toilet after him when he retired.

"Hank, did you just laugh?"

Garcia's eyes widened. Did he laugh? "I don't think so, sir."

"This isn't a laughing matter. Let me tell you what I think

is going to come down in the next twenty-four hours. But you can't hold me to it, okay?"

"Aye, sir."

Holman started in about the talks in Beijing involving the Americans, Russians, Indians, and British. The Chinese, the old crimes of World War II never far from their eternal minds, had unilaterally barred the Japanese. Holman expressed his tongue-in-cheek belief that the Great Wall of China was maintained not for tourism and historical significance, but because the Chinese still suspected the Mongolians of preparing to invade them. Only the North Koreans, who believed everyone hated them, surpassed the xenophobia of China. Most likely, the North Koreans weren't wrong.

Garcia thought of his own career. One where he'd opted out of the mainstream Surface Warfare Officer community to pursue a career of taking new systems and ships to sea for operational tests and evaluations. He had never been in a combat situation until last month, when the North Koreans attempted to board and capture Sea Base. The emotional feeling afterward showed him why people like Holman sought out the dangerous challenge of wagering their own war-fighting skills against any opponent regardless of their level of competence.

Holman had seen the age of warfare change a lot in his years, Garcia realized. The man had been around for the Cold War and then the War on Terrorism. The admiral had seen warfare go from fighting an enemy who was easy to find and hard to kill, to an enemy that was hard to find but easy to kill. Now, they were face-to-face with the Chinese. Was warfare about to change again? He thought of the Gulf Religious Wars as some called it. The Persian Gulf War was another name.

". . . the Rivet Joint?"

Garcia jumped. "I'm sorry, Admiral, you were garbled."

"Hank, are you listening to me? I get the impression that either you're asleep or daydreaming; if you're doing either, then go back to your stateroom and do it there. I asked if the fighters and the Rivet Joint had linked up."

Garcia put his hand over the mouthpiece. "Commander, what's the status of the reconnaissance mission?"

"We have data links with Weasel, sir. Major Johnson's formation is flying escort. The British fighters are four hundred miles ahead orbiting and waiting to take over. We have . . ."

Garcia nodded and made a chopping sign across his neck. He repeated the information to Holman.

"Keep an eye on the aircraft orbiting over the coastline, Hank. According to the information from the RJ and confirmed by the Taiwanese, those aircraft are the new Chinese J-12 stealth fighters."

"Yes, sir. We'll watch," Garcia answered, knowing all they could do was watch. Then, he thought of his laser cannons, wondering just how effective they would be beyond the curvature of the earth.

FIVE

Andrew stepped onto the main deck of Sea Base. He had walked from *Altair,* which held the forward starboard position of the eight ships holding aloft the Sea Base canopy. As he traveled from one of the Fast Sealift Ships to the other, he glanced often at the bottom of the dark gray canopy that stretched outward as far as he could see. He wondered if he would find his compartment where he had dropped off his seabag in the vast metal jungle, but God's Will would take care of that small problem.

When he reached the *Algol,* he opened the hatch leading upward and climbed to the top of the canopy onto the huge flat deck of Sea Base.

The devil-man Taleb had told him the top of Sea Base was four stories high from the main deck of the ships. He looked down. This is the main deck, he thought, taking a small bit of pride in remembering the Navy term without having to search for it in his mind. It had taken a month of listening to Steve Bucket talk about his years in the Navy. A month to teach him about the maelstrom of sea life he would have to face. Knowing the test of his faith was to be performed here.

He wondered if the times of confusing nautical terms with

landlubber talk—he smiled—were gone. Andrew walked along the side of the ship, keeping a couple of feet between him and the safety lines marking the edge of the deck. He knew others who believed in the sanctity of the Holy Spirit would be here, even if they worshipped the same Lord and God in different manners. Eventually, the evil ones who forsake the Lord, those who were nothing more than Satan's spawn, would discover him—one of God's angels in their midst. He shut his eyes and sent a short prayer of thanks to God for this opportunity to prove his faith.

Splashing from the ocean drew Andrew to the edge of the deck. He grasped the safety lines and nervously glanced down at the water. The water bubbled and cascading upon itself as weaving dark shapes drove against each other at the surface. The turmoil ceased abruptly and the area of disturbance disappeared, melding into the waters around it.

Dark shapes appearing beneath the surface briefly before disappearing beneath Sea Base—these would be the sharks he'd overheard sailors talking about in the berthing area while he was stowing his seabag. Sharks had appeared soon after Sea Base was raised, and now they swam beneath this manmade evil wherever she went.

If anyone in God's Army doubted his father's vision, the presence of the sharks and the death of Joshua on board Sea Base would have erased the doubts. No one but his father would have had the vision to recognize this Navy experiment for the threat it was to global anarchy and the next coming.

Epiphanies were more than religious visions. This one washed over him. It was a combination of his father's vision, Steve Bucket's knowledge of the United States Navy, and him walking the deck of this huge experiment of American technology and projection of Navy might that allowed the true threat to be seen. The threat was not just Sea Base. The threat was not just the U.S. Navy or the Navies of the world. The threat was that control of the seas truly ensured global stability. Armies won wars, but Navies ensured stability throughout the world. They isolated pariah nations and kept the global economy moving. He looked along the safety line running from over a thousand feet aft to a thousand feet from where he stood before it curved right and left, heading toward the runway that marked the center of Sea Base. He uncurled his fingers from the safety line, and then gripped it again. Sea Base represented all of this epiphany in its hugeness. Stability threatened the vision of God's Army. The destruction of Sea Base would start the dominoes of anarchy falling.

Unconsciously, he straightened while he gave thought to this epiphany. His hands rested on the safety line, the grip loosening. His eyes narrowed and his lips pursed as Andrew tried to determine how he was to use this knowledge that God had just now bestowed on him. Another series of splashes from below drew his attention.

He leaned forward, gripping the safety line firmly. His head and shoulders stuck out from the side of the ship, his body pushed against the safety lines. A slight breeze rode across the ships underneath Sea Base, starting from the rear of the ships. The breeze bathed his face with a mixture of oily smells and the garbage that was continuously dumped unceremoniously into the ocean beneath. The odors assailed his senses, causing him to shut his mouth as if somehow this kept the smells away. A shiver ran up his body. This was God's way of offering one more proof of the danger Sea Base presented to his father's vision. God was calling to him.

Along with the realization that Andrew was the angel in the midst of the devil's workshop came an unanticipated thrill over the adventure of what awaited. He had never seen so many powerful things in the few hours he had been on board. This ship. Sea Base.

Laser weapons and things called rail guns. Later, he might try to find out how they worked. A weapon carried its own seed of destruction. The congregation would never believe America had a ship the size of this. Then, he wondered, is Sea Base really a ship, or a metal island as he overheard one sailor call it?

Until this mission, Andrew had never been near the water other than the rivers and ponds of West Virginia. Was he capable of fulfilling his father's instructions? Would he disappoint God's will and be unable to send to the devil those who'd killed his anointed brother? He would pray. Through prayer, God's will be done.

Andrew turned back to the open hatch and started back

down the ladders to the ship beneath him. Minutes later, he stepped onto the main deck of the *Algol.*

Laughter and shouts riding the odorous breeze drew his attention. They came from behind the aft forecastle. He continued walking aft toward the noise, wondering what other proof of the devil's work waited.

Minutes later, Andrew emerged from the covered walkway beneath the aft forecastle. A group of sailors and merchant marines stood inside a huge yellow line painted in a semicircle on the deck. They were talking and smoking. He took a deep breath, knowing he had to meet others to do his assignment—mission—job. His father called it God's will.

He moved to the edge of the crowd. Counted about ten people congregating there, and at the very edge saw Taleb. Taleb was staring directly at him. When their eyes met, Taleb smiled, raising his eyebrows and giving a short wave as if they were old friends. Here was truly a man of Satan.

Andrew's heart fell when Taleb headed his way. This was God's will showing him Satan's demon. He had been unsure when Taleb was at the aircraft, but for the man to know he was coming here told Andrew this Taleb had Satan's ear. He would have to be careful, he told himself.

This Taleb had cursed God several times earlier when they made their way to the office of the Master-at-Arms. He had felt relief earlier, as if a dark cloud had lifted, when Taleb had left him at the berthing area and gone on his way. Andrew expected to never see the man again on something the size of Sea Base.

"Well, how about this, Al," Taleb exclaimed when he reached Andrew. Grabbing Andrew by the shoulders, Taleb turned to the crowd.

"Hey, everyone, this is Al Jolson, new arrival and a member of First Division. Anyone here from First Division?"

"I am." A short squat woman wearing a second-class patch, or crow as sailors called them, pushed her way to the front. She looked Andrew up and down as if she was assessing a bull at an auction. "Guess you'll do," she announced, stepping forward. "Turn around."

Andrew turned around.

"What'd you think, Mad Mary?" someone said, laughing from behind him as he turned.

"He'll do," she replied.

When he had come full circle and faced the woman again, she stuck her hand out. For a moment, Andrew drew his hand back. Men in God's Army never touched a woman out of wedlock unless they were family members. Almost imperceptibly, he stuck his hand out and shook hers. She squeezed his hand much like the men did back home.

"Welcome aboard, sailor. My name is Mary Showdernitzel. Some call me Mad Mary; you can't. The master chief calls me Stella; go figure he'd be the only one to know my middle name." She glanced around at the others, smiling at them. "I'm the leading petty officer for First Division." She jerked her thumb into her amble bosom a couple of times. "Means you'll be working for me, so welcome to hell."

His eyes widened and fear shot through him. He was right! The devil's presence rode this evil thing in the middle of the ocean, hiding from Christian righteousness.

"Hell," he confirmed aloud.

"Hell, yeah! You know, the hottest place around," Showdernitzel answered, mistaking Andrew's comment as a question. "It may be October, but we're heading south beneath this heat collector above us."

He nodded, his eyes returning to normal, and turned away. Moving away from the demon in front of him to look at the others standing around the stern. Only a few glanced at him; a couple of the sailors nodded with a greeting. Most of them stood in their dungarees in small groups talking. A couple of sailors leaned against the safety lines, flicking ash into a breeze that blew it back onto the gray deck, and against their uniforms.

"What's your name?" Showdernitzel said, causing him to jump.

Andrew looked over his shoulder. Both Showdernitzel and Taleb were walking along with him.

When he failed to answer, Taleb jumped in. "It's Al Jolson. Remember the person who made the first talking movie?"

Showdernitzel drew back as if a most odorous smell had washed across her nostrils. Shaking her head vigorously, she snarled, "No, and why would I want to?"

Taleb shrugged. "Just thought you might have heard."

"Porno?"

"Naw, ain't porno, Mad Mary," Taleb snarled. "Not every movie you've never seen is a porno."

"Is it something that has to do with nautical shit, or is this just another example of you trying to show everyone how much you know, shitbird?"

The words! The evil! It was everywhere. Andrew basked in a mix of glory and fear at being chosen for this. Not fear of the evil surrounding him, but the fear he might fail to do God's will.

She looked at Andrew. "What is your name again? You got one, don't ya?"

"It's Al Jolson."

She slapped him upside the chest with the back of her hand. "Well, welcome to First Division, Asshole Jolson. I'm heading up to do my rounds. As you probably know, right now with the master chief still recovering from his wounds—remind me to tell you how he and I saved this contraption—I'm running the division." Showdernitzel cocked her head to one side. "For the good order and discipline of the First Division, you may call me Petty Officer Showdernitzel." She leaned forward smiling, revealing a missing tooth on the left side of her mouth. "Unless I decide you can get to know me better." She leaned back, laughing, her eyes traveling up his body. "Yep, unless we decide to know each other better."

"Did you see the look on his face?" Showdernitzel said to Taleb. She turned back to Andrew. "Just call me Petty Officer Showdernitzel, Jolson. On second thought, I doubt you and I will get to know each other better."

"Call you Showdernitzel? No one can pronounce it, much less rattle off something that long," Taleb said, turning to face Andrew. "Have fun. Mad Mary will take care of you or kill you."

"Hey, Taleb. I told you, you don't know me well enough to call me Mad Mary. Only my friends call me that, and the master chief calls me Stella, unless he's upset then he calls me—"

"Then you probably don't hear Stella often."

"I'm going to throw Otis's hairy ass overboard one of these nights, Jolson."

"He said his name was Jaime," Andrew said.

Showdernitzel wrinkled her face. "The man is a dickhead. He told one of the junior officers his name was Jerry. He don't even know his name. It could be Jaime. Or it may be Otis. And he could have been telling the truth to the officer and he's really Jerry Springer."

He looked at Taleb.

"Personally, I think his Goddamn name is Richard Whiskey," Showdernitzel said in a low voice.

"Richard Whiskey?" Taleb protested.

"With a name like Richard Whiskey, we could call you Dick Liquor."

Andrew's stomach knotted. Blasphemy! He would have been the only one unsurprised if a bolt of lightning had struck the demon at that time.

Taleb waved her away. "Mad Mary, I'm leaving. You're something men of the world such as Al and I fear."

"Fear?"

"Yeah, fear our moms might think we're going to marry you and immediately disown us before they collapse from a heart attack."

"Screw you, Taleb. Go take a short walk off a long pier, bucko!"

"Damn, Mary, you can't even get your—"

"Oh, eat shit and die; you know what I mean."

Taleb turned to Andrew. "Al, good luck. I hope you find the incentive needed to work with this woman, or else make sure you have your page-two next-of-kin card filled out with Personnel. Working alongside God's gift to man may cause your heart to give out."

"I don't believe in incentives, Al. The only incentive you need is to keep me happy."

"There goes an impossible dream," Taleb sang as he walked away.

"Come on, Al. Let's get you topside so you can meet our hero master chief and then I'll help you check in. I won't assign you anything today because it's your first day. Give you a chance to get settled and get your bearing on this floating bucket of bolts. But what I will do is show you where to report for work tomorrow morning."

As he followed the broad-hipped sailor along the port side

of the ship, he found himself looking forward to going topside. The lower decks of Sea Base brought visions of how a trip to Satan's domain would look; a world of constant shadows filled with those destined for hell breathing in the horrid fumes of oblivion. He wondered if somewhere topside he could find more fitting accommodations for the messenger of God.

Twenty minutes later with little conversation, the two emerged on top of Sea Base.

Showdernitzel turned to him, her breaths coming in rapid gulps. A couple of joggers passed. "Don't need to jog to stay in shape," she said, slapping her flat stomach. "Several trips up and down the stairwell every day will be all the exercise you need." She cocked her head to the side, eyes wide, and smiling. "This your first ship?"

Everything Steve Bucket taught him to say came easily to his lips. Everything a lie, but to lie to Satan's helper was not a sin. But he didn't lie. It was hard to lie, but he told her this was his first ship. Bucket said that would cover any slipups he made. He explained he had made third-class petty officer out of A school. That would cover the fact he was a petty officer and not a seaman. Petty officers had more freedom than seamen.

Showdernitzel shook her head, putting her hands on her hips. "Well, shipmate, looks as if we will have to start work on teaching you what life as a real boatswain mate is all about. Book learning don't do nothing but produce word fairies that have little to do with the real world of the sea."

"SENIOR Chief," Seaman Gentron said, turning from the AN/SQR-25 Sonar console. "Glad you're back. I'm getting sporadic contact on that submarine again."

Agazzi pushed the lever down securing the watertight door. This was his domain. The lowest deck on board the USNS *Algol*. He quickly moved across the top level of the compartment and slid down the few steps to the lower level where the row of consoles was located.

"Diagnostics check out?" Agazzi asked.

"I checked them when I changed the watch, Senior Chief.

No problems then." Gentron pointed to the readouts above the console. "The data is basically the same. Same hertz readout indicating a non-Western submarine. Doesn't jive with marine environmental noise. Whatever it is, it's man-made and it's not American."

"Where's Petty Officer Keyland?" Agazzi asked.

"He, Taylor, and Bernardo are in the UUV Compartment over on the *Bellatrix,*" MacPherson answered.

"They haven't finished reloading the firing cartridge?"

"Nope," MacPherson said, tapping his computer screen. "But I've been watching them through the cam. I think Bernardo is ready to return." He chuckled.

"Why?"

MacPherson shrugged. "No reason other than body language, Senior Chief. Can't hear anything through these devices," MacPherson said, reaching up and tapping the cam on its own console. "All they do is let us guess what the other guy is thinking."

Agazzi patted MacPherson once on the shoulder. MacPherson was draped over his chair like a thrown blanket. His right leg rested on the chair arm, his foot swinging slightly back and forth. His right arm was up and over the high back, while his body rested awkwardly against the left arm.

"More likely he just don't want to be doing hard work," Gentron added.

"That's enough," Agazzi said.

"Good point," MacPherson added. He winked at Agazzi, then returned to watching the video image in front of him. His left hand moved the mouse gently, guiding the deployed UUV on its patrol.

Agazzi smiled. He could see why women fought over this young sailor. Dark hair and blue eyes that could "freeze a lady at twelve paces and cause her panties to disappear," as Bernardo said kiddingly.

Agazzi turned to Gentron. Gentron was still the new kid on the team even after five months on board. Seamen were always the new kids at sea.

Agazzi had seven sailors, including him, to fight an underwater war. They'd had eight for a while, but the eighth sailor had been no sailor. He'd been some sort of religious fanatic with a fatal design to sink Sea Base. No one knew why, or could even figure out what Sea Base had to do with this religious notion of starting Armageddon. Agazzi's thoughts went back to the one moment when he looked up from the walkway in the UUV compartment and saw this Smith bringing the metal bar down on him.

"Senior Chief, you listening?"

"Tell me what you have," Agazzi replied to Gentron's question.

"Same thing as Petty Officer Bernardo had yesterday. A contact bearing 220. It stays around for a few seconds and then disappears."

"Same contact?"

Gentron shook his head. The light brown hair cropped close to the head had grown in the months at sea. Grown too much for Navy regulations, for it touched the man's shirt collar. Agazzi made a mental note to mention it to Petty Officer Keyland, the Leading Petty Officer of the division. The seaman was spending too much time with Bernardo.

"Different contact, Senior Chief. The passive noise spikes show slight differences in the signature. I'd say we have at least two submarines out there."

"Two submarines?" Agazzi grew interested. They had had one submarine shadowing them since they departed the Sea of Japan a month ago. Naval Intelligence had given a probable identity as Chinese. Now that they were shifting their operations area to support the growing Taiwanese crisis, maybe the Chinese had decided to put another submarine out here with them. Maybe the submarines were relieving each other on station like American submarines sometimes did. "You pass it along to Combat?"

"I was just going to do that, Senior Chief," Gentron answered.

Agazzi knew Gentron was waiting for him or Keyland to show up before telling Combat. Combat Information Center was located on the second deck of the tower on the top of Sea Base. Combat never let a piece of reported information go without a multitude of questions, and Gentron would have been a basket of nerves within two seconds of their questions.

"Petty Officer MacPherson, why didn't you pass this along to Combat?"

MacPherson brought his leg down onto the deck. "Senior Chief, every time Seaman Gentron said he had something, I looked. Didn't see the contact."

"But the SQR-25 still had the traces running down it, Senior Chief," Gentron objected.

Agazzi looked back at MacPherson.

"He's right," MacPherson agreed. "I did see the traces, but Senior Chief, we only had two contacts and both were light traces. I wanted to see a third trace."

"Next time, report it and worry about confirmation later." Agazzi reached over and pushed the button on the intercom. At least the communications problems within Sea Base were being corrected by ship's force. The Navy had generated a request for contractors to propose corrections, but then after the commercial world provided their own recommendations, the funds had been de-obligated.

His thoughts wandered for a minute as he recalled overhearing Admiral Holman in a tirade with Captain Garcia about the internal communications problems plaguing Sea Base. Rear Admiral Dick Holman had been told about the funds being "de-obligated" that had been earmarked for Sea Base. The admiral had launched into a tirade about Washington rear-echelon so-and-sos not knowing where their balls were located. What was it the admiral said? Agazzi tried to recall, then he remembered. The admiral said something about politicians like, "To them, every program is the same; so when they get down to two, they cut one—but they always cut the nice one and kept the ugly one. Then, everyone spends the rest of their time trying to put the red lipstick of the good one on the ugly one." After a few minutes of listening to Admiral Holman, Agazzi came to believe the worst curse word in the Navy was "de-obligate."

But the admiral had acted. That's what leaders do when faced with a problem; they make decisions even if sometimes the decision is wrong. The key attribute of good leaders is willingness to change their minds when they realize they're marching toward the wrong decision.

Holman had shouted for the Communications Officer and given him a week to correct the problem. The Information Technicians from the Radio Shack and every sailor who had the word "technician" in his rating spent a week working the problem. Even Petty Officer Taylor, the maintenance technician for ASW, had spent two days helping hook up a legacy "push-to-talk" intercom system. Agazzi scratched his head. He wondered where they found all this old stuff, but at least it worked.

"Combat, this is Sonar; we have a contact, bearing 220 degrees, range unknown."

"Roger," came the scratchy response through the jerry-rigged voice box. "Wait one."

"Wait one" meant the young sailor on the other end was getting someone more senior, which was most of Combat.

"Sonar, TAO here; what you got?"

"Commander Stapler, Senior Chief Agazzi here. Same direction of the contact we had yesterday, but the signature is different. Looks as if we may have two submarines out there trailing us."

"Any idea of the range?"

Agazzi shrugged. "Hard to say, Commander. I would guess no closer than fifteen nautical miles, sir. But if we are picking them up from a convergence-zone hop, then they could be double, even triple the range."

Gentron touched Agazzi's arm. Agazzi leaned down. "I would say it's between twenty to forty nautical miles, Senior Chief. The noise is too strong to be from a second convergence zone," Gentron whispered.

Sound waves under the water oscillated when they traveled, bouncing off the layer beneath until they reached the surface, to be bounced back toward the bottom. A good sonar technician could recognize a convergence-zone contact by the losses and gains of passive noise as the ship sonar sailed in and out of the zone. A continuous contact usually meant the contact was within striking distance because the noise was direct. Passive sonar techniques involved listening to the underwater sounds and deciphering them. Sonars seldom went active like the ones seen in old World War II movies. An active sonar was an invitation for an adversary to track the return back to you.

Agazzi nodded, thinking of Gentron being new to the AN/SQR-25. Only last month Gentron had been the backup for MacPherson, and in the confrontation with North Korea, Gentron had been the pilot of the second UUV. Seaman Gentron had very little experience in passive sonar techniques, but then Gentron had been the one who had successfully identified the class of the North Korean submarine.

"Commander, my sonar tech believes the noise is too strong for the contact to be any farther away than forty nautical miles, but that's an educated guess, sir. I wouldn't hold us to that maximum range."

"Thanks, Senior Chief. You got a UUV out there somewhere. Why don't we send it down the line of bearing and see what it finds?"

"We can do that, sir," Agazzi said with hesitation, looking at MacPherson, who nodded and immediately leaned forward toward the UUV console. "Commander, if I may, I understood Admiral Holman to say we wanted to do nothing that could be misconstrued as hostile. If I send the UUV . . ."

"I understand, Senior Chief, but I'm not saying attack the damn thing. Just go out far enough to see if you can refine the range of this submarine from Sea Base . . ."

Agazzi stood back from the speaker, recognizing Stapler's anger.

". . . so we don't get a torpedo up our ass. You understand?"

"Aye, aye, sir." Stapler was going to get them sunk one of these days.

"Let me know when the UUV is outgoing on the line of bearing."

Agazzi acknowledged the order.

"Vintage Stapler," MacPherson said without looking up. "Didn't like what the admiral told him to do?"

"He's got a better idea of what is hostile and what isn't," Agazzi answered, silently agreeing with the second-class petty officer.

"Then he hasn't looked in the mirror lately."

Agazzi pointed at the console. "Aren't you supposed to be sending the UUV down the line of bearing?"

"You sure that's what you want me to do, Senior Chief?" MacPherson asked.

"Gentron, you keep tracking the contact."

Gentron's eyebrows rose. "Don't have to do much to track

a submarine on the AN/SQR-25 sonar in passive mode, Senior Chief. The system works itself."

"Well, you help it work itself." He looked up at the maintenance table where his other seaman, Calvins, sat on a stool silently watching everything. "Calvins, go ahead and set up the sound-powered phone watch."

The lanky kid from New Oxford, Pennsylvania, jumped down from the stool, nearly falling. "Aye, Senior Chief."

Without looking up, MacPherson added, "And watch your step, Calvins. Don't want you killing yourself and getting blood over everyone."

Agazzi picked up the telephone and dialed the UUV Compartment. Stapler was the only qualified Tactical Action Officer on board Sea Base. The TAO was someone the Captain trusted enough to give him or her a letter authorizing the TAO to fire weapons and fight the ship if attacked. Stapler took seriously anyone trying to tell him what he could and couldn't do when it came to protecting Sea Base, including the venerable Admiral Holman.

Holman was the Commander, U.S. Seventh Fleet, embarked on board the USS *Boxer,* an amphibious ship accompanying Sea Base. He was a hero within the warrior ranks of the Navy, and much hated by the political flags who made up most of the senior ranks of the military.

"Senior Chief, didn't mean to upset you," MacPherson added as Agazzi held the telephone to his ear.

Agazzi nodded. They both knew the game of leadership. Regardless of what you might have in negative thoughts toward your seniors, you keep them to yourself unless there's something illegal involved. When you retired is when you could gripe, complain, and write editorials against the politics of command.

Three minutes later, Agazzi finished his telephone call with Keyland. The three men in the UUV Compartment would be back on the watch in the ASW Control Center soon. Even if they left the *Bellatrix* immediately after his telephone call, it would take them fifteen to twenty minutes to climb up six decks, cross two ships, then climb down another six decks to Sonar. As soon as they reloaded the UUV on the transom, then the three would head back.

Five minutes later, Gentron had the contact back on his scope. After working with MacPherson, Agazzi called the TAO and told him the UUV was heading out on the line of bearing. He glanced at Gentron's console, where a trace of steady noise ran down the rainfall display. What would the submarine do once it heard the noise of the UUV approaching it? Last month in the Sea of Japan, from the reactions of the North Korean submarine, its captain must have thought the UUV was a torpedo heading toward it. It had been the wrong decision.

SIX

"Weasel, Black Leader checking in."

"Looks as if the British have arrived," Johnson broadcast to Franklin.

Franklin nodded. "Yes, ma'am." He glanced out his cockpit, but the glare of the sun hid Johnson's outline so he couldn't see if she was looking in his direction or not. He glanced ahead and down. The huge RC-135 aircraft flew straight and level a couple of thousand feet below them. Slowly, as they flew along the mission track, Johnson and he had ascended in altitude, wanting to put some distance between them and the huge Rivet Joint aircraft. When the equivalent of the commercial Boeing 707 decided to turn or make a rapid change in course or altitude, the rules that applied to surface ships around an aircraft carrier applied in the sky. When a large aircraft is maneuvering, all other aircraft stand clear. Large aircraft and aircraft carriers do not change courses as rapidly and easily as fighter aircraft or smaller surface ships.

The bagpipe sound of secure communications broke the circuit.

"Black Leader, Weasel; welcome to the club. We hold you

dead ahead five-zero miles at two-eight thousand feet. We are changing our course to one-nine-zero true for rendezvous. Be advised we have two Foxtrot 22s as escort two thousand feet above us at angels three-two."

"Roger, Weasel; we have been copying your comms. Break-break. Raptor Formation, this is Commander Tyler-Cole of His Majesty's 801st Naval Squadron. From the chatter, I presume that's you, Major Johnson."

Franklin smiled. She must be having a conniption. No one broadcast real names while in flight, and here was the British commander as nonchalant as if they were out for a day in the park. Of course, they were on secure communications, so it mattered little other than Johnson was a stickler for protocol.

"Roger, Black Leader; good to hear your voice again," Johnson broadcast.

The smile grew wider on Franklin's face.

"Raptor Formation, unless you want to continue along with us, Black Formation will assume escort duty from you—should give you an additional few minutes for your refueling bingo."

"Roger, Black Leader, but our orders are to hand off at ten miles. We have forty to go."

Two clicks came across the circuit acknowledging the exchange.

"Weasel, Black Formation consists of four F-35 fighters. We are prepared to accept data link at this time."

The F-35 fighter was also known as the Joint Strike Fighter. The F-35 was a stealth fighter developed by the Pentagon for the purpose of a single stealth fighter for the four services and selected allies. While the Navy and Marine Corps quickly backed the program, the Air Force argued convincingly within the hallowed halls of the Pentagon for the F-22A. The behind-the-scenes arguments with Congressional leaders ensured both aircraft entered the defense inventory.

Franklin looked at his display, wondering what would happen once the British joined the network-centric operations of the United States military. He watched his heads-up display waiting to see what the British data would bring online. He didn't have long to wait. Within a minute, the exact location of the four Royal Navy fighters jumped onto the display. They had been there all along, but identified as unknowns. Now, the Tactical Data Display icon that had been a square box over a sporadic radar contact changed to a circle. Surface contacts had full circles for friendlies, boxes for unknowns, and the dreaded diamonds for known hostiles. Air had the top halves of the symbols, while the bottom halves identified submarines. The six Chinese J-12 stealth fighters orbiting along the coast were marked with the top half of the diamond icon.

Ten minutes later, the Royal Navy fighters had taken escort duty and the Raptors were heading north toward the KC-10. The KC-10 had the commercial DC-10 airframe. It had replaced the aging KC-135 tanker fleet as the Air Force's primary air-to-air refueling aircraft. But unlike the KC-135, the KC-10 was also capable of carrying the ground crews for an Air Force deployment.

The Air Force enjoyed pointing out that with the KC-10 providing support, the Air Force could deploy anywhere in the world within forty-eight hours. On site, in the fight, by night. The Navy saw this capability more as an Air Force attack on their carrier fleet, so the counterargument had always been that the Air Force needed another nation's airfield to operate, while the aircraft carrier was on American soil. The Air Force always argued they could orbit and flight until they had to land.

Sea Base was another affront to Navy aviation even if it was a Navy program. The unexpected Congressional mandate that Air Force fighters operate on board Sea Base had not been well received on the fourth deck of the Pentagon by the Navy flag officers. The Air Force always seemed to do better on the hill than the Navy.

But the Navy had cut its own throat in the early years of the twenty-first century. It had willingly given up its reconnaissance mission to the Air Force saying it wasn't a Navy core competency needed for control of the seas. Then, it had given the Air Force the mission of air-to-air refueling, chuckling behind the scenes about how that freed up more carrier space for fighters.

Slowly, the Air Force had received the mission of providing aerial support to the joint services. It had willingly taken the reconnaissance missions. The Navy only wanted fighter aircraft—all else was superfluous, and besides that, was boring.

The KC-10 flown by the Air Force was now used by all the services for in-flight refueling.

"Blackman, let's turn our radars back on. We're heading away from the mainland."

Franklin glanced at the clock on the heads-up display. He hit the switch, and almost immediately heard the beep announcing the radar back online. Flying northeast kept the radar beeps from being detected by sensors along the Chinese coast.

"Damn glad to have my radar back," he said to himself. Data links were nice. Data links connected all the sensors together in what the Department of Defense termed net-centric warfare.

There was one element of net-centric operations that bothered Franklin. It was this concept of "reach-back." Reach-back meant forces, resources, and assets that used to be on the front lines with the war-fighter were now located in the United States or elsewhere far, far away along the yellow brick road. He liked the idea of having what he needed with him. Most fellow fighter pilots felt the same way. If you were exposed to the dangers, the bullets, and the stress of combat, you had a better appreciation of what the war-fighter really needed.

Unfortunately, no one could pinpoint examples of when reach-back failed. It just failed to make sense to those putting their lives on the line why everyone was not at the front with them. Franklin shrugged. He and his fellow warriors had this paranoia that whoever was providing whatever reach-back capability might be more interested in getting his or her son or daughter to a Little League game than providing what the warriors needed in the middle of a fight.

The intelligence, the data links, the communications, logistics, and a myriad of other "just in time" efficiencies had never failed him. Maybe they had failed him and he just didn't know. Bottom line for him was if he couldn't touch the person providing the service, then how did he know that person really existed? Shit if he knew.

In his earphones, he listened to the chatter between the RC-135 and Commander Tyler-Cole. The British commander was quite the character, as Franklin had discovered when the man landed on Sea Base after the fight with the North Koreans.

Narrow of waist, broad of shoulder, and with a lower lip that seemed always tucked tightly against the upper. There was a touch of vanity in that the commander combed his hair forward, trying to cover a receding hairline.

The career Royal Navy fighter pilot had landed announcing he and his wingman would be aboard for a week. Two days later, only the wingman remained. Discovering Sea Base was like the rest of the United States Navy—dry—was sufficient for other duties to demand Tyler-Cole's presence back on the Royal Navy aircraft carrier *Elizabeth*. There was only so much a man could take at sea. So Tyler-Cole had launched back to the *Elizabeth*, the wardroom pub, and the English soccer matches.

"We should reach the anchor area shortly," Johnson said on their private circuit, referring to the geographical area where the tanker would be orbiting. "Keep a good lookout."

Franklin keyed his mike twice in acknowledgment. If his radar failed to pick up the KC-10 before he saw it, then he had problems with the radar.The Air Force fleet of modified Boeing C-10s had entered the fleet in 1981. The Air National Guard had inherited the venerable KC-135 tankers. He shook his head. *Of course, we're still flying B-52s, only not as often,* Franklin thought.

With the catastrophic economic collapse of 2015, funds to purchase new ships and new aircraft were hard to come by. The Navy had the same problem as the Air Force. With the exception of this Sea Base experiment, both services were using out-of-date aircraft and ships. Even the F-22A needed upgrading to more modern technology, but each year Congress voted down the funds.

The tone of the voice on the secure tactical frequency grabbed his attention. It was Weasel transmitting.

". . . disappeared. One moment they were there, and now the radar video is gone!"

"Roger, Weasel. Maybe they've returned to base for refueling or maybe they've called it a day," came the calm voice of Tyler-Cole. "After all it is getting late. . . ."

"Not likely! Not all six at once. One moment they're in a nice racetrack pattern edging closer to the coast, and the next they're gone. Something's not right."

"It is four o'clock, mate. I think they've gone home for a bit of tea."

"You serious?"

There was a chuckle on the circuit. "My fine American friend, we British have been trying to figure out the Oriental mind for centuries with as much luck as trying to figure out a woman's."

"I heard that," Johnson broadcast.

"With you as an exception, Commander."

Johnson heard two clicks on the circuit.

Does that mean he's figured Johnson out? Franklin thought.

"Contacts don't just up and disappear. They're up to something."

"Roger, Weasel. What would you like us to do?" Tyler-Cole asked.

Several seconds passed with no answer from the RC-135.

"Weasel, Black Leader here. Unless you object, I am going to dispatch two of my flight to take a position twenty-five miles west of us at angels twenty-eight."

"Roger, Black Leader."

"That will bracket you with me and my wingman above you, while the other pair will fly the right flank as early warning at two thousand feet lower than you."

"LOOKS like those Chinese stealth fighters have disappeared," Johnson said on their private circuit.

"Maybe they went low. Maybe ground clutter is obscuring them from the Rivet Joint."

"I doubt it. The RJ has so many sensors, and access to so many other sensors we don't even know about, that if the aircraft went low or high, they'd pick them up. They have a better reach-back capability than we do."

Franklin imagined Johnson shaking her head as if lecturing a student pilot. "Think we ought to go back?" he asked.

"No," Johnson answered. "If they need us, then it'd be nice to have a full fuel pack."

A blip appeared on Franklin's radar, almost immediately covered by a half circle. The automated Electronic Warfare suite on the F-22A identified the radar return as the KC-10.

"I got the tanker," they both broadcast almost simultaneously.

"Change to secondary tactical frequency," Johnson ordered.

Franklin reached over and changed the settings of his secure communications, listening to the Key Material Infrastructure within the radios synchronize. KMI was the key to secure communications throughout the military.

He pressed the button beneath the Communications-Navigation-Integration system—fondly called CNI. Pressing the button, he froze the frequency onto a specific channel. If he needed to switch between tactical-one and tactical-two, all he had to do was press the button. CNI was the key to the net-centric capability of the F-22A. The data link they had been using for the past two hours was part of CNI.

While he keyed the radio, Franklin flipped the range of the radar so the data link from the Rivet Joint blended into the heads-up display. He glanced at the location of the tanker, then to the Rivet Joint heading south away from them. Two of the F-35 British fighters were diverting westward separating from the RC-135. He wondered what they were doing, then decided they were just doing some due diligence in positioning some protection between the high-value target—the RC-135—and the Chinese threat to the west.

Trailing the Air Force reconnaissance aircraft were the other two F-35 aircraft. An upside-down half circle covered each of the friendly aircraft with a slight line leading from the icon, pointing in the direction of travel with the length of line indicating the speed of each of them.

"Jolly Roger, this is Raptor Leader; we hold you five-zero miles. We bear one-eight-zero true from your orbit position. Estimate five minutes your location."

Five minutes later, Franklin and Johnson were maneuvering toward the wings of the tanker.

"Raptor 10, I'll drink first," Johnson said.

He clicked his transmit button twice. *Of course she'd drink first. She's the DETCO—oh, no! Not DETCO. "I'm the Commander and don't forget it—so get the hell out of my way and let me refuel first. After all, you're just a lowly captain while I am a senior major."* Franklin let out a deep sigh. "Fast Pace, I hope you recover soon and get the hell back out here."

"Raptor Leader, course will be zero-one-zero at angels twenty-seven," the tanker broadcast.

Air-to-air refueling was dangerous, but it was the critical node in the Air Force's capability to reach globally anywhere, anytime. Air Force pilots could do it in their sleep. Hence, their explanation for the bumper sticker that read: "Fighter Pilots can do it in their sleep." The same bumper sticker the Air Force Chief of Staff banned from his bases.

"Jolly Roger, Raptor Leader; can we do the refueling on a southerly course?"

Several seconds passed before a deep Southern voice answered Johnson's request. "Ma'am, we'd like to, but our orders are to steer clear of the strait. Not to enter it. We have to go northeast. Would you secure your radar during refueling? Thanks."

Franklin shook his head and smiled. *Dumb shit tanker jock,* he thought. *Saying 'ma'am' told her you're junior to her. Now, you have to live with what's coming.*

"Roger, Jolly Roger," came Johnson's voice, a little stiffer in tone than the previous transmission. "As the senior officer here, we need to head south. We may have a situation where we have to break off. If so, we'd like to be nearer the area."

"But Raptor Leader . . ."

"That's an order, Jolly Roger. You may enter it in your log and explain to your superiors when you return."

Franklin laughed. *Give it up, tanker lad. You're outmatched and outgunned.*

Several seconds later: "Jolly Roger, I am ready for new course," Johnson said.

As the tanker and F-22A fighters maneuvered to the new course, Franklin put his radar in idle as Johnson eventually ordered.

Five minutes later, the three aircraft were heading 190. Franklin watched from a thousand feet higher as the drogue emerged from the KC-10.

It was an untidy ballet between the fighter and the drogue in in-flight refueling. Franklin watched as Major Johnson approached the bell-like end of the refueling drogue slowly. Every aspect of in-flight refueling was critical, but none more so than the approach. It was here that a miscalculation, an air pocket, or high-altitude wind shear could send the drogue crashing into the fighter aircraft.

Johnson's male probe slid into the refueling drogue smoothly—almost like teenage sex, thought Franklin, recalling his first time. Daydreams and fantasies helped pilots pass those boring moments of level flight. *Wow!* he thought. *Those tanker and RC-135 pilots must need more flight suits than fighter pilots.*

Thirty minutes later, Franklin had replaced her. Both of them ignored the continuous complaints by the tanker pilot as they entered the Taiwan Strait. After all, Franklin reasoned, Jolly Roger had two of the world's most powerful fighter aircraft accompanying it, and afterward, hundreds of miles for the glazed-eye flight back to Okinawa.

"SENIOR Chief!" Bernardo shouted, waving four fingers above his head. "I have four contacts out there now." Bernardo dropped his hand and leaned closer to the AN/SQR-25 sonar display. "Gentron, you Christly twit! What the hell did you do to my screen?"

"Nothing, Petty Officer Bernardo," Gentron stuttered from the other side of MacPherson.

"Bullshit!"

"Leave him alone," MacPherson interjected. "We're trying to set up the controls for another UUV."

Bernardo grabbed a tube of wipes from beneath the console, ripped one out, and started wiping down the display. "Looks as if he rubbed his greasy hair against it."

MacPherson reached over and ran the back of his hand up the side of Gentron's close-cropped hairline. "Yeah, too much hair, Gentron."

"Okay, everyone, let's concentrate on the ASW picture. Tell me about the contacts," Agazzi interrupted as he jumped up from his desk, heading toward the lower level.

"Four of them just popped up. Popped up within seconds of each other."

Bernardo stuffed the wipes beneath the console, never taking his eyes off the display. He reached up and pointed. "I have two strong ones and a weak one that could be convergence-zone jump. And, of course, this one that's been there all along."

"Location?"

"We have the original two southwest of us. One is bearing 225 and the other is 240 degrees." His finger pointed to two new trace marks inching down the rainfall display. "This one is north of us bearing 010 degrees true, with a buddy coming from the east at 080 degrees."

"East! That would mean they . . ."

Agazzi reached the console, touched Bernardo's shoulder, and interrupted Gentron's comment. "Any indications of their presence prior to this?"

Bernardo looked toward Gentron, straining his neck for a glimpse of the young seaman. "Gentron! Did you see anything other than the original submarines?"

Gentron looked at Agazzi. "Senior Chief! I only saw the ones Petty Officer Bernardo detected yesterday: those bearing around 240. All they did was show up on the console and then disappear, as if they knew how close they could get before being detected."

"Senior Chief," MacPherson said. "You want me to keep our UUV searching southwest of us?"

"Taylor and Keyland still in the UUV Compartment?"

MacPherson looked at the small cam picture. "I see Elvis, but Po-Boy must still be fiddling with the UUVs."

"Tell Petty Officer Keyland to prepare to launch another two UUVs."

"Senior Chief, we're launching the second one now. Two more means Gentron or I am going to have to handle two on each console. We've never handled more than one at a time."

"I've got confidence in your ability, Petty Officer MacPherson. It's time to test your professionalism," Agazzi said. He leaned down and watched the noise trace of the four contacts trickle down the rainfall display. "Petty Officer Bernardo, start a time-motion analysis on those four contacts. I need to know their course, speed, and distance from us."

"Can I help?" Calvins asked from where he sat on the stool near the maintenance desk. Agazzi looked at him for a second before his attention returned to the contacts.

"I can do the TMA, Senior Chief, but the signal strength is

increasing on each and each is on a continuous bearing. I may not know how far they are from us, but they are definitely closing."

"Where's our submarines when we need them?" MacPherson asked.

"We have five and every one of them is somewhere in the Taiwan Strait."

"How about they *Taiwan* one of them out here with us?" MacPherson added.

Agazzi pushed the MC button for Combat. "Combat, Sonar here; we have four—I say again—four unidentified contacts. . . ." He repeated the initial analysis to the Tactical Action Officer. Responding to the peppering of questions by Commander Stapler, Agazzi told him that based on constant bearing and increasing signal strength, the contacts might be approaching Sea Base.

A constant bearing, decreasing range meant the submarines were on a collision course with Sea Base.

"We're surrounded," Bernardo said with a sigh. He looked toward the young sailor from Pennsylvania, who was now standing beside the maintenance table, his body half-blocking the security camera screens. "Okay, Seaman Calvins, get your ass down here and I'll show you how the SQR-25 does time-motion analysis."

Agazzi leaned forward as the young sailor squeezed by him. With only seven of them, it helped that each learned something about every job in Sonar. "Okay, Calvins, if they sound General Quarters, you will have to stop and man your sound-powered phone position," Agazzi warned as he left the console.

He was halfway up the ladder from the console area to the upper level when Bernardo shouted, his voice trembling with emotion.

"I got torpedoes in the water. Jesus Christ! They're coming from every direction."

Agazzi gripped the railings and slid down backward to the bottom level. He pushed Calvins out of the way as he leaned over Bernardo's shoulder. The normal dark green background of the screen had turned pale from the number of noise signatures filling the ocean beneath Sea Base.

"Eight. I got eight! Eight torpedoes inbound, Senior Chief!"

"Calvins, get your ass up there and man your position!" Agazzi shouted, pushing by the seaman as he hurried to the MC console.

"SHOWDERNITZEL!" Jacobs shouted, waving her toward him. Who was the sailor trailing behind her?

"That's the master chief," Showdernitzel said, her hand shielding her mouth. "Whatever you do, don't let his bluster scare you. It's his bite you have to worry about."

Andrew stared at the man standing near the rail gun. "Is that Jacobs?" he asked quietly, bending down near Showdernitzel's ear.

"Master Chief Jacobs to you. The rest of us call him Bad Ass, but not to his face. It'd make his already too large ego bigger."

Jacobs! Andrew straightened, his eyes narrowing as he absorbed everything about this man who had killed his brother. His father had read in the papers about Jacobs's act. But none ever knew the whole story of his brother's death. He glanced down at Showdernitzel. This woman would tell him. She'd tell anything about anybody if anyone even pretended to listen to her babble. He shivered at the idea of spending unnecessary time with this woman of sin. The left side of his lips curled in disgust.

"What was that?" Showdernitzel asked, laughing as she looked up at him. "You think he's bad from here, wait until you see him up close. Then, you'll really shake." She laughed again. "You look as if you smell a skunk. You'll get used to the odors of the flight deck after a while. Most of us never notice them."

He bit his lower lip, forcing down the urge to shout for her to shut up. Spending time with Steve Bucket learning about the Navy was book learning. Anyone can do book learning, as his father liked to say, but real learning was by doing. Her two chevrons meant she was senior to him within the military. He wondered what she would say if she knew how close she was standing to one of God's saints? He imagined her on her knees kissing his feet and worshipping his presence. Someday, many would.

"You don't talk much, do you?"

"Showdernitzel! You going to meander and mosey over here, or you gonna get a step on it? You think I got all day to stand here and wait for you to stroll by?"

"He's a darling, ain't he? I like it when he's in a good mood such as now. When he's in a bad mood, he's been known to throw people into the water like that asshole Smith. Other divisions have mellow people-persons such as that friend of his Senior Chief Agazzi." She mimicked, *"Oh, are you okay, Petty Officer Spuckitelly? Do you need some time to yourself, Petty Officer Spuckitelly? Can I get you some coffee, Petty Officer Spuckitelly?* Give me a break," she finished, taking a deep breath, and smiling. "Not our master chief. He'll slap you silly if he caught you trying to find the inner you. That's what I like about him. None of that shitty psychotherapy-babble leadership touchy-feely bullshit or 'I'm your friend' crap. You know where you stand. You start off on his shit list and seldom have to worry about getting off it. Plus . . ."

He tuned her out, catching his breath. Smith had been Joshua. Joshua; his brother and the chosen one before he was selected to replace him. Unconsciously, Andrew's hands turned to fists. An inner fire of righteous fury urged him to run at the man who had killed his brother. The man stood there less than thirty feet from him with his arm in a sling. The knowledge of this man killing his brother was common on board Sea Base. And they praised a man who had killed one of God's chosen. Sea Base and all who rode her were damned.

"What's wrong with you, Jolson? You going through hot flashes at your age or something?" Showdernitzel shook her head, and then looked straight ahead at Jacobs. "I can tell you he don't like things that ain't ordinary. You one of these druggies with their ups and downs of bipolarism, you gonna join—"

"I don't do drugs," he said angrily. He opened his mouth to continue, but all he could do was stutter. He wanted to punch her.

"Okay, okay, okay," she said, reaching over and patting him on the arm.

He jerked his arm away.

"Jolson, I can tell you ain't gonna last long in this man's Navy. Or this woman's." Showdernitzel stopped, grabbing Andrews's arm and turning him around. Poking her thumb into her chest, she said, "You're too moody. You'd better get over it, and stop acting strange. We got enough strange on board without me having to add you to it." She poked him in the chest. "You understand me?"

"Showdernitzel," Jacobs shouted before Andrew answered.

"Get your butt over here, quit lollygagging, and who in the hell are you beating up?"

The two turned. Several seconds later, after the two were near him, Jacobs pointed at the dark area on the port side of the runway that split the centerline of Sea Base. "Showdernitzel, how do you think we are going to get this stain off my deck?" Jacobs took his arm out of the sling, wincing slightly from the dull pain it brought.

"Ought to leave it in the sling like the doctor told you."

"Showdernitzel, when I want a mom, I'll send for you."

"Ah, come on, Master Chief; you and I know you never had a mother."

"Focus on my deck that you let get cruddy, Showdernitzel, and who in the hell is he?"

"This is Petty Officer Jolson: Allan Jolson. Taleb said he was a singer."

"A singer? Let's hope you aren't a boatswain mate."

"I'm not a singer. Taleb says my name Al Jolson is the name of a singer who lived a hundred years ago. I've never heard of him."

Never heard of Al Jolson, Jacobs thought. *If my name had been Al Jolson, someone would have kidded, badgered, and beaten me so many times in school, I'd've never forgotten the man's name.* But then that was *his* day, when boys were boys and sheep were nervous. He smiled at his unspoken joke. *Kids aren't learning what they should in school nowadays anyway.*

"Are you one of my boatswain mates?"

"Yes, Master Chief; he arrived on the noon flight. He's berthed on the *Algol* and I'm showing him around."

"And you're not a singer, a ballet dancer, or one of those sons-of-a-bitch who finished college but can't decide what they want to do so they think they can go to sea to discover themselves, are you?"

Andrews's eyes widened slightly at the verbal blast. He shook his head.

"Good, welcome aboard." Jacobs stuck out his left hand. "Sorry, but my right hand is being repaired by Navy medicine. Most likely won't ever work again."

"Master chiefs aren't supposed to whine."

Jacobs's eyebrows arched over his eyes, nearly hiding them from sight. "Showdernitzel, you and I have to have a come-to-Jesus chat about respect." He turned back to Jolson, his hand still out.

Jolson was staring at his hand. *What's this man's problem?* Then, the new sailor reached forward and took Jacobs's hand. His lips curled. *What a shitty handshake,* Jacobs thought. *Like shaking a wet fish.* He nearly wiped his hand on his khaki pants, but he didn't need anything human on the trousers.

"So, you all squared away and ready to start working?"

"Yes, I think so."

"It's yes, Master Chief," Showdernitzel corrected.

"Well, welcome to First Division," Jacobs said. "Glad to have another hand to help keep this floating bucket of bolts afloat and looking halfway decent." He nodded at Showdernitzel. "She'll get you settled and tell you the routine. It's a big island and bigger than anything you've ever been aboard. If you get lost, just work your way topside is the best recommendation for finding your way around."

"Yes, Master Chief."

"You should have some time to get the hang of Sea Base. It isn't your conventional warship, but it's still a warship. Don't let anyone tell you different." Jacobs put his hands on his hips, quickly dropping the right one. "Showdernitzel, see what you can do about this stain. Maybe get some of the hands to help you and try a few different methods on swatches of it to see what happens. Check with supply and see how much nonskid they have. I don't want to remove the fire stain down to white metal only to discover we don't have enough nonskid to cover it."

"You could paint it," Andrew suggested.

"Oh, yes, we could paint it, and the first time there's another fire on this deck, it would burn right alongside whatever else was burning." Jacobs shook his head. "No, we need something nonflammable, within Naval regulations, and gray: Navy gray. And Showdernitzel, none of that Air Force wimpy blue shit."

Showdernitzel opened her mouth to say something. The bongs of General Quarters drowned out whatever she was going to say. The three looked toward the speakers mounted on the top deck of the tower. "This is not a drill; this is not a drill: General Quarters, General Quarters; all hands man your battle stations!"

"Showdernitzel; get to the port-side damage control station! I'll be there shortly." He pointed at Andrew. "Keep Jolson with you." He looked at Andrew. "You stay with her!" Then he shouted as they took off running, "Start the muster as soon as you get there!"

Jacobs headed toward the tower. What the hell was going on now? He reached over with his good hand and eased the right back into the sleeve. He hated this. Not having control over his hand bugged the crap out of him. Maybe the doctor could give him a pill or shot to hurry up this healing shit.

SEVEN

Franklin broke away from the refueling drogue, thanking the pilot, who verbally blasted both of them for taking him nearly a hundred miles from his anchor orbit.

"Reform, Blackman," Johnson broadcast, ignoring the complaints.

To their left, the KC-10 aircraft banked left away from the Raptor formation. There was no wish for luck from the tanker as it quickly disappeared behind them. Franklin smiled. Got to hand it to Johnson; if pissing off people is a core skill, then she graduated top of her class.

Franklin had been in focused communications for the past fifteen minutes with the tanker. Refueling operations were fun, or so he thought, but all you needed was a fraction of a second of inattention and that drogue would pop out like a missile ripping through your cockpit or slamming into one of the jet intakes.

"Roger, Commander."

"Reform left side, one hundred feet. I'm on course one-nine-zero degrees at angels twenty-six."

He clicked his transmitter twice.

A few minutes later, the two F-22A Raptors were formation-flying.

"While you've been having your drink, Raptor 10, the Rivet Joint reached the southern leg of its track and is now heading north. We are to relieve the British in forty-five minutes so they can refuel. You synchronized with your data links?"

Sometimes during refueling operations, the closeness of so much metal treated the data links as if they were in the middle of an antenna jungle. Franklin flipped the switches, synchronizing the secure communications, hearing the telltale bagpipe approval as the data links established connections. Seconds later, his heads-up display looked like a Disney cartoon with different colors, shapes, and outlined landmasses.

"I've resynch'd, Raptor Leader."

"They don't know what happened to the Chinese J-12s that were flying the racetrack. Rivet Joint figures the stealth fighters have returned to base."

"One moment they have them on radar and the next they're gone. Doesn't sound to me as if they've gone home. Sounds more to me as if they have some sort of stealth technology to help the antiradar skin of the aircraft."

"You could be right, Blackman."

He keyed his mike twice. What the hell was he doing? This was Major "Call me Commander" Johnson he was gabbing with. She might be friendly with the two of them out here, but once they touched down, she'd be the hard-nosed bitch everyone expected.

"Raptor Leader, Raptor Haven; how do you read?"

"Raptor Haven; I have you fivers," Johnson replied.

"Be advised, we are at General Quarters with multiple torpedoes inbound. Your nearest bingo field is Taipei."

"Roger, Raptor Haven; say again why GQ?"

"Inbound torpedoes."

Shit! thought Franklin. *That can't be good.*

Johnson keyed her mike twice.

"Maybe those stealth fighters didn't return to base," Franklin transmitted on their private circuit.

"Coordinate into the computer directions for Taipei, in the event we have to bingo without much warning."

"Yes, ma'am." Franklin keyed in the coordinates and saved the data.

For the next minute, they double-checked the coordinates

and data, knowing if they became separated or damaged, they could flip on the autopilot that could grab the data and take them to the bingo field.

Afterward, they flew in silence, listening to Black Leader and Weasel passing status reports. Franklin thought of Walters and his wingman's young family. Ideas for what he wanted to do with his Air Force career careened through his thoughts, and in the background he listened to the communications chatter filling the air, watching the heads-up display much like a driver in Washington beltway traffic glances at his dashboard. Every few seconds he checked his distance to Johnson, and all of this was going on almost as a second thought, unconsciously, as they flew toward the rendezvous spot. He had lost count of time until Johnson broke his reverie. He glanced at the clock and saw five minutes had passed. It seemed longer.

"Weasel, this is Raptor Leader; did you copy Raptor Haven's transmission?"

"That's a negative," the communications officer on board the RC-135 replied. "Was it to us?"

"Negative; Sea Base has gone to General Quarters due to . . . They are under attack."

That's not what Raptor Haven said, Franklin thought, his eyebrows rising at Johnson's transmission. *Slight difference between "Torpedoes inbound" and "We're under attack."* Though he couldn't really see the difference other than semantics.

"Roger, Raptor Leader; we copy."

"Who or what is attacking them?" interrupted Commander Lester Tyler-Cole. "Air or sea?"

"They report torpedoes heading toward them, so am presuming submarine attack."

"I would say," Tyler-Cole added, "this puts a different picture on the disappearance of those six contacts, Weasel. I think it might be time for you to disappear."

"Roger, Black Leader; hold one."

Franklin knew that on board the RC-135, the officers would be racing up and down the long fuselage toward the mission commander's spot, wherever that was inside the aircraft. Must be nice to stretch your legs, drink a cup of coffee, and stand up to take a leak. It takes practice to learn how to pee sitting down while fully dressed.

"Weasel, this is Raptor Leader; we are increasing speed and expect to rendezvous with you and Black Formation within three-zero minutes."

The bagpipes of encryption erupted in Franklin's ears for a second, followed by the British accent of Tyler-Cole. "Roger, Raptor Leader; we are four F-35 fighters coming toward you. Two are overhead Weasel with other pair taking station between big boy and the Chinese coast."

Franklin wished Walters were here now. They'd be bantering snide comments and humorous shit back and forth, excited over the possibility of air combat. The banter would be to convince each other they weren't scared to death also. He listened with his finger off the transmit button as Johnson, Tyler-Cole, and the RJ exchanged courses, headings, and positions, though everything they passed was easily discernible on the heads-up display. *Why in the world do we have this information technology if we still trust our hearing better?* Well, he had no intention of trying to change it. Nothing wrong with someone confirming the data. Look at those five Navy aircraft the Bermuda Triangle ate.

KIANG was gasping for breath by the time he reached the top of Sea Base. His binoculars and camera swung from leather straps rubbing around his neck. He bent over, putting his hands on his knees, catching his breath, ignoring the tramping of metal-toed shoes slamming down on the metal deck as hordes of sailors ran around him, racing toward their battle stations.

A half minute later, he raised his head. He glanced up at the mast above the tower. A maze of antennas decorated the arms like Christmas tree icicles. Several radars turned like ornaments twirling among the limbs. Those antennas and radars were the only official reason he was on board Sea Base. The Layer Institute of Research in downtown San Antonio had been awarded the noncompetitive contract. They had been the only technical organization with the professional depth and expertise to meet the requirements.

He stood staring at the mast as his thoughts turned to Jack Sward. He had run into Mrs. Sward during his short trip back to San Antonio at a ceremony honoring her husband. She had been kind saying how much Jack thought of him. If Jack had not been chosen over Kiang for this trip, he'd still be alive.

Kiang thought briefly of the meeting in Pearsall Park where the colonel had instructed him to ingratiate himself with Sward. Two months before Sea Base was to sail, Jack Sward died in a car accident and Kiang was catapulted to where he stood now. The Institute had taken care of Mrs. Sward and their small children.

He started walking, putting his hand over the binoculars and camera to keep them from swinging, listening to the rapid beating of his heart. Running up four flights of near-straight stairs was no mean task.

Kiang glanced up again, squinting at the metal crow's nest nestled in the center of the antennas and radars. He sighed, hoping he was not going to discover himself trapped aloft again with the sailor who never stopped talking.

Motion to his left drew his attention. Two pilots were scurrying up the ladders into their F-22A fighters. Most of the Air Force contingent was at the flight line. Others scrambled around the two aircraft much like ants swarming over a fresh piece of bread.

Kiang walked toward the tower, his eyes watching the activity along the flight line. People passed him at the run. There were thirty-two Air Force enlisted and twelve officers according to his count. At least ten of the officers were pilots. Most of the enlisted were members of the ground crew. He stared for a moment at a group of officers standing out of the way of the activity, their eyes fixed on the two aircraft being readied for launch. He counted seven. That meant one unaccounted for.

He looked at the tower ahead of him. Near the base he saw the sailor. He was talking to one of the Air Force women at the base of the tower. The ladder leading up to the crow's nest was beside the two. A slight moan escaped Kiang. What was the man's name? Taleb?

The idea of spending hours listening to the sailor talk about his plans and baring his soul caused Kiang's stomach to churn. He had never enjoyed small talk nor social mingling, but to be forced onto a small metal platform with a man who constantly invaded his personal space both physically and verbally was atrocious. His attention turned to the woman. The woman was dressed in Air Force cammies and wearing white sneakers. Most of the Air Force, including the ground crew, wore flight suits. She walked away as he watched, heading inside the tower. He wondered briefly if she was part of the Combat Information Center on the second floor, one of the Air Tower personnel on the top floor, or just using the stairwell in the tower to go belowdecks.

Kiang stopped and raised his binoculars. With the activity ongoing around him, he doubted anyone would notice or care. He trained the glasses on the Raptors, watching the two cockpits close. The tall bald-headed chief master sergeant seemed to be an island within the storm of moving bodies. Every minute or so, one of the ground crew would run up to him, listen to what he said, and hasten off. Kiang trailed the glasses right, stopping the lens on a small group of Air Force flight suits. The dark splashes of color on top of each of the shoulders confirmed these seven as officers.

He dropped his glasses for a moment and looked at his watch. Two minutes remaining until the six minutes needed for GQ passed. The average time for Sea Base to set General Quarters was six minutes. He'd read it in the Plan of the Day. Captain Garcia was demanding half that time. Kiang raised the glasses again and spun them toward the tower, the glasses passing briefly over where, moments earlier, the sailor and Air Force woman had stood. The sailor was gone now. He focused upward, expecting to see Taleb climbing toward the crow's nest, but saw no one.

He sighed. His eyebrows furrowed and eyes narrowed as he thought about the woman. Had he seen her elsewhere? There was something about her that seemed familiar. Wherever it had been, it had been something pleasurable, he decided from the faint feeling when he saw her. His lower lip pushed into his upper. Where was it?

"Hey, buddy! Aren't you supposed to be somewhere?"

Kiang dropped the glasses.

Master Chief Jacobs stood there. Jacobs glanced at the

badge hanging around Kiang's neck. "Contractors are to be either at a specific location, in their staterooms, or in a designated space. You're crowding my deck, sir, so please do one of the three."

"Yes, Master Chief," Kiang said, nodding a couple of times, noticing the right arm in the sling. His eyes went back to the master chief's eyes. So this was the venerable Jacobs who'd saved Sea Base.

"Bad enough I got every Air Force zoomie out here crowding my deck, but now I got sightseers." Jacobs jerked his thumb to the open hatch leading down. "Hit the lower level now."

Kiang turned and headed back down the ladder. A feeling of relief rushed over him. He now had a reason for why he was not where Office of Naval Research wanted its consultant, and he'd avoided being trapped with the sailor. At the bottom of the four-story ladder, Kiang found himself on the main deck of the *Pollux. Pollux* was directly astern of the lead ship *Altair,* ahead of the *Antares,* and on the starboard side of *Regulus,* where his stateroom was located.

Pollux also had its main cargo hold filled with the servers that controlled the varied computer orders that kept Sea Base afloat against the ever-changing tempo of the sea. Since the explosion on the *Denebola* that destroyed the main server farm, armed masters-at-arms guarded the entrances to the cargo hold on board *Pollux.*

Kiang turned toward the passageway leading to the *Regulus* and his stateroom, but near the entrance stopped. What was it the master chief had said? He said all the Air Force were topside. If they were topside, then there was a good chance no one was in their offices. Their offices and berthing areas were on board the USNS *Antares* located astern of where he was now. He might never have a better opportunity to see what they had in the way of technical documents.

It was an assignment given to him that he never expected to have the opportunity to carry out. An assignment filled with the danger of being caught. He wasn't in the crow's nest where he was expected to be. That he could explain, but he would be unable to explain why he was in the Air Force spaces.

He turned, saw no one around, and headed aft toward the

passageway that would take him to the *Antares*. He could visit the *Antares* cargo hold and take a better look at the Air Force portable offices. He grunted. Kiang might have an opportunity or not, but he would definitely not have one if he at least did not take a look at the spaces while he had the opportunity.

Ten minutes later, Kiang reached the end of the mobile passageway that ran from the stern of the *Pollux* to the bow of the *Antares*. The temporary nature of these passageways crisscrossing between ships allowed movement beneath the Sea Base canopy. Because they were temporary and built to break away if necessary, there were no watertight hatches at each end. The ships held aloft the metal canopy of Sea Base, but the metal canopy served as one more anchor in keeping the ships in a coordinated location. One more thing holding this seagoing island together and functioning. These passageways would fall into the ocean if Sea Base fell apart. In which case, it wouldn't matter where you were when this scientific marvel started spiraling downward into the dark Pacific.

When Kiang stepped onto the forward deck of the *Antares,* he immediately looked up at the darkened bridge and glanced at his watch. No one was around. It was if he had stepped onto a deserted ship where everyone had mysteriously disappeared, but he knew everyone on Sea Base was entombed behind watertight hatches or manning positions designed to help this floating island fight and stay afloat.

If anyone saw him from up there, they'd probably dismiss him as another lost soul in the confusion of General Quarters.

It had now been ten minutes since the GQ alarm had sounded. He was probably one of only a handful still walking the decks of Sea Base. He thought most likely he was the only one unauthorized to do so. He was wrong.

Kiang moved cautiously through the covered walkway to the main deck, which was covered with supply pallets stacked on top of each other. He stepped carefully along the deck, not looking up to see if anyone watched. If he looked up, they would see his face; this way, only the top of his head was visible.

When he reached the forward forecastle, he took a deep breath of satisfaction because he had encountered no one.

He opened the nearby hatch on the forecastle of *Antares*

and entered, wincing at the screeching of the metal catch freeing the rubber seals from their watertight suction. White lights blazed inside the passageway. On warships, they would have been red during GQ. He turned and pushed the metal bar down, feeling the hatch tighten around the rubber seals, securing the door, making it watertight once again. Kiang looked both ways, reached up, and pushed his sweat-matted black hair away from his eyes. He ran his fingers beneath the leather straps of the binoculars and camera, easing the weight slightly around his neck. He felt the tender skin beneath them, knowing later he would have blisters.

Satisfied no one was moving in the passageway, Kiang started downward, ladder by ladder, quiet as possible, moving toward the main hangar—the cargo hold—where the Air Force had loaded mobile office buildings in Pearl.

He opened the hatch to the huge main cargo hold of the *Antares*. The Fast Sealift Ships had two main cargo holds. The largest one was located beneath the main deck between the two forecastles of the ships. A smaller bay was in the aft section of the Fast Sealift Ship directly beneath the helicopter pad. Kiang entered the larger of the two cargo holds—the forward one located between the fore and aft forecastle.

The sound of voices came from the aft portion of the cargo hold. The main cargo hold was so large that echoes could be heard when it was empty and rumor had it that small clouds were known to condense in the overhead and produce rain. A short burst of laughter and the conversation continued. He couldn't make out what they were talking about, but could tell from the laughter and the number of voices that the group was doing little but talking.

His attention went to the starboard side of the cargo hold, where a two-story white mobile facility had been fitted. Air-conditioning units projected from each office. Small curtained windows allowed light into the offices. It made Kiang compare the situation to someone putting a house trailer inside a massive cave.

On shore, the two-story mobile facility would have fit comfortably along the side of an aircraft hangar. Here inside the bowels of one of the Navy's largest supply ships, the two-story mobile facility barely made a dent in the available space of this cargo hold. One of the many Morale, Welfare, and Recreation tours he had taken when Sea Base first stood up, to get an idea where his targets were located, had taken him through the bay of every Fast Sealift Ship. This ship could carry seven hundred Army vehicles when fully loaded for its primary job of quickly transporting large mechanized equipment to support the Army and Marine Corps at war.

Kiang secured the hatch as quietly as possible. He listened to the voices talking and laughing on the far side of the hangar. Walking quietly, he stayed near the forward bulkhead in the shadows as he neared the Air Force spaces. He could read the sign on the doors of the offices—large red letters blazed AUTHORIZED PERSONNEL ONLY. He took a step forward. The maintenance and ground crew occupied the bottom offices. Officer country was the second floor. He looked up in that direction. The Ready Room, where the pilots hung their helmets, the offices that were most likely to have classified material, and the offices of the senior officers were on the second floor.

A loud burst of laughter caused him to jump. Kiang pulled back into the shadows of the forward bulkhead as he moved, his head turning from the mobile offices to the unseen group at the other end of the cavernous cargo bay. He looked around the cargo hold. The huge steel frames running up the sides of the cargo hold bulkhead created numerous shadows where anyone could be hiding. He paused for several seconds, trying to see if anyone else hid in the shadows.

Satisfied he was being overly cautious, he let out a quiet sigh of relief and continued. Seconds later, he passed into the alleyway created by the forward bulkhead and the mobile office complex. Metal stairs led up.

THE two ready-alert Raptors taxied to the end of the runway. Willard stood with his feet apart and arms crossed. Large hearing protectors were pulled down over his ears, shielding him from the noise of the jet engines revving up for takeoff.

A moment later, the two aircraft sped down the runway. The lead pilot was nearly two aircraft lengths ahead of the wingman. When they lifted off together, the wingman eased forward slightly, closing the distance. Willard watched it with the same awe today as he did as a young airman at Nellis when he helped launch his first aircraft. The Air Force had come a long way since the F-15s of yesteryear, and he, by the grace of God, had been part of it.

"Chief Willard!"

He turned at the muffled shout. Master Chief Jacobs approached. Willard smiled, lifting the ear protectors off his ears.

"Hi, Jerry. What brings you out here on this bright sunny afternoon?"

"You and General Quarters do. Johnny, do you need all these people topside? I know you have to launch aircraft, but can't some of them clear the decks?"

Willard looked at the officers standing off to one side, talking with each other. "I guess I could ask some to go below until we need them, but you know how fighter jocks are, Jerry. They gonna want to stay up here and provide us with all the advice and assistance they can."

Jacobs looked to where Willard pointed and smiled. "I see they're having a conference about it now."

"Conferencing is something officers do well, my fine squid friend."

"Well, my zoomie comrade, can you ask them to do their conferencing in the Ready Room? Tell them they're too valuable to be topside. Tell them the Navy loves them and wants to cradle them inside its protective arms."

"Pardon me, Jerry, while I throw up."

Jacobs waved the comment away. "The Air Boss is going to say something soon if everyone remains topside, Johnny. Just trying to save you and me additional General Quarters angst."

Willard crossed his arms and looked at the officers again. "I can send a few belowdecks, Jerry, but we've been told to launch all of them, so we'll need the ready pilots available topside."

Jacobs looked over toward the starboard aft side of Sea Base and saw his First Division personnel forming up. He pointed them out to Willard. "Thanks, Johnny; I got to go and distribute my people." He looked at his watch. "You got about a minute before GQ is fully set. I recommend getting them belowdecks ASAP."

"How's the arm?" Willard asked.

"It's okay," Jacobs said, lifting the right elbow, dragging the sling upward. "But can't talk right now, but you need to get your people into life vests."

Jacobs started to walk away, but Willard grabbed his sleeve. "What's going on?"

"Torpedoes are what is going on. One of the sound-powered phone talkers told me Sonar had eight of the bastards inbound."

"Torpedoes? If they hit, it won't matter where everyone is," Willard objected. "Maybe keeping them topside is safer?"

"It will matter if they're in the way of us fighting to keep Sea Base afloat. So do me the favor of one E-9 to another; get them belowdecks and out of the way."

Willard watched Jacobs leave. Lou Thomas ran up to him, the man's mouth open to speak.

"Are the next two ready, Lou?" Willard asked before the technical sergeant could say anything.

"Chief, our aircraft are always ready."

Willard held up one finger.

"With the exception of 223," Thomas added reluctantly.

Willard looked at the pilots milling about to the rear of the flight line. One thing he liked about the Air Force was how officers knew when their advice was needed and when they needed to stay out of the way. Well . . . most times. Christ! He'd hate to be in the Navy where you got advice all the time. He watched Jacobs's back as the Navy master chief hurried across the runway portion of Sea Base.

"Lou, get our people into life vests."

"Why?"

"Why! Because I said so."

"Okay, Chief," Thomas replied, glancing behind Willard. He opened his mouth, but shut it. "I'll go get them into life vests, Chief. They aren't going to like it. It's hot enough out here."

"Lou, is there something else bothering you?"

"I'm going to get them into the life vests, Chief. What about the other people problem we're getting here? I got more people than I need and the officers are starting to get antsy. They want to fly and fight."

"You know something, Sergeant Thomas? You are right on target. Tell the officers to get on their life vests or go wait in the Ready Room. Tell them how valuable they are and all that other stuff they like to hear. Then, tactfully—you know that word: tact? Then, tactfully, suggest they wait in the Ready Room rather than sweat up their flight suits beneath the life vests."

"Ah, come on, Chief. Why should I ask them? You're the chief master sergeant."

"Everyone accounted for?"

"Everyone but Sergeant Norton. She didn't show up for muster and no one has seen her since four o'clock."

Willard nodded, his lower lip pushing into his upper. "She's new. Most likely she's locked up somewhere in some passageway wondering why the Navy kidnapped her. I don't think she's fallen overboard."

"The bridge is asking for muster reports, do I report her UA?"

Willard nodded. "Well, she is, isn't she?"

"Yeah, but . . ."

"No buts. Just report her UA. She won't be the only one the Navy is missing. Never pass up the opportunity to do what is right, Lou. In the long run, you'll sleep better at night."

"And the officers? You'll talk to them? They won't listen to a tech sergeant. Everyone listens to a chief master sergeant."

Willard uncrossed his arms and shook his head. "Flattery will get you promoted, Lou, one of these days. All right," he said with a sigh. "I'll tell them the choices." He glanced at the gaggle of pilots. "We'll send four down; keep the next two pilots to launch up here." He sighed again, reached out, and touched Sergeant Thomas. "I'll take care of them. I doubt all of them will go belowdecks, but I'll convince Captain Nolan to lead some back to the *Antares*."

"Thanks, Chief. You're one swell guy."

"Sergeant Thomas, eat my shorts. Now go get the crew into life vests before the Navy comes back."

EIGHT

"They're gone, Senior Chief. They're gone!" Bernardo shouted, whipping around in his chair to stare at Agazzi for a second before returning his attention back to the display. "They're gone," he said in a quiet voice. "One moment they were there, heading toward us, and the next they just poof—disappeared." Bernardo threw his hands up spreading his fingers. "Just poof."

Agazzi leaned over the shoulder of the petty officer, his eyes squinting as he searched the rainfall display trying to find the noise trace of the torpedoes. The passive noise spikes of the four Chinese submarines were there on their respective lines of bearing. The eight fast-moving torpedoes disrupting the rainfall display of noise were gone. Nowhere to be seen. The last trails of their tracks were disappearing at the bottom edge as the rainfall display continued its slow move down the screen.

"Can you hear them?"

"That's just it, Senior Chief. One moment, the noise in my ear set matched the visual trace on the console. Then—poof!" Bernardo flicked his fingers into the air again. "The sound of the torpedoes' propellers turning and the trace on the console disappeared—ceased at the same time."

"Could they have gone beneath the layer?"

Bernardo reached up and hit several buttons. "Here are the returns from the dipping sonars beneath Sea Base, Senior Chief. See? Nothing. I'm telling you they're gone."

"Maybe they were fired too far out and ran out of steam?" Calvins said.

Bernardo grimaced and shook his head. "They weren't in the water long enough to run out of fuel, and when torpedoes run out of fuel, what do they do?"

"Explode?"

"Nope." He made a circling motion with his finger. "They start circling as they sink, hoping for a last-minute target to strike. And when they start sinking, the motion of the water hitting their propellers keeps them turning so they still make a signature. This didn't do any of those things, Senior Chief. They just stopped."

"I don't know either," Agazzi admitted, a slight chill going up his spine. The good news was the torpedoes were no more. The bad news was he had no idea why. Whys bothered him. Was this some new technology? Maybe the torpedoes were still inbound, but running so quietly the passive sonar was unable to detect them.

"It wasn't one, then two, then three disappearing in a row, Senior Chief. All eight disappeared at the same time—in unison—as if coordinated somehow."

"If they were coordinated to switch to a different type of propulsion . . ." Agazzi thought aloud.

"I don't think so, Senior Chief," Bernardo said, shaking his head, his long hair cascading over his ears. "The sound signature was of the newer YU-6 torpedo, and what we have on that shows it has a long-range capability exceeding forty kilometers, single screw, electrically propelled. It should still be running."

Petty Officer Keyland leaned over the safety rails running along the top level. "Maybe they're designed to drift."

"Drift?" Bernardo said, frustration showing in his voice. "What do you mean drift? Torpedoes don't drift. Most are wire-driven as far as possible, then once the wire breaks, they become fire-and-forget weapons."

"Unless they turn back toward you. Then, I bet you remember them," MacPherson said.

"Oh, eat shit and die, Jenkins. This isn't funny."

Agazzi put his hand on Bernardo's shoulder. "Stay calm. We're as perplexed over this as you."

"By drift I mean, what if you had a torpedo that was meant to be launched . . ."

"All torpedoes are meant to be launched," MacPherson interrupted.

". . . and after the torpedoes reached a certain distance from the target, they were programmed to stop." Keyland made a chopping motion with his hand. "If the targets were warships, then the submarine would know they detected the torpedoes. When the torpedoes seemingly disappear from Sonar, then everyone relaxes. Later . . ."

"How much later?" Bernardo asked.

Keyland shrugged. "I don't know. I'm just thinking out loud—voicing alternatives as to why you lost the torpedoes. . . ."

Bernardo spun around in his chair. Poking his thumb in his chest, he growled, "I didn't lose them. They disappeared."

"Watch the console," Agazzi said.

Bernardo's breathing was rapid. The young man leaned closer to the console.

"Petty Officer Keyland, did you read or hear about this?" Agazzi asked.

Keyland shook his head. "No, but every 'why' has an answer."

"Maybe they weren't torpedoes," Gentron said.

Everyone looked at the young seaman manning the second UUV console.

"What do you mean?" MacPherson asked.

"What if the submarines never intended to fire on us, they just wanted to make sure we knew they could if they wanted? What if what we thought were torpedoes were no more than sophisticated practice or decoy torpedoes?"

"And what if they are still alive like Elvis . . ." MacPherson added.

"Don't call me Elvis," Keyland rebuked.

"This time I'm talking about the real Elvis," MacPherson continued, waving the Leading Petty Officer off. "But what if Petty Officer Keyland is right? What if those torpedoes are out there waiting for us to relax our guard; then they'll rev back up and hit us before we could do anything."

Gentron shook his head. "Doesn't make sense."

"Why?" Keyland asked.

"The database said they were YU-6 torpedoes," Bernardo said.

"We couldn't have done anything anyway if they had been live torpedoes. If they have gone quiet like Petty Officer Keyland offers, then what they've done is give us time to get UUVs and decoys out in front of them."

"It also gives us time to mount a counterattack," MacPherson added.

Agazzi's eyes widened. "Gentron's right. While we're sitting here arguing about what happened, we have to assume the worst case. Worst case is Petty Officer Keyland's. Petty Officer MacPherson, how far away are we from having another UUV in the water?"

MacPherson looked at his console. "We can launch a second one in two minutes."

"Tell Taylor that we are going to launch six more."

"Six! Senior Chief, Gentron and I have never handled more than two. You want us to handle six?"

"I want eight. One for each torpedo. Now, get busy doing it." He looked at Gentron. "Seaman Gentron, you're doing a hell of a job, sailor."

The man blushed. "Thanks."

"Senior Chief, Combat?" Keyland asked.

"Calvins, you been passing this along to Combat?" Agazzi asked, looking at their youngest sailor who was encumbered inside the sound-powered telephone apparatus.

Calvins shook his head. "Didn't know what to tell them other than we'd lost the torpedoes."

Agazzi took a couple of steps to the right, his back to the consoles. He grabbed the rails of the ladder, and in three steps was at the upper level. He pushed the MC button for Combat, and in seconds was talking to the TAO, Commander Stapler.

"CAPTAIN, Admiral Holman is on secure voice, sir," the First Class Operations Specialist said, handing the telephone to Garcia.

Garcia uncrossed his legs and leaned forward. He had been in the Captain's chair in Combat since GQ had been sounded minutes ago. He had also asked himself about two minutes into it why the venerable hero of the Mediterranean hadn't called to offer his advice.

"Hank, Admiral Holman here."

For the next few minutes, the two men exchanged information on what was going on. With eight torpedoes heading toward Sea Base, when did they expect impact? It had been nearly fifteen minutes since they were detected. The two senior officers decided the torpedoes were fired too far away and most likely would run out of fuel before they arrived. Both knew they were trying to assure each other of a scenario neither believed.

Stapler ran over and tapped Garcia on the arm. "Captain! It's important."

"Wait one, Admiral." He looked at Stapler and raised his eyebrows.

"Sonar reports the torpedoes have disappeared. They aren't sure why."

"All eight?"

"That's what they said."

"And the submarines?"

"They still have them. They are concerned—"

"Later, Commander; let me finish with the admiral."

"But—"

Garcia smiled, slid the handset back to his mouth. "Thanks, Commander Stapler."

"But there's more."

Garcia waved him away. "Looks as if you are right, Admiral, once again. Sonar reports every one of the torpedoes has disappeared from the scope. They've lost them. They still have the submarines, but not the torpedoes."

"Good. I have our two destroyers, USS *Gearing* and USS *Stripling,* launching their SH-36 helicopters along with torpedoes. Since they fired on us, the field is open. I want to put our forces in place to take them out. I don't want them to close their range to us. How stupid can they have been to fire so far away?" Holman chuckled. "A Third World nation in a First World ocean."

"That's good news, Admiral. I don't know how Sea Base would survive eight torpedoes."

"Hank, Sea Base wouldn't survive a well-placed lone torpedo, much less eight."

AGAZZI hung up the handset. "Commander said they were going to remain at General Quarters for the time being. He wanted to know how far out the torpedoes were when they disappeared. Told him that passive sonar doesn't give us that ability. He wanted to know why we don't go active. Told him we didn't have an active capability through all this metal floating around us."

"I still think they were decoys. They were meant as a warning for us to stand clear of Taiwan," Gentron said.

"It would be nice to know how we can be sure you're right," Keyland said.

"Second UUV in the water!" MacPherson announced. He leaned over to Gentron. "You got it?"

"Got it."

"Where to, Senior Chief?"

"Give me the location of the first one again."

"First UUV is heading toward the contact along bearing 225 degrees."

"What's your recommendation for this one?"

"I'd recommend," MacPherson said, pausing. He bit his lower lip.

"I'd recommend sending this UUV against the target at 010," Bernardo interrupted.

"Why?" Keyland asked.

"It's going to be the easiest one to get the UUV against. Gentron is going to have to drive out the stern area of Sea Base, which is pointed in that direction. Plus both it and the contact at 080 are on the open-ocean side. To return to Mainland China, they have to cross our wake. That transit is going to be their most vulnerable."

"But we are heading toward the two targets at 210 and 240 degrees," Keyland argued.

"You mean Sea Base?" MacPherson asked, shaking his head. "We're only doing eight or nine knots—that's not like we're going to run over them. We have a UUV traveling in that direction."

"Only one?" Bernardo asked with slight sarcasm.

"Petty Officer Bernardo is right," Agazzi said, surprising the young AN/SQR-25 operator, who was trying to figure out what he said that was right. Agazzi continued. "We only have two UUVs available for the next few minutes. Put one in each sector. If the UUVs don't do anything else other than keep the contacts busy trying to avoid them while we work to get six more UUVs in the water, then it's worth our time."

"010 it is, Senior Chief," Gentron said. "Plus, if we have to beat feet for the open ocean, those two stand in our way."

Quiet descended on the ASW Operations Center while everyone watched and waited as Seaman Gentron eased the UUV through the underwater maze of sea anchors and dipping sonars until it emerged free into the open ocean.

"I have UUV Two on course 010, Senior Chief," Gentron announced.

"I still show four contacts remaining on same lines of bearings," Bernardo added. "010, 080, 210, and 240."

"I can answer your question now, Petty Officer Keyland," Gentron offered.

"What question?"

"How we can tell if they were decoys meant to show us they could sink us if they want."

"And how would we tell?"

KIANG turned the doorknob, surprised when the door opened easily. The lights were on, but in the cargo hold where the lights remained on twenty-four hours a day, it was not unusual. Scattered across the tables were diagrams and schematics. Kiang closed the door behind him and quickly sorted through the papers. His heart soared over the gold mine in front of him. This was too easy.

He jumped back, glancing around the room, looking for a security camera or some sort of recording device. A chill went through him. Had he allowed the thrill of doing this to override caution? Kiang took a deep breath. It was a bare office room that fit the idea of a mobile office in a mobile building. No obvious cameras, motion detectors, or other security devices.

Satisfied, he lifted the edge of a huge sheet of paper, looking for the title in the top right-hand corner. The word "Confidential" was printed in the familiar block. Some security officer had taken the time to stamp the same classification in bright red across the printed word. Kiang flattened the sheet, read the title. This was the fuel-flow diagram for the F-22A. Kiang lifted his camera and took two photographs. He took a photograph of the left side of the sheet and then a second of the right side. He wanted to ensure he photographed every bit of information he had. The Ministry of State Security could figure out how to meld the two photographs.

A burst of loud laughter caused Kiang to move away from the table. He eased over to the window and parted the blinds slightly. A group of merchant marines walked along the deck of the cargo hold, heading toward the aft section of the ship. They must have come down the same way he did. He quietly eased the blinds down and returned to the table.

He folded the sheet halfway over and shoved it to the side.

Beneath it was a paper listing the maintenance work schedule for the week. It was a personal effect of one of the officers or senior noncoms. He lifted the paper. It had today's date on it. He folded it and stuck it in his pocket. Personal papers such as this went missing all the time. Whoever it belonged to would assume it had gone missing during the confusion of General Quarters.

He took a couple of more photographs, and then looked at his watch. How long before someone came? Kiang glanced at the door. Anytime, one of the Air Force personnel could open the door. What would he say? *"Hi! Got lost during GQ and decided this looked like a good place to stay until it was over."* He shook his head. Since he was Asian, that would make it harder for them to believe the lie.

The other course was unthinkable to him. He didn't think he could kill anyone to protect his espionage. This was the first time he had given thought to what he might have to do to save his own life and the lives of his parents. He never thought of the killing of Jack Sward as his responsibility. It was the colonel who arranged the death.

Kiang moved away from the pile of classified schematics to the desk in the back. On the seat of the chair lay a folder stamped "Top Secret." Someone was going to be in a lot of trouble when GQ was secured and they discovered they forgot to lock it away. Kiang moved around the desk, looking for the safe where the document should have been stored, but couldn't see it. Must be in another office space. He lifted the folder. Maybe the safe had already been locked by the time the person who had possession of this top-secret document tried to store it, and the person thought it would be safe here. Couldn't very well be tramping around topside with a top-secret-stamped folder tucked under your arm.

He laid it on top of the desk and opened it. He scanned the documents, realizing quickly that it detailed the F-22A's weapons systems avionics. He flipped through the pages quickly. The bottom of the last page read "Page 22 of 22 pages." He started snapping pictures. Ten minutes later he had all twenty-two pages committed to digital imagery.

Kiang took a deep breath and went to the door. There was so much here he would like to photograph or take, but the longer he stayed the more likely he would be discovered. He put his ear to the door, straining to hear any noise outside. He slowly lifted the edge of the nearby blinds. Satisfied no one was around, he opened the door and stepped onto the narrow walkway. A minute later, he was on the cargo hold deck walking quickly toward the hatch leading up.

His heart pounded with excitement over his success and with the thrill of fear of being caught. Kiang was beginning to understand how much this forced espionage was beginning to excite him. It was a game. A game between him and Zeichner, a game between him and the unsuspecting crew who surrounded him, and a game between him and the colonel. Espionage eventually became a game of intellect. He shivered over the idea of the colonel winning the game. Maybe it was a game of brawn and fear over intellect and bravado.

Maybe the colonel knew instinctively that Kiang would stay and do what was expected regardless of what happened to his parents. He could understand why the thrill of espionage could become addictive. In that moment, Kiang hated himself for what he was doing.

He stopped at the hatch and shook his head. His eyes misted up. No way he would do this forever. He told himself he loved America. It was blackmail that made him do what he just did.

The hatch opened.

"Pardon us," an Air Force officer said as he stepped through the hatch.

Kiang recognized the officer as Captain Nolan. He knew more about the officers than they could ever guess. He knew that Major Johnson, the female detachment commander, and the lone Afro-American, Franklin, had taken the first formation off earlier in the afternoon. He had seen the number-two officer, Major "Tight End" Crawford, crawl into the F-22A that led the second formation into the air.

"Hey, how long do you think we'll be down here before Chief Willard calls?" a young first lieutenant asked as he stepped through the hatch.

"Who knows what lurks in the shadows of the mind of a chief master sergeant?" the third officer through the hatch said, turning to Kiang and nodding. "Excuse us."

Kiang nodded back.

"Well, I for one am glad they let us come back. Too much coffee and I understand the Navy frowns on people who pee on their decks."

"Zimmerman, you are getting too much like a sailor out here. Air Force officers never pee. We void water."

Kiang stepped through the hatch and turned. Instead of pulling it shut, he stood inside watching the Air Force pilots. Two of the officers went into the Ready Room on the lower floor, but the one they called Zimmerman scooted up the steps to the second floor. Zimmerman touched the doorknob to the room Kiang had just left. Kiang breathed deep, waiting to see the man enter, when another officer called Zimmerman and motioned him to the Ready Room with the rest.

Kiang pulled the hatch shut and secured it.

As he climbed the stairs, confusion climbed with him as he tried to sort out what he should do. Maybe it was time to turn the tables on the colonel. Talk with American intelligence and see if they could help rescue his parents while he became a double agent. If being an agent was additive, being a double agent must be orgasmic. But then again, he would sleep better at night without worrying which intelligence agency was about to burst into his bedroom.

Seconds later on the far side of the cargo hold, Sergeant Norton rose from the squatting position and stepped out of the far shadows of the starboard bulkhead. She watched the metal rod swing down inside as Kiang secured the hatch on the other side. Norton watched the officers enter the Ready Room. Then, she turned and braced her left foot on the bulkhead. Norton leaned forward and retied her sneaker, revealing a small tattoo of a bird on her right ankle. Finished, she straightened and looked down at her feet for a moment, then up at the second floor of the Air Force offices, before dashing across the deck toward the mobile office. Quickly and quietly, she ran up the metal stairs and entered the office where Kiang had been. Moments later, she emerged and dashed down the stairs.

At the bottom, she stopped and adjusted the folder jammed inside her cammie shirt. The words "Top Secret" were facing forward. She pulled it out and turned it around to hide them, then buttoned her blouse.

Stepping away from the mobile offices, Norton walked rapidly aft, trading barbs with the group of merchant marines sitting on crates, sharing cigarettes in an unauthorized smoking area. She would have enjoyed staying and bantering with the grizzled men of the sea, but right now she had more important things to do. Grizzled men of the sea cut to the chase; no mincing of words or politically correct shit. With banter, humor, and an overabundance of flirting remarks, they knew how to make a woman feel like a woman. She enjoyed it occasionally, but would never want to live it on a continuous basis.

When she emerged on the main deck of the *Antares,* Petty Officer Taleb waited.

"Well?" he asked.

She nodded without replying and walked away.

"Damn! Too easy," Taleb said, snapping his fingers as he fell in alongside her.

NINE

"Black Leader, this is Weasel; we are breaking off track at this time, heading east."

"Weasel, be advised we can only follow you to the territorial limits of Taiwan and then must break off. His Majesty's Government restricts us to international waters at this time."

"Roger, Commander; we understand and do appreciate your escort."

"Weasel, Raptor Leader here; we are on our way. Fully armed and refueled."

"Roger all. Black Leader, we are about two hundred miles from the coast. Estimate crossing the twelve-mile coastal line in forty minutes. Can you stay with us until then?"

"Of course, Weasel. The Royal Navy has never left an ally in its hundreds of years of tradition . . . unless, of course, they were French."

Franklin looked at his heads-up display. They were one hundred miles from where the four British F-35 fighters escorted the American Rivet Joint reconnaissance aircraft. The torpedo attack on Sea Base had changed everything out here. It meant the Chinese were serious this time and not just pounding their chests.

"Raptor 10, Raptor Leader," Johnson broadcast on their private channel.

Franklin rolled his eyes. "Yes, ma'am," he replied.

"Check your weapons systems."

He reached over and touched an icon. The diagnostics cycled quickly.

"Captain Franklin, did you read me?"

"Yes, ma'am. I am checking system at this time."

Motion caught his eye, drawing him to the heads-up display. He blinked. For a fraction of a second he thought he counted a fifth aircraft off to the west, nearer the RC-135 formation. Then, the blimp disappeared. Things such as that occurred sometimes when aircraft were maneuvering. A radar return takes a few hits, and the next thing you know the sky is filled with aircraft as radar smears dot the screen. But the F-22A technology was supposed to compensate for that phenomenon.

"Did you see that?" Major Johnson broadcast on their personal frequency.

"See what?"

"I thought I saw an unidentified aircraft near the Rivet Joint and the British. Didn't you?"

Franklin bit his lip for a second before replying. "Yeah, I saw something on my heads-up. Don't you think it could be a radar smear or some electromagnetic thing caused by them turning?"

A few seconds passed. "You could be right."

"They should have seen it too."

"They could have, but they're in a right-hand turn toward Taiwan, so their radars aren't pointed in that direction."

"I thought the Rivet Joint radar was omnidirectional; could see 360 degrees regardless of its heading." Franklin lifted his fingers off the throttle and stretched them. If Johnson hadn't said anything, he wouldn't be worried right now. What if those were stealth bogies. . . . He shook his head. He hated what-ifs.

He looked at the heads-up radar display again. It amazed him how technology could take a radar picture or pictures of his instrument readings and project them onto his windshield below his line of vision. It took only a second or two to read them, and the whole time his eyes never left the front of the aircraft.

Another blimp popped up farther to the right of the first one.

"Did you see that?" they both asked simultaneously, their broadcasts overriding each other. The shrill of the comms hurt Franklin's ears.

"I said, did you see that one?" Johnson asked again.

"Yes, I did," Franklin replied, reaching up and rubbing his right ear. "That one was farther south than the other one."

"If that second one is heading east, it is going to get inside the turning pattern of the Rivet Joint. It's going to cut the formation off before they get near Taiwan."

Before Franklin could answer, Johnson hit the common tactical frequency. "Weasel, Black Leader; this is Raptor Leader. We have two unidentified bogies nearing your position. One is directly west on your six, Black Leader. The other is south and heading east."

The original two blimps popped up again along with two others. The two new ones were near the originals.

"I have new data. I show minimum of two formations of two aircraft bracketing your location. Recommend you turn north. We are increasing speed and expect to be in your position in seventeen minutes."

"Raptor Leader, Weasel; be advised we show no bogies. I am looking at your radar information being downloaded via data link. I don't show—"

"Listen, Weasel, the data link won't send sporadic or unconfirmed contacts. We're seeing them here."

"Maybe they are radar smears."

Franklin's lower lip pushed into his upper and he shook his head. That's what he'd thought until Major Johnson questioned it. Maybe he and the Rivet Joint were right. Maybe the major was grandstanding. He rolled his eyes. God! He hoped not; he'd never hear the end of it.

"Weasel, you could be right. But what if you're not and those so-called smears turn into Chinese J-12s? What you going to do then? What happened to them when they disappeared?"

"We decided they went home. Their fuel should have been getting low."

"Do you know how much fuel they burn?"

Franklin's eyes lifted. *Be careful, Weasel, you're pissing her off.*

A couple of seconds passed. "No, we don't have exact figures; it is just our analysis that the J-12s went home because they were getting low on fuel."

"And what if you're wrong?" Johnson answered, irritation showing in her voice.

"Weasel, this is Black Leader. I recommend we err on the side of caution and turn left—head north. If the radar returns are smears, then you have not lost much time. If they are real, then it would be nice to outnumber them."

Nearly a minute passed before the RC-135 Mission Commander spoke. "Roger, fighter formations; Weasel is turning left onto course zero-one-zero, maintaining angels thirty."

"Watch for those blimps again, Blackman. If they're the Chinese J-12 stealth fighter and are trying to intercept the reconnaissance bird, then they'll have to turn. When they turn, they'll be standing on their wings, which will decrease their stealth capability for a few seconds. Our radars should get them—"

Before Johnson finished talking, across Franklin's heads-up display eight radar returns emerged. Four formations of two aircraft each. They had been encircling the RC-135 and British fighters from the rear and from the south. The turn north had pulled the American and British aircraft out of the box being closed around them, but now the Chinese J-12 stealth fighters were in pursuit.

"Be advised—" Johnson broadcast.

"We got them! You're right! Damn it, we got them!" shouted the RC-135 controller. "We count eight! We only had six of them on the defensive fighter patrol earlier."

"Roger, Weasel. Looks as if you have eight now. Black Three and Black Four, reform on my wing."

What is Commander Lester Tyler-Cole up to? Franklin asked himself.

"RAPTOR 10, Raptor Leader; let's put some speed on and catch up with them. I show fifteen minutes to rendezvous. Increase speed to Mach 1.2."

The F-22A was the only aircraft in the world with the capability to reach maximum speed with full arms and full tanks. Most of that, thought Franklin, was thanks to the stealth technology hiding everything internally and creating a smoother fuselage. The missiles couldn't slow you down while tucked inside the stomach of the Raptor.

"Weasel, Black Leader; can you give me a vector to the bandits?"

A few seconds passed. "Black Leader, we do not have the air-intercept skills to provide a controlled intercept. Sorry."

"Roger, understand. Then guess we will have to wait until they reach us. Black Formation, this is Black Leader; armament switches on."

"Raptor Leader, this is Raptor 20," came the voice of Tight End Crawford over the F-22A tactical frequency.

Franklin let out a deep sigh. *Finally, company is coming.*

Johnson acknowledged with two clicks. "What is your location, Tight End?" she asked.

Franklin looked at his heads-up display. The two friendlies were southwest of Sea Base.

"We are 230 miles from your location. Fully armed and fueled. Unless otherwise directed, my intentions are to join your formation."

"Roger, be advised we are—"

"Roger," Crawford interrupted. "We have been following the chatter. You have the lead."

"Of course—" Johnson snapped, but quickly let go of the transmission button before she finished whatever she started to say.

Franklin grinned. God! He'd hate to meet her in a dark alley if he ever pissed her off. Come to think of it, he hated to meet her in daylight when she wasn't pissed off.

"What's going on at Sea Base?" she asked.

Crawford spent a minute relaying what he knew.

Franklin was pleased the other Raptors were being launched. Even as he thought about it, two other F-22A icons suddenly appeared on the display. He grinned.

"Screw you, Chicoms," Franklin whispered to himself. What a hell of a surprise they were going to get when six F-22As popped into the middle of an airspace already filled with Royal Navy F-35s. It was going to be one hell of a party. "It's missiles in summertime for you and for me," he sang.

ZEICHNER leaned against the bulkhead. His breaths came quick and shallow. *Didn't this woman ever walk to where she wanted to go?* White spots danced across his vision.

"You okay, Mr. Zeichner?" Montague asked, pausing halfway up the ladder. Kevin stood two steps behind her, heading up.

He motioned them onward. "You and Kevin go ahead. I'm not as young as you two. I'll meet you at the tower."

"You sure? You look awful pale. Maybe we should call someone?"

Zeichner saw her and Gainer exchange "the look." He had seen "the look" from others during his trip from lithe and lean to slow and fat. Almost a combination of concern and pity. He hated both.

"Go on," he growled. "We need to know what he's doing."

"He's in the crow's nest like last time," Gainer added. "At least, he should be."

Zeichner took a deep gasping breath. "If you haven't seen him," he gasped, "doesn't mean he's not there. Last time we had no idea where he was."

"But, the Watch-Quarter-Station bill from Combat shows him as the tech rep for the antennas. When General Quarters is sounded, he's supposed to be in the top of the masts," Montague agreed, nodding once to Gainer. "It would be a bright red flag for him not to be there. Foreign agents tend to follow all the rules."

"If they were following all the rules, they wouldn't be spies," Zeichner said. *What are they doing?* he asked himself. *Ganging up on me?* "Listen! I said go ahead. If I'm not there in fifteen minutes, you can send the corpsman to find me. You both have done your duty."

"Let's go, Kevin," Angie Montague said with a sharp nod. "Mr. Zeichner is right." She grabbed the railings of the ladder, and then looked at Zeichner. "Fifteen minutes and then we call the corpsman," she said. Then she quickly disappeared up the ladder.

Gainer looked questioningly at Zeichner. Zeichner leaned forward putting one hand on his knee. He waved Gainer onward. In the back of his mind, he knew the leadership of the team had passed in those few seconds to Montague, who had only arrived a few hours ago. Her original idea had merit, but while they waited to discuss it with the Air Force, they should keep an eye on Dr. Zheng. He doubted the Chinese-American was unaware they were suspicious of him. If the man was a foreign agent, then there was no doubt Zheng was aware and had taken some precautions. Zeichner wondered what precautions *he* would take if he were betraying his country.

Nearly five minutes passed with Zeichner resting at the bottom of the ladder leading to the top of Sea Base. He raised his head, happy the spots had disappeared, and his breathing was even. Maybe he wasn't in such bad shape. After all, it only took five minutes for his heart rate to slow and normal breathing to return. He slipped a finger around the waistband of his pants, surprised to see it slide in without forcing it. She's only been on board less than a half day and already he could feel the difference, he told himself. He ignored other times in the past few months when he had been able to do the same thing. He pushed away from the bulkhead and walked to the bottom of the ladder. Zeichner slapped his hands together and smiled.

He grabbed the railings for a few seconds, released them, and then sat down on the second rung. By the time he climbed four flights of ladders, he was going to be in the same state he'd just spent five minutes recovering from. For a moment, he looked over his shoulder and up the ladder, nearly convincing himself to give it up and return to his stateroom. The idea that Montague would take charge and take credit for their hard work irritated Zeichner even if he was unsure whether a foreign agent even existed on board Sea Base. Headquarters had sent her to take credit. He could roll over and let her do it, return to his nondescript job in Chicago, or . . .

Zeichner freed his handkerchief and wiped the sweat from his forehead. What if he had a heart attack here? He glanced around. No one to be seen, and other than the background sound of ventilation and hydraulics, there was no noise. In this heat, it wouldn't take long for a fat man like him to fade in with the ever-present odor of exhaust and fuel oil.

He glanced at his watch. Fifteen minutes he'd been here. By now, Montague and Gainer will have notified the corpsman. *How embarrassing*. He pushed himself up, grabbed the railings, and started the climb, taking it slow. If he died, his nephew was going to be one lucky bastard, meager estate though it was. He had to start taking better care of himself. And he had to prove Headquarters was wrong. Who did Montague have as her mentor to get her sent out here? She wasn't sent to help him and Kevin. She was sent out here to help her career.

At the top of Sea Base, his breath was rapid, but the white spots weren't there. He congratulated himself on taking his time. His watch showed twenty minutes since he'd sent the two ahead of him.

"Testing, one-two-three," he said aloud. "Now is the time for all good men to come to the aid of their country." He smiled. No one in shape could appreciate the joy of climbing four floors and still being able to talk. His heart skipped a beat, causing a quick falling sensation, before it returned to normal. His legs ached and his breathing was rapid, but he could talk in a normal voice.

Zeichner started toward the tower. Ahead, he recognized Gainer climbing the ladder leading to the crow's nest above the tower. On the deck stood Montague, her hand shielding her eyes, staring up as the former soldier climbed.

Gainer reached the crow's nest just as Zeichner walked up alongside Montague.

"What's he doing?"

She dropped her hand. "Oh, Mr. Zeichner. How are you feeling, sir?"

"I'm fine. What's Kevin doing?"

"He's checking to see if our suspect is on the mast platform." She shielded her eyes again and looked up.

"Wouldn't that tell our suspect that we suspected him?"

She opened her mouth to reply, her brow wrinkling downward as she tried to think of an answer.

"Never mind," Zeichner said, the edge of his lips curling left. Just like two young agents to think of the moment instead of a long-range plan. If this guy was a foreign agent, which Zeichner doubted, these two had just confirmed any suspicions Zheng might have had. Zeichner thought about shouting up for Gainer to come back down, but the noise of the flight deck preparations ongoing with the launch of the F-22As would have drowned out his words. Besides, if he shouted, he ran the risk of bringing on the fatigue he had just conquered.

Gainer's head disappeared into the floor opening of the crow's nest. A few minutes later, he started down.

"Well, Dr. Zheng should have no doubt now we are on to him," Zeichner said.

She dropped her hand and shook her head. "He's probably like most spies and thinks he's invincible. He probably doesn't even know what you two look like."

"He knows. We've had too many 'serendipitous' encounters since we set sail for him not to know. He'd have to be a pretty stupid spy to not be aware of the law enforcement people around him."

She bit her lower lip for a moment. "How did he act?"

Her expression told everything. She was trying to cut Zeichner out. As a young A-type personality, she needed to make the capture. Zeichner was a legacy; a passed-over ancient who could upset this applecart of hers. He smiled.

"He acted like most people you pass in the passageway of a ship or meet on a street. Greetings and so-longs. His eyes didn't widen and he didn't try to bolt for it when we stumbled into each other. He acted like every innocent person I've ever met."

"Did he act anything like some of the guilty ones you've met?"

Zeichner thought about it for a moment. "Yes, he did," he agreed reluctantly.

Her eyes widened. "Mr. Zeichner, I think . . . well, I'm sure," she stumbled.

He waved her down. "Not to worry, Angela. I've been there, done that." Zeichner looked up at Gainer, who was climbing down. "The important thing is that Kevin not fall. He's a good agent; quick to do anything required to meet the needs of the case."

Montague looked in the same direction. "Yes, he is. He's very good. New, isn't he?"

Zeichner sighed. She's trying to assess her competition, he told himself. So young. She'll go places. Her arrival was no coincidence, nor was it a coincidence Angela Montague was chosen. He knew a potential espionage case on the Navy's foremost scientific project was a career catapult for whoever solved it. Not for him. Once you reach your fifties, your experience is valued, but leadership opportunities go to the groomed coming up rapidly behind you on the ladder of success. You had your turn. These thoughts went through his head rapidly, and what surprised him was the lack of emotion he felt on knowing his own place. He glanced at Montague and back to Gainer. Both of them would move up the NCIS ladder. Gainer would stop climbing long before this hungry agent standing beside him.

Gainer jumped the last few rungs, landing with bent knees near them.

"What did he do when you got up there?" Montague asked.

Gainer shook his head and looked at Zeichner. "He's not up there, Boss. There's a young sailor up there—a boatswain mate—who said Dr. Zheng had not arrived yet but he expected him."

"Where do you think he is?" Montague asked.

"His stateroom?" Gainer asked.

Zeichner nodded. "He could be in his stateroom, or he could be using this lockdown time to do a little free-time espionage. We know he's interested in the Unmanned Underwater Vehicles and the F-22A Raptors if we read the classified intelligence reports—"

Montague interrupted. "I don't recall reading anything about the suspect indicating his interests, Mr. Zeichner. Are there messages or reports out here that I'm not privy to?" There was a hint of anger in her voice.

Zeichner nodded. "You think he's a spy for the People's Republic of China. Right?"

She nodded.

"Then, you read what interests the Chinese Ministry of State Security. We know from their own open source and our own information that laser weapons, rail guns, UUVs, and stealth technology are fields resident on board Sea Base that are of interest to the Ministry of State Security. Ergo, they are of interest to our suspect."

It always gave him professional pleasure when he saw a

light go off in a young agent's head. She would never forget that tidbit because it was a logic trail she would use up her ladder.

She glanced around the deck. "You think maybe he's over at the rail guns or the laser weapon?" She pointed at the remaining F-22s parked on the apron. "Too many Air Force personnel around the Raptors for him to be there."

"So, here goes," Zeichner said, holding up his fist. "Let's assume he is a foreign agent. Let's assume he is using this opportunity to gather some intelligence for his bosses. If the assumptions are correct, then we can end this now without having to ask the Air Force to stage-set one of their aircraft."

Gainer and Montague exchanged glances, and then looked back at him. "How?" they asked in unison.

"Well, if he hasn't already, he will finish his intelligence gathering. We know he carries a camera and binoculars with him everywhere he goes." He saw Montague open her mouth to ask something. He held his hand up. "We asked, and he said the binoculars allowed him to watch the electronics and antennas on the mainmast without having to climb it every time. The camera was for taking photographs of the systems he was responsible for so that he and the Institute would have photographs of 'befores' and 'afters.' "

"Where do you think he is going?" Montague asked.

Zeichner had a momentary inclination to send her off on a wild-goose chase to one of the engine rooms of the Fast Sealift Ship, but quickly put his pique back in its mental case.

"It's not where we think he has gone, but where we know he will have to come back." He cocked his head and grinned.

"His stateroom," Gainer said.

"Right. When he finishes his expedition, he will return to his stateroom. Most likely, he is using the camera for what it was meant to be used for—taking photographs. He is going to have to be converting whatever he photographed into some sort of data format for transmission. He is going to want to get whatever is on that camera out of that camera. As long as the photographs are in that camera, they are evidence of his treason—if he is in fact a traitor."

"We should go to his stateroom?" Montague asked. "Won't that tell him we're onto him?"

Zeichner nodded. "Kevin going up that ladder has already blown any semblance of cover we may have had. It's over with. You think that sailor is going to come down after General Quarters is secured and keep quiet about why an NCIS agent was climbing up to the highest point on Sea Base and asking about the good doctor?" His lower lip pushed his upper lip up as he shook his head. "No way. It's going to be all over Sea Base within hours after GQ is secured."

Montague seemed to turn white, Zeichner thought with a bit of enjoyment over bursting her bubble. *Only aboard a few hours, and already you've blown any chance of catching the good doctor through subterfuge.*

"Number one: Whatever he is doing, eventually he is going to end up at his stateroom. Two, he's belowdecks somewhere nosing into the laser or rail gun weapons." He nodded at Montague. "You indicate Headquarters believes his primary interest will be the UUVs and the F-22As. He could be nosing around the Air Force offices on *Antares* or over at *Bellatrix* trying to force his way into the UUV compartment. Of the two, I don't think he is in *Bellatrix*." He shook his head again. "No, he wouldn't be at *Bellatrix*, since we have a Marine guard down there."

"That leaves the Air Force offices. We should go check."

"Wait a minute, Angie, and let me finish. Three, he could be down in the *Algol* to see how our ASW operations center works; four, he could be inside Combat." Zeichner nodded toward the tower beside them. "Observing how we fight the weapons systems on Sea Base. Or five, he could be below the decks near one of the weapons systems collecting information on their individual operations."

Montague swept her right hand down her left arm. "Where should we look first?"

"Well, we're only going to do one. We're going to step inside the tower and search the Combat Information Center because it's here and we're here. I don't think he'll be here, but we'll do it." He started toward the door leading to the ladder, wondering again why the Navy doesn't call them stairs. That's all they were. Thank God, he thought, Combat is only on the second deck.

"And the second?"

Zeichner paused on the second step and looked back at them. "Second what?"

"Second place we're going to look," Montague said, her eyebrows crunched into a deep V.

Zeichner grinned. "I'll tell you if he isn't here."

"You think he's here, Boss?"

Zeichner shook his head. "Nope, Kevin, I don't. If he was here, they would have already thrown him out." He turned and started up the stairs to the second deck. Dr. Zheng could be anywhere on this huge thing. Zeichner's grin grew into a broad smile even as his breathing increased in tempo. Leadership had shifted back to him. It amused him that the game was just that to him. Ten, twenty years ago, it would have been a web of anguish as he tried to figure out the next move. Now, it was just a game. He'd fought to keep NCIS headquarters from sending anyone, but they had. He wished her well, but had no intention of helping her career.

"How many floors?" Montague asked.

"There are four in the tower, but we are only going to the second deck," Zeichner answered.

"OK, Showdernitzel, is everyone present and accounted for?" Jacobs asked. His eyes roamed over the two rows of eight boatswain mates standing in loose formation, hopping from one foot to the other, turning right and left to whisper to their buddies. Damn! He was proud of these sailors.

"Everyone, including Petty Officer Jolson."

Jacobs glanced at the tall newcomer standing in the back row near the far end. He was surprised to find the sailor staring at him. One thing about this guy; he didn't seem to be afraid of him like a lot of first-timers. Maybe Jacobs was reaching the point where he reminded sailors more of their granddaddy than their father.

"They should be back soon with the weapons."

Jacobs shook his head. "Who is going to be back soon with what weapons?"

"Leary and Dickens."

"Dickens isn't one of my boatswain mates; he's a master-at-arms."

Showdernitzel shrugged. "After last time, Master Chief, they decided we needed an MAA when we were armed."

"What!"

"Safety and all that bullshit."

"Write yourself a note to remind me to rip someone's throat out when GQ is over," he growled, making a mental note to talk to the new senior chief master-at-arms who had reported on board last month. No one in the goat locker had much affinity with the new man. Too impressed over his new senior chief star. Now, he had gone too far. Don't screw with Jacobs's First Division without discussing it with him. He'd rip his lips off.

He looked down at Showdernitzel, who was grinning from ear to ear.

"What the hell are you laughing about?"

"I'm not laughing, Master Chief; I'm just wondering what torture you're dreaming up for whoever put an MAA to watch over your boatswain mates when they're armed."

"That's none of your f'ing business, Showdernitzel. So, wipe that smile off and tell me the disposition of the security details."

Mad Mary Showdernitzel faced the formation and started reading off the security detail assignments. As she spoke, the third-class boatswain mate Leary and the second-class master-at-arms Dickens arrived with the weapons. Fifteen shotguns, one .45-caliber pistol, and an M-16. Dickens grabbed the M-16 and handed the pistol to Jacobs.

"Good thing it isn't loaded." Showdernitzel spoke.

The roar of another pair of F-22A aircraft thundering down the deck drowned out any conversation. Showdernitzel motioned the sailors into a line, and watched as Dickens handed out the shotguns along with shells from an ammo bag.

Jacobs took his eyes off the distribution of the weapons. Showdernitzel had it in hand. He had mixed feelings about the weight she had started shouldering during his convalescence and his reduced involvement in the day-to-day supervision of the sailors. He watched the two aircraft lift off near the end of the runway, their wheels disappearing into the fuselages before the pilots hit afterburners and zoomed for altitude.

Behind him, Andrew drew a bead with his eyes on the small

of Jacobs's back, marking the spot where he would put the bullet. He had wondered how he was ever going to find a place to reassemble the torn-apart pistol he had brought on board. He glanced forward. Four sailors ahead of him, and they would give him a weapon more than capable of accomplishing his assignment. God would be pleased he was able to finish everything on the first day. The second part of the assignment, doing it without being caught, was something he would work out later.

Jacobs turned just as Andrew's eyes moved forward. Jacobs caught the movement. The sailor had been staring at him. Something about this young sailor looked familiar. His face scrunched as he thought about it. Could he be a son of a former shipmate? He had run into others. He had even run into a first-class petty officer whose diapers he had changed the day after the man was born.

At this moment, Jacobs realized it was time to retire. He had heard others say that you'd know when it was time. It would leap out at you one day like a cougar off a rock. He'd never expected what they told him to be true. It was as if a greater weight had just lifted from him. Helen would be pleased. As soon as GQ was secured, he was going to march down to Personnel and put in his papers. When he stepped off the gangway in Pearl Harbor from whichever Sealift Ship he was riding, it was going to be with his seabag over his shoulder, the Navy to his back, and a song in his heart. The song might be a dirge, but in these few minutes as his boatswain mates were grabbing their pieces, he found himself looking forward to civilian life.

"What's wrong, Master Chief?"

"What do you mean, what's wrong?"

"You're smiling. I thought maybe someone had died."

"Showdernitzel, make sure your page-two next-of-kin data is up to date."

She laughed. "Sure thing, Master Chief."

Yep, time to retire. Couldn't even frighten a second-class petty officer. But first, he was going to chew ass on that new senior chief master-at-arms. Who the fuck did he think he was screwing with his division?

"All right, you dirt bags!" shouted Showdernitzel. "Listen up, Master Chief has something to say."

Jacobs shook his head, bringing his thoughts back to GQ.

A couple of seconds passed. Showdernitzel glanced over her shoulders at Jacobs, jerking her head, her eyes questioning. "Master Chief?"

Jacobs cleared his throat. "Okay, listen up. Most of you have gone through this drill in the Sea of Japan. And you all saw how it paid off having you topside with weapons. I doubt seriously our men in light blue will allow any aircraft to get that close again, but just in case, be alert. Your job is to ensure we fight Sea Base as best we can without someone trying to sabotage the effort or landing another force on board it. You are the last line of defense and the first line of security. You are the security force for GQ. That means you also have the authority to stop anyone who isn't where they are suppose to be. It's not for you to make a unilateral decision on whether someone is right or wrong; innocent or guilty; lost or found. Just bring them to quarterdeck."

The sailors glanced at each other. A hand went up along the back row.

"Yes, Potts; you have a question?"

"Yes, Master Chief. Which quarterdeck?"

"What do you mean which quarterdeck?"

"Do you mean one of the ship's quarterdecks?" Potts stuttered.

Jacobs sighed. Eight quarterdecks below them and there really wasn't one topside. The tower was the nearest thing to a real Navy quarterdeck they had. He had slipped. He never slipped, and here he had. Yes, it was time to retire.

"Good question, Petty Officer Potts. In fact, it is such a good and easy question that I am going to let Petty Officer Showdernitzel answer it." He smiled as her smile disappeared and her eyes widened. "Petty Officer Showdernitzel, I'll be at the quarterdeck when you finish. After you make your security rounds, provide a report to me."

He turned and started to walk away.

"Okay, dirt bags; right where you are standing is the quarterdeck."

Jacobs stopped walking and turned around. The quick turn brought a sharp pain to his recent wound. He winced, but thankfully the pain quickly subsided. Jacobs looked up for a moment toward the hot sun. He reached over with his left hand and rubbed his right arm, leaving it in the sling.

Showdernitzel had maneuvered him into being out here on the aft starboard quarter. He squinted as he looked up at the hot sun.

Showdernitzel looked over her shoulder, grinned, and turned back to the boatswain mates. "Didn't want to tell you, but that's the truth. This is the quarterdeck and this is where our boss, Master Chief Petty Officer Jacobs, will take your prisoners. Petty Officer Potts, you're paired with me."

Jacobs saw Potts blush. The two of them had been spending a lot of time together since the brush with death last month in the Sea of Japan. It had been Potts whose body had protected Showdernitzel from the blast of the exploding North Korean Y-8 transport. Potts had had a crush on Mad Mary since he'd stumbled on board out of the mountains of Pennsylvania six months ago. Jacobs wondered how Mad Mary might have rewarded that worship, but then shook his head, thinking *Too much info.*

"Okay," she continued. "You've got your assignments, now get on with them."

ANDREW'S fingers wrapped and unwrapped around the shotgun. His eyes narrowed as he looked at Jacobs. He wished it were night. He could accomplish both sides of his mission.

"Hey, you're with me. I'm Quincy Stonemeyer," the sailor standing beside him said. The man raised the shotgun. "I'd offer to shake hands, but they're kinda full right now." The sailor laughed self-consciously.

Andrew looked down at the man. His face wrinkled in disgust at the acres of acne that covered Stonemeyer's face.

"It's an oily-skin thing, the doctor says," Stonemeyer replied.

Andrew leaned back. "Sorry."

The sailor nodded at him and smiled. "Don't be. I'm used to it. It's just acne, but it shocks people the first time they see my face, but—believe it or not—it's getting better. Doctor told me not to squeeze them and eventually they'll go away."

"I apologize," Andrew stuttered. "I did not mean to stare."

"That's all right. I've grown used to it. It is a burden given by the Lord. If He didn't want me to learn from this travail, He would not have given me this burden to bear."

"Amen," Andrew said, nodding in agreement. "The Lord asks a lot of His followers."

"Well, we have to start our rounds or the master chief will hang our privates on his mantle. You want me to lead?"

Andrew nodded. "I'm new on board."

"I know. Follow me. We have the rail gun over there and the forward starboard side of Sea Base." Stonemeyer pointed toward the weapon mounted forward on the starboard side of Sea Base. "Not too far to walk; just the length of the deck."

"How long is Sea Base?"

"You mean the top part?" Stonemeyer laughed again. "Sorry, of course you do. It's about 3,500 feet." He hefted his shotgun and slung it over his shoulder.

Spots of acne appeared under the short sleeves of the dungaree shirt. Andrew shuddered, imagining the man's body covered like his face, and the damage caused by the simple act of putting a sling across his shoulder. Maybe acne was the leprosy of the twenty-first century? He wondered if God would one day give him the power to heal such afflictions.

Stonemeyer motioned toward the projecting end of the runway. "If you include the ends of the runway that project out over the ocean both forward and aft, then it's 4,500 feet." Stonemeyer's arms were white, covered in cream.

Andrew pulled his eyes away from his partner. He took in the massive man-made island. Was it really an abomination as his father called it? An abomination because to destroy it would hasten Armageddon and with Armageddon would come the chaos needed for God's Army to assume its rightful leadership over the world? As he grew older, he had more questions about how things he seemed to see conflicted with those that he heard.

". . . to join us. There's about six of us who get—"

"What did you say? I'm sorry I was taking in the massive size of Sea Base."

"It is huge, isn't it. You can get lost on it. I heard of a sailor who came on board five months ago when we set sail and they only found him last week. He had been missing that long, lost in the engine room of one of the Fast Sealift Ships." Stonemeyer shook his head. "Hard to believe." Then he leaned forward and whispered, "He was being held as a . . . you know . . . sex slave." He straightened up and shuddered. "I would rather kill myself than have the Lord's Temple—my body—violated."

Andrew nodded. He could see someone losing themselves in this maze of metal. Sex was God's reward for a pure life. Sex was not something abhorred by God's Army, unlike the majority of religions on this earth. He doubted the story Stonemeyer told, but he was curious. If someone could get lost for five months on Sea Base, what was stopping him from killing Jacobs and this other person—Agazzi—and then disappearing until the ships returned to Pearl Harbor. The only thing stopping him was that he needed to know more about the layout of Sea Base. You can never hide in a strange forest.

Stonemeyer moved toward the starboard edge of Sea Base. "You seen the sharks yet?"

He had, but he shook his head, shocking himself. He'd just lied when he had no reason for it.

"Well, you have to see them. Within moments of Sea Base unfolding, they filled the ocean beneath us. All sizes," Stonemeyer said. Whenever Stonemeyer spoke, he turned to face Andrew as they walked. The young man bubbled with enthusiasm as he shared his thoughts with the new shipmate.

When the two reached the safety lines running along the edge of Sea Base, there were no sharks to be seen. Stonemeyer whined that most likely it was too bright for them out here. Maybe they're only in the shaded areas of Sea Base. He promised to show them to Andrew after GQ was secured.

As they turned toward the rail gun, Stonemeyer continued. "What I was saying was that we have a Bible study group on board, if you're interested. Only about six of us, but we try to meet every night."

Andrew smiled. God had sent Stonemeyer to him. He was not alone. "I would be honored to speak to all of you tonight."

Stonemeyer's face scrunched in confusion. "Speak to us?"

"Of course. That's what you wanted, isn't it?"

Stonemeyer smiled and looked uncomfortable. "Of course. We'd love to have you speak with us tonight. It would be good to hear your experiences." Then, almost in a conspiratorial whisper, he added, "Not many such as us make time to study His words."

"I can understand that," Andrew said, reaching out and patting the man on the shoulder. "Into every flock a shepherd must come. As much to lead as to protect." He let out a deep breath. "Brother, I am glad God has brought us together. He has so much love and I have so much to do in His name."

"I'm happy too. You will be the first newcomer to our group in over a month," Stonemeyer replied too quickly.

Andrew heard the joy in the man's voice. Is this man a disciple sent from God, or only a dove to lead him to others who could be molded into an arm of God's Army? Thoughts of killing Jacobs and Agazzi were still there, but the thrill of meeting other worshippers overrode the immediacy of the deed. His father had his flock and Andrew needed his. He wondered how many tonight would recognize his omnipotence when he arrived.

After a while, it became obvious to Andrew that this Stonemeyer had no close friends. He hoped the others at tonight's Bible group were of similar nature to this Stonemeyer. Lonely people turn to God more often, and are always looking for a shepherd to help with their burdens.

TEN

Garcia leaned forward; his elbow bumped the empty coffee cup lodged in the holder on his Captain's chair. The electronic hum of background noise mixed with the soft patter of voices in the blue light of the darkened Combat Information Center. Long wires ran from sockets in the bulkheads crisscrossing the deck like giant vines in some cavernous fantasy, until they leaped upward to the headsets of the sound-powered telephone talkers.

Sound-powered telephone talkers dotted the area within Combat, one hand always on the button of the mouthpiece, pushing it down when they talked quietly into it. The slight clicks reminded Garcia of crickets. His eyes went from one sound-powered phone talker to another. The most junior sailors usually manned the sound-powered phones, which were the last vestige of a technology long superseded by a rapidly changing world of information. As much as information technology and communications continued to advance in the twenty-first century, the risk of it all coming down to these simple early-twentieth-century devices for internal communications existed. They had not changed much since World War II. Bulbous helmets with protruding mouthpieces and earpieces made you think of soldier ants with giant mandibles. But those cumbersome helmets, trailing wires, and junior sailors were the last and final line of maintaining communications within the ship. The antiquated sound-powered telephones gave the Captain the ability to fight and save the ship regardless of battle damage.

The overhead speaker squeaked, drawing his attention back to the situations unfolding in front of him.

"Black Formation, Raptor Formation, and Weasel; this is Mother, I have control, report status."

Garcia bit his lower lip and nodded once. The words came from the red speaker mounted overhead to his left. Red meant the transmissions were protected by secure enciphered communications. Only those with the right security keys could hear it. Mother was the call sign for the British carrier *Elizabeth*. The Sea Base F-22A Raptors had crossed out of Garcia's area of operations and into the British area of control.

"Raptor Haven, Raptor Leader; formation of two F-22A fighters switching to Mother control."

"Roger, Raptor Leader; good hunting. Check in with Raptor Air Intercept Control upon commencement of return flight."

Garcia nodded once in silent acknowledgment to that broadcast transferring the final two fighters to British control. Major Johnson and her formation were heading south into the Taiwan Strait because the Chinese were trying to encircle the Rivet Joint bird. Major Crawford and his wingman were only minutes behind her. Now, Captain Nolan and Captain Delaney were heading into the fray. Meanwhile, Garcia had eight missing torpedoes to add to the mystery of these tactical dances between the Chinese and them.

"Roger, Raptor Haven."

Garcia motioned Stapler over.

"Stan, I want to listen to the TACAIR channel even though I know they've transferred under the control of the *Elizabeth*. I want to keep us aware of the ongoing action with the RC-135."

Stapler twisted his head slightly and nodded at the speaker. "No plans to change it, sir," Stapler replied. "All our F-22s are launched. Only the Air Force hangar queen left on the deck.

Nothing left to do but handle our submarine problem and listen to them."

Garcia nodded. "Good," he said, his tone firm. He was enjoying this role of a war-fighter. A month ago, he was a Navy captain whose whole career, since XO on a destroyer as a lieutenant commander, had been taking ships out to sea to test new programs, equipment, and systems. In this past month, he had fought a major sea battle and an attempt to land forces on Sea Base. He smiled until he thought of the young pilot in the burn unit in San Antonio. A breath of fear traced across his conscious. He began to recite the Rosary silently. At about the third Hail Mary, a slight smile spread for a moment across his face as the peace in his prayer eased his guilt over the proud feelings of his performance in the Sea of Japan.

"SHIT," whispered the first-class petty officer to a second class standing nearby.

"What's wrong?"

"Iron Man smiled," he replied, nudging the other sailor to look at Garcia.

The sailor visibly shivered. "Shit, man. He's not smiling now. You sure he smiled? Maybe he yawned."

"Man, I know the difference between a yawn and a smile. He smiled. Ain't good."

"Means he's looking forward to whatever shit is about to happen."

"Torpedoes coming at us. Invisible aircraft trying to shoot down our invisible aircraft and he's smiling." The first class let out a big sigh and grinned. "Damn glad I'm on his side of this."

"Me too. I'm about ready to change my skivvies and he's sitting there, legs crossed and smiling. Almost as if he wants someone to fuck with us."

"They don't know what sex is until Iron Man fucks with them."

"Yeah, man."

THE main war-fighting consoles were aligned like slot machines in a semicircle directly across from Garcia's chair. He could easily sit here, sip coffee, and fight this humongous floating island without ever leaving his seat. He lifted his cup, noticed it was empty, and put it back in the holder.

"HE'S out of coffee," the first class noticed.

"I'll get him some."

They nodded as the sailor hurried to the aft bulkhead where a coffeepot percolated continuously. Fresh coffee happened mostly in the mornings. After that, it was happenstance if the pot was ever started anew. Most times, someone just poured more water into already overworked grounds.

GARCIA eased back in his chair, resting his elbows on the arms of the chair, clasped hands arched above his lap. He leaned forward and rested his chin lightly on his hands, watching the green-tinted screens of the consoles arrayed in front of him.

He tuned to the chatter between the SH-60 antisubmarine helicopters as they headed along their varied courses, two for each submarine contact out there. If the Chinese torpedoes had not run out of fuel before reaching Sea Base, he and everyone in this compartment would be either dead or floating in the Pacific. The Naval Research scientists believed it would take substantial battle damage to sink Sea Base. Of course, they based that on their mathematical models and statistical analysis.

He had overheard a master chief voicing what most believed. Sea Base was a floating accident waiting to happen. He dropped his hands and leaned back. He shut his eyes for a moment trying to recall how the boatswain mate master chief had phrased it. After a couple of seconds, the two words came to him: dark Pacific. Sea Base was another man-made accident waiting to join the others along the bottom of the dark Pacific.

To the far right along the port bulkhead sat a lieutenant commander manning a single computer console. The young lady's job was to monitor the readout from the Sea Base servers and computers located in the main cargo hold of the

USNS *Pollux*. Those servers and computers kept this floating eighty-plus-acre man-made island afloat. So much could go wrong—so much already had.

So far, all that had gone wrong had been man-made. He had been pleasantly surprised at how the complex algorithms racing at near light speed through the IT bowels of the *Pollux* had not produced a major catastrophe. Way beneath the hulls of the eight Fast Sealift Ships were sixteen gigantic sea anchors rising and falling as the Sea Base servers compensated for the ever-changing dynamics of the sea. But here they were five months into a six-month operational test and evaluation and they were still afloat. During those five months they had fought sabotage, North Koreans, and aircraft crashes, but not once had they fought the danger of a server malfunction.

His face crunched, lips pushing out, eyebrows pulling into a deep V. They were at General Quarters because the Chinese were trying to sink them. What next? He wondered for a moment if at the end of the next thirty days they'd be allowed to return to Pearl Harbor. That is, if Sea Base was still afloat. He knew the answer was no if the Taiwan crisis wasn't settled.

Commander Stapler walked up and stood in front of him.

"What's the status?" Garcia asked.

"USS *Stripling* will have its LAMPS helicopters over the contact datum within three minutes. We will need your orders to drop the torpedo."

"Which contact is that?"

"Bears northeast of us, Captain; 010 degrees."

"Has it turned away? I would think—"

"No, sir," Stapler interrupted. "According to Sonar, there has been no course change. Sir, we will need your orders to attack. I could do it as the Tactical Action Officer, but you're here, Skipper."

Garcia nodded. He ignored the implication by Stapler that he should turn over the fight to him as the TAO. While he had confidence in Stapler to fight the ship, he knew the officer would fight first and worry about consequences later. He bit his lower lip.

"Sir?"

My orders. Someone always has to give the order to destroy or kill. This was his ship regardless of how little like a ship it looked.

"They'll be overhead the datum any moment."

When Garcia gave the orders, a helicopter outside the detection envelope of the Chinese submarine would drop a Mark-46 torpedo. The Chinese would pick up the splash. A fraction of a second after hearing it, they'd know what it was. The Chinese submarine would immediately start executing maneuvers to avoid, fool, or outrun the torpedo. It would fill the waters with decoys in an attempt to pull the torpedo away from the true target. Everything the Chinese Captain did would be designed to keep him and his crew alive. The Chinese Captain could also fill the waters with torpedoes aimed at Sea Base.

And through all of this, Garcia's simple order would be directly responsible for killing a bunch of Chinese squatting and sweating inside a tube called a submarine somewhere hundreds of feet beneath the surface. Scientists, engineers, and he had tested the technology in the logic heads of those torpedoes in an attempt to defeat it. When the testing had been finished, the probability of a kill when he gave the order was ninety-nine percent.

"Sir?" Stapler asked, impatience bursting through the thin veneer of the war-fighter.

All of this because they tried to kill us. *To the victor goes the first kill,* he thought. Who said that? His eyebrows furrowed as he tried to recall. After several seconds, his face relaxed and his smile spread. *He* said it. It was his saying.

"OH, man, we must really be going into some shit stuff," the first class said softly.

The other sailor shook his head, standing there with a paper cup full of hot coffee. "He's almost laughing, man. If it was anyone else, I'd be nervous."

"Well, it's not anyone else, it's Iron Man. Look at Stapler, the asshole. He looks as if he's about to wet himself the way he's dancing from foot to foot."

"I think Iron Man finds him funny."

"That's because he's the Captain and he doesn't have to put up with Stapler's shit. Let him work for Stapler for a day."

"He'd grab the lanky zero and toss him overboard is what

he'd do, then wipe his hands against each other and walk away whistling. We got one hell of a Skipper, Smuckers."

"If he can smile when the rest of us are scared shitless, then he must have it under control." The first class looked at the cup of coffee. "You're not going to give Iron Man coffee in a paper cup, are you?"

The sailor shook his head. "No man, I ain't that brave. I'm gonna lift his cup and pour it into it."

The first class nodded in approval.

"What should I say?"

"What you talking about? You don't have to say nothing. Just do it. You watch now," the first class said, pointing at Garcia. "Iron Man cares for the troops. When you do it, he'll be so calm, he'll thank you."

A minute later, the younger second-class petty officer was back alongside the first class.

"Well?"

"You were right. He said thank you, took a sip, and then told me it was good coffee."

"He is the Iron Man, ain't he? That coffee has been there all day. It'd take paint off a bulkhead if someone spilled a cup on it, and he thinks it's good."

They both shook their heads in amazement. "He's a braver man than me."

"SIR? Do you want to okay the attack now?"

The smile dropped and Garcia shook his head. "Let me know when they have positive contact, Commander. Until then, weapons tight. They are not to fire until I give the order."

Stapler rolled his eyes slightly and sighed loudly. "Aye, sir, but we may only get one chance once we have contact," he said, and walked back to the console.

Garcia leaned back and looked at the huge screens mounted on the bulkheads in front of him. He lifted the coffee and sipped the acidic aged mixture. Whoever brought it to him knew to put only the powdered stuff in it, no sugar. The blue light hid the grayness of the day-old liquid within his cup. He set it back in the holder. Wonder the stuff hadn't chewed a hole in his stomach.

He focused on the console to the right. Computer icons moved across the screen. Each represented either a Chinese submarine or the eight helicopters out to fight them. The center of the screen was Sea Base. The amphibious carrier USS *Boxer* steamed off the port quarter of Sea Base. Around the two of them, the three destroyers USS *Gearing*, USS *Perry*, and USS *Stripling* bored through the ocean waves, weaving between the higher-valued units of Sea Base and *Boxer* in an attempt to be in position to take out another torpedo attack.

He moved his attention to the middle screen as the operator zoomed out. This was the Air Intercept Controller watching the unfolding scenario of the Rivet Joint as it fled possible hostile aircraft. A round icon northwest of the action identified the Royal Navy aircraft carrier *Elizabeth* and its battle group. The British were entering the Taiwan Strait, nearly four hundred miles from Sea Base, which loitered northeast of the northernmost tip of Taiwan.

The red handset rang. That would be Admiral Holman on the *Boxer*.

The nearby sailor picked up the telephone and handed it to Garcia. Stapler, standing in front of the ASW console, glanced at Garcia, but turned away when he saw the handset handed to the Captain.

"Yes, Admiral."

"Hank, how are you doing?"

Garcia took a deep breath and explained the situations as he saw them to Holman. Every so often the three-star Commander U.S. Seventh Fleet would add his opinion and insight. They talked for several minutes and during the talk, it dawned on Garcia that unlike the fight in the Sea of Japan, Holman was speaking to him as an equal. It was in the tenor, tone, and words. It was something human nature allowed you to recognize, but left you unable to describe.

Finally, Garcia heard Holman take a deep breath. "Hank, your helicopters are reaching the estimated positions of the four submarines. What are your plans? Do you intend to launch your weapons when you reach best position?"

Garcia opened his mouth to speak, then shut it. Until this minute, he had not decided what he was going to do. He pushed the talk button. "I still have weapons tight, Admiral."

"You can never go wrong keeping weapons tight until you're ready to launch."

Garcia nodded. "Yes, sir. Admiral, my orders are not to fight unless attacked. We've been attacked, but the torpedoes were launched so far away they ran out of fuel before they even reached us."

"If they had reached us, they could have done an awful lot of damage, Hank."

"Yes, sir. My thoughts are to keep weapons tight and revert back to my initial orders, Admiral," he said, waiting for Holman to revert back to the mentoring voice from the Sea of Japan.

A couple of seconds passed.

"I think that is a wise choice, Hank. So far, we haven't exchanged a real blow against each other. Once we do, the gloves are off. So, if you don't intend to launch immediately, what do you intend to do?"

Garcia looked at the large black numbered Navy clock on the bulkhead to his right. He knew what he was going to do. An epiphany of events unrolled in his mind as he saw the various logic trails of results roll out as clear as the Rockies on a bright summer day. He pushed the talk button and shared his plan with the admiral. When Garcia handed the handset back to the first class, he was smiling.

"HE'S smiling again."

"We're probably under attack again."

"Could be that coffee you brought him."

"It was fresh."

"Hot it was, fresh it ain't."

"You told me to."

The first class sighed. "Next time we make a fresh pot."

"COME on, Seaman Gentron," Bernardo urged. "You going to tell us or not how you know they weren't real torpedoes?"

Gentron nodded toward Bernardo. "If they had been real torpedoes, those contacts would not have remained on our passive sonar. They would have run."

"What if you're wrong? What if they are some sort of stealth torpedo waiting for us to relax a little before they restart and hit us?"

"You could be right, Petty Officer Bernardo."

"Oh, now we start getting proper military etiquette."

"Pope, give the boy a chance to answer," MacPherson snapped.

"Okay," Bernardo said with a show of arrogance. "Go ahead, Gentron."

"If they are stealth torpedoes, which I don't think they are, then the Chinese would not have to hang around to see what our reaction is. They could leave the area confident in the knowledge that sometime in the future the torpedoes will restart and do their job. They'd be safely away somewhere out of range of our antisubmarine forces."

"They didn't leave. They're still here."

Gentron nodded. "If they are decoys meant to warn us away . . ."

"No one fires decoys."

"Of course they do, Pope," MacPherson said. "We fire decoys all the time to lure torpedoes or ships away from our own submarines."

"I don't think that's what Gentron meant," Agazzi said. "Go ahead, Seaman Gentron."

"If they had been torpedoes, they would have done a little intelligence-gathering on our reaction and then depart the area. That's another alternative to why they haven't disappeared yet. Most likely, they're a warning. Kind of like someone aiming a gun at you and shooting blanks. Still scares you, but doesn't kill you. Now, what if they take that gun after they've scared you, warning you off, and replace the blanks with real bullets? The first salvo was a warning to us. The next salvo will be real torpedoes," Gentron finished as his voice trailed off as if where his thoughts took him scared him. "Then, they'd disappear from sonar."

For nearly a minute, no one spoke in the ASW operations center as Gentron's words soaked into their thoughts.

"Naw, what do you know?" Bernardo asked, motioning Gentron away. "You're just a seaman."

"A seaman who was able to tell us that we had a North Korean submarine trying to sink us," MacPherson said. "I didn't see any of us coming up with that answer."

Agazzi nodded. "Thanks, Seaman Gentron. Let's see what happens." He turned to Keyland. "How about you? Does Seaman Gentron's hypothesis sound good?"

Keyland nodded. "It makes sense to me. If they are intent on sinking us, then I think they would have already fired a second round. If you had eight more torpedoes inbound, it would draw our attention to them and away from the first salvo. Worst case is that Pope is right and the first eight were some sort of stealth torpedo. With our attention drawn to the new inbounds, if the other eight suddenly reactivated, then we'd have a hell of a story to tell our grandchildren."

"I think the first eight were duds, maybe exercise torpedoes," Gentron said softly. "I don't think the first eight were some sort of stealth torpedoes."

"You mean the survivors would have a hell of story to tell their grandchildren. I don't think we'd be in that number," MacPherson replied to Keyland's comment.

The exchange reminded everyone they were in the lowest level of the USNS *Algol* holding up a metal canopy called Sea Base that would crush everything beneath it once it started falling.

MacPherson pushed his earpiece against his head. "Roger, we're ready here," he spoke into his mouthpiece. He turned to Agazzi. "Senior Chief, Mort says the UUV firing cradle is locked in place—finished its cycle. We can launch the third UUV anytime."

Agazzi gave permission to launch. His mind meshed the two theories of Bernardo and Gentron. What was his theory? Both of theirs made sense. But the best case for determining who was right would be whether the submarines remained on sonar. As Agazzi thought about the problem, searching for a third alternative, he was unaware that in Combat, Garcia had already reached the conclusion that the first salvo were live torpedoes that had run out of fuel.

Topside within Combat Information Center, the ASW air controller continued vectoring SH-36 helicopters with their torpedoes along the lines of bearing provided by Agazzi.

* * *

"BLACK Leader, Raptor Leader!" shouted the voice of the RC-135 controller. "I have multiple bogies bearing one-nine-zero and two-one-zero from us."

"Roger, Weasel," came the calm voice of Tyler-Cole. "We see them on our heads-up display. I think you have found the missing J-12s, sir."

"Black Leader, this is Mother; we are showing multiple air targets emerging off the coast of mainland China. We are turning into the wind to launch the ready CAP. Recommend a quick escort of the heavy away from the area." Aircraft carriers in times when a quick reaction against an approaching hostile force might be required kept two fighters ready for immediate launch. This pair was usually referred to as the ready combat air patrol: CAP.

"Roger, Mother; that is what we've been doing for the past few minutes," Tyler-Cole replied in a sharp tone.

Franklin listened as Tyler-Cole discussed a new flight course. A course that took the Royal Navy fighters and the American reconnaissance aircraft closer to the Taiwan landmass. On his heads-up display, the data link showed the six contacts behind them in formations of two. He didn't have them on his radar, but the data link from the Rivet Joint was providing the locations. "How are you doing that?" he asked aloud.

The Chinese aircraft had almost encircled Weasel and Black Formation before they had been detected. He smiled. Their stealth technology wasn't as good as ours.

As suddenly as they appeared, they disappeared. In their stead, twelve smaller bogies appeared.

"This is Weasel; we have multiple missile seekers and radar returns. Long range, but heading our way."

"Have they locked onto you?"

"That is a negative, Black Leader. We are being painted, but the seeker is still searching. Activating countermeasures at this time."

"This is Mother. I have control of all aircraft within my area of responsibility. Weasel, come to course zero-six-zero, and descend to three thousand meters altitude. Taipei control has been notified of your approach. You can expect a flight of Taiwanese F-16s to pick you up by the time you reach the coastline."

"Tight End, this is Pickles; you copying this?"

"Affirmative, DETCO. We are about one hundred miles behind you. Go for it and we'll catch up."

"Roger. Captain Franklin, let's put some speed on and join them."

Franklin looked up as Johnson's aircraft pushed the afterburner to maximum. A second later, she was a mile away as he pushed the throttle forward. The jolt of speed pushed him back into his seat.

"Black Leader, Mother; reform and prepare to engage."

Franklin's attention switched between the heads-up display showing him the changing air scene and keeping visual track on Johnson, who seemed hell-bent to be in the middle of the action even if she was alone. This could be the first air combat action between three sets of stealth fighters from three different nations. He took a deep breath. Someone else would have to write this history.

"Weasel, Mother; continue descent to five hundred meters altitude."

"Roger. Let me know when the paint of the missile seekers disappears."

"Roger, Mother."

The F-35 Joint Strike Force Fighter flown by the British was a stealth fighter like the United States Air Force F-22A, but not on a technological par with the Raptor. The U.S. Navy and Marine Corps flew the F-35 fighters also. Franklin allowed himself a slight smile. Just ask any Air Force pilot if you wanted the truth. It was only right the Air Force had the better fighters. Franklin's eyebrows lifted for a moment. The air was their sea and they controlled it.

"Weasel, this is Mother; do you have missile identification yet?"

"That is a negative, Mother. These missiles are not in our database. They were fired long range, subsonic, active mode. They are continuing to paint us. No lock-on at this time. Diving past cloud layer—ten thousand feet at this time."

"Roger, continue on to five hundred meters—make that fifteen hundred feet. Report when missile seekers have been lost."

When air-to-air missiles are fired, they are usually configured with an infrared seeker designed to home in on heat signatures. Those type missiles are very effective for rear-hemispheric attacks against a fleeing aircraft or against an enemy where the shooter pilot is behind his or her target.

The other type of seeker was one with high-frequency band radar in the cone that put out a directional beam, searching for a return to guide it to its target. These missiles employed active seekers that searched for their target and once it was found, the radar signal locked onto the target and wherever the target went, the missile followed.

Then, there were missiles with both capabilities, such as the venerable American Sidewinder that could switch between active-seeker radar and infrared-seeker. Those were the hardest missiles to defeat.

Aircraft had antimissile capabilities. The Air Force RC-135 Rivet Joint reconnaissance aircraft could drop magnesium flares to draw away the infrared missiles. Other countermeasures included decoying the active seekers with radar countermeasures such as jamming or deflecting the return. Stealth fighters such as the F-22A and F-35 Joint Strike Fighter depended primarily on their stealth technology to defeat the active seeker, but even they had flares and electronic countermeasures in their basket of defense.

"Do you have a jamming capability against the missiles?"

"We are scrambling now, Mother. No joy at this time."

"Mother, this is Black Leader; Black Formation reformed and ready for direction." After the Royal Navy aircraft carrier *Elizabeth* acknowledged Tyler-Cole's report, the commander passed the fuel and armament status to the controller.

"Roger, Black Leader; come to course two-zero-zero for intercept. Be advised we have nothing on radar to guide you toward the targets except last bogie location. Estimated range to interception is one hundred kilometers. Descend to five thousand meters."

Franklin's eyebrows wrinkled as he tried to convert five thousand meters into feet. The rough estimate used by American pilots was 3⅓ feet for every meter, even though everyone knew a meter was 3.28 feet. The British formation was descending to around seventeen thousand feet. Close enough for air combat, he figured.

As if reading his mind, the British Air Intercept Controller on board the Royal Navy aircraft carrier *Elizabeth* came on the circuit. "Raptor Formation, this is Mother. Black Formation is being vectored for interception of hostile targets. They are descending to five thousand meters, which is about 16,500 feet. Request you take altitude angels twenty-five; 25,000 feet or about 7,500 meters. I am showing two Raptor formations about seventy-five miles apart on the data profile. Third Raptor formation has been launched from Sea Base. We have control of it also."

"Roger, Mother; this is Raptor Leader—lead formation. We are on intercept course to the heavy," Johnson broadcast using the cover term "heavy" to describe the RC-135 reconnaissance aircraft. "Second Raptor formation is Raptor-30 Formation."

"Roger, Raptor Leader; request you break off interception course to Weasel and come to course one-nine-zero, angels twenty-five. We have asked the Taiwanese Air Force to take over escort of the heavy. They have F-16 Falcons en route. My intentions are to put our F-35 and Raptor fighters between the hostiles and the reconnaissance aircraft. You are being vectored to southeast flank of Black Formation. Black Formation will have initial point."

Franklin heard the two clicks as Johnson acknowledged the direction. He nearly laughed. Those two clicks sounded as if she was pissed off, if that was possible. Only a personality such as Pickles could show her emotions through the clicking of an acknowledgment. Pissed off at the idea that the British were directing them into the first air combat of the twenty-first century and, no doubt in his highly tactical mind, pissed that she might not be part of it.

He listened as the British Air Intercept Controller maneuvered Tight End and his wingman onto a course and altitude that would place the second Raptor formation center rear to the lead British and American fighters. The second Raptor formation was what history always called the reserve force. Reserve forces never fared well in history.

Franklin wriggled in his seat, changing his position slightly. He discovered the bravado from the officers club, the desire to shoot down an enemy fighter in the clenched-fist orgasm of air-to-air combat, had morphed into anxiety mixed with a tinge of fear. He wriggled the fingers on his hands, one hand at a time, and took a deep breath. Franklin wondered if all the pieces of his training and flight time would be the edge so when the fight was over, he'd be the one watching the other guy's parachute open on the way to the sea. "You fight like you train," he said to himself—the mantra of every training course he ever took.

"Bring them on," he said softly to himself, stretching his shoulders, trying to force that feeling of confidence back into his body. "No way, Bubba," he mumbled, thinking of his Chinese opponent.

He went through the various combat maneuvers he knew by heart. He glanced around the cockpit. This was his cockpit. He knew it as well as he knew his own body—better even because he could see every bit of the battle space. The anxiety of a moment ago became replaced by eager anticipation. He was going to kick some Chinese butt.

ELEVEN

Kiang paused outside his stateroom door. Without touching the knob, he looked at the wire in the crevice of door facing. It was still there. He pulled the key from his pocket and opened the door, glancing around the compartment before entering. Everything appeared to be where he left it. The radio was still in the middle of the table. He closed the door, making sure it was locked, before walking to the center of the stateroom. His fingers trailed across the gray-topped metal table. He leaned down close to the radio, his face almost touching the table. The radio remained within the light pencil lines that traced an outline of the corner edge of the radio.

Since that time months ago when Zeichner and Gainer had secretly searched his stateroom, he had failed to find evidence of a second entry. Didn't mean someone had not been there to search it again, but if so, that someone wasn't either of these two. He smiled, his lips tight. Zeichner and Gainer were a joke. Sea Base was in its last month of deployment, if you believed everything said when they set sail from Pearl Harbor. Five months with him having the run of Sea Base, photographing and gathering intelligence, and not one time had anyone questioned him about what he was doing. That stupid sailor in the crow's nest had even asked for copies of the photographs Kiang took during the North Korean fiasco.

The only one who had ever reacted to his presence had been that master chief today who graciously ordered him belowdecks, giving him an excuse to . . . He hugged the camera to his chest. "Thanks, Master Chief," Kiang mumbled.

Espionage was ninety percent luck and ten percent skills, Kiang had come to realize. Most of what he gathered while on board had been because of ongoing operations, combat, or just plain serendipitous luck. Luck was the true God of success.

Kiang lifted the camera and binoculars from around his neck and set them on the table. He checked the lock on the stateroom door and wedged a chair under the knob. It wouldn't stop anyone who really wanted to come in, but it would give him the seconds he needed to destroy the evidence gathered from the Air Force office.

He went to the head, washed his hands, and then returned to the table, where he lifted the radio. He pulled the sidepiece out to reveal the hidden transmission device. Underneath the top part of the radio, using his thumb and forefinger, he found the thin wire. He pulled the wire, letting it unwind as he walked backward to the nearby electric plug-in. He wrapped the wire around the electrical cord of the tall lamp beside the recliner. Satisfied the makeshift antenna was ready, Kiang went into the head and brought the electric razor out. It took a few seconds to open the back of the razor.

He undid the cover to the camera, and within a few seconds had the camera connected to the transmitter. He pulled another wire and connected it to the operating controls hidden within the back of the electric razor.

Even if they discovered the radio, they'd find no evidence of what had been transmitted. The original method of using underwater delivery devices had failed early in the deployment, so the Ministry of State Security had gone back to the old tried-and-true method of radio transmissions.

Kiang visually checked the antenna, the operator connection, and the camera settings. The photographs would be transmitted directly from the camera. They would disappear from the camera as little bits of data, hit the radio transmit device, travel along the antenna, up the electric connections within the ship to the antenna topside of Sea Base. From there, they would burst into the electromagnetic spectrum, where the Ministry of State Security would pick up the data signal. It was a matter of seconds and not minutes before this data would be in the hands of the analysts in Beijing.

He hit the download button on the camera. The transmitter inside the radio lacked controls. External devices such as the camera provided the data, while the operation controls within the razor gave the digital instructions to tell the radio what to do. If, or when, he was captured they'd discover the transmitter, but there would be no frequencies; no controls; nothing to show what was transmitted or how. Without the camera and his electric razor, the radio was nothing but a radio with a hidden compartment filled with wires.

Kiang leaned forward and checked the digital readout of the camera. It was counting down and as he watched, it reached zero. He counted to ten, as if the espionage unit needed additional time for the data to transmit. He disconnected the radio and camera. Went over to the electric cord and disconnected the wire. He dropped the wire and watched the tiny automatic winder inside the radio retract the thin antenna wire. Then, Kiang closed the radio and set it carefully back within the pencil traces. He quickly moved the chair away from the door.

He used the head, closing the door behind him even though he was alone within his own stateroom. Coming out, the flush of the toilet filling the compartment, he put the binoculars and camera around his neck. Less than a minute later, he was out the door, heading toward the top of Sea Base.

He was toying with the idea of climbing to his designated spot in the crow's nest. But the idea of sharing it with that sailor again appalled him. Social interaction had never been a strong suit in his limited personality arsenal. He had no way of knowing that the sailor was no longer in the crow's nest. The sailor's abandoned sound-powered headset lay in a disorganized heap near the foot of the ladder leading up to the crow's nest.

* * *

"BLACK Formation, Mother; armament switches on."

"Roger, Mother; armament switches on. Gyro on," came the voice of Commander Tyler-Cole.

What the hell is a gyro? Franklin asked himself.

"Maneuver sharp, ready?"

"Ready."

Franklin listened as the British Air Intercept Controller on board the Royal Navy aircraft carrier *Elizabeth* vectored the four F-35 fighters toward unseen targets. What the hell was a maneuver sharp?

"Black Leader; right turn now!" came an explosive command.

Franklin felt chill bumps race up his spine. What was happening? Were they firing missiles, or what? Damn, he hated not knowing. He looked at the heads-up display on the cockpit. Black Formation was making a sharp right turn. Franklin shook his head. What the hell were they thinking? That turn was going to expose their belly to the hostiles and degrade their stealth coatings, making them susceptible to radar detection. He didn't like things happening in the air that he didn't understand or that were surprises. This was both.

"Flares now, Black Formation!"

Flares would not be reflected on the data link display racing across the heads-up he was trying to follow while keeping his eye on Johnson's Raptor and the sky ahead of him. Christ! He hated this. *What the hell are the British doing and why aren't they telling us?* There were no other missiles in the air, so why the flares? Flares were part of the antimissile decoys for fighters.

"We have contact!" Tyler-Cole transmitted. "I have them on my radar. Mother, good call."

"They have you also, Black Formation. Good hunting. Level off and immediately descend to two thousand meters."

"Damn," Franklin said aloud when he realized what they had done. Flares burn brightly when released to decoy infrared missiles, but in the few seconds when they first ignite, they create a virtual presence in the air. A presence that could be misinterpreted, if unexpected. Stealth fighters have to open their weapons bay door to fire missiles and when they do, they are detectable.

The flares had been picked up by the Chinese stealth bomber and misinterpreted as missiles being fired. The sharp turn by the British fighters had broken their stealth-ness just enough for the Chinese to pick them up also. Radar video returns can tell you a lot. A quick detection may mean the release of decoys such as flares. The longer detection caused by the sharp turn exposing the reflective underbelly of the Joint Strike Fighter caused the Chinese to believe the British had fired missiles at them.

To counter infrared missiles meant stealth aircraft had to break the radar reduction signature along their fuselage long enough to fire their own flares. Those small seconds gave the British an opportunity to detect and locate the Chinese fighter formations.

"Black and Raptor Leaders; we hold two formations of hostile fighters. Three per formation. Black Leader, come left, steady on course two-two-zero, maintain current altitude. Raptor Leader . . ."

Raptor Leader? That was Johnson and him. He leaned forward, listening intently to the Air Intercept Controller. Johnson did tell Mother she was the lead formation.

". . . ease to course one-eight-zero, maintain current angels twenty-five."

How were the British doing this? He could never imagine an American air intercept controller switching seamlessly between kilometers, meters, feet, and miles. That impressed Franklin more than the fact the British and Americans were in a joint engagement against the number-one military power in Asia.

"WHERE are the helicopters?" Agazzi asked, looking at Calvins, who was entombed in his sound-powered telephone talker outfit.

"I can switch off the UUV for a moment so we can see the Naval Tactical Data System, Senior Chief, if you want," MacPherson said, glancing over his shoulder.

"No, need to keep the UUV steady on course. What course are you on now?"

"220 and 010 true."

Behind him, Calvins was relaying the question to Combat.

"Okay, Gentron, how are we going to know if the Chinese really mean to attack us or just showing us they could if they want to?" Bernardo asked. "You said they'd sneak away. Well, they're still there."

"Hey, don't be snotty with my seaman," MacPherson interjected.

"I'm not being snotty. He said if the torpedoes were fake, the submarines would leave. Well, they haven't." Bernardo turned. His eyes traveled from Keyland to Agazzi. "Come on, Senior Chief, Petty Officer Keyland; you both are curious also, aren't you?"

Keyland crossed his arms and nodded. "Seaman Gentron, you want to share any other ideas? You were pretty good in the Sea of Japan—" Bernardo interrupted. "Yeah, Mertz; you were the first to figure out it was a North Korean submarine that sunk the Chinese sub. Not that we wouldn't have figured it out, but you did it first."

At the second UUV console, Gentron smiled, his face darkening in the blue light of the ASW Control Center as he blushed. "I did, didn't I?" he said quietly.

"Ah, Christ," Bernardo said. "Now we'll have to widen the hatch to get his head through it."

"Seaman Gentron," Agazzi said. "What do you think we should look for?"

Gentron cleared his throat. "I think that if they were trying to sink us, they would have already fired another salvo."

"They're still out there. Maybe they're preparing to fire another round and just coordinating," Keyland offered, leaning forward and putting his hands on the safety rail above the lower level of the compartment.

"That is true. I thought if they were firing to let us know they could sink us, then they'd fade away having accomplished their mission."

"They haven't. Therefore, maybe they're going to fire again?"

"You could be right, Petty Officer Bernardo," Gentron continued, "but don't you think they've had sufficient time to fire again?"

Agazzi nodded. He came down the ladder, moving toward

the AN/SQR-25 passive sonar console where Bernardo sat. "That is true."

"Unless they are less competent than we think," MacPherson added.

"I don't think they are," Agazzi answered. "These four submarines are out in the open ocean. China is no longer a coastal Navy." He turned, glancing up at Keyland and then at Gentron. "It could also be China demonstrating to us that they can go anywhere in the world with their Navy."

"They've done that before, Senior Chief," Keyland added. "They've taken a small task force and circled the globe."

"But they didn't take their submarines with them and that was nearly ten years ago. Since then, they've been poaching on our and other nations' technology, putting their own scientists and engineers to work, and now they have a second aircraft carrier being built alongside the first."

"They have over sixty SSNs and ten SSBNs," Gentron said. "They're already a force to be reckoned with with that many attack and ballistic nuclear submarines."

Bernardo twirled around in his chair and started typing something on one of the data icons. A moment later, he stared back in Gentron's direction, then at the senior chief. "They have sixty-two attack submarines and ten ballistic missile submarines," he said quietly.

"Where'd you get all this knowledge?" MacPherson said, reaching over with a friendly push on Gentron's shoulder. "You trying to be an officer or something?"

"They taught us in A school," Gentron replied somberly. "The Chinese would have more submarines if during the Cultural Revolution . . ."

"What's a Cultural Revolution?" Bernardo asked.

"It's you understanding what a movie is without sex in it," MacPherson replied.

"Because during it, 1966 through 1969, Mao purged over eleven thousand Naval officers, of which eleven were senior admirals. He closed down the submarine force and the submarine force languished. . . ."

"Languished?" Bernardo asked.

"It's what you do afterwards when most men would tell her

how wonderful it was and have a cigarette," MacPherson shot back.

"Jenkins, bite me!"

"You two shut up and let Gentron finish," Keyland ordered from above them.

"But since 2002, China has done a massive military buildup fueled in part by its gigantic economic growth. They either felt they couldn't afford aircraft carriers, or believed their national interests would never be threatened sufficiently for them to have to project power away from their shores. So, they started building an oceangoing submarine force. Kind of reminiscent of Germany's strategy of controlling England . . ."

"Germany?"

"Pope, keep quiet!" Keyland said sharply to Bernardo.

". . . by building a gigantic submarine force. If you don't have the antisubmarine forces capable of defeating them, then a country is unable to control the seas until those ASW forces reach a level of capability and competence to do it."

"They're still out there and they still can attack us, Seaman Gentron," Agazzi declared.

"I don't think they want to attack us unless we attack them. I think they're just making a point." Gentron nodded toward MacPherson and then his console. "When these UUVs reach a certain point, the submarines will disappear. The ones north of us may cross our bow heading back to the mainland, but most likely will disappear out to sea. The ones on our southwest will just disappear. We won't know if they have left us or are just languishing . . ."

"Languishing . . ."

Agazzi put his hand on Bernardo's shoulder and gave him a sharp look. Bernardo nodded and made a motion of zipping his lip.

". . . outside detection range."

"How do they know our UUVs aren't torpedoes coming at them?" Keyland asked.

Gentron shrugged. "I'm not sure."

"I'll tell you," Calvins said from behind them, raising his hand as if still in high school.

"What is this, seaman intellectual day?" Bernardo asked.

"Petty Officer Bernardo, what are the contacts doing?"

"Same thing as before, Senior Chief. They are steady on bearings 225, 240, 010, and 080. No change in cavitations. They could be approaching, but if they are, they're doing it at a constant speed. I have not detected any increase in decibel level to indicate they're closing, but then I don't know how far out they are." He turned and looked at Agazzi. "How's this for a guess? They fired torpedoes and the torps ran out of fuel?"

"We've discussed that option already," Keyland replied. "If they meant to sink us, they would have already fired another salvo."

"Well, I think that is what they're going to do."

"You could be right," Agazzi said, patting Bernardo on the shoulder. "Let's hear what Seaman Calvins has to say." Agazzi nodded at the sound-powered telephone talker. "Go ahead."

"We've been conducting UUV operations for over five months. And during our fight with the North Korean submarine, we used UUVs. This isn't our first contact that was a Chinese submarine. What if they've been shadowing us this whole time? If so, wouldn't they have a database like the Office of Naval Intelligence database that Petty Officer Bernardo uses? Wouldn't they know the difference between a torpedo and a UUV by now?"

Agazzi nodded. "Good logic trail, Seaman Calvins. You are probably right, but then they would also know that these UUVs have an explosive warhead of five hundred pounds that would sink them."

"I think Tommy is right," MacPherson added. "The Chinese know we have UUVs in the water. They also know the speed of them and the speed of the UUVs is slower than a torpedo. They have an idea how far away we are, probably a better idea than we do as to their location because we are on top of the water. Since they know where we are and they know when we launched our UUVs, they can extrapolate the speed from the cavitations of the screw and know how far away the UUV is from them."

"When they think we've come as close as we should, they'll disappear," Gentron added quietly.

Agazzi looked at the young seaman.

Calvins pushed the right side of his helmet against his head.

Then he pushed the talk button on the cumbersome mouthpiece. "Roger, Combat." He looked at Agazzi. "Senior Chief, they expect the helicopters overhead to contact in the next couple of minutes. Then, the helicopters are going to launch a sonobuoy barrier prior to dipping their sonars. They are going to pinpoint the submarines' locations."

Gentron turned in his seat. "Are they going to attack them?"

Calvins shrugged. "There are two helicopters per submarine. At least one in each of the four formations has a Mark-45 torpedo."

Gentron looked at Agazzi. "If we go active on those submarines, Senior Chief, they are going to think we are preparing to launch an airborne torpedo against them. They know our tactics."

"That should make them disappear quicker," Bernardo said.

"That could also make them launch another salvo."

"Just because we go active?" Bernardo asked, disbelief in his voice.

"They may not fire when we go active," Agazzi said. "But they'll recognize when a torpedo is dropped and it goes active. They'd still have sufficient time to fire another eight."

"They could fire 32," Gentron said.

"32?"

"Yes, Senior Chief. They have eight torpedo tubes each in the bow. What if they fixed all of them at once?"

"We couldn't stop 32 torpedoes," MacPherson said.

"Senior Chief, wouldn't you say that is another reason that shows Seaman Gentron is probably right?" Keyland added. "If they had wanted to sink us, they could have fired a massive torpedo attack against us."

"It's hard to fire eight at one time. Too much intensity in the bow, but they could have fired them one after the other," Agazzi added.

"We shouldn't fire on them, Senior Chief," Gentron added. He looked up at Agazzi, his eyes shiny.

The young man has scared himself, Agazzi thought. *He has also frightened all of us.*

Agazzi eased by the consoles to the ladder leading up, quickly climbing to the top level and moving to the intercom system connected with Combat. A moment later, he was talking with Commander Stapler.

ZEICHNER walked across the canopy of Sea Base, heading toward the hatch they originally came up. It had been easy to take back leadership from Montague when they discovered Dr. Zheng was not in the crow's nest. He knew when they entered the tower that Dr. Zheng would be elsewhere, but the exercise pulled them back together as a team with him in charge. He had to get them to willingly follow him. Not run off on wild-goose chases or unorganized searches.

"Where are we going, Boss?" Gainer asked from his left.

"If he wasn't in the crow's nest and not in Combat Information Center, where do you think he is?" Montague added.

Zeichner smiled at both of them. "I have no idea."

"No idea! Then we should stop and think about where we think he could be, prioritize the options, and search each one in order," Montague said, slowing her walk.

Zeichner kept ambling forward toward the hatch. Out of the corner of his eye, he saw Gainer glance at Montague and then back at him. When Gainer disappeared from his peripheral vision for a moment, Zeichner thought the impetus had shifted back to Montague, but the man quickly regained step with Zeichner. Zeichner let out a mental sigh. A second later, Montague joined on the right.

"I don't understand how we can find him if we don't know where he is," she said.

Zeichner stopped at the hatch and looked directly at Montague, his back to Gainer. "Where does everyone go when they have finished work, whether the work is legal or illegal? Where do they go?"

She shrugged.

"They go home," Zeichner said. "Home is where you sleep. Home is where you have your belongings. Home is where a man, or a woman, feels safe and able to relax."

"Home? On Sea Base?"

Zeichner smiled. "You're new to the game, Angie. Home can be anything from a million-dollar mansion to a homeless campground on the banks of the Mississippi. It's where you sleep. It's what you call your place."

"Then he's heading back to the *Regulus*," Gainer offered.

Zeichner took a step back so both Gainer and Montague were beside him. "Right on target, Kevin. He may not be there when we get there, but eventually, Dr. Zheng is going to return to his quarters. When he does, we'll be waiting."

Montague's eyebrows furrowed. "But if he isn't there, then he could be anywhere." A motion with her arm encompassed Sea Base. "And doing anything while we wait in his state room. Don't you think that is risky?"

Zeichner nodded. "If we don't go where we definitely know he will show eventually, we'll be wandering around this huge man-made island searching for him forever."

"What if he is intent on sabotaging Sea Base; blowing it up?"

Zeichner's lower lip pushed into the upper for a moment as he thought about her question. "We have not had any problems since the death of the God's Army person over four months ago." He put his hands on his hips and shook his head. "No, this man doesn't want to blow up Sea Base. He just wants to get as much intelligence and data as he can for his country. If he wanted to blow up Sea Base, he could have done it many times during the past five months."

"He's an American citizen," Gainer said.

Zeichner shook his head. "He may think so, Kevin, but in my book, when the man started giving away our technology and secrets to another nation, he lost his right to citizenship. He lost his right to freedom. And he definitely lost his right to get off Sea Base before we catch him."

"So, you're convinced the spy is Dr. Zheng?" Montague asked.

Zeichner looked at Gainer and pointed at the hatch. The younger man opened the hatch, lifting the heavy door. Zeichner started down the ladder with Montague following. Zeichner was on the first platform of the four-story-high ladders leading down when the hatch clanged shut behind him. He heard Gainer twist the watertight lever securing it before starting down toward the main deck. They were silent as they descended, the clanging of the metal steps mixed with the noise of Zeichner's rapid breathing.

At the bottom of the ladders, Zeichner stopped. The others waited for him to catch his breath. A couple of minutes passed before Zeichner turned to Montague. "Angie, I heard your question. No, I don't know if he is the one Headquarters thinks is on board. I'm not even sure we have a foreign agent on board, but they think we do and obviously you think we do also."

"But . . ."

Zeichner held up his hand. "Kevin and I have given all eight suspects an in depth look. Four of them have no access to any classified material. They are seldom topside where the most sophisticated weapons systems are located. And none of the four have any reason to be near the UUV compartment—the other new technology we are testing.

"Two of the remaining four are providing technical assistance in the engine rooms of the Fast Sealift Ships. Both of them are in their mid-sixties because they are the only ones who have any experience with the 1970s engines steering those ships.

"That leaves two: Dr. Zheng and a David Bassett. Mr. Bassett is handicapped, but he does work in the server farm. He is in the right place where a foreign agent could download everything he or she would want, and then sink Sea Base by pulling the proverbial cord."

"Maybe we should be looking at him instead of Dr. Zheng?" Montague asked. "Sounds as if he might be . . ."

Zeichner shook his head. He lifted his hand and waved it a couple of times while glancing down for a moment at his feet. "No way. Mr. Bassett has been doing this work for over thirty years. He has been investigated more times than the two of you put together. He is in a wheelchair most of the time because of severe joint problems, and the paucity of handicapped facilities within Sea Base precludes him from ever leaving the vicinity of the server farm in the main cargo hold of *Pollux*.

"Additionally, during his thirty-plus years with the Defense Information Systems Agency, Mr. Bassett has been polygraphed a minimum of four times. And not just your counterintelligence polygraph, but the full-scope polygraph."

"Full-scope polygraph?"

"Yep, sometimes referred to as the lifestyle poly."

"Then, that leaves Dr. Zheng."

"That leaves Dr. Zheng."

Zeichner held up one finger. "Though we are barred from racial profiling, Headquarters believes the agent is Chinese. Dr. Zheng is Chinese American. Two . . ." A second finger went up. "He has a job that keeps him topside as much as he wants. He doesn't have the highest security tickets to get him into some of the more restricted spaces, but he has unfettered access to any ship, most compartments, and anything topside." Zeichner lowered his hand. "Look at where he had himself assigned for General Quarters; the highest point on the ship where he could photograph and see everything."

"You're right, Boss," Gainer said. "When I talked with the young sailor in the crow's nest earlier, he said Dr. Zheng should have been there."

Zeichner lifted three fingers. "A third indicator."

"Did the sailor know where he was?" Montague asked.

"I asked if he had seen him. He said no, but that he'd be easy to spot because Dr. Zheng was never without his binoculars or camera strung around his neck."

Zeichner chuckled. "Something, isn't it? Here we are in the Pacific Ocean where we may have to fight the most populous nation on this planet. A country that is the economic powerhouse of the world and that holds nearly a third of the United States debt, and they have someone walking freely about Sea Base watching everything and photographing anything he wants."

"How does he get the information to them?"

Zeichner looked at Gainer. "We'll know that when we arrest him."

"I would like to try the ploy Headquarters proposed before we arrest him," Montague said. "That would be the fourth nail in his coffin, if he is truly the person we want."

"We will have to ask the Air Force and get their buy-in. Asking them to leave the panels of one of their stealth bombers open without anyone around is like asking . . ." He glanced at Gainer and then Montague. "I don't know, it's just they won't like it."

"I would still like to discuss it with them."

Gainer scratched his head. "Angie, you wanted to find him and arrest him a few minutes ago. If we arrest him, how are we going to have time to arrange the Air Force trap?"

"Well, we should arrest him if we discover him spying," she said, the words coming in jerks. "But the trap we planned at Headquarters would prove it."

Zeichner nodded. "Okay, we can try that if you want, but for now, let's go see if he's in his stateroom. And if he isn't, then we may invite ourselves inside to wait."

TWELVE

"Raptor Formation, this is Mother; steady on course one-nine-zero, descend to angels twenty."

"Roger, Mother," Johnson acknowledged. "Descending to twenty thousand feet."

Franklin was glad Johnson confirmed Mother meant feet and not meters, though meters would have meant them ascending. Fighting in the four-dimensional battle space of air meant that course, speed, altitude, and time were everything. They were the four guiding principles of knowing where everyone was at, where everyone was going, where everyone was leaving, and what the hell was going on at what time.

"Mother, Black Leader; leveling at two thousand meters. Steady on course two-two-zero."

"Roger. Raptor-10 Formation; request you slow your speed to allow separation to increase to fifty miles between you and Raptor Leader Formation."

"Roger, Mother," came Crawford's deep bass voice over the airways.

Separation! Franklin's eyes narrowed. Separation, hell; he wanted the two additional Raptors right up here alongside him—not sitting on some aerial grandstand watching the fight.

"Raptor 10; you are the reserve force. Shortly, I will be fully engaged with Raptor Leader and Black formations. You are to take whatever actions necessary to maintain this constant separation, but prepared to engage when I so order. Copy?"

"Roger, Mother. I copy."

On Franklin's heads-up display in the cockpit, the distance between the two Raptor formations began to increase. He hoped the British knew what the hell they were doing, because he sure as hell didn't. The more F-22A fighters around him right now, the better he'd feel. A vision of a pregnant Connie standing alongside Fast Pace's hospital bed, holding his hand while she held their daughter's hand in her other hand, intruded for a few seconds into his thoughts.

"All fighters this circuit," the Air Intercept Controller on board the British aircraft carrier broadcast. "Situation report. We have multiple bogies—estimate sixteen, emerging from land splatter along the China coast, heading toward the engagement area. The six J-12 fighters continue to approach Black and Raptor Leader Formations. Raptor-10 formation is in reserve. Sea Base is shifting control of additional F-22A fighters under call sign Raptor 20 to Mother control. Raptor 20 is two-fighter formation that will not arrive in engagement area prior to the approaching aircraft from the mainland. *Elizabeth* has launched four fighters for overhead combat air patrol and to protect the fleet. They are to your north. *Elizabeth* battle group is turning to course zero-two-zero at this time."

Franklin looked at the heads-up display on his cockpit windshield and saw the friendly icons about two hundred miles from his location orbiting to the north. The British had their battle group protected, while it increased distance between the ships and the approaching aircraft. He glanced to where Sea Base should be on the display, and saw a lone fighter orbiting overhead. With six of the seven operational Raptors on board Sea Base heading toward this center of gravity, it meant only one remained to protect the vulnerable Navy experiment from air attack.

"Mother, this is Raptor Leader; what are your intentions?"

Franklin was slightly startled by the question, but not surprised Johnson was asking. Patience was a virtue little enjoyed by Johnson and few who believed it existed. But at this time and in this place, information was something he wanted also. Being a mushroom and kept in the dark was unlike what he or other Air Force pilots were accustomed to. Usually, everyone knew everything. You kept to a pattern until you were fully engaged. Then, combat became a personal thing between you, your enemy, and whatever God you worshipped, though God was the wingman few thought about until after the engagement.

"Raptor Leader, my intentions are to control the sky. At this time, we do."

"Roger, but shouldn't we make arrangements for engaging the approaching bogies?" Johnson asked. "Sixteen would vastly outnumber us."

"Yeah," Franklin said aloud. "Ought to send Tight End and his wingman up to join us." That would be a sight to behold when those conventional fighters were splashed by the F-22As.

Seconds passed before the AIC answered. "Raptor Leader, understand your concern, but real danger to control of the sky are the J-12s approaching you. Coastline bogies will not arrive in engagement area for twenty-five minutes. We are in process of launching additional fighters to assist with that engagement."

"Our data links are not showing those J-12s, Mother. We show no bandits approaching," Johnson replied. "We do have Black Formation on display."

"Bandits are approaching. On this you have to trust me. At this time, the bandits are less than sixty miles away on course zero-four-zero at an estimated altitude of 6500 meters. For certain reasons, we are unable to enter them in the data system."

"Roger," Johnson replied.

"How do they know that?" Franklin asked on the formation circuit. He knew Crawford and his wingman heard his question.

"Must be something with their data systems."

"Or they have something we don't," Franklin added.

"Sixty miles is about five minutes at this speed," Johnson said.

"Black Leader, this is Mother; prepare for rapid ascent at my command."

Two clicks came across the frequency.

"Raptor Leader Formation; worst case approaching you is a quick missile release. Engagement in less than four minutes."

"Worst case? What's best case?" Johnson broadcast.

"Best case is they pass by you before their controller tells them to launch."

Two clicks on the microphone acknowledged the AIC's comment.

"Black Leader, stand by."

Two clicks on the microphone acknowledged the AIC's order.

"What the hell is going on?" Franklin asked himself. Here they were fighting the first stealth air-to-air combat in history and he had no idea where the enemy was, but the British controller apparently did. And all they were getting was a bunch of verbal warnings without any data stream to show them the battle space. Black Formation was below and headed up toward the approaching bandits. Crawford and his two F-22As were northwest and above Black Formation about fifty miles away—five minutes of fast flying time. Five minutes was forever in air combat where an engagement was measured in seconds.

A glint of reflected sunlight to his right caught Franklin's attention. He squinted through the sun visor of his helmet. The glint happened again. Then, two bright reflections occurred simultaneously.

"Major, two o'clock. I have a flight of two aircraft." He touched his throat. Was that his voice with the slight tremor in it? Franklin cleared his throat. "Me, me, me, me," he said aloud. *Better not be me.*

A moment later, Johnson hit her transmit button. "Mother, Raptor Leader; we have visual. Bandits are less than thirty miles from us off to our southwest."

"Roger, Raptor Leader; you are clear to conduct a left-angle approach to intercept on your visual. Keep them on your forward right as you approach."

"They'll see us."

"That's the plan."

"That's the plan!" Franklin transmitted to Johnson and the other Raptors. "What the hell kind of plan is that?"

"Stay off the circuit, Blackman," Johnson replied.

"Hostiles are believed to be at seven thousand meters altitude," the AIC broadcast across the tactical action frequency to both Raptors and Joint Strike Fighters under his control.

23,100 feet, Franklin mentally calculated. On Franklin's heads-up display, two hostile icons appeared near their position. He wondered who put it into the system, whether it was Mother or Johnson. Or even Tight End could have done it, but somewhere someone was thinking. Mother said she couldn't.

"Energize weapons systems, everyone," the AIC broadcast.

This was a load of bullshit as far as he was concerned. Without some sort of valid data profile, they were flying blind.

"Black Leader, Mother; come to course zero-four-zero, rapid ascent to 6500 meters, weapons free, rear-hemispheric approach."

"Holy shit!" Franklin said aloud. "That's about twenty thousand feet."

Franklin pushed his transmit button, glancing once to ensure he was on the formation frequency. "Pickles, we're the bait. The damn British are using us as bait!"

"Bait?"

"Yeah, bait. The J-12s are going to see us, if they haven't already, and they're going to come right at us."

"Good," Johnson said emphatically. "I'm glad something's about to happen. I'm tired of this chasing."

"Chasing? We just saw them a second ago."

"A second here, a second there, and the next thing you know you're talking real time."

She sounded almost giddy with anticipation.

"There's a third one out there somewhere," Franklin added.

"No, there are four more out here. We've just got one formation. There's another formation with three aircraft."

"Then where's the third one of this formation?" Franklin asked.

"Probably near the two we saw."

Franklin leaned as far forward as the straps allowed and

glanced behind him and to his sides. The air was clear as far as his quick glance could tell. But he knew it meant nothing. Aircraft were hard to spot unless you knew exactly where to look or something such as a sunlight reflection or contrail gave them away. Then, you wondered why you didn't see them in the first place.

"Looks as if we are going to be the first to engage," he said.

"Captain Franklin, someone always has to be the first to engage. We're not bait. We are the best of the fighters out here. If someone has to distract them, then it should be us. Think of us as more of the first wave to splash their silly asses."

"Black Formation, this is Mother; steady up at altitude 6200 meters. You are fifteen miles from bandits. Raptor Formation, you have weapons free, and we hold you ten miles from bandits. You are authorized to engage at your convenience."

As Franklin watched, contrails emerged from the rear of the two Chinese fighters as the bandits turned right, heading directly toward them. No doubt about it. They were going to be the first on the scene. Damn! He hoped Black Formation wasn't too far behind them.

"We count two bandits," Johnson broadcast.

Suddenly, Mother erupted over the tactical frequency. "Weapons tight! Weapons tight! I say again to all formations, weapons tight!"

Weapons tight! What the hell was the AIC thinking? The Chinese were coming right at them and they couldn't fire? Franklin reached up to turn the weapons switch off. An inch from the switch, his fingers rubbed together, and then he returned to flying the aircraft. If he needed to fire a missile, it would only take a quick flick of the wrist, and he wouldn't have to rearm the weapons system. It achieved the same thing, and besides, the AIC only said, "Weapons tight"; he did not say to turn the weapon system off.

"Mother, Raptor Leader; I have three bandits dead ahead approaching. Request weapons free."

"Raptor Leader, request denied. Orders are weapons tight. You are authorized to fire only if they fire on you first."

In a near scream, Johnson shouted, "They have already fired on us. They shot twelve missiles at Weasel."

"Negative, Raptor Leader, twelve bogies were in the air that we interpreted as missiles. We have no confirmation they were missiles."

"Weasel said . . ."

"Raptor Leader, Mother; descend to angels thirteen immediately, diving turn to the right."

Without thought, Franklin flipped his fighter to the side. In front and on his right, Johnson's fighter dove also. In tandem formation, the two Raptor fighters headed nearly vertically toward the new altitude. Why in the hell they were diving, he had no idea. Without warning, a single bandit emerged through the sparse cloud cover at twelve thousand feet in a rolling turn, heading upward toward them.

Johnson broke right, Franklin left. The Chinese fighter zipped between them. The turbulence of the air wake shook Franklin's aircraft as the bandit passed behind him.

"Steady at current altitude," the AIC ordered.

Franklin pulled back sharply on the stick, leveling the aircraft up.

It was the missing third J-12 of the approaching formation. If they had not been in a rolling dive, the Chinese would have surprised them from the rear. How in the hell did the British know where the Chinese fighter was? They were stealth fighters and neither he nor any of the other Raptor pilots knew where the J-12s were. Must be an overhead something or other they were using, he told himself. When mysterious stuff happens, it's always the eyes in the sky that know the truth.

"What the fuck!" Franklin shouted.

"Keep off the circuit!" Johnson shouted back. "Reform, level up. I have angels ten."

"Raptor Leader Formation, report status."

"One Chinese fighter came up beneath us, Mother. We do not have a visual. Believe we have lost him. He was ascending when we passed. Request weapons free to engage."

"Negative, Raptor Leader. You are at angels ten; steady up at current altitude and report. Turn to course one-six-zero. Formation of three J-12s is attempting rear-hemispheric approach on your formation. Follow my orders explicitly, please."

"Roger, Mother. Steady at ten thousand feet."

Franklin eased up on the left of Johnson's aircraft, slightly to the rear of her aircraft about one aircraft length. She started to turn left; he turned left with her, trying to keep her in sight as his view of her became obstructed in the turn.

"Black Leader, increase speed. Raptor Formation is about to engage. You will be coming from above. For both formations, please do not collide with each other. Raptor, you are occupying the horizontal plane in this engagement. Black Formation will be shooting through on the vertical. If both will listen to my instructions, we will send the Chinese running for cover with their tails between their legs."

"How about we send them swimming for the coast?" Franklin asked himself.

"I see the Chinese fighters," Johnson broadcast. "They are approaching our left side. About ten miles from us."

"Roger, Raptor Leader; they are in the system. You should be seeing them on your display."

"That's a negative, Mother. I have nothing on my display since the visual we reported earlier."

Suddenly, on the display, the three bandits appeared. There was no radar video return beneath the hostile icons, but at least it gave Franklin some satisfaction as to where they were.

"Raptor-10 Formation, this is Mother. You are to start descent and close the engagement area to twenty-five miles."

"Roger," Crawford acknowledged.

"Glad someone remembered the reserves."

"Raptor-20 Formation, request you increase your speed. Steady up on course two-four-zero, angels fourteen."

"Mother, Raptor Leader; this will increase separation between us and Raptor-20 Formation."

"Roger, Raptor Leader; that is my intention."

The British had the skies filled with aircraft and from the voice of the Air Intercept Controller, you would think it was a bright afternoon walk through Hyde Park. No excitement in his voice. Everything calm. Maybe the AIC was coming from the pub. Franklin knew they had pubs on board Royal Navy ships. From what the Navy officers on board Sea Base told him, every Navy in the world but the American Navy had pubs on them. Places to have an after-work drink and build camaraderie. When this was over, he could use a little camaraderie-building.

"Mother, Raptor Leader; steady on course one-six-zero, angels ten."

"Roger, sharp ascent to angels sixteen, please. That is angels sixteen in feet."

"Black Leader, do you have visual on bandit formation?"

"Negative, Mother. We have them on the heads-up display."

"Status?"

"Black Formation steady on course one-four-zero at six thousand meters."

"Start slow descent, but prepare for quick adjustment depending on imminent engagement between Raptor Leader and bandits."

Two quick clicks acknowledged the command.

"Raptor Leader, weapons tight?"

"Roger, Mother; weapons tight," Johnson replied sharply.

Franklin grinned at the thought of all that anger encapsulated within the glass bubble that made up the 360-degree cockpit windshield of Johnson's Raptor.

"Raptor Leader Formation, at my command, you will do a sharp left turn, ascending rapidly."

Before Johnson could ask why, the AIC broadcast the command. "Now, Raptor Leader; sharp left turn to course one-eight-zero, near vertical ascent."

Franklin flipped his aircraft to the left. He lost visual of Johnson, but knew she was in front of him but hidden by the bottom of his fuselage. His right hand pulled the stick back while his left pushed the throttle forward. The Raptor responded smoothly sending his aircraft heading upward. Franklin pulled the stick back slightly. He told himself that no aircraft in the world could catch him now. But running wasn't something he wanted to do.

"Raptor Leader Formation, be advised you have three J-12s on your tail. They are separating from you at this time.

"Black Formation; Raptor Leader and hostile formation have passed your altitude. Start rapid ascent, come to course one-four-zero during ascent."

"Mother, Black Leader; we have them on visual. They have passed by us. Request visual intercept."

"Roger, Black Leader; cleared for visual intercept.

"Raptor 10, do you have battle-space awareness of the players?" the AIC asked Major Crawford.

"Roger, Mother. We are approximately twenty miles from engagement at angels sixteen."

"You are to ascend to angels thirty and close the engagement. Here is the plan . . ."

"There's a plan?" Franklin asked aloud, his body pressed against the seat as his fighter flew at a near-vertical angle. He glanced to his right. Johnson had come up alongside and moved ahead of him about one aircraft length. They were back in formation. Instead of him maneuvering for position to reform the formation, she had done it.

"Raptor Leader Formation is in rapid ascent, passing angels twenty at this time. When they pass you, you are to conduct an active and intrusive identification pass through the center of the Chinese formation."

"Intrusive identification pass?" Crawford asked.

"Roger, that is correct. That is a pass where one formation is traveling vertical while the other is traveling horizontal. The intent of your pass is to break apart the hostile formation."

"That seems dangerous," Crawford replied.

"Oh, yes, it is very dangerous, so be careful when you fly through the Chinese formation."

"Roger, Mother."

"After the pass, Raptor-10 Formation, you will continue outboard and establish a combat air patrol twenty-five miles from the engagement area. Do you understand?"

"Roger. One pass. Break up enemy formation. Survive it and then set up CAP between engagement area and mainland."

"Very good," the AIC acknowledged. "Raptor Leader Formation, as soon as Raptor 10 completes the disruption, you will flip from ascent to descent and engage the bandit formation. Weapons are to remain tight. You are not authorized to fire."

"Can we use our fire-control radar?" Johnson asked. "At least scare them?"

"Negative. To all flights, no fire-control radar, no missile fire-control seekers, and weapons are tight." Without waiting for a reply, the AIC continued. "Black Leader; upon the intrusive identification pass by Raptor-10 Formation, you are to engage the Chinese formation from the rear. Both Raptor Leader and Black Leader Formations; once again, be advised you are not to collide as you pass each other."

Multiple clicks hit the tactical frequency.

Franklin's lower lip pressed into his upper as he smiled and nodded. *Wow!* he thought. *What a great way to mess up a pilot's day.* He hadn't figured out what the Royal Navy AIC was doing with all this maneuvering. *Wonder why Raptor-10 Formation is not reengaging.*

"Passing angels twenty-nine," Johnson reported.

"Roger, Raptor Leader; bandit formation is still trying to catch up, but have dropped behind you about six thousand feet."

"Angels twenty-nine," Franklin said aloud.

"Mother, Raptor 10; we are five miles from engagement zone. We have the contrails in sight. Request permission to engage."

"Roger, you are cleared for intrusive pass-through, Raptor 10. A pass and identification that disrupts their formation will most likely cause them to break off Raptor Leader. It will also break up their formation integrity."

"Roger; misspoke."

"Roger. You are cleared for intercept and pass-through."

"Say again?"

"I said you may conduct your pass and identification at your convenience, but right now would be a great time," the AIC said, speaking so quickly the words ran together.

Franklin watched the icons approach in the heads-up display. What he wouldn't give right now to be able to see what was going on behind him.

"Raptor Leader Formation, at my command. Three, two, one . . . Now! Direct reverse course and start descent. Weapons remain tight."

Six thousand feet behind them were the Chinese flying upward; Major Crawford and his formation flying across; and beneath those two formations, four Royal Navy F-35s heading toward them. This was going to be one crowded piece of air real estate in about thirty seconds.

* * *

BEHIND Franklin, the three J-12s had a visual on the two Raptors. The Chinese leader had the aircraft at full throttle knowing that the J-12 had altitude superiority over the Raptor. When they passed 35,000 feet, that superiority would allow them to start closing. He smiled as he thought of the look on the Americans' faces when the J-12s rolled through their formation. He said as much to his two wingmen, who were enjoying this combat action even if they had been refused permission to fire on the Americans. Nothing would give him more satisfaction and honor than to land with two kills for the side of his cockpit. He glanced down at his weapons panel. He'd never secured the weapons panel as ordered. Keeping it armed and ready was the same thing. But, if needed, it would not require him to go through the seconds of motion necessary to arm and fire. This way, all he had to do was flick a switch, hit a button, and missiles would fill the air. Air combat was quick, rapid, and those who made the right first decision lived. He took a deep breath and told the wingmen to keep in formation. He wondered briefly where the British fighters had disappeared to, but Ground Control would tell him where they were when they found them. He looked up at the heat signature coming from the exhausts of the F-22As. What mattered were the targets dead ahead of him.

A dark shape flew past in front of him. He pulled the stick to the right, nearly hitting the wingman on that side. He pulled the throttle back. The J-12 dropped downward. He rolled the aircraft to the right, shouting into the microphone at the two wingmen to take evasive action. Where did that aircraft come from?

A second aircraft zoomed between him and the wingman on the right. They were F-22As. The distinctive cockpit was an easy identifier during that split second as the American fighter flew by. Where was his wingman on the left? The J-12 on the right disappeared in a burst of speed, heading upward. The Chinese leader rolled the fighter to the left. His left wingman was gone. Did they shoot him down? He was shouting into his microphone for answers. Both wingmen answered, but neither of them knew where the others were. In that brief moment when Crawford's Raptor-10 Formation flew through the bandits, the integrity of the hostile fighter formation had been lost just as Mother predicted.

Mainland Ground Control came onto the circuit, ordering everyone to be quiet as he began re-forming the Chinese J-12 formation.

The Chinese leader saw a wingman ahead of him and started toward the other J-12. Two were better than one, but not as good as three.

Then, between the two of them, a pair of Raptors appeared. He pulled back on the stick, shouting for the other wingman to ascend and re-form on his left side. Behind him somewhere were the two Raptors. Were they the same ones he had been closing on? Couldn't be. He had had them visually and they were running for altitude. There must be a second—even a third American formation out here. He pushed the transmit key and told Ground Control. Where was the other J-12 formation?

The left wingman appeared alongside him. The leader saw a shadow on his right, smiled, and let out a sigh of relief. His other wingman had found them. His formation was back together. As the aircraft eased up alongside, the smile faded. It was a British-marked F-35 fighter. Where did he come from? The leader looked to the left, and on the other side of the J-12 wingman, a second F-35 flew in formation. The Chinese leader quickly looked back to the right. The pilot in the aircraft raised his hand and did a two-finger salute. the Chinese leader didn't know what else to do. He returned the salute. At least the enemy recognized him as a fellow fighter professional.

He looked at his weapons panel. He could easily engage, but they had his formation bracketed. Four—maybe six Americans, and he could see three British fighters. His missiles wouldn't be out of the bays before they shot the two of them down.

The Chinese fighter pilot relayed the situation to Ground Control, who ordered them back to the mainland. He turned and nodded to the British fighter pilot, gave him another two-finger salute, and turned the J-12s toward the mainland. Five minutes later, two other F-22As flew by him. By now, he had lost count of how many fighter aircraft were between him and the coast of Taiwan. It could have been any number between six and ten. How this happened would be a question he would be fielding in the days to come.

"MOTHER, this is Black Leader; the Chinese are turning toward the mainland."

"Roger. Raptor Leader Formation, join up with Black Formation. Raptor 10, this is where we confuse them further. What is your current altitude and course?"

"We are at angels twenty-eight and in a racetrack orbit about thirty miles from where Black Formation is located."

"Roger, ascend to angels thirty and come to course one-one-zero. The Chinese formations are returning to the mainland. Keep weapons tight."

"You said formations."

"Roger, the second J-12 formation was south of you and unable to participate in the exercise. The formation Black Leader passed down the sides is the one you disrupted minutes ago."

"Roger."

Franklin watched the icons close on his heads-up display even as he followed Mother's directions bringing the two pairs of allied fighters into one four-aircraft formation. He was thoroughly impressed. Their tactic had always been to hit the enemy head-on and splash their asses. This had been more fun, more aerially challenging, and knowing how he would feel, those Chinese pilots were going to be one embarrassed bunch of fighter pilots at the officers club tonight. His eyebrows bunched. Do the Chinese have officers clubs?

THIRTEEN

"What do you think is going on?" Stonemeyer asked Andrew as the two started their umpteenth circuit of their area. "Have you ever been in combat? I was on this in the Sea of Japan when the Koreans tried to board us. You should have seen the master chief. He was a hero. Fought them single-handedly with the help of Potts and Mad Mary."

"Mad Mary—don't you think that is a horrid name for a woman?"

"Petty Officer Showdernitzel?" Stonemeyer asked, shaking his head. "Naw, she likes it . . . sometimes. Besides, it fits her. Her first name is Mary and she is as mad as the Mad Hatter."

"She is crude," Andrew said with a trace of disgust. "She curses, she smokes, and she acts as if she is a man. She is an example of what is wrong with our nation today. God never intended for women to be . . ."

Stonemeyer put his hand on Andrew's arm, causing Andrew to jerk away.

The look on the sailor's face caused Andrew to realize his involuntary reaction hurt Stonemeyer's feelings. "I'm sorry. I'm not used to people touching me."

Stonemeyer looked down at his feet and continued walking.

Andrew walked alongside the young man, saying a silent prayer of forgiveness for his actions. Stonemeyer's affliction of massive acne was God's gift—God's burden. It was the leprosy of the modern age. If God decided Andrew was to wear that burden, then he would be honored. He reached over and touched Stonemeyer on the shoulder. "I apologize, brother. When you touched me, I jumped. I should recognize that you are blessed by Him whom we worship with all our might." Andrew pointed skyward.

Stonemeyer shrugged. "That's okay," he said with a shrug. "I should be used to it by now." He waved his hand in a circle in front of his face. "I have used every cream they have in sick bay." One arm cradled the shotgun, so he stuck out the other arm. "I cake myself with sunscreen every morning before I come out." He dropped the arm and shrugged. "It does no good. It is as if I have these small volcanoes beneath my skin sending bubbles of oil erupting over my body." He let out a self-conscious laugh. "You should see my sheets in the morning."

Andrew dropped his hand from the man's shoulder. The image caused him to shudder. God was a loving God, but then why did He demand so many sacrifices from His followers? He shut his eyes for a moment and begged forgiveness for such a question.

Stonemeyer shifted the weapon to the cradle of the other arm, raising his left wrist to glance at his watch. "Mad Mary will be here soon," he said. His head spun toward Andrew. "I'm sorry. Petty Officer Showdernitzel will be here soon."

Andrew glanced around, seeing no one. "How do you know she'll be here soon?"

"She likes to make the rounds during GQ. Check on *her* boatswain mates . . ." He raised his two hands, nearly dropping the shotgun, to make a sign of two quotation marks. "To make sure they have enough water. You watch. Some may call her Mad Mary, but she sure as hell can be like a gruff old mother when she lets her guard down."

"She should be on land, bearing children and taking care of her husband."

Stonemeyer laughed. "You really believe that, don't you?" He shook his head. "I think you may be of a different religion than most of us." Stonemeyer's eyes scrunched as he looked at Andrew. "What religion are you? You're not Mormon, are you?" When Andrew failed to answer, Stonemeyer continued. "Showdernitzel; she is the same age as most of us, but for all her grossness and profanity, down deep, here"—Stonemeyer patted his chest a couple of times with his left fist—"she has a heart of gold."

Andrew felt the man's eyes on him, but continued to look straight ahead.

"Do you think it is possible to have Christian values and not be a Christian? I think of Petty Officer Showdernitzel that way."

Andrew shook his head. "I'm of a Protestant sect from West Virginia." He continued walking, ignoring that Stonemeyer had quit walking. "We have members in West Virginia, Kentucky, and Ohio. We are the true religion. Dedicated to the facts of the Bible and dedicated to hastening the return of Our Lord Savior. We believe you can have Christian values and live a Christianlike life, but if you don't accept Him, God, and the Holy Spirit, then you are not a Christian and all the good deeds pale beside the atrociousness of walking outside of His word."

Stonemeyer again walked silently alongside him.

Andrew would have expected nothing less.

After a couple of minutes, Stonemeyer said, "I think you may be more extreme in your views than we six who get together every night." He poked his chest. "I'm Catholic. We have a couple of Southern Baptists. . . ."

Catholic! Popery, as his father intoned at every meeting. Popery heretics who have stolen God's words for man's gold. Popery where a single man determines God's word on earth. He shuddered at the idea of being in the vicinity of a pagan. No wonder Stonemeyer could bestow God's love on . . . what did the demon call her, Mad Mary? He looked at the edge of the deck ahead of them and thought of how many heretics filled the decks of Sea Base.

"And I think Damon is Methodist. So, there you have it. With you, there will be six Protestants and me—the lone Catholic fighting to show you Protestants the right way to God's salvation." Stonemeyer's laugh was cut short when he saw the expression on Andrew's face.

"You know, Al Jolson, you make me nervous," he said quietly.

"You have seemed nervous since I met you."

Stonemeyer nodded, then tripped over one of the raised tie-downs on the deck. He quickly recovered. "Not only am I the nervous sort, but I'm sort of clumsy also," he said with a nervous laugh.

"What are those?" Andrew asked, pointing at the tie-down.

At equal distances across the expanse of the Sea Base canopy, small holes in the deck crisscrossed by two stout metal rods covered the deck.

"Oh, those," Stonemeyer said with enthusiasm over being able to show his knowledge. "They are used to tie down stuff such as aircraft, equipment—you know? Keeps the wind from blowing them away and holds them in place until we need them."

Stonemeyer pointed toward the quarterdeck area that had been roped off by the boatswain mates. Less than thirty minutes ago, they had been standing in formation in that area. "Petty Officer Showdernitzel and Jaime are coming."

Andrew grunted in acknowledgment. In that moment, he understood the danger of Sea Base to God's Army. A microcosm of what America had become where equality existed across all diversities and sexes. Completely counter to what the Bible demanded in God's word. He understood better than his father why this floating island was one more of man's follies delaying Armageddon.

AGAZZI put the telephone down. "Combat says when the helicopters reach the search area, they are going to deploy a sonobuoy barrier along the line of bearings."

Bernardo reached up and pressed an icon above the console. "The sonobuoy receiver is still active, Senior Chief. When they deploy them, we should receive the signals and the SQR-25 will integrate them into the rainfall display."

Sonobuoys were small, long devices dropped from antisubmarine helicopters and aircraft and designed to pick up the passive noise of a submarine. With sufficient sonobuoys deployed in a pattern, the detections can triangulate a contact and provide the information back to a system such as the AN/SQR-25 manned by Bernardo. The system would take the noise signals, their signal strength, and the lines of bearings from the sonobuoys to identify the location of the submarine. And all of this was done most times without the submarine ever knowing they were being targeted.

When the SH-36 LAMPS helicopters worked in pairs, one usually carried a torpedo. After locating the submarines, the armed helicopter could scoot ahead to where the contact was located. Once there, it could launch its Mark-45 torpedo immediately, or most likely, it would dip its own sonar from the helicopter to beneath the waves to confirm the location of the submarine.

Two tactics were available for the launching helicopter. It could launch based on the passive information, or it could turn on its active sonar and ping the submarine. The ping gave the exact location. The ping also told the submarine it had been detected, and like most submarines, it would go into a dive, maneuvering, changing speeds in a race to lose contact.

The SH-36 and the P-3C Orion ASW patrol aircraft were two of the most powerful antisubmarine assets in the United States Navy. They were also two of the oldest and with no replacements in sight, eventually they would reach an age where they too would join the aircraft graveyard at Davis Monthan Air Force Base just outside Tucson, Arizona. China, following the path of history for new wannabe superpowers, had turned to submarines as the first phase of developing an oceangoing Navy: a world-class fleet capable of projecting its power anywhere in the world.

"I'm getting their signals," Bernardo said.

"Flip the screen," Agazzi said to MacPherson.

"I can't, Senior Chief. I'm trying to control two UUVs right now." He turned in his seat. "How about Calvins? He can remote the screen to one of the screens at maintenance."

"Seaman Calvins," Agazzi said. "How about rigging up one of your spares so we can see the Naval Tactical Data System display?"

The young man smiled. "Sure thing, Senior Chief. I can do that." He reached up to remove the sound-powered telephone helmet.

"Keep that on," Keyland said. "You can do it without having to take that off. Just pull your cord with you."

"Sure thing, LPO."

A couple of minutes later, one of the screens arrayed on top of the maintenance desk showed the remote picture of the NTDS. On a bearing of 240, small blinking icons representing sonobuoys flashed.

"They're bearing 240," Agazzi said.

"Roger; bearing 240. They also have a contact, Senior Chief. How far out are they?"

"About twenty-five nautical miles."

"The submarine is bearing 220 from sonobuoy number one and 190 degrees from number five," Bernardo said, his voice trailing off. A moment later, he shouted, "Contact is bearing 240; range thirty-two nautical miles. Wow! I love it when a plan comes together."

"Calvins!" Keyland shouted. "Pass that to Combat."

At the maintenance desk, Agazzi listened as Calvins passed the information along to Combat. At the AN/SQR-25, Bernardo was passing the computations directly into the NTDS database. The information reached the U.S. units first. Fractions of a second later, the same data was flashing on the British version of NTDS. Two nations; two Navies; one fighting force.

"Senior Chief," Calvins said. "Captain wants to know if we have any refinement on what we think the submarines are doing."

Agazzi looked around at the team, all of whom were staring at him. "Well, team. Do you think they are going to fire or flee?"

"I think if we fire on them, we are going to have one hell of an exciting five minutes until their torpedoes reach Sea Base, followed by pants-filling screams as we go down," Bernardo offered.

"If they fired torpedoes earlier, Senior Chief, those torpedoes never reached us. I think they are just watching us, gathering intelligence," MacPherson said. He looked at Gentron. "Okay, Brain; what do you think?"

Gentron's face turned darker in the blue-lighted space. "I think you're right. I also think they want us to know they're out there. Otherwise, why would they fake a torpedo attack against us?"

"Who said it was fake?" Bernardo snarled. "It could have been one they screwed up."

"That's enough, Pope," Keyland ordered. "If you can't contribute something positive, stay quiet."

"They're just showing us they can do it," Gentron finished.

"They can do it," Agazzi repeated.

"Sometimes, we like to do things just to show people we can do it," Gentron expounded. "That's what they're doing. Maybe this whole military thing is nothing more than China showing the world they can do it."

"Okay, thanks," Agazzi said. He turned to Calvins. "Tell the Skipper we show no further indications of hostility from the contacts. We think they're watching and waiting to see what we do, but we do believe that if we attack, they'll retaliate."

Sweat ran down the young telephone talker's face and Calvins's tongue ran across his lips. Agazzi leaned under the safety rail, reached out, and touched him. "Stay calm," he said quietly. "Just repeat what I told you."

Calvins nodded, pressed the talk button, and relayed Agazzi's words to his counterpart in Combat. Moments later, he told Agazzi the Captain sent his regards.

Agazzi watched the NTDS console as helicopters began laying sonobuoy patterns along the lines of bearings of each of the four contacts. Within ten minutes, Bernardo had inputted the near-precise locations of each of the four submarines. On the NTDS console, Agazzi watched the helicopters move toward those locations. In his mind, he knew each unarmed helo would lower his dipping sonar and keep track of the submarine, while the armed one would be ready for an immediate attack if the Skipper ordered. He hoped it wouldn't come to that. He mentally crossed his fingers. If they had to drop the torpedo, it would take nearly a minute for the Mark-45 to hit the target. In combat, a minute was a very long time, and if the submarine was sitting there with the weapons officer's finger on the launch button, even if they destroyed all four submarines, he would be surprised if most of them failed to launch some torpedoes.

Maybe he should retire after this trip. Then the thought of

putting on those two stars of a master chief petty officer wove across his mind. Becoming one of the top one percent of the military services had been his goal for years. Sometimes, fate has other ideas.

"OKAY, you two," Showdernitzel said from about twenty feet away. "Lay below and take a head break, get yourselves a bottle of water, then get your asses back up here."

Stonemeyer smiled. "Like a mother, I told you," he whispered to Andrew.

Andrew grunted, his eyes narrowing. He would do God a good deed by taking this woman out along with Jacobs. What was he thinking? He took a deep breath and let it out, forcing himself to relax. He had one job assigned by his father. Kill Jacobs and the other man—Agazzi—was the first half of his mission. The second half was to return alive. But since he was a prophet, God might have other ideas for his mission.

"*Capella* is directly below you," Showdernitzel said. "You got thirty minutes to make a head call and get your asses back up here. Potts and I will stand your watch, but others are waiting to take a break too."

Stonemeyer smiled as the two pairs reached each other. He turned to Andrew. "I don't need to go. I'm going to go over to the quarterdeck and tell Damon about you joining us tonight."

Andrew failed to catch the apprehension in Stonemeyer's voice. He had no way of knowing the young sailor regretted inviting him to the Bible study group. Neither could he know that Stonemeyer wanted to warn the other members of what a bad mistake he might have made. Plus, Stonemeyer also wanted reassurance from a fellow worshipper that he had not made a mistake. He wanted someone to remove this apprehension wrapped around his acne-covered body.

Andrew nodded. "How do I get down to the *Capella*?" he asked, trying to keep his voice normal.

"Well, Petty Officer Jolson, you can go down that hatch over there as long as you seal it behind you." Showdernitzel leaned close. "Or we could leave Potts up here and I can show you the way."

His eyes widened in horror at the offer. "I have to go to the bathroom."

She smiled, a gap from a missing tooth along the right side catching his attention. "I think I can find it," he said firmly.

Showdernitzel laughed. "You don't have much of a sense of humor, do you, Al?" She reached out and patted him twice on the shoulder, laughing for a moment before her face hardened. "Listen to me, Al. If you don't relax, you're going to have one lonely deployment. We're all in this together. You don't have to worry. I'm not going belowdecks with you to watch you pee." She shook her head and glanced at his crotch. "Besides, not sure it would be worth the effort."

He took a deep breath. All these shouts of blasphemy and damnation welled up inside of him, but he fought the urge, concentrating on his mission. He had been aboard Sea Base less than a half day, and already knew he could never survive out here away from God's paradise for six months. All he had to do was survive for a month, until they reached Pearl Harbor. Then, he could disappear into the wilderness of West Virginia.

"Well? Are you going to the head or not?"

Stonemeyer started walking toward the quarterdeck. "I'll be back soon."

"Yes," Andrew managed to gasp out.

"Then, go!" Showdernitzel said sharply. "And hurry your ass back."

As he walked away, he heard her say to Potts, "What a dickhead."

It took several seconds for him to figure out how to work the lever to go belowdecks. Once in the stairwell, closing the hatch was easy. A few minutes later, he was stepping onto the main deck of *Capella*.

He did have to go to the bathroom, but how do you find a bathroom on board a ship? He lifted his helmet and scratched his head before stepping off to the left, heading toward the safety lines. Might be a men's room sign somewhere along the sides of the ship. Seeing nothing, he turned aft, heading toward the stern of the ship.

His only familiarity with ships had been the one gained from these hours on board Sea Base. He knew that behind the aft forecastle was a broad area where sailors gathered for their smokes and conversation. Where there is a crowd, there must be a nearby bathroom.

As he neared the covered passageway of the aft forecastle, another person stepped onto the main deck and followed. Andrew stepped onto the aft deck, wondering briefly what the large painted circle on the deck with an X in the center meant. There was no one there. He looked along the bulkhead, and only saw some hatches leading inside. Maybe the bathroom was behind one of these hatches. Andrew glanced at his watch. Ten minutes had passed. The madwoman had told him thirty minutes. If he needed more time, it was his right to take it. It was God's right and God's right was the same as his.

He swung the lever down and pulled open the nearest hatch. He stepped forward, the hatch blocking his vision to the right. But there was no passageway—no bathroom. The hatch opened into a storage compartment filled with lines, buckets, swabs, a couple of fire extinguishers mounted on the back bulkhead. There were some things he had never seen.

Andrew stepped back, grabbing the edge of the hatch, and shoving it shut. Hiding behind the open hatch was Taleb. Startled, Andrew stepped back. "What are you doing here?"

"I should ask you the same thing," Taleb said. "Aren't we at General Quarters?"

Andrew relaxed slightly. "I am on a break and looking for a bathroom."

"A head we call it at sea." Taleb cocked his head. "You don't really know too much about the ships, do you, Al?"

"First time . . ."

"First time for a third-class petty officer? A boatswain mate at that? Kind of hard to believe."

"I've been in school."

"School for a boatswain mate is the deck of a ship. They don't really have a school, but then you know that, don't you?"

Andrew tightened up. He sensed danger. What was this man's problem? He measured their difference, realizing he was taller and heavier than Taleb.

"I know why you're here," Taleb said. "I've known before you boarded that C-130. Not only have I known, but others know also. Did you actually think we would stand aside and let you come out here for whatever nefarious reason you may have?"

Andrew's eyes narrowed. "Why do you think I am out here?" He reached up and pulled the lever down, securing the watertight hatch.

"You are God's Army, aren't you?"

Andrew gasped, his eyes widening. How did he know? "Why do you think that?" he asked, his voice shaken. His mind whirled, trying to figure out how this demon . . . That was it! A demon of Satan confronted him. "God give me strength."

Taleb laughed. "I say that every day when I run into assholes such as you who think they know better than anyone else how we should live our lives. You should have stayed in the hills of West Virginia sowing your seeds of hatred. You should have let your brother . . ."

Brother! He knew about Joshua? Andrew's breathing increased. He was confused. This demon confronting him . . . Confidence flooded Andrew's body and mind. This was part of God's test. Part of God's plan to see if Andrew was a true prophet for the Lord.

". . . Joshua's death go. If you had, you'd be in West Virginia now, being arrested with your father and his followers. . . ."

Andrew looked up, his eyes locking onto the eyes of the demon in front of him. Looking at the abomination of the dark skin shaded by white blood. Brown eyes staring at him, Taleb's face relaxed while Andrew felt his body tensing, ready for the coming battle. Taleb's words broke through his internal battle with one word bubbling to the top: "arrested."

"You arrested my father?" he asked. "God will stop you."

"God is helping us. He doesn't like you any more than you like me or any other person who wants to live their lives as they see fit. You have been responsible for a lot of deaths, Andrew." Taleb shook his head. "Not as many as your old man and his cronies, but you are as responsible as they." Taleb reached forward and tweaked the shirtsleeve of Andrew's dungaree shirt, jerking it a couple of times. "Until you decided you'd avenge your brother's death, we had nothing on you." Taleb laughed. "I'm not even here for you. We didn't even know about you or that you were coming until you arrived in Hawaii. Department of Homeland Security tipped my Ag—people off about you booking a west Pacific voyage to Sea Base." Taleb's lower lip pushed upward into the upper as he nodded a couple of times, looking downward. "You are just an added side benefit."

Without warning, Andrew lunged forward, pushing Taleb backward. Taleb tripped over a rough spot on the deck and fell hard. Andrew jumped on top of him before he could move. "Die, demon!" he said through clenched teeth. "As God—"

Taleb brought his knee up between Andrew's legs, throwing the bigger man off balance. Andrew rolled to the side. The knee had caught him in the upper thigh, missing his crotch by inches.

Taleb rolled to the left away from Andrew, coming up onto his knees in one smooth motion. Andrew pushed himself upright. Taleb stood, his arms and hands out like some wrestler waiting for his opponent to charge.

"I wouldn't do that," Taleb said, flexing his outstretched fingers. "I don't want to hurt you."

Andrew crouched, spreading his hands out also, preparing to get the smaller man within his grasp. He knew his muscles built from years of farmwork and country living were more than a match for the thin frame of the man circling across from him. He turned his head slightly to the right and left. No one to see him kill this man. God works in mysterious ways.

"There's no one here but you and I, Andrew. No one to help you and no one to help me. Just you and I."

"You are a demon. You are my trial sent by God."

"God didn't send me, asshole. I come from a much more worldly group and my mission—unlike yours—is to stop assholes such as you from doing stupid things."

"I will never be arrested."

"I already told you, I'm not here to arrest you. Bring you back to justice? Why? So you can shout your religious bullshit on television and encourage other nutters? No, if we take you, you'll disappear from the face of the earth, or in this case, shipmate, from the face of Sea Base."

"God's justice is the only justice I recognize."

"Stand down, Andrew."

Andrew rushed Taleb, jumping at the last moment to grab the man. Taleb stepped to the side and slammed the back of his hand down on Andrew's neck, near the shoulder. Andrew fell to the deck, his momentum rolling him forward. *He called me by my name,* Andrew thought as he hit. The rough nonskid of the gray metal deck scratched along his face, drawing blood and leaving lines of scratches down his cheeks.

"That must have hurt," Taleb said with a laugh. "I'm so sorry."

Andrew pushed himself up on one arm. He ran his hand along his face, bringing it away covered in blood. Blood of Christ.

Taleb shifted sideways, stepping nearer the safety lines.

Andrew smiled. Hitting the man square would catapult him overboard. Overboard to where sharks weaved their demonic path back and forth in the shadows of the ships. Would the sharks eat the demon or protect him as one of their own?

"I know what you are thinking," Taleb said.

"God is protecting me." Andrew crouched, letting one leg stretch behind him, bending the toe of the boondocker against the deck for traction.

"God didn't do too good with that face. You got blood all over you. Why don't you give up, come with me, and let's get off this contraption they call—"

Andrew launched himself, running at Taleb. He opened his mouth and screamed at the top of his voice. His shoulder caught Taleb on the side, knocking the man against the lines. Taleb used the tension of the line to spin him away from the heavier Andrew. Andrew spun, reached out, and jerked the collar of Taleb's dungaree shirt. The shirt ripped. Taleb's elbow came back and caught Andrew in the nose. The crunch of bone seemed loud between the grunts of the two.

Andrew's grip lessened as the pain of the broken nose roared through his body. Tears streaked from his eyes. He looked up, trying to see Taleb through the red haze of blood and tears.

Taleb stepped back several feet. "Well, look at yourself now, Andrew. The side of your face is ripped and you made me break your nose."

"You are a demon," Andrew said, a whistle through the broken nose accompanying the words.

"That's what my wife says too."

"You are an abomination in the sight of God."

"If it's the God of God's Army, then I consider that a compliment. You people are as dangerous as Al Qaeda. You go through America and through the world blowing things up and killing people because of some misguided belief that if you kill enough people and blow enough things up, Armageddon will happen. You think a bunch of virgins are waiting on the other side for you also?"

"I will kill you," Andrew mumbled.

"What was that?" Taleb asked, placing spread fingers on his chest. "You're going to kill me? Andrew, I think you have the right idea, but I view the scenario differently. I told you, I'm here for another reason. You have drifted into my mission. You complicate it. I could have killed you minutes ago. The choice is yours."

Andrew walked away from the safety line, shifting to the right, trying to line himself up with Taleb. God wanted him to kill this demon. He must fight the good fight for in God's eyes, Andrew knew he was the prophet. "I am the prophet," he mumbled.

Taleb shifted to the left, keeping his distance from Andrew. Every so often, he glanced downward. The aft deck was also the helicopter landing pad. Tie-downs decorated the deck. He had already tripped over one of them.

Andrew never looked down. His gaze was fixed on Taleb. His mind raced trying to figure out how to get a death grip on the demon. Once his hands were around Taleb's neck, the fight would soon be over. Grace would be his with the death of this Taleb.

Taleb tripped again, the man glancing downward as he stepped backward. Andrew leaped forward. He was faster than Taleb expected.

He caught Taleb by the neck. Taleb stomped on Andrew's left foot, near where the ankle connected. The pain caused Andrew to stumble to the left, but his grip remained. He never let go of the man. He had his massive hands around Taleb's neck, squeezing the breath from the demon. God's will filled his being. Taleb was pounding Andrew in the stomach, bringing his knee up, trying to kick him in the crotch. He pulled

Taleb closer. The pain became pleasure with the knowledge of his own personal strength augmented by God's.

Andrew felt Taleb slowing. He was winning. God's will. Andrew stopped moving. He spread his legs to put more strength into the choke hold. Andrew looked down. Taleb's face was turning blue and the man's eyes bulged. He brought his face within inches of Taleb's. "You are dying," he spit into Taleb's face through clenched teeth.

Taleb's lips moved.

"Are you praying?" Andrew gasped out. "You should pray. Maybe God will forgive you for the demon you are."

Taleb's lips moved again. Andrew heard the word "Joshua." His brother's name. He leaned closer; simultaneously, he heard the rattling of the man pulling some air through the choke hold, so Andrew tried to put more strength into it. "What—" he started to say.

Taleb's head came up, the forehead slamming into his broken nose. Simultaneously, the knee came back up, catching him in the crotch.

The pain was excruciating. Andrew stumbled backward a few steps, releasing his grip in the process.

Taleb fell to the deck on one knee, gasping for breath. His eyes watched Andrew, for he knew he could not survive another grip from this wild man. White stars dashed across his eyesight for several seconds.

Andrew reached up to touch his nose, but then saw Taleb watching him. Dropping his hand, he took a flying leap, his legs kicking out, intending to knock Taleb flat. His 220 pounds would knock most any man prone. He bent his legs in the air, and at the last minute shoved them outward.

Taleb rolled to the side, coming to rest on his back. He brought both legs up at the same time, bending them at the knee. He caught Andrew in the buttocks, knocking him toward the safety lines of the ship.

Andrew's knees caught the top line, sending him over the side. He caught the bottom line, holding on. He looked below him at the water, seeing the demons swimming back and forth. "God . . ."

A hand came over the side. "Here, grab my hand."

Andrew glanced at the demon above him. The black face

stared back at him. He looked below. Demons on both sides of him. He had failed his God.

He felt Taleb's hands grab his right wrist. Andrew grabbed Taleb's left hand with his left one, letting go of his grip on the bottom line. Now, he could go to his death taking the demon above him with him into the waters below. God would protect him. God would raise him above the demons below. God would know how Andrew had fought the demons in God's name.

Taleb put his boondockers against the narrow lip along the edge of the deck. "Let go. Don't do this, Andrew." He strained. Taleb was still weak from Andrew nearly choking him to death.

A shadow passed over them. Andrew looked up as something swung and hit him across the face. He let go. As he passed into unconsciousness, he felt the freedom of falling.

"ABOUT time you got here," Taleb said. A hand reached out and pulled him to his feet.

Sergeant Norton tossed the piece of metal over the side. "You're too good of a man to let him feed you to the sharks."

Taleb bent over at the waist and put both hands on his knees, catching his breath. He stuck his head over the side and vomited.

Finished, he apologized.

"You all right now?" Norton asked.

"Yeah," Taleb said, grabbing his handkerchief and wiping his face.

"I take it he didn't want to come peacefully?"

Taleb straightened, grabbed the safety lines, and looked down at the water below, expecting to see blood, or see the body, but there was nothing. "He's gone."

"He's shark food now."

"I don't see him."

"Maybe they ate him," Norton said, joining Taleb alongside the safety lines. After a minute, she stepped away. "Come on. We did what the boss wanted. Now, we need to get back to our primary mission. Let the Department of Homeland Security worry about God's Army. We got a bigger fish to fry, and with luck we'll be off this thing by tonight and sleeping in real beds for a change." She touched Taleb on the arm. "You sure you're all right?"

He nodded. "Man had a death grip on my throat. Luckily, he was an amateur who had no idea of how to do it properly."

"Seems he did pretty good to shake you up this much."

Taleb shook his head. "He did that for sure. Strong as an ox. If he had been like some we'd faced, I'd be the one below the waterline."

"There you go speaking Navy again," she said. Norton looked at her watch. "We have to go."

A minute later, the two disappeared through the covered passageway of the aft forecastle of the *Capella*. Behind them, with the exception of a few spots of blood on the gray deck, there was nothing to show what had happened.

FOURTEEN

"Hank, I've been watching everything on NTDS and it looks as if you have those contacts bracketed. What now?" Admiral Holman asked from the other end of the secure telephone.

Garcia shut his eyes for a moment. The what-nows are the big questions of every operation. "Admiral, I still have weapons tight. I think in the half hour since they fired torpedoes at us, if they had intended to sink Sea Base, they would have fired multiple salvos."

"I can see the reasoning, Hank. That being said, can we afford to let them think we have no capability to return the favor? I don't think I want them leaving Sea Base believing we are defenseless."

Garcia squirmed in his seat. He slid forward and stepped down on the deck. Glancing up, he saw several pairs of eyes watching him, and he wondered for a moment if anyone was listening to the conversation. If so, what they hard would be one-sided, and what would they take away to spread throughout Combat and ultimately Sea Base?

"Admiral, we have four UUVs out there. Each one is heading toward a contact. I have four pairs of SH-36 helicopters hovering over each of the Chinese submarines."

"Chinese submarines?"

"Contacts, Admiral. We are presuming they are Chinese."

"You are probably correct, Hank, but we should call them unidentified contacts until we know for sure."

This was the three-star side of Holman that Garcia had not seen. The political side. The side thinking about what would happen long after this was over and the two countries were being skewed by the public. A short time in the early years of Holman's career had been spent learning what the Cold War was like and pursuing the Soviets around the globe.

"Roger, Admiral," Garcia acknowledged, and then continued as if the rebuke had never occurred. "The UUVs could be misinterpreted by the submarines. They might even believe that what is coming at them are torpedoes fired by us, but I don't think so."

"Why not?"

"If the submarines thought we had fired torpedoes, they wouldn't still be hovering in the same location with their bows pointed at us. They'd be taking evasive action."

"Ergo, they must know they're Unmanned Underwater Vehicles."

"Yes, sir."

"They've been trailing us for five months and have seen what we can do with our Unmanned Underwater Vehicles."

"I would think, with that knowledge, they would turn away."

A chuckle came from Admiral Holman. "Those Captains must be feeling their sphincters tightening about now."

"If they feel that way, Admiral, why aren't they either heading away . . ."

". . . or firing torpedoes at us? They must have different orders."

"Orders that tell them to hold their position and be prepared . . ."

"To sink us, or fire another warning shot," Holman interrupted.

"You could be right, Admiral. Warning shots could be what those torpedoes were, or they could have run out of fuel from thirty-five nautical miles away."

"I think they knew they were too far away for a torpedo to

reach us. Maybe they want us to know how far away they are from us."

"What do you think we should do, Admiral? Have any suggestions?"

"Glad you asked, Hank. We need to make sure they know we know exactly where they're located."

Garcia nodded. "I don't want to drop a torpedo or change the speed of the UUV so it replicates an inbound Mark-45. I am concerned . . ."

"No, that's not what I'm thinking. What do we do with our LAMPS helicopters right before we launch a torpedo from them?" Holman continued, referring to the SH-36 by its cover term. "We take a ping to make sure we have the location pinpointed. In this instance, we are only going to do one ping. One ping that bounces off the submarine and gives us the range and bearing from the dipping sonar of the helicopter."

Garcia smiled even as he realized he should have thought of that instead of having Holman tell him.

"HE'S smiling again."

"If I was those submarines, I'd get out of Dodge now."

"THE unarmed LAMPS has its dipping sonar in the water. We have sonobuoy barriers between Sea Base and each of the submarines. If we pinged them, Admiral, and they decided it was hostile, the sonobuoys would be the first to detect any torpedoes fired. The UUVs have proven effective in taking out torpedoes."

"Unfortunately, they can fire as many as 32 torpedoes simultaneously if they thought they were under attack."

"Admiral, they wouldn't if we did one ping, stopped, and waited. They'd be waiting for the splash of the torpedo hitting the water and the next sound of high-speed revolutions caused by the small propeller as the torpedo headed toward it. As long as they didn't hear the splash, they would interpret it as a warning from us much like the one they sent our way."

"Hank, you are one smart fellow."

"I think I had help heading in that direction," he laughed.

"I'll never tell."

"I don't think you'll have to."

"HE'S laughing," the petty officer whispered to the second class.

The second class turned away.

"Where you going?"

"To put on that fresh pot of coffee that I should have last time and find my life vest."

"SENIOR Chief," Bernardo said. "No change in the speed and bearing of the four contacts. I am showing the last of our four UUVs has cleared the baffles of the *Bellatrix*."

"Surface ships have baffles?"

"Be quiet, Seaman Calvins," Bernardo said.

Agazzi scratched his head. "What's going on?"

"Senior Chief," Calvins called, "Combat says they're going to ping the contacts in two minutes."

"All right!" Bernardo exclaimed. "We're going to sink the motherfuckers."

"Combat says they want to ensure they have the right location."

This isn't good, Agazzi thought. *If the SH-36s are pinging, then that means we are preparing to launch torpedoes. If we launch torpedoes, even simultaneously, most if not all of the Chinese submarines would get theirs in the water before ours locked on and hit. We might sink them, but their torpedoes would still be heading our way.*

"Petty Officer MacPherson, how far away are the UUVs?"

"UUV one and two are about fifteen miles from the contacts bearing 010 and 240. UUV three is about twenty-four nautical miles from the contact bearing 225, and the UUV four has just entered the open water, so it is easily thirty-five nautical miles from the fourth contact bearing 080."

"What are our options if they fire an eight-torpedo salvo from each contact?"

It was several seconds before MacPherson answered. The petty officer looked at Gentron for a couple of seconds before turning to Agazzi. "Not a lot that we didn't do in the Sea of Japan, Senior Chief. If the Chinese know what we did there, they will have a snapshot of our UUV tactics. I can mimic any type of ship you want and may draw some of them away."

"What if they're wire-guided?" Keyland asked from the upper level.

MacPherson frowned. "Then the torpedoes follow the guidance of the operator until the wire breaks."

"Which means the operator won't be guiding it long," Bernardo interjected, "because the submarine is going to be heading down. Heading down to the dark Pacific."

"But while it's wire-guided, we have to fool the operator."

"The wire guides are only good for about fifteen nautical miles," Agazzi said. "Then they'll break, and the torpedoes are on their own."

"Maybe we ought to keep our UUVs twenty nautical miles from the submarines," Keyland offered. "It would give us more time to react. If we get too close and they fire, then we will be inside the envelope where we can employ all the toys of the UUV."

Agazzi nodded. "Petty Officer MacPherson, let's stop UUVs one and two at the fifteen-mile range and put them in orbit."

A couple of minutes later, MacPherson reported, "UUV one is in a racetrack orbit. Gentron, your status?"

"Same with UUV two. Doing an oval circle."

"Let's speed up UUV three and four until they're twenty miles from their contacts and do the same. Seaman Calvins, relay the information to Combat," Agazzi ordered.

Agazzi stepped over to his desk and grabbed a plastic bottle of springwater from his desk, taking a deep drink before hurrying back to the safety rail that encircled the lower level of the ASW operations center.

Keyland slid down the handrails of the ladder to the lower level. Bernardo was slouched in his chair, right leg cradled beneath his left knee. Keyland stopped behind the AN/SQR-25 operator, standing ramrod straight, his slight stomach touching the back of Bernardo's chair.

Agazzi grabbed the top safety rail, his eyes going from console to console as he tried to figure out what else they could do.

MacPherson's face was the epitome of concentration, the tip of his tongue caught between his teeth, while his right hand spun the ball that guided two UUVs. Sweat rolled down Gentron's cheek as the young wizard guided his pair of UUVs. Complicating both sailors' job was the knowledge that both of their UUVs were operating independently, so they had to switch back and forth between each UUV as they maneuvered them to position.

Agazzi looked behind him at Seaman Calvins, who grinned back at him. Calvins's fingers opened and closed on the mouthpiece, ready to push the talk button if told.

"How is Taylor doing?"

"I have him on the line," MacPherson said without looking up. "He is maneuvering a fifth torpedo into launch position."

"Tell him to let us know when it is ready."

"Senior Chief, we can't handle five UUVs," MacPherson said, almost apologetic in the admission. "I know they say we can handle up to four at a time, but Gentron and I are doing everything we can to keep these four moving in the right direction."

"You can preprogram them," Keyland said. "We can preprogram them prior to launch to do a preset series of maneuvers as well as tactics."

"That's right, but we can't turn them loose on automatic until we clear Sea Base. Too many things bopping around under Sea Base like sea anchors, dipping sonars, keels, and props. If we preprogram them, Gentron and I are going to have to use about five minutes of our time maneuvering them clear of Sea Base. In those five minutes, we will be unable to control the four we have out there." MacPherson glanced at Agazzi. "Dangerous to do, Senior Chief."

"We could preprogram them to dive beneath the layer."

"The layer is at one thousand feet according to today's oceanographic report," Gentron added.

"We could do it," Keyland said with a sharp nod.

Bernardo laughed and uncrossed his legs, sitting forward with his elbows on the narrow ledge of the console. "Unfortunately, the dipping sonars are below the layer and the sea anchors pop up and down through the layer all the time. We preprogram to do a set of routines and they will do that set of routines." He leaned back in his seat. "Won't matter to the routine they are following if a sea anchor or dipping sonar gets in its way." Bernardo made an exploding sound, throwing his arms outward. "We could sink ourselves."

"Tell Petty Officer Taylor to let us know when the fifth UUV is in place. If we lose one of the four UUVs, I want the fifth one launched immediately," Agazzi said.

"You're a bunch of good news," Keyland said to Bernardo.

"But Pope is right," MacPherson said. "I understand the next generation of UUVs will have better logic in them so they can avoid underwater things you don't want them to hit."

"Senior Chief," Calvins said.

Bernardo threw down his headset. "Damn! Calvins, why didn't you tell us they were about to ping?"

"I was trying," Calvins protested.

"He did—earlier," Keyland said.

"Yeah, but he didn't say they intended to do it now. He just said—"

"That's enough," Agazzi said. "Focus on your contacts."

"WE'VE pinged," Commander Stapler said to Garcia.

Hank nodded as he acknowledged the statement. Now, they waited.

A half minute later, the antisubmarine warfare controller turned toward Stapler and Garcia as he lifted his headset off one ear. "Skipper, Commander; three of the LAMPS report exact locations on their contacts. Fourth one reports no joy."

"Which one?"

"Contact 7311; the one bearing 225 degrees. According to the LAMPS, they show nothing in the water. The helo is requesting permission for another ping."

Garcia turned to the sound-powered telephone talker. "Ask ASW what they have on the contact bearing 225."

Almost immediately, the phone talker reported Agazzi and his team still holding the contact hovering in the exact location on a bearing of 225.

"If that's true, then why didn't our active sonar pick him up?" Stapler argued. "There is no way we can have all this passive shit detecting them and then they not be there. It doesn't compute."

"What is the depth of the dipping sonars on the four helicopters?" Garcia asked.

He waited patiently as the ASW controller gathered the information. Meanwhile, he could feel the anxiety building within him. What were the Chinese doing in these vital minutes as he rushed to find the fourth submarine?

The second class who earlier had brought him a cup of coffee came up silently to his chair. The young sailor lifted Garcia's cup and disappeared. Someone must really want to test his bladder control, he thought, bringing a slight smile to his lips. He basked for a few seconds in the deference being shown by the sailor. Respect from sailors was always earned and never freely given. He frowned for a moment. There was an aspect to war-fighting that made you feel a little "John Wayne-ness."

The sound-powered telephone talker lifted his headset again and talked with Stapler, Garcia's Tactical Action Officer. Tactical Action Officers were officers whose skills U.S. Navy Skippers had such confidence in that the Skippers signed written orders authorizing them to fight the ship in the Skippers' absence. With that order, Stapler could legally fire weapons, mount an attack, or run from one. Right now, Garcia was glad he was here because Stapler was not the running type and the man's short patience had become apparent during these past two months.

Stapler came over to Garcia. "The three reporting sonar contact had their sonars below the layer at 1100 feet. The LAMPS hovering over the contact bearing 225 degrees had his dipping sonar at six hundred feet. I have ordered him to take it beneath the layer, let us know when it is there, and then I recommend we authorize him to do the single ping again."

Garcia rested his elbows on the arms of his chair, his hands gripped as he rested his chin on them. He raised his head off his hands. "What would you do if you heard the first ping and that ping was a ways from you? Then, you hear a second ping. The second ping is stronger." He made a fist. "And it seems right on top of you." Garcia leaned back. When Stapler failed to answer, he asked him again, "Commander Stapler, what will the Captain of that submarine think? And more important, what will he do?"

* * *

"RAPTOR Leader Formation, this is Mother; turn to course two-six-zero and form up to the south of Black Formation. Raptor 10, turn right onto course three-zero-zero and form up north of Black Formation. Raptor-20 formation, continue on course one-nine-zero and report when you're twenty miles from your current position."

"What are we doing now?" Franklin asked on the formation circuit.

"I'm not sure either," Johnson replied. "Tight End, what do you think?"

Franklin's eyes widened. She's asking someone their opinion and using their call sign?

"I don't know, Pickles," Crawford replied. "I have you on my radar, if you want to call it that. I expect to form up with you within five minutes."

"All formations, this is Mother; the two formations of J-12s are running for base. Well done. They have passed the sixteen contacts we have coming your way. Request expedite formation. Black Leader, report when ready."

"Ready for what?" Franklin asked.

"We must be going to meet those sixteen bandits," Johnson replied.

"Good news is we still have all our missiles and our guns are fully loaded," Crawford added.

"So far, we haven't fired a shot, sunk a ship, nor destroyed an aircraft and we're winning. What kind of war is this?" Johnson asked.

"My kind," Commander Lester Tyler-Cole said.

"Black Leader, didn't know you were on our circuit."

"You gave me your formation frequencies last month when we were busy with our old enemy the North Koreans. I apologize for intruding, but I've been on your circuit since I recognized the griping and complaining of my friend Blackman. Captain Franklin, how are you?"

Franklin shut his eyes and shook his head. He wondered if he had said anything derogatory about the commander or the Royal Navy. "I apologize, Commander. I thought Major Johnson and I were on private circuits."

"Not to worry, Blackman. This time you said not one disparaging thing about your Royal Navy counterparts."

"Black Leader, Raptor Leader here; what is Mother up to?"

"I think we are going to do some churning and burning where our stealth capabilities convince the approaching bandits that we are a superior in number force."

Franklin's eyebrows arched in a V as he thought about the sharp maneuver Black Formation did when they launched the flares. It had momentarily exposed the Royal Navy F-35 fighters to radar detection. The turn accompanied with the flares had convinced the Chinese J-12 stealth fighters that missiles had been fired against them. The Chinese had launched flares against nonexistent missiles. When anything emerges from a stealth fighter such as missiles or flares, it involves opening something on the fuselage of the aircraft that increases radar detection.

The F-35s' deliberate turn sideways exposed their undercarriage, increasing their radar cross section and allowing them to be detected for a moment before they leveled off and disappeared from the radarscope.

"Like the flares?" Crawford asked.

"Exactly. We call that 'churning and burning' the air. Once we form up, Mother will have us flipping and rolling so the enemy sees multiple radar returns giving a fleeting impression we are a significantly larger allied force than they think. We'll appear in the sky somewhere, disappear to race to another section, where we will appear there. To the enemy, it will seem like multiple aircraft. The automated coastal air defense system will go wild assigning multiple contact numbers to a single aircraft."

"What if it doesn't work?"

"Then we may actually find out how superior our stealthness is to their superior number. Exciting, isn't it?"

Franklin took a deep breath. As long as he had stealth as a tactic, he was confident in winning the air combat battle from a distance. Way back in his psyche was also confidence that if he had to run, he could hide in plain radar view. It was a little harder to hide if they were in the middle of air-to-air combat.

"I think we would prefer to be superior numbers," Crawford added.

"Of course, chaps, we would also, but unfortunately, we have discovered that the Royal Navy tends always to be outnumbered, so we have to add a little British tactical ingenuity to the mix of technological superiority."

"YOU okay?" Norton asked Taleb. She reached up and touched Taleb's cheek.

"Ouch!" Taleb exclaimed, jerking back and gingerly putting his hand where she touched. "What you trying to do?"

"He did do a little damage to you. Here, let me see," Norton said, pushing Taleb's head to one side.

"You are going to have one hell of a bruise around that thin neck of yours." She removed her hand and started walking again. "You are lucky I came along when I did or else it would be you dodging sharks below the waterline."

"Yeah, and you have my undying thanks and admiration," he said, stretching his neck. "He was just lucky I hadn't started getting serious with him."

"If he had gotten any luckier, you and I wouldn't be walking together right now."

He dropped his hand by his side as they passed through the covered passageway between *Capella* and *Algol.*

"I think you'll live," Norton said, looking at him. "How do you feel? Anything hurt more than it should?"

"My ego hurts more than anything else. I am going to swing by my rack and grab a few personal things." He glanced at his watch. "Thirty minutes."

She looked at hers. "Thirty minutes. Let's hope everything goes according to plan this time. This General Quarters helps. How long until they miss him?"

Taleb shrugged. "Just because I'm wearing a Navy uniform doesn't mean I know everything. I would say several hours after they secure from General Quarters. Large organizations have large gaps of missing information and few ways of putting it together."

"Was he shocked when you told him we knew he was coming?"

"Yeah. This Andrew . . ."

"Does he have a last name? Even the short reports referred

to the family members by their first names. I don't recall ever seeing a last name."

Taleb shook his head. "I'm sure they have one, but God's Army isn't in our sector. It belongs to Shenk and Williams. I'm sure we'll know what it is soon when I file my report. Right now, across America, the leaders of God's Army are being rounded up. By this time tomorrow, CNN and the press will be having cataclysmic orgasms about homegrown terrorists gone international." He held up one hand. "On one hand, they'll talk about how the Federal Government has broken up a homegrown terrorist group." He dropped the hand and held up the other. "Then a few days later—by Sunday—the talk shows will be discussing whether this really broke up a terrorist group or was it government interfering with freedom of religion."

"Our job is to do and die, not to—"

"I know, I know," Taleb said, quickly changing the subject. "Next time, they shouldn't go around blowing up foreign embassies. Where you want to meet?"

They stepped onto the bow of the *Algol*. Norton bent down and pulled her sock up, covering the small tattoo of a bird on her right ankle. Standing, she pulled her Palm Pilot from her pocket, pulled out a thin wire from it, and held the wire against the nearby mast. "Target is topside near the *Regulus* or heading in that direction." She shoved it back into her pocket.

"Fifteen minutes. Give me five minutes at my rack and I'll meet you on board the *Regulus*. From there, we'll catch up with him."

She reached out and tugged his shirt. "What will we do if it doesn't go down right? We got those security patrols to worry about."

"I have passed it along to Langley. They know. It's their responsibility to take care of it."

"If they don't?"

"I take it you haven't been with the organization long? They always get it right."

"Lots of things have to happen here." She made chopping motions with her hand. "One after the other, in order—in proper sequence."

"And they will. They always do." He looked at his watch. "Ten minutes on *Regulus*. We need to get that radio."

Taleb glanced over his shoulder at Norton, who stood watching him walk toward the stern of the *Algol*.

"They always go right?" she shouted after him.

He shrugged. "Well, sometimes . . . but not often."

He picked up the pace and was soon out of sight. Damn. He hoped everything went right this time. Most times, the operational planning became general guidelines as the intensity and timelines converged. He was still wondering where they were going to find their man and how they were going to get him topside.

FIFTEEN

"Mother, Black Leader; I have Raptor Leader Formation on my left flank and Raptor-10 Formation on my right."

"Roger, Black Leader; Raptor-20 Formation is twenty miles behind you in an easy turn toward you."

Two clicks on the microphone acknowledged the Royal Navy Air Intercept Controller's transmission. Franklin looked out his right side. Johnson's Raptor was several hundred feet ahead on his right with a five-hundred-foot higher-altitude separation. He looked past Johnson to where, in the distance, he could make out the two F-35 aircraft of Commander Lester Tyler-Cole's formation. There were two other F-35s out here somewhere, or so said Mother when he was packing and stacking the aircraft during the past few minutes. Franklin looked to his left; clear sky as far as the horizon. Ahead, off the horizon, clouds marked where land started. Somewhere between those clouds and their own westerly subsonic heading were sixteen bandits heading their way. At this speed, he doubted it would be long until they either passed each other with wide-eyed shock, or found themselves dodging hastily fired missiles and bullets.

As if reading his thoughts, the Royal Navy AIC keyed his

microphone. "Black Leader, Raptor Leader, and Raptor 10; bandits are twenty-five miles from your position. We are going to do some churns and burns. For Raptor formations, churns and burns will involve exposing your undercarriage for a couple of seconds. Be aware of where your wingman and other friendlies are in the area. I will call a sharp right-hand or left-hard turn. You are to flip the aircraft so the wings are vertical with the ground. I will then almost immediately say level off, followed by a level turn. In the level turn, you will increase speed and put a mile from the churn position. Then we'll do it all over again. Any questions?"

"I have one," Franklin said aloud to himself. "What happens to our formations after we do these things?"

"Good," Mother said. "Raptor 20; you are now ten miles from the main formation. Maintain your position. You are not to churn and burn until I tell you to. Do you copy?"

Franklin heard the acknowledgment. He wriggled his fingers, visually checked his harness to make sure everything was tight and shipshape. Shipshape! "Tell me I did not think shipshape," he mumbled. "I have got to get off this floating island and back to the real Air Force before I have to go through rehab."

"Black Leader, Raptor Leader, and Raptor 10; for the next few minutes you three are known as Main Formation. Copy?"

Tyler-Cole, Johnson, and Crawford acknowledged the AIC.

"Okay, Main Formation; sharp turn to the right, ninety degrees . . ."

Franklin whipped his Raptor to the right, turning the wings vertical with the ground. He could look down and see through the sparse twelve-thousand-foot cloud level to the sea. He thought he saw the wake of a ship.

". . . now. Sharp turn now; then immediately level off."

He felt a slight drop in his stomach. He had turned too soon. Franklin looked at the heads-up display and saw good separation with Black Leader. Raptor-10 Formation was way off to the right. He couldn't see Crawford and his wingman, but they were far enough away from Franklin that he knew there was little opportunity for a mishap with them.

Johnson, on the other hand, was a different story. She was somewhere nearby. He looked at his heading. "Whoops!" he said aloud. Mother said a ninety-degree turn. Ninety plus 240 equaled 330. He still had the fighter in a turn and it had passed 330 degrees and was approaching 000. He eased back on the throttle and shifted the flaps slightly to bring the aircraft around to 330. He was dead on course when Mother came back on the circuit.

"Main Formation; level off. Level turn to course two-five-zero, afterburners on for one minute."

Franklin eased the Raptor into a left-hand turn, his attention flipping between the heads-up display and the compass. He pushed the throttle forward, shifting to afterburner. He checked his altitude: 18,500 feet. He had gained five hundred feet. He started a slight descent to his assigned angels eighteen. As his nose dropped, Raptor Leader shot up from below, filling his view for a fraction of a second. His heart reached a new speed. Franklin shoved the Raptor into a dive, pulling up sharply a thousand feet later. Above him and separating to the right was Johnson's fighter.

"Wow!" she said over the formation circuit. "That was close."

"Close!" Franklin broadcast. "Too close for comfort, ma'am." His breath was coming in short, rapid gulps.

"Okay, Main Formation. Take a second to check your position with your fellow fighters."

Franklin looked at his display.

"Okay, we look okay from my position," the AIC said. "On my command this time, sharp sixty-degree turn to the left and when we come out, we will be turning to the right."

Franklin glanced quickly around the cockpit. His right hand was on the stick and the left on the throttle.

"For you Yanks, in churns and burns, if you overshoot your turn radius or fail to achieve it, you run the risk of a midair bump with your wingman."

"Now he tells us," Franklin griped. He'd nearly got both of them killed.

"Sharp turn now!"

Franklin flipped the Raptor on its side. Once again, the undercarriage of the stealth fighter was pointed toward the Chinese mainland. His sensors were useless in this position. While in the turn, there was no way to tell if radar was painting him or not. He assumed it was. This tactic was something he and the others would have to take back with them. He thought of how close he and Johnson had come to colliding. It would take lots of practice so they didn't destroy a squadron learning it.

He looked at his gyrocompass. He was nearing 270 degrees. Franklin eased back on the stick. He glanced down again, wondering where the wake of the ship he saw earlier had gone. He looked up, searching west of him, hoping to catch a glimpse of Raptor-20 Formation. Still flying with his belly exposed, Franklin leveled the aircraft on 270-degrees heading. He hoped Johnson, wherever she was, had done the same. He looked down at his feet, thinking that somewhere beneath the undercarriage or nearby was Pickles. He hoped the last thing he saw wasn't the nose of her aircraft coming up through the cockpit floor.

"Main Formation; level off, level turn to the right; steady up on course three-zero-zero true."

For the next sixty seconds, Mother brought the formation closer together, almost back to the original disposition. Franklin's heart beat rapidly. The tactic was both exhilarating and dangerous. He wondered how this "here we are; here we aren't" tactic was being interpreted by the Chinese.

What he didn't like was not knowing how close they were to the approaching fighters. It had been nearly three minutes since the AIC had given them tactical information. He looked at the radio, considered calling Mother himself, but Air Force training overrode the professional urge.

"Main Formation, be advised the Chinese formation is doing maneuvers of their own. Separation remains nearly the same."

Franklin frowned. *How did the Brit know my curiosity about the range?*

"Okay, Main Formation; let's do it again. Raptor 20; it is your turn to join the maneuvering. Please join along."

Franklin went through the same sequence of events as the last time. Checking his position, checking his handholds on the stick and throttle, and waiting for the "now." He gained confidence with the third churn and burn. The fourth was in the same direction and when they came out, they were heading on course 240 again—right where they'd started. The display had them scattered across the battle space.

He thought of the approaching fighters and wondered what happened to them. They should have been here by now. What if he had to engage? It would be a single-fighter battle against the incredible odds of a coordinated sixteen-fighter formation.

"Main Formation; be advised the approaching bandits went into a racetrack orbit thirty miles from your position on the third churn and burn."

"Thirty miles?" Franklin asked on the formation circuit. "We were twenty-five miles from them a few minutes ago."

"Mother has been using speed and turns to increase separation while creating the illusion for the bandits that we were approaching them," Tyler-Cole answered. "Nothing really fancy about it, wouldn't you say?"

"Yeah, yeah. I understand completely," Franklin answered, not understanding at all these Royal Navy maneuvers, but knowing he'd figure them out once he had an opportunity to think them through. He looked at his GPS reader and saw the Royal Navy commander was right. How did they do that? One moment they're driving right toward a massive engagement, and the next they're dodging the engagement without the enemy being aware of it. He bit his lower lip. If you used this tactic correctly, you could suck an enemy's fuel dry before they realized it. He smiled. He was enjoying this. He wriggled his fingers ready to do it again. Then he frowned. *Wait a minute, it sucks our fuel dry also.* He looked at his fuel gauge, but the Air Intercept Controller interrupted his attempt to contact Johnson.

"Main Formation and Raptor 20; I am going to reform the Main Formation and integrate Raptor 20 into it. Should take about five minutes. Main formation, come to course . . ."

Minutes later, Franklin eased into the left wingman position, two aircraft lengths back from Johnson, with five-hundred-feet altitude separation. He slowed his speed to match hers. Mother had them in a racetrack orbit, matching the Chinese fighters thirty-five miles away. Franklin looked constantly for the opposing force hoping for a flicker of sunlight off a fuselage or a contrail—then, he looked over his shoulder to make sure he wasn't leaving a contrail.

"Okay, Main Formation, Raptor 20; Raptor 20 is located north of Raptor-10 Formation. All aircraft are now Main Formation. Main Formation, steady on course two-four-zero and maintain assigned altitude separation."

Nearly thirty seconds passed before the four leaders acknowledged steady on course 240.

"Jolly good, everyone. You Yanks are getting the spirit of this exercise. Now comes what we hope is the coup de grâce, so cross your fingers. We are going to do one churn and burn, but instead of to the side, we are going to do this one vertically. When I give the order, you will turn on your tails and ascend at current speed. Thirty seconds into the ascent, I will give the order to level out. You are to level out back onto course two-four-zero. All leaders will level out on triple-zero altitudes plus five hundred feet, while wingmen are to steady up at the triple-zero."

"Triple-zero, five-zero-zero plus I understand," Franklin said aloud. "But it sounds strange over a tactical frequency."

"Hopefully, this will keep you from colliding with each other. Everyone understand?"

A series of double clicks went through the airways, reminding Franklin of crickets.

"Good. Now, within thirty seconds of leveling off and steadying up on course two-four-zero, we will do it again. Then again."

"Mother, Raptor Leader; I thought you said we were going to only one churn and burn. We are approaching a fuel problem."

"Roger, Raptor Leader; this is one churn and burn, but it involves three maneuvers. We have confidence you can do it. I am told by our wardroom that the odds have dropped to three to one on the Americans successfully completing this multiple maneuver. Now, Main Formation, after the third leg of this one churn and burn, we will turn toward the orbiting bandits and engage."

Engage! They were really going to fight them? A fresh wave of adrenaline rushed through Franklin's body. This was what he was trained to do: fight and win. Then the thought of the three-leg churn and burn had him wondering how dizzy he was going to be coming out. He looked at his weapons system. It was still ready-energized. A flip of the switch and he'd have weapons filling the sky with "howdy-dos."

"Do not energize your weapons systems until I tell you to do so."

Franklin looked at his energized weapons systems. Seemed foolish to turn it off now since they were going to engage the bandits. He reached forward to flip it off, thought about it, and left it on. It had been on throughout the time they'd been weaving and dodging the Chinese Air Force. Why turn it off now?

"Okay, everyone, wait for my command. You Yanks who haven't done this one, for it to succeed means everything has to be done in seconds, not minutes. It means you are going to go on an aerial roller-coaster ride. Every time you ascend, coastal radar is going to pick up you. They're going to count you; then you're going to disappear from their radar. When you do it the second and third times, their automated system is going to count you as new contacts. It won't take an astute radar operator long to figure out the first contacts are the same as the second and third. But in those minutes while they are deconflicting their system, we will have perceived tactical superiority over the enemy. Any questions?" the AIC asked, and then without waiting for an answer, he said, "Okay, jolly good. All aircraft sharp ascent, now!"

Franklin pulled up. Ahead of him, filling his vision was nothing but blue sky—from the Air Force anthem. A few seconds later, Mother gave the order to level off. Franklin rolled left, pulling a few Gs as he checked his altitude, made a slight course correction, and steadied up on 240. About a mile ahead was Raptor Leader. He smiled. She's as nervous as I am about us colliding with each other. Then, suddenly, he was in the second vertical ascent and without much thought about it, the third series came and went. He checked his altimeter each time, making sure the last three digits were around 000.

"Jolly good . . ."

They really do say "jolly good," he thought.

"Main Formation, start steady descent to 18,500 feet. All leaders to take five-hundred-foot altitudes and wingmen steady at eighteen thousand. Maintain course two-four-zero. Energize weapons systems, but weapons tight unless I give a different order, understand?"

Several clicks filled the air.

Franklin noticed that the AIC was using feet instead of the metric system. More likely for the safety of us *"Yanks"* than for the British formation.

"Roger, everyone. For the weapons-tight order, I would like a verbal acknowledgment from everyone."

Franklin listened to everyone acknowledging the weapons-tight order. He waited until a moment presented itself, and then acknowledged the order also. Mother wanted to make sure no one misunderstood the weapons-tight order. Weapons tight meant that no matter what happened, unless it was an emergency self-defense issue, they were forbidden to fire.

"Report when weapons systems energized," the Royal Navy AIC broadcast.

The same sequence occurred again with each pilot reporting compliance.

"Okay, here comes the fun, my illustrious fighter pilots. We will start with Black Formation, followed by Raptor Leader, Raptor-10, and then Raptor-20 Formations. We are going to illuminate the battle space with fire-control radars. Red Formation is approaching your position from the northeast. . . ."

"Red Formation? Where in the hell did they come from?" he asked himself, immediately realizing that while they had been doing this churn-and-burn tactic, the *Elizabeth* had launched an additional formation of F-35 stealth fighters.

"They have not been detected by our opponents. They will add their fire-control radars to the mix. Should be a fine electromagnetic mess for my counterparts along the coast. Black Formation, you may start emitting fire-control radar emissions."

"What if we paint a target?" Franklin asked himself.

"You are not to lock onto any target, but if your system should malfunction and you achieve lock-on, Main Formation, you are not to achieve it for longer than two seconds. No longer than two seconds. Would hate for the Chinese to fire real missiles in self-defense, now wouldn't we?"

"But, when we lock on, that is an act of war and they are allowed to fire at us," Crawford broadcast.

"Yeah, you tell them, Tight End," Franklin mumbled.

"Yes, it is, and they may opt to fire on you. Let's hope they don't," the AIC replied calmly.

Franklin thought he heard the AIC chuckle just as the man cut off his transmission. It confirmed to Franklin that the AIC was showing a bit of sadistic pleasure about this whole thing. *"Oh, well,"* Franklin imagined the AIC saying to a fellow sailor, *"looks as if we screwed this up. See if any of the ships can recover anyone alive."*

The Raptor-only circuit tweaked in Franklin's ear.

"Tight End, this is Pickles; the bandits are still in racetrack orbit. They'd have to break out to fire. I don't think a two-second lock-on will give them time to fire."

"Raptor Leader; you and wingman are now clear to illuminate your fire-control radar."

Within two minutes, the four F-35 Royal Navy fighters and the six F-22A U.S. Air Force Raptors were filling the sky with airborne fire-control radar. Seconds later, the fire control from the British Red Formation joined the fray.

On Franklin's electronic warfare scope, only the fire control from Red Formation was reflected. All the other fire-control emissions were heading west. He smiled. *Sneaky little devils, these British. Remind me not to play poker with them. Good argument for having booze at sea.*

"Looking good," the AIC announced.

"It should," Franklin said aloud. "We haven't fired a shot and if I was on the other end and had teeth in my butt, I'd chew a hole through my seat."

Seconds passed as the AIC quizzed the formation on fuel, data link, and positional status. The AIC on the *Elizabeth* double-checked altitudes and speeds. Then, with each aircraft, he tweaked their altitudes and positions as he aligned the aircraft in a line-abreast formation that stretched for twenty miles across the sky. He might be sadistic, but he knew his job.

"Okay, Main Formation; we are going to reverse course shortly—" The transmission stopped abruptly. "Gentlemen, it appears the bandits are turning toward us. Without any violent maneuver and keeping a level turn, let's come to course—" Once again, the transmission stopped.

"Well, well, well," the AIC finally said. "It looks as if they have flipped their course and are heading toward the mainland."

"I have missile radar!" Tyler-Cole interrupted. "I now have multiple missile seekers."

"Me too," Crawford announced.

"Main Formation; damn the bad luck. It appears our opponents fired missiles at us before bolting for the mainland. No talking," the AIC continued. "You will follow my instructions explicitly. Come immediately to course zero-eight-zero. We are showing multiple missiles heading toward your formations."

Franklin flipped the aircraft to the right, keeping his eye on Johnson as she did the same; he tried to keep the bottom of the Raptor hidden as much as possible in the tight turn.

The bandits had not turned to engage. They turned to fire their missiles. A fire-and-forget tactic to discourage anyone from engaging them as they put on full speed headed for home.

Flares were effective against infrared seekers. His integrated Electronic Warfare System was sending a cacophony of alerts to his headset. He reached down and hit automatic on the system. If the electromagnetic intensity of the seekers increased to a certain point, the system would deploy chaff. Chaff was tiny bits of metal that would spread in the air behind the aircraft creating false targets for the air-to-air missile. Simultaneously with the chaff would be magnesium-burning flares to decoy the infrared seeker of the missile. Right now, the missiles heading their way were active seekers. If the active mode failed or lost contact, Franklin knew the missiles would switch automatically to infrared.

"Red Formation, this is Mother; come right to course two-zero-zero. You are cleared to fire your missiles at this time."

The Brits are attacking! Franklin thought. *Why the new formation and not us?* Then he quickly rationalized that the Chinese attack was directed at them and the F-35 formation outside of the line-abreast Main Formation was not in the path of the missiles. But was Red Formation close enough? Wouldn't the missiles run out of fuel before they reached the bandits?

"Main Formation; descend quickly to six thousand feet and

steady up course zero-eight-zero. Watch your fuel and report when low."

"We're low," Johnson reported.

"Roger, continue to six thousand feet and steady up on heading zero-eight-zero."

Franklin grinned. Their orders had always been not to engage the Chinese unless in self-defense or unless freed to do so. The British were one smart bunch of cowboys. The missiles fired against the Chinese were to shock them with a return volley from a different direction than they'd fired. Make them think they'd wasted their missiles. God, he hoped they'd wasted them.

A minute later, after he, Johnson, and Crawford had exchanged positional data and discussed FUREMS—fuel remainders—Franklin had some time to think about the past minutes. Maybe the Chinese missile launch from so far away was the same thing the British had done. Neither side wanting to engage, but both sides wanting to show they could if the occasion mandated it. Franklin knew that once one or the other shot down an aircraft, the military situation would change, and it would change for the worse for both sides. It's easier to start a war than it is to disengage.

"Blackman!" Pickles screamed. "Behind you!"

"SENIOR Chief, I just lost the contact bearing 010," Bernardo said. Then, before Agazzi could reach the bottom level of the ASW operations center, he added, "And the contact at 080 is gone now."

Agazzi looked at Gentron and then back to Bernardo. "How about the other contacts?"

"I still have the two at 225 and 240. Wait one!"

Agazzi leaned forward, watching the rainfall display of the AN/SQR-25 sonar system. The two remaining noise traces from the 225 and 240 contracts were bending to the left. "They're . . ."

". . . turning," Bernardo finished. "They are in a left-hand turn."

* * *

"SIR," Stapler said. "The helicopter has its dipping sonar below the layer and is reporting 1100-feet depth. Request permission to do a second ping."

Garcia sipped the fresh coffee, feeling the rich taste of fresh industrial-perked coffee washing across his tongue and the sides of his mouth. He swallowed. "Permission granted, Commander. Only one ping, though," he said, holding up one finger.

ALONG bearing 225 from Sea Base, the Chinese Skipper was tense. The earlier ping had been interpreted correctly according to undersea tactics. Everyone on board the Han-class nuclear attack submarine knew the ping had to have come from an American ASW helicopter. It had come from above, hitting sensors near the conning tower. He had no way of knowing whether the ping had hit his submarine. He thought now. The layer was thick enough to stop the return signal. If he were the American Skipper, what would he do?

What he did know was the Northern Fleet Headquarters in Quigdao had sent immediate directives for the four submarines to break off and increase the distance from Sea Base to two hundred miles. They were ordered to keep their torpedo tube doors closed. He had yet to give that order. What if he needed to ensure the survival of his boat and crew?

The problem, he knew, was there was nothing here he could destroy except Sea Base. He reached up and grabbed a handhold in the conn as the submarine continued deeper, turning away from the American intruder. If he had to fire, it would be retaliatory fire against Sea Base.

The only tactic to fight helicopters was to surface, open the watertight hatches, and get his man-pack air-to-air surface missiles topside. Wasn't a smart tactic unless it was a last resort. A submarine on top of the water is nothing more than a bobbing, waffling target.

Fifty feet above the surface of the water, the helicopter pilot turned in his seat and gave the sonar operator a thumbs-up.

A second later, the second ping hit the side of the Han submarine. It was much louder than the first one. The acoustic signal reverberated throughout the hull. Dishes rattled in the sink of the galley and the boat vibrated once. The Skipper saw the XO leap quickly to grab his cup of tea as it bounced near the lip of a small nearby shelf. Hot tea spilled across the younger man's hand.

The Skipper's eyes met the XO's. "They are about to launch," the XO said, setting his cup down quickly and shaking the hot tea off his hand before wiping it.

The Skipper nodded. One ping. What would he do if the roles were reversed? He listened to the XO preparing to launch the preprogrammed torpedoes. It would only take the Captain's word. He let the preparations for launch continue, knowing no firing would occur until he personally gave the order. Everything he'd studied about American antisubmarine warfare tactics indicated two pings were needed for an accurate targeting solution. One ping to establish depth and location; the second ping to determine course and speed.

"Ready to fire all tubes," the XO said.

This time he did not nod. He held up his hand and told them to wait.

"THEY got him, sir!" Stapler said with a hint of satisfaction. "We got all three of them." He put both hands on his hips. "What now, Skipper?"

Garcia set the cup down in the holder. "Not a thing, Commander. We wait . . ."

"Excuse me, Captain," the sound-powered phone talker interrupted. "Sonar is reporting loss of the two contacts bearing 010 and 080. They also report the two remaining contacts at 225 and 240 are in a left-hand turn away from Sea Base."

Garcia smiled. "Looks as if we have scared them away."

Stapler's face clouded as he frowned. The faint wrinkles on his forehead creased downward like deep crevices. "Sir, those two may be drawing our attention away from the two Sonar lost. Maybe we should do second pings on them?"

Garcia's lips pressed together. Second pings were for final firing solutions. He had already done it once. To do it against the others might be pressing their luck. He shook his head. "No, not at this time. *Gearing* is the ASW commander; tell him to try to locate the two missing submarines, but via passive means, not active. Don't want the Chinese to think they're under attack."

"SENIOR Chief," Calvins reported, his eyes looking up from under the lip of the large sound-powered phone helmet. "The second ping confirmed the located of the 225 contact."

"Senior Chief," Bernardo called. "I'm going back through my noise library. I show three of the submarines with noise associated with closing their torpedo tubes. That submarine bearing 225 either still has its tubes opened, or our sonar array missed him closing them."

Agazzi nodded. Most likely they missed the closing.

"My UUV is about five miles from the contact bearing 240," MacPherson said. "My second one is eight miles from the contact bearing 225. Want me to continue pursuit?"

ON board the Han-class submarine along the 225 bearing, the Skipper agonized over whether to fire the torpedoes or not. Quigdao's orders were to conduct no hostile act against the Americans unless in self-defense. The last thing they wanted was to give the Americans a reason to become more involved in this operation off Taiwan. But he was not going to stand here as they ran from the Americans and let his boat be sunk.

The sonar operator turned from his console, his left hand pressing the headset against his ear. "I have a possible torpedo bearing 045. Very faint at this time. If we continue turning, it will disappear into our baffles."

The Skipper twitched slightly as he felt his stomach tightening. They had fired on him. He had not heard the torpedo hit the water. It should have been overhead. He ordered the weapons officer to lift the red protection devices from the firing button. He ordered the submarine to shift its rudder, turning the Han to a new course and uncovering the baffles.

"We should fire now, sir," the XO protested.

The Skipper's steely eyes punctured the XO's protest. "We will fire when I say fire."

"Yes, my Captain," the XO answered, his eyes cast downward.

"Can you hear it better now?" the Skipper asked, licking his lips slightly.

"Yes, sir," said the sonar operator. "The torpedo continues on course toward us. I do not have any sonar activity from it. Most likely passive, steering toward our propellers."

The Skipper ordered an increase in the speed, and then snapped at the helmsman for a sharp right turn. As soon as the turn was executed, he ordered all stop. Behind the Han-class attack submarine, churned water roiled upon itself, creating an underwater knuckle that masked the fading presence of the Han.

It was quiet in the conn. Everyone waited to see if the American torpedo would be fooled and steer toward this knuckle. The Skipper directed the conn to nine-hundred-feet depth, taking the submarine above the layer away from the torpedo. Since the helicopter's dipping sonar must be below the layer, maybe this would blind them from passive detection.

It also blinded the submarine if the torpedo shot through the layer in pursuit, but he counted on the layer hiding him if the torpedo went into active seeking mode, searching with its fire-control radar, trying to lock onto him.

"I'VE lost the submarine," Bernardo said.

"Which one?" Keyland asked.

"The one bearing 225," Agazzi answered. "What do you think happened?"

Bernardo shrugged. "One moment it was there, the next it was gone. It put on a burst of speed and I think it was executing a sharp turn at the time." He chuckled. "Must have thought a torpedo or something was after him."

Agazzi jumped back. "MacPherson! Put that UUV into a racetrack now! Do it quickly!"

"What's wrong?" Keyland asked.

Agazzi turned to Calvins. "Tell Combat the submarine at 225 degrees may be positioning for a torpedo attack."

"Wait!" Keyland shouted. "Senior Chief, you tell Combat that, they're going to tell the helicopter to launch its torpedo."

"That's the Captain's decision, not mine. Calvins, tell Combat."

* * *

"SIR, we need to launch the torpedo now. Sonar is reporting the submarine in a launch maneuver."

Garcia nodded. "I know, Commander, but we're not. Tell the *Gearing* if a torpedo is detected in the water, then he has permission to attack. Otherwise, we sit and wait."

"But Skipper . . ."

He nodded again. "Commander Stapler, I know how hard it is to wait, but sometimes patience and time together cause a crisis to go away. He hasn't launched his torpedoes yet. We haven't launched ours."

"Sir, with all due respect, they did launch torpedoes."

Garcia shook his head. "I am coming to think, Commander Stapler, that maybe what they launched was a warning. Some sort of fake torpedo to show they could have sunk us if they had wanted."

Stapler took a deep breath, his gaze glancing one way and then the other, before he turned back to Garcia. "Sir, you may be right, but until Naval Intelligence does its analysis, we won't know."

"Commander, if they were hell-bent on sinking us, they would have cranked out more than one salvo of torpedoes, and most likely we'd be seeing our friends beneath Sea Base long before we experience the dark Pacific."

"Sir, if we attack now, we might be able to sink or cripple him before he can."

Garcia frowned. "I disagree. As soon as he hears the splash of the torpedo hitting the water, he'll launch his torpedoes."

"But Captain Garcia, the submarine is below the layer. He won't hear the splash. He won't hear anything until the torpedo penetrates the layer at one thousand feet. He's at twelve hundred feet. The torpedo will hit him before he can fire."

"What if he does fire? What if we sink him? What about the other three contacts out there? Just because they've disappeared from our sensors doesn't mean they won't hear what happens to their sister boat." He shook his head, slid forward, and stepped down from his chair.

Garcia leaned toward Stapler and whispered, "Commander, I know you are doing what I expect and giving me your heartfelt and best tactical opinion, but you are close to stepping across the line." He raised his hand and placed it on the taller

Stapler's shoulder. "It would be bad for morale and the fighting spirit of our men if I had to relieve you." He dropped his hand. "Do we understand each other?"

Stapler opened his mouth to reply, thought better of it, nodded, and in a quiet voice said, "Aye, aye, sir." The taciturn Tactical Action Officer turned away and walked to the bank of consoles in front of the Captain's chair. Garcia watched and listened as Stapler relayed his orders to the Skipper of the *Gearing*. After a couple of minutes, Garcia reached around and lifted his cup. The coffee seemed to taste much better.

"IT'S in a racetrack, Senior Chief. Estimate distance to the contact as ten thousand yards: five miles. What now?" MacPherson asked.

Agazzi moved along the consoles until he stood between MacPherson and Gentron. "We wait. Keep every UUV in a racetrack between the submarines and Sea Base. Don't take them any closer."

"Kind of hard for me to do, Senior Chief," Gentron said. "I've lost contact with all my contacts until Bernardo restores contact."

"Wow! Another poet in ASW," Bernardo sniped. "Anyone got one of those airline barf bags?"

MacPherson leaned over to Gentron's console. "Here," he said, punching in the "main menu" icon. Then, for the next couple of minutes, he instructed Gentron in how to use preprogrammed patterns for the UUVs such as racetrack, figure-eight, weaving course, and others.

Agazzi listened. He knew you could preprogram the UUVs to do certain functions on their own to reduce the piloting complexities for the operator. It was nice to know MacPherson knew how to do it.

FRANKLIN hit the flare dispenser and dived toward the surface of the water. He flipped the Raptor into a left-hand turn. Watching the approaching water and his controls, out of his peripheral vision he saw the contrail of a missile about a mile behind chasing his tail.

"I have a missile—" he started to broadcast.

"I'm coming!"

What the hell can you do, Pickles? Franklin thought. The fight against a missile locked onto you was yours alone. He deployed chaff, even as he knew the EW system showed no active lock-on. He increased his turn ratio, jerked the stick, and felt the Gs push him into his seat as the F-22A shot upward. Either the missile would have gone into the drink by now, or he still had a problem.

"Blackman, Pickles; keep ascending. The missile is closing. Increase speed."

He glanced at his fuel. He was going to be running on fumes again if he managed to evade the missile. If he didn't, it wouldn't matter.

"Flares . . . more flares!" Johnson said.

He hit the dispenser. Flares filled the space behind him and the attacking missile. The missile shot through several of the flares, bending its course slightly, but without the aircraft maneuvering away from the aligned flares, the missile shot through the decoys and immediately relocked onto the heat of the engines.

"It still there?" he asked.

"It's still coming. I'm nearly there," Johnson broadcast.

"Stay away. Nothing you can do."

"I saw this once in a training film."

"A training film!" Franklin asked incredulously. "A training film?"

His Raptor vibrated, growing to a rough shaking for a few seconds before stopping. He glanced over his shoulder and then to his right. Johnson's F-22A shot across his path, between him and the missile. Behind her, the missile left Franklin and took off after her.

"Pickles! What the hell have you done? The missile is locked on—" He never finished. As he turned the aircraft to the right to follow Johnson, the missile exploded several feet from the tail of her aircraft.

The Raptor started spinning in the air—over and over—the tail and nose exchanging positions as the aircraft started downward toward the water.

"Eject, eject, eject," Franklin kept repeating, his throat constricting. *She killed herself,* he thought.

Then the cockpit exploded outward as Johnson ejected. The aircraft was still turning, and Franklin thought he saw the tail hit the seat as it rocketed upward. He put the aircraft into an orbit around where Johnson ejected.

A moment later, the parachute opened, but he saw no movement from the figure strapped to the seat.

"Raptor down," Franklin broadcast on the tactical circuit. "Major Johnson's Raptor was hit by a missile. She has ejected. Parachute has deployed." He looked at his GPS, then broadcast the exact location.

"Roger, Raptor Leader. A Canadian destroyer is in the area and en route to recover."

"She was Raptor Leader," Franklin objected.

"Roger; understand, Wingman."

THE Han submarine slowed as its momentum decreased, the water passing through the propeller leaving a minor, hardly detectable wake behind the light gray boat as it drifted toward all stop. The Skipper glanced at the weapons officer, whose eyes were locked on him. The man's thin piano-player fingers rested on the top two buttons. The XO stood beside the weapons officer staring at the Skipper. Both were waiting for the one word that would allow them to launch torpedoes. Neither knew he wanted to say that word. What submarine captain didn't want to sink something on the surface? But he was a professional Navy officer. He kept coming back to his orders to avoid direct confrontation with the Americans. One word from him and those fingers would launch a full salvo of torpedoes and some would hit this thing they called Sea Base. And he so wanted to say that word.

The XO spoke up, bringing the Skipper's attention to the sonar operator, who said the torpedo appeared to be circling ten thousand yards to their southeast. He smiled. Five miles was not much maneuvering room. A circling torpedo was a searching torpedo, a torpedo that had lost its target. The next action would be for the Americans to launch other torpedoes. With them losing him, they would ping again.

He assumed the helicopters were still above searching for him. After reflection, he decided if they pinged a third time, he would launch the torpedoes and then sprint for the open ocean. Thinking ahead, he believed the Americans would believe he would head for the shelter of the mainland, so he would seek the vastness of the Pacific in which to disappear. But only if they pinged again.

He dropped his hand from the leather strap he had been holding onto. The Skipper of the Han submarine stepped over to the officer of the deck and ordered him to increase speed to eight knots, one knot at a time, and to make sure the speed did not create any undue cavitations. The course kept the propeller away from the direction of the circling torpedo, so he maintained it, slowly increasing distance between Sea Base and the Han. Twenty minutes later, he let the weapons officer take his fingers off the red buttons and ordered the safety guards across the switches lowered.

When they were fifty nautical miles from Sea Base and the passive noise of the circling torpedo had long faded, he closed the torpedo tube doors. Taking a longer route than planned, hours later the Han-class submarine was heading back toward station in the Taiwan Strait.

SIXTEEN

Garcia set the handset back in the cradle and stood there for a minute wondering about what he had just been told. No explanation. He had heard stories of such things about other admirals. It had just never happened to him where an admiral ordered him to do something without some sort of explanation. Nothing illegal, just do something and ask no questions. Out of the corner of his eye, he saw Stapler staring at him. He let out a sigh.

Stapler was a problem he would address later; then again, sometimes problems went away without any intervention. Stapler had proven himself adept at running Combat, getting weapons systems on line and ready, and in the myriad of other things a Navy officer must know to fight the ship. But Stapler would have attacked the submarines regardless of what the orders had been, which were to avoid open conflict with the Chinese. It is hard for some officers in the confusion and emotion of battle to remember the strategic picture and bend the tactical moment to it.

Garcia turned and walked toward his chair, nearly tripping on one of the sound-powered wires that trailed across the deck. Regardless of how well your eyesight adjusted to the blue-lighted darkness of Combat, you were still working in the dark. The cords pursuing the sound-powered phone talkers shifted and curled across the deck as the young sailors moved within their assigned watch stations. Then again, Garcia thought, until this deployment, his own career had been one as a desk jockey except for those short excursions off the coast to test new systems for the Navy. Maybe every war-fighter has shortfalls, which others around them compensate for.

Garcia motioned Stapler over to the chair. "Commander, I've changed my mind," he said, looking at the analog Navy clock on the bulkhead. "We'll stay at General Quarters for the time being."

Stapler nodded with a grimace. When Garcia started to climb back into his chair, Stapler spoke up. "Sir, they've been at it for over six hours. This hot sun and closed spaces are starting to take their toll on the troops. Sick bay already has twelve people down there with some degree of heat exhaustion."

Garcia sat down. "I understand, Stan, but until I say differently, we will stay at General Quarters."

"May I ask why, sir? And for how long you envision us staying at GQ?"

Garcia gripped the arms of the chair and shook his head slightly. "Are you questioning me, Commander?" He touched his chest a couple of times. "I am the Captain, so we'll stay at General Quarters until I decide it's safe to stand down."

Stapler colored. "My apologies, Skipper. I'm not questioning your right about making the decision on General Quarters or anything else having to do with commanding Sea Base. Sir, I was thinking of the crew. They have been at GQ most of the day. This heat—and body functions—will take their toll on the crew. Additionally, if we are going to be at GQ for the next few hours, we have to start thinking of feeding the crew. It's after dinnertime and most missed lunch."

"You're right," Garcia answered, his temper abating when he realized Stapler was thinking ahead. Maybe they do complement each other. Maybe every level-headed officer needed a hot-tempered firebrand alongside to fight wars.

"Sir?" Stapler asked.

"I was just thinking, Commander Stapler—maybe you and I working together really did a great thing with this contraption called Sea Base."

Stapler smiled. "If that is a compliment, Skipper, my thanks. But sir, about the crew."

Garcia nodded. "You can secure the mess crew from General Quarters, but tell them to stay belowdecks while they're moving to their stations." Garcia frowned, dark eyebrows furrowing into a deep V. He didn't think this slight modification to GQ would violate what the admiral told him.

Stapler turned to execute Garcia's order.

"Commander, wait a moment," Garcia said, reaching out as if to touch Stapler. Stapler turned. "I want everyone, including the security force, to clear the port side forward of midships. Everyone topside who doesn't need to be, I want belowdecks."

Stapler looked questioningly at Garcia. "Sir, what is going on?" He nodded at the red handset. "What is it that Admiral Holman told you that is causing us to stay at General Quarters?"

When Garcia failed to answer immediately, Stapler continued. "Sir, I am your TAO, I should know."

Stapler was right. If whatever the admiral was asking could endanger Sea Base, then it was his—Garcia's—responsibility to take actions to protect it. He motioned Stapler closer. For a couple of minutes, he gave Stapler as much information as he knew. Clear the topside of Sea Base on the forward port side. Move everyone away. There was a helicopter coming; it would touch down, and once it lifted off, Garcia could secure from General Quarters.

"I don't think he's coming back," Montague said, pacing the stateroom deck of Dr. Kiang Zheng.

Zeichner folded his hands on top of his stomach, raising his head so the air from the fan blew beneath his chin. The evaporation of sweat felt cool. "He'll be here," he said. "He might be waiting for General Quarters to be secured. Once the captain sounds All Clear, we'll be able to move freely about Sea Base; so will Zheng." He pulled his already soaked handkerchief from his back pocket and ran it around the folds of his neck. He was too comfortable in the air-conditioning to want to move anywhere.

The sound of water flushing came through the closed door to the small head. A moment later, Gainer emerged, checking his zipper with one hand as he closed the door behind him. Both Zeichner and Montague looked at him. Montague shook her head and looked back at the door.

"What?" Gainer asked, glancing down to make sure his zipper was up.

Montague continued with her pacing. "I am concerned that while we sit here"—she looked at her watch—"for over an hour now, our suspect is running about Sea Base gathering intelligence."

Zeichner laughed. "I don't think he's running amok anywhere, Angie. Too many watertight doors and too many barriers to give him free rein. He has to come back here."

"How much longer are we going to wait?"

"As long as it takes. Patience, my young agent. He has to come back here." Without knowing why, Zeichner pointed at the radio. "He has to come back because the radio is here."

Gainer picked it up, turned it every which way, looking at it. "It's just a radio, Boss." He turned it on. The music from the internal radio station came from the channel. He turned the knob, moving the channel selector through the spectrum, getting other local stations.

"I could be wrong, I have been before," Zeichner said. "If he is any kind of spy, he is going to have to have something to transmit his intelligence to his masters." He pointed at the radio Gainer was holding. "That's the only thing in here that could be the device. It was sitting in the center of the table the last time Kevin and I were here. And it was sitting at the same angle and position this time," he guessed. He failed to recall how it was sitting last time, but the angle and profile of the radio seemed familiar. His lower lip pushed into his upper. *Yes,* he thought, trying to convince himself he was correct, *Definitely the same place on the table and the same angle.*

Gainer bent over the table. He kept the radio in his right hand as he softly moved his left hand along the table. Suddenly, he set the radio down on the edge of the table and laid his head on the table. He shifted his head slightly as he sighted along the table. "Damn, Boss. There's a faint ninety-degree mark on the table."

Montague stopped her pacing and moved to the table. "Mark?"

"Yes," Gainer said, straightening. He ran his finger along the faint pencil tracing. "See? A straight line running here a few inches, then one at a ninety-degree angle to it about an inch long."

"I don't see it," she said.

Damn, I was right, Zeichner thought. He smiled. "Set the radio along those marks." He stayed seated, the comfort of the recliner drawing him more than the curiosity of Gainer's discovery.

Gainer set the radio within the ninety-degree trace. "It fits."

"Of course it would," Zeichner said, amazed with himself. "How else would he know if someone had been searching his stateroom?" He reached over and pushed the lever of the recliner, lowering the leg rest. Placing both hands on the arms, Zeichner grunted as he pushed himself out of the chair. "You know what this means, don't you, Kevin?"

Kevin looked at him.

"It means Zheng is no longer a suspect. He is our spy. And he's known since you and I were in here five months ago rambling through his stateroom that we were onto him."

"If we were onto him and he knew it, then why didn't he do anything?"

"Maybe he did. Maybe that was why he flew back to Texas the other month."

"Why would anyone go to Texas in the middle of the summer?" Montague asked.

Gainer laughed. "You've never been along the Riverwalk in San Antonio."

"Well, he must not have thought it through thoroughly," Montague added, ignoring Gainer. "He came back."

"Maybe he had no choice," Zeichner said.

"Maybe he did," she countered. "Maybe he is as patriotic to China as we are to America."

Gainer's eyes roved the compartment with a new intensity. He looked at the space beneath the bottom bunk. "When I left here last time, we could see the shoes."

Zeichner and Montague both looked at the deck beneath the narrow bottom bunk.

"I don't remember, Kevin."

"I do because I'm the one who searched beneath his bed."

"It's a rack," Montague said.

"Okay, I searched beneath his rack. I moved those shoes, but when I finished, I couldn't recall whether they were shoved back out of sight or shoved back just enough so he wouldn't trip over them. In hindsight, I may have guessed wrong when I put them back."

Zeichner smiled. "It wouldn't matter, Kevin. I bet he knew from when we opened the door to this stateroom that someone had been here. Besides, he's a bachelor; there is no rhyme or reason as to how things are organized in a bachelor's suite."

"Smell," Montague said.

"Smell?"

"Well, yes. Look at the three of us. Our clothes are wet through and through with perspiration from running up and down Sea Base. It smells like a locker room right now. If this man is so organized he lines his shoes up, then he'd smell the presence of someone else in his compartment."

Zeichner lifted his arms out from his sides. Both sides of his shirt were matted to his body. "I don't smell anything."

"Well, duh. If you had my feminine nose, you would."

Gainer moved to the stateroom door and opened it. He scanned the door facing and lock, looking for something. He shut it. "I don't see anything."

"It's there somewhere. A piece of string, a speck of dust near the floor or on top of the door. Something we wouldn't notice, but he would. Something small and insignificant unless you were looking for it."

Montague put her hands on her hips. "If you knew this all along, Mr. Zeichner, why didn't we take better care coming in here? Why didn't we look?"

He smiled and turned away. He'd opened himself up for that scrutiny, he told himself. Why didn't he do all these things that he seemed to be dredging up from some deep epiphany somewhere inside of him? Why didn't he stop now while he was ahead? He sat back down in the chair, his feet flat on the deck. His thighs touched starting just above the knee.

"Sir?"

He looked at her. "Good question, Angie. You are probably right, but the radio was something that came from sitting here in the stateroom looking at things and letting the mind come to terms with what was possible and what was probable." He waved his hand in a circular motion above his head. "Sometimes, you just have to be patient and let your mind figure out what the details mean."

"Good point," Gainer said. He turned around the chair he had been sitting on and straddled it, placing his hands across the top of the back and leaning his chin on them. His eyes traced the stateroom, inch by inch.

Montague watched him for a few seconds. "My God," she said finally, and started her pacing again, head down, not talking to either of them.

Five minutes passed before Gainer stood and walked back into the head. He emerged a moment later with the electric shaver.

Zeichner pulled the lever up again, lifting his feet off the deck. "What you got?"

"I saw this earlier, but it never dawned on me until now that the electric razor doesn't have one of those Navy safety tags on it." He reached over and lifted the electric cord of the radio. "Even the radio has a safety tag, but the razor doesn't. Now why would the good doctor get his radio tagged, but not his razor?"

"Probably didn't want to have to do it twice," Montague snapped. "But it would be an additional reason for wandering belowdecks."

Gainer pulled the blade off, holding it up to look at it closely.

Zeichner pushed the lever of the recliner down. He leaned forward, putting his hands on his knees, resting his stomach on his thighs. He really had to do something in this last month at sea. He caught the disgusting look on Montague's face when she glanced at him. The young have no appreciation for the spreading bulge of growing old. An old, balding fat man leading two young agents. Must bug the shit out of her.

Gainer lifted the back, easing it off the razor. He looked at Zeichner and smiled, setting the open razor on the table. "Voilà!"

Zeichner pushed himself out of the chair and reached the table about the same time as Montague. "What?" he asked as he bent over the open razor.

Gainer pointed to the inside. "See these three chips aligned in these slots?"

They both nodded.

"Why does an electric razor need computer chips?" He lifted the razor. "Look at it. On the outside it's just a cheap electric razor one plugs into the wall. Bulkhead," he added, correcting himself. "And runs around his face removing the morning whiskers. This one has chips." After several seconds, Gainer straightened and in a profound voice announced, "This is the transmitting device."

"Are you sure?" Zeichner asked. *What about the radio?* he asked himself. He was wrong. He waited for Montague to point it out.

Gainer nodded with a smile. "Look here, Boss. The radio is the antenna. You figured that out."

I did?

Gainer lifted the radio. "Somehow, these two things have to connect. The razor is the operating half. Separate, neither the radio nor the razor is anything more than what they seem. But once the razor is connected to the radio, it provides the transmitting instructions."

"So, whatever intelligence Zheng has collected is sent out via the radio," Montague finished.

"Right!" Gainer exclaimed. He looked at Zeichner with admiration.

Montague nodded, but didn't say anything. "If we are right, then how did the two things connect? They would have to connect with each other—a wire or line or something."

Zeichner nearly smiled. She was definitely destined for greater stardom. He wondered if she'd consciously thought of the switch from the "I" to the "we"?

"I don't know," Gainer said, bemused. He set the two things on the table and walked away. "They have to connect someway. But how?"

Zeichner looked at Montague. "Think we ought to go searching for him now?"

She bit her lower lip and then smiled. "No, Boss; I think he'll be back here soon. Regardless, he cannot send anything he has gathered today until he comes back to his radio." She reached out and touched the small radio.

ZHENG hurried toward his stateroom, working his way through the deserted passageways and closed hatches, trying to avoid anyone else who might be violating General Quarters. He was hot and craved a quick, cool shower. He had toyed with the idea of taking some photographs of the weapons systems topside, but he had so many, he didn't know what else more photographs would show.

The noise of people approaching caused him to walk along the bulkhead of the connecting passageway. There was no place to hide.

Ahead of him came the Air Force crew led by the tall bald-headed chief master sergeant. They surged by him, none of the uniformed personnel acknowledging his presence. His stomach tightened as he waited for them to ask why he was in the passageway during General Quarters, but no one did.

Instead, they were talking to each other as they passed him. He listened to a shorter sergeant arguing with the taller chief master sergeant. The chatter told him they had been ordered belowdecks. They didn't like it; they had aircraft out there, and what if one of the aircraft had an emergency and had to land. What would it do without the ground crew there to secure it? The chief master sergeant was leading them toward the Fast Sealift Ship *Antares.*

Zheng slowed his pace, turning to watch them until they disappeared. Then, he quickened his pace, wanting to get into his stateroom and away from any other encounters. Ahead was the ship *Pollux;* then he'd hang a left through the connecting passageway and be at the *Regulus,* his ship. About another ten to fifteen minutes and he'd be in his stateroom. He wondered why that third agent, Angela Montague, had been sent? He had gathered enough information to know he was a suspect, but since the search of his stateroom months ago,

Zeichner and Gainer had not returned. Maybe the work of the colonel had sidetracked their investigation?

Twenty minutes later, he stepped onto the deck of the *Regulus*. He pulled his handkerchief from his pocket and wiped the sweat from his face. The reflection of his face in the glass of a nearby hatch showed hair glistening with perspiration. He hated the feel of being in sweat-stained clothing, but the thought of his time in the cell in what seemed years ago erased the uncomfortable feeling. There were worse things than heat, sweat, and odor.

Zheng looked both ways. The main deck was empty. Jamming his soaking handkerchief into his back pocket, he started along the edge of the deck, head down, watching for things that could trip him, reaching out every now and then to touch the top safety line.

Reaching the forward forecastle, he grabbed the lever to open the watertight hatch.

Two sets of hands slammed him against the hatch. Fear sent adrenaline racing through his body. He pushed, kicking backward.

"Now, Dr. Zheng, why would you want to do that?"

A hand pushed his face against the hatch. The hot metal burned his cheek as he twisted his face to the side. The face of the sailor from the crow's nest came into view.

"Hi there, Doc. Remember me? Didn't see you at your battle station today." The face disappeared.

"Doc, put your hands behind your back."

He fought to free himself. A third hand slammed his face against the hatch again.

"Don't give us a hard time," a female voice commanded.

He looked down and caught a glimpse of a small bird tattooed on the woman's right ankle, just below the camouflaged trousers. Visions of the park in San Antonio rushed through his mind, of a similar tattoo on the ankle of a sunbather. Small nipples that had made the white shirt tent and had drawn his attention every day when he visited the park, waiting for the colonel. She had been there when the colonel finally showed. He had no idea what her face looked like, but the tattoo told all. He relaxed, hoping they would relax. Better to go over the side than endure the shame of interrogation by a country he loved.

"That's better, Dr. Zheng."

Plastic handcuffs tightened on his wrists. Even if he wanted to fight now, he couldn't. He squeezed his eyes shut. Not right now, but someday in the near future, he saw his parents standing before an open hole as the colonel, laughing, pulled the trigger that would send them both tumbling lifeless into an unmarked grave. Remorse filled his being and what little strength he had gave way to great weakness.

He always knew it could end like this, but deep inside was a hope that one day the colonel would disappear; his parents would be freed; and he could return to the normal life of work, sleep, and eat.

He was an American. He loved his country. It was to protect his parents he did this, but in protecting them he had brought great shame upon himself and his family. In the days to come, an opportunity would present itself and in that space of a moment, he would do the honorable thing. An honorable thing he probably should have done earlier.

"Okay, Doctor, don't pull that relax crap on me. I've seen it before and if you try anything, I have this shock thing here that will send you into unimaginable pain . . ."

He grunted in reply. There was nothing that could compare to his time in the colonel's cell. Nothing was unimaginable as the pain suffered in it.

". . . and render you unconscious. Then, we'd have to drag you topside, bumping your head along the way. It'd just make it harder on you and us."

For a faction of a second, he thought of baiting them into doing it, but what if they broke his arm or leg? He needed his body whole for when the opportunity presented itself.

"Now, turn around. There are two of us."

"CAPTAIN, we have a helicopter approaching," Stapler said. "And it's not responding to our transmissions."

"I know."

"It's what we've been waiting for?"

Garcia shrugged. "I expect so. We aren't to ask questions. Tell the Air Traffic Controller to stop interrogating it."

"Aye, aye, sir."

* * *

THE dark, unmarked helicopter landed on the far side of Sea Base.

Jacobs watched from the quarterdeck area on the aft starboard side, wondering where it came from and why there were no markings.

"What do you think, Showdernitzel?" he asked.

"What do I think?" she asked back, placing spread fingers on her chest. "You're asking me what I think?"

"Showdernitzel, one of these days I'm going to take you across my lap. . . ."

"Master Chief, don't try to turn me on. . . ."

"Oh, shut up," Jacobs said, walking away. *Try to be nice, just once.* He lifted his hand, shading his eyes, as he watched several figures in gray uniforms leap from the helicopter, weapons cradled in their arms.

"Showdernitzel! Ask Combat about that helicopter," he shouted, recalling the experience last month in the Sea of Japan with the North Korean Y-8 transport that tried to land troops on Sea Base. A slight chill went up his spine. He shook his head. No way this could happen twice in one person's history. He squinted. It was an American helicopter, not one of those old Soviet has-beens.

Two people across the deck opened the watertight hatch leading down to the *Pollux* and disappeared. Two others remained near the open side door of the helicopter.

"Master Chief, Combat said to ignore them."

"What type of helicopter is that?" he asked.

Showdernitzel lifted her hand to shade her eyes. She shrugged. "Damn, Master Chief, if you don't know, how in the hell can you expect me to know?"

"You are one smart-ass, you know."

"I know; that's why you love me so."

"Don't bet on it. It's an awful big helicopter."

"Then it's most likely a BOH," she answered.

"BOH?"

"Yeah, Big Old Helicopter." She laughed.

"Showdernitzel, go check on our security guards."

"I did. That Jolson who flew in today is missing. He never

returned from his twenty-minute break to use the head. Went down below and never returned. When I get my hands around his arrogant neck, I'm going to break it."

As they watched, the two uniformed men emerged through the watertight door. They were holding someone between them. In less than five seconds, the captive was bundled from the hatch to the helicopter and tossed inside.

"Did you see that?" he asked.

"Looks as if they are taking someone with them."

"Get our security team on the circuit and tell them to stand by. Then call Combat and tell them that helicopter they told us to ignore is kidnapping someone."

"Now, you're talking."

TALEB looked at his watch. "We got three minutes before they have to launch," he said to Norton.

They glanced at their teammates, who were hustling Kiang up the stairwell.

The two hurried down two decks to the main deck of *Regulus,* opened the watertight hatch, and hurried along the passageway. At Kiang's stateroom, Taleb grabbed the knob and turned. The door opened. Three people stood there with weapons pointing at them. Behind him, Norton had her weapon pointed into the stateroom.

"Looks as if it's a standoff," Taleb said.

"Drop your weapon!" Montague commanded, shifting her open-leg stance to the right, increasing slightly the space between her and Gainer. Zeichner eased to the left, putting the table between him and the two in the doorway. His shoulder nearly touched the starboard bulkhead.

"We can't and we don't have much time," Taleb said. He nodded at the table. "We need the radio and the electric razor. The rest of this stuff, NCIS can have."

"NCIS already has it," Zeichner said. "Who are you? You're not military or else you wouldn't—"

"It doesn't matter who we are, we need those two items."

"Well, you aren't getting them," Zeichner said. "If you want them that bad, then answer some questions."

Norton leaned closer. "One minute," she whispered.

"Mr. Zeichner—"

"I know you," Gainer interrupted. "You're the sailor who was in the crow's nest. You and Zheng have the same General Quarters stations. You and him are—"

Taleb slammed the door shut. "Let's go!"

The two raced down the passageway, barely reaching the watertight hatch before Montague and Gainer burst into the passageway, one with a weapon pointed right and the other looking to the left.

"There they are!" Gainer shouted. "Halt or I'll shoot!"

Taleb and Norton leaped through the hatch. Taleb slammed the hatch, looked around for something to wedge against it.

"Not enough time," Norton said, grabbing him by the sleeve. "Let's go."

The two started up the ladder, running, glancing over their backs.

"Here they come," Norton said, seeing the two younger agents emerge carefully onto the main deck.

The two reached the stairwell. Taleb opened the door, held it until Norton was through. "Run," he said.

Up the stairs they ran, their metal-toed military shoes clanging on the metal rungs as the four stories of steps led upward.

"Stop or I'll shoot," came a masculine shout from below.

Taleb knew they could see them, but the maze of metal steps and railings created a place where if either fired, the ricochet effect could just as easily kill the person who fired.

They passed the third story. Taleb was surprised to feel his breathing starting to intensify. It had to be these months at sea instead of ashore, where he could jog and work out. He could have done it here, but when you're undercover and on assignment, your whole attention is on the mission.

Bright light came from above. Norton had reached the watertight hatch. Taleb was a few seconds behind her. He heard the helicopter revving up for takeoff. They'd leave him if they had to. This wasn't hostile territory, but they would just as soon take him with them to avoid later explanations.

He pulled himself up the last few steps.

A gunshot rang out behind him. A sharp lightning of pain raced through his shoulder. He saw the deck racing toward his face as his eyes shut. The pain was overwhelming. He knew he had been shot. Why would they shoot him? He always knew his missions ran risks. He had never expected to be shot by someone on his side. Hands grabbed him beneath the arms and just before he faded into unconsciousness, he felt the familiar lift of the helicopter as it rose into the air.

GAINER emerged onto the deck first. The helicopter was already off to the port side at sea level.

"Who were they?" Montague asked as he ran up beside him, gasping for breath.

"I think they were comrades of Dr. Zheng," he said softly.

A few minutes later, Zeichner emerged from the hatch. While he recovered his breath, Gainer and Montague brought him up to speed on what happened.

Zeichner looked at Gainer. "I think you may have shot someone on our side. There is a possibility you may have missed."

Gainer pointed at the deck. "Blood," he said.

Montague nodded across the deck at a bunch of sailors running toward them, their weapons at port arms. "I hope they're friendly."

In seconds, the sailors had them surrounded with their weapons.

"Put those weapons down!" Zeichner shouted between gasps for breath. He pulled his wallet out of his pocket and held aloft the NCIS badge. "We're NCIS."

A Taiwanese fishing vessel pulled alongside the body in the water. Two fishermen lifted the body onto the deck, dropping it when it vomited up water. The bright blue eyes blinked several times as Andrew fought to breathe. He glanced at the Oriental features surrounding him. God was merciful, he thought. Hundreds of sharks swimming around him and not one had touched him. Some brushed against him, but throughout the ordeal, Andrew had put his faith in God. He was prepared for whatever God had to offer, and this rescue was God's way of saying Andrew's mission was here, on earth. He pushed himself off the slick wooden deck; the odor of fish swept over him. At a distance, the massive bulk of Sea Base filled the horizon.

Andrew fell back onto the deck. He touched his head. Inside there were the codes needed to warn his father of what Taleb had said. Money and passports would wait for him at whatever airport he could reach. He smiled and drifted off to sleep.

The fishermen shrugged. A couple of them pulled Andrew off to the side so he would be out of the way for the rest of the day until they returned to their small village. Then the elders would decide what to do.

"CAPTAIN, radio sent this, sir," said the second-class petty officer, handing a metal clipboard to Garcia.

Garcia mumbled thanks and flipped open the top cover. A red-striped cover sheet with the words "Top Secret" embossed across it covered the message. He lifted the cover sheet and read it. Then he read it again, before dropping the metal top of the clipboard down. He handed it back to the sailor, who handed Garcia a pen and had him initial that he had read the document. Security was something taken seriously by those who handled classified material.

When the sailor left, Stapler walked over. "What was it, Skipper? Something about the helicopter?"

Garcia smiled. "Nope, Stan. Good news this time. The talks have produced a breakthrough. The Chinese have informed our State Department that this was a major exercise for homeland defense and will be finished by tomorrow."

"So, they're not going to invade Taiwan?"

Garcia shook his head. "Not this time."

"You think they ever will?"

He nodded. "Ever read the history of the Arab-Israeli War of 1973—some call it the Yom Kippur War?"

Stapler shook his head. "Wasn't even born back then."

"Neither was I, but the Egyptians were led by a man named Anwar al-Sadat. For three years leading up to 1973, the Egyptians used to have a 'crossing the Suez Canal' exercise. In the third or fourth year, whichever it was, the exercise turned into a real operation. The Egyptians were nearly at the Israeli border before the Israelis recovered enough to force them back."

"You saying one day what they say is an exercise will turn real?"

"This may have started out real, but turned into an exercise because we and the British were here. One day we won't be and there will be nothing to stop them."

JACOBS stood at the aft safety line as Agazzi approached. It had been several hours since Sea Base had secured from General Quarters. The sun was disappearing off the horizon.

"Looks as if the China crisis has resolved itself," Jacobs said between puffs.

"Until next time."

"We'll have to fight them eventually."

"We may not have to, but our children might."

"Or we may decide it isn't worth the blood necessary to be involved."

Agazzi nodded, gripping the safety lines with both hands. "You find your sailor?"

Jacobs shook his head. "Nope. Don't know if he's knocked out somewhere; lost belowdecks, groping for topside; or fell overboard. They're still looking, which is why I'm still here."

Agazzi looked around. "Here?"

"Yep, this is our quarterdeck during GQ. Makes it easier for my sailors to find me when they need me."

"You can't stay up here all night by yourself."

Jacobs pointed to the shadows off to his right. "I'm not. Got Petty Officer Todd over there with his brick keeping contact with the search party." He glanced at his watch. "Showdernitzel is coming back later tonight and will take the midwatch. If we haven't found him by tomorrow afternoon, then we'll list him as missing, presumed overboard. The Skipper has the helicopters and ships out looking for four people who are missing."

"Who are the others?"

"One is an Air Force sergeant who had been on board about a week, and the other one is another boatswain mate named Taleb. And we have a civilian contractor who is missing also."

"You have two of your troops reported overboard?" Agazzi asked in amazement. "Two seems . . ."

"He's not mine." Jacobs shrugged. "Seems no one knows where he was assigned. He was on the Watch-Quarter-Station bill for the crow's nest during GQ, but no one knows which division he was assigned." He paused for a moment, then continued. "Showdernitzel knows this Taleb, but she thought he was assigned to Combat. Combat has never seen or heard of him."

"A mystery?"

"Or associated with the helicopter."

"What helicopter?"

Jacobs spent the next few minutes telling Agazzi about the strange helicopter that landed, and then quickly took off. He also told him about seeing men from the helicopter toss someone who seemed to be reluctant to go with them on board the departing craft.

"Wow! Quite a tale for the grandchildren," Agazzi finally said. "Might have been one of the four missing?"

"That's why I don't think we'll find all four. I think one or two of the missing is still on board, but I think a couple of them probably flew off on the helicopter. With the gunfire surrounded the liftoff, might be dead for all we know."

"Gunfire?"

"Yeah, Mr. Zeichner and NCIS was shooting at them."

"Zeichner!" Agazzi shook his head. "I'm surprised at a man his size being in a gun battle." He looked at Jacobs. "You're friends with Zeichner; did he say anything or tell you what happened?"

"No, I got to the location with a few of my armed-to-the-teeth boatswain mates, but by then the helicopter was off the deck and gone. Mr. Zeichner was trying to catch his breath and the other two, Kevin Gainer and some woman whom I had never seen on Sea Base, refused to comment." He shrugged. "Still a mystery, but with some of the secret laws we have for terrorism and such, I think the gunfight was between two different sets of police."

"You got to be kidding me."

"Would I kid you?"

"All the time."

Jacobs sighed. "We'll find out what happened eventually. Meanwhile, let's hope we find the ones who are really missing."

"Hope you're right."

"I think this Taleb had to be one of those on that helicopter. No one has heard of him officially on Sea Base and now that he's gone, no one can recall him reporting on board. He just appeared one day."

"What about the others?"

"The new kid who landed this morning I think fell overboard, but I hope we find him knocked out or lost belowdecks on one of these massive Sealift ships. I would like to know where he is. He has a family and loved ones who are going to be devastated when they are told. Chief Willard, the Air Force senior enlisted person, says they have already submitted their presumed lost report on their—What was her name?" Jacobs reached up, pulled a three-by-five card from his pocket, and read from it. "Her name is Sergeant Kathy Norton." He slipped the card back into his pocket.

"How about the missing civilian?"

Jacobs shook his head. "Not my problem," he said, taking the cigar from between his lips. "NCIS is handling it. I offered to help as much as we could. They thanked me and went off. I think he might be another one that left in that helicopter."

The conversation faded after a while. On the other side of Sea Base, a Royal Navy helicopter approached for landing.

"CHIEF!" Technical Sergeant Lou Thomas shouted, holding his radio aloft. "They're bringing Major Johnson aboard!"

Willard hurried over to where Thomas stood, wiping his hands on a faded red rag jerked from his back pocket. "Does the Ready Room know?"

"Major Crawford broadcast it. They're on their way up. She's early."

Willard shoved the rag back into his pocket.

"Wonder how banged up she is," Thomas said.

Willard looked down at the young airman. "She didn't have to be banged up at all. Captain Franklin says she saved his life."

"Wonder if she did it intentionally."

"Who knows?"

"She would."

"There will always be someone who will doubt she did it to save her wingman."

"Everything we'd heard about her—"

"Shut up, Lou. Whatever we heard is bullshit. What you do in the heat of the moment, in the chaos of an air battle, and without regard for your own safety is the true measure of your grit. Johnson has grit, even if she lacks some of the social graces we enlisted like to see in our officers."

"You mean like courtesy and respect."

"Didn't I tell you to shut up?"

"Yeah, Chief, you did, but you only told me once."

THE helicopter touched down. The sailor guiding the helicopter down crossed the lighted flashlights—*torches, they called them*—telling the pilots they were down, chocked, and could secure their engines.

As the propellers wound down, other members of the Air Force detachment surrounded Willard and Thomas as if they had marked the spot for the crowd to wait.

Corpsmen from Sea Base hospital facilities waited with a wheelchair near the helicopters. Finally, the side door opened. A couple of crewmen jumped down, reached inside, and helped Johnson onto the deck. They held her as the corpsmen approached. Johnson stood up and waved them away.

Franklin started forward first, soon the others joined, and by the time they reached Major Johnson they were a laughing, congratulating, and happy group of flyers who recognized heroes in their midst. Shouts of "Commander" and "Pickles" and "Welcome back."

Franklin stopped a couple of feet from her, snapped to attention, and saluted. "Welcome home, Commander."

Johnson nodded. In the faint light of the setting sun, moisture glistened in her eyes as she looked around her detachment. The initial noise quieted for a moment. She looked back at Franklin. "Are you all right?"

"Am I all right?" Franklin laughed, poking himself in the chest with his index finger. "I'm fine, thanks to you, Pickles."

She smiled.

JACOBS lit a cigar and the two shipmates stood at the safety line, watching the fluorescence of the sea grow as the darkness grew. Periodically, one of the boatswain mates would wander by to report the lack of progress in finding Petty Officer Jolson. Each time, Jacobs's voice seemed lower in his response.

"Nothing you could have done, you know," Agazzi said finally after the sailor delivering the report walked away out of earshot.

"Knowing it and feeling it are two different things. If one of my sailors fall overboard, it's still my responsibility regardless of how short a time he or she is on board."

The two friends stood there for a while longer. Agazzi looking out to sea, knowing something more was bothering Jacobs, but also knowing that when Jacobs wanted to tell him, he would. The smell of cigar smoke whiffed by every few seconds as the evening ocean breeze shifted upon itself.

Jacobs opened his mouth to say something as two F-22A Raptors did a low overhead flyby of Sea Base. Both men turned at the noise, watching the two aircraft fly by. The white-orange glow of the engines highlighted the dark silhouettes as the aircraft crossed the bow, turned on their tails, and disappeared into the night.

As the noise faded, Jacobs went back to his cigar. "Must be entering the landing pattern," he remarked.

"How can you tell?"

"You stay topside enough instead of hiding belowdecks in the cool air-conditioned spaces of ASW, you learn the routine."

Agazzi watched the Air Force ground crew on the other side of Sea Base, chocking down two Raptors that had landed earlier. He counted five of the stealth fighters on the deck. The faint noise of jet engines drew his attention to the port side of Sea Base. He squinted, and motion finally drew Agazzi's attention to the two aircraft in the pattern as they made their final turn. "Short final" was what he thought the pilots called a modified landing pattern.

The noise picked up in intensity as the two aircraft approached the end of the runway, their wheels down and locked. Any hopes of conversation drowned in the wash of noise rushing across them.

Agazzi watched as white smoke burst from wheels squealing as the two fighters touched the deck. At the forward end of the runway, a pale blue Air Force pickup truck with flashing lights reading "Follow me" led the two fighters toward the ground crew. *"How come the Navy doesn't have pickup trucks on its carriers?* he asked himself.

He turned back to the safety line, looking out to sea. Jacobs's hand was empty. He had tossed the cigar overboard.

"Alistair, bad news today."

"I know, but you may find him tomorrow, or even tonight. Probably lost belowdecks."

"No, that's bad news, my friend, but more bad news." He put his hand on Alistair's shoulder. "The master chief list was released by Chief of Naval Personnel today."

Agazzi nodded, feeling the disappointment well through him. "I wasn't on it."

Jacobs removed his hand and looked down at his shoes. He scuffed the soles on the nonskid deck a couple of times. "No, you weren't. But I wouldn't give up. I think once they see your fitness report next year and see the battles you've been in, they'll have no choice but to select you. Give it another year."

Agazzi nodded. He took a deep breath. "I don't think there will be a next time, Jerry. Frieda and I discussed it before I sailed. If I made it, I would stick around. Been in twenty-two years. Twenty-two years is the right time for me to make it. It would have been right on time."

"You should have made it."

"You're only saying that because we're friends, and I do appreciate it. I thought I stood a chance this time. I thought having a bachelor's degree and being a division officer—"

"Other bad news also," Jacobs interrupted.

Agazzi stopped. "More?"

"Yeah, when they secured from General Quarters, I went

down to Personnel and put my papers in. They said it'd take about six months to process and then I'd be retired."

"No wonder you're sad. You sure you want to do this?"

"Lots of things happening at once can make your mind up for you. You not making master chief was one of the things."

Agazzi frowned. "Don't get out of the Navy because of that," he said, miffed over the idea his friend was using his failure to be selected as a reason. "There has to be something more important than that."

"I didn't say I was getting out just because you failed to select, Alistair. Don't go trying that psychological bullshit on me or I may have to gangsta-slap you," Jacobs said humorously. "It's time. They say when it's time to retire, it's like an epiphany. One moment you love it, and would fight anyone who tried to throw you out or even suggest retiring. Then, in a matter of moments, you're watching the calendar for that magic day when the Veterans Administration takes over your health and welfare. Just another reason added to many others."

"Does Helen know you've done it?"

"Not yet."

"She will be ecstatic. She's been wanting you to retire for years."

Jacobs laughed. "Yeah, I can hear her now after the first few months. It'll be something along the lines of having twice as much husband and half as much pay. I think she'll get tired of seeing my ugly puss around the house."

"Think you'll have a little Sea Base to play with Deep Freeze, Deny Flight, and the others you keep naming after your deployments?"

"Naw," he said with a laugh. "I can't see the horizontal mambo creating a Sea Base. Besides, you heard her when she was throwing my stuff out the window—she is closing the port down for any more production—thinks six kids is enough. Most likely, once I retire, she's going make me call them by their real names instead of my deployments. She said Deep Freeze came home from school crying the other day because the teacher corrected her, telling her that her name was Joyce, not Deep Freeze."

"You sure you going to hang around the house after you retire? Maybe you'll discover like so many others that there is life after the Navy, but it involves working elsewhere?"

"Well, I also found out that if I change my mind, all I have to do is call the Bureau and they'll tear up the papers."

The two men laughed, drifting back into that silence of the sea shipmates understand so well. Off in the distance, the faint lights of the fishing fleet of Taiwan were disappearing along the horizon as they headed back toward their port. Behind the two friends, the engines of the Raptors abruptly fell silent. And beneath them the sharks swam vigilantly, marking the boundaries of the surface from the dark Pacific below.